OXFORD WORLD'S CLASSICS

# ABOUT LOVE
## AND OTHER STORIES

ANTON PAVLOVICH CHEKHOV was born in 1860 in Taganrog, a port in southern Russia. His father was a former serf. In 1879, after receiving a classical education at the Taganrog Gymnasium, he moved to Moscow to study medicine. During his university years he helped support his family by writing stories and sketches for humorous magazines. By 1888 he was contributing to Russia's most prestigious literary journals and regarded as a major writer. He also started writing plays: his first full-length play, *Ivanov*, was produced in 1887. After undertaking a journey to visit the penal colony on the Siberian island of Sakhalin in 1890, he settled on a country estate outside Moscow, where he continued to write and practise medicine. His failing health forced him to move to Yalta in 1898, where he wrote his most famous short story, 'The Lady with the Little Dog' (1899), and two of his best-known plays: *Three Sisters* (1901) and *The Cherry Orchard* (1904), written with Stanislavsky's Moscow Art Theatre in mind. In 1901 he married the company's leading actress, Olga Knipper. He died from tuberculosis in Badenweiler, Germany, in July 1904 at the age of 44.

ROSAMUND BARTLETT lectures in Russian and music at the University of Durham. She has published *Wagner and Russia* (1995), *Literary Russia: A Guide* (with Anna Benn, 1997), *Shostakovich in Context* (2000), *Chekhov: Scenes From a Life* (2004), and *Anton Chekhov: A Life in Letters* (2004).

# OXFORD WORLD'S CLASSICS

*For over 100 years Oxford World's Classics have brought
readers closer to the world's great literature. Now with over 700
titles—from the 4,000-year-old myths of Mesopotamia to the
twentieth century's greatest novels—the series makes available
lesser-known as well as celebrated writing.*

*The pocket-sized hardbacks of the early years contained
introductions by Virginia Woolf, T. S. Eliot, Graham Greene,
and other literary figures which enriched the experience of reading.
Today the series is recognized for its fine scholarship and
reliability in texts that span world literature, drama and poetry,
religion, philosophy and politics. Each edition includes perceptive
commentary and essential background information to meet the
changing needs of readers.*

OXFORD WORLD'S CLASSICS

━━

ANTON CHEKHOV

*About Love*

*and Other Stories*

━━

*Translated with an Introduction and Notes by*
ROSAMUND BARTLETT

OXFORD
UNIVERSITY PRESS

# OXFORD
## UNIVERSITY PRESS

Great Clarendon Street, Oxford OX2 6DP

Oxford University Press is a department of the University of Oxford.
It furthers the University's objective of excellence in research, scholarship,
and education by publishing worldwide in

Oxford New York

Auckland Bangkok Buenos Aires Cape Town Chennai
Dar es Salaam Delhi Hong Kong Istanbul Karachi Kolkata
Kuala Lumpur Madrid Melbourne Mexico City Mumbai Nairobi
São Paulo Shanghai Taipei Tokyo Toronto

Oxford is a registered trade mark of Oxford University Press
in the UK and in certain other countries

Published in the United States
by Oxford University Press Inc., New York

British Library Cataloguing in Publication Data

Data available

Library of Congress Cataloging in Publication Data

Data available

ISBN 0–19–280260–7

1

Typeset in Ehrhardt
by RefineCatch Limited, Bungay, Suffolk
Printed in Great Britain by
Clays Ltd., St Ives plc

# CONTENTS

# INTRODUCTION

## *Evolution as a Writer*

Chekhov became a writer at an inauspicious time in Russia's history. Alexander II had initiated a series of long-overdue reforms at the beginning of his reign, the most important of which was the abolition of serfdom which took place in 1861, when Chekhov was 1 year old. By the time Chekhov published his first story in 1880, when he was 20, however, Alexander's modernization programme had ground to a halt. Growing unrest at its slow progress had led the most radical of Russia's young revolutionaries to resort to terrorism, and a year later the Tsar was assassinated. Contrary to their hopes, however, the assassination of Alexander II in fact brought an end to any possibility of further reform. It was also the end of an era in literary terms. The 'age of the great novels' was brought to a close by the deaths of Dostoevsky in 1881 (shortly after the publication of *The Brothers Karamazov*) and Turgenev two years later. Tolstoy, meanwhile, had decided to abandon fiction-writing in favour of fighting moral causes—such as vainly appealing for clemency to be granted to Alexander II's assassins, who were all hanged.

Alexander II's successor, his son Alexander III, reacted to the violent circumstances of his accession by increasing censorship and and introducing measures which actually attempted to undo some of the 1860s reforms. His highly reactionary policies caused widespread despondency amongst the educated population, who came to see Alexander's reign as a sterile era of 'small deeds'. The stultifying atmosphere of prohibitions and denunciations is well evoked in Chekhov's satirical masterpiece 'The Man in a Case'. It is no coincidence that the voluminous, soul-searching novels of the 1860s and 1870s gave way to less ambitious short stories after Alexander III became tsar. The government's closure of the country's leading literary journal in 1884 was a further blow to morale. In the doldrums of the 1880s and the 1890s, Chekhov was almost the only young writer to appear on the literary scene who was of international calibre.

Even Alexander III could not completely halt the wheels of change, however. Industrialization belatedly reached Russia at the end of the nineteenth century, and with it came the inevitable mass exodus from the villages, where it was becoming increasingly difficult for Russia's peasant population to earn a living. Urbanization was also a direct consequence of the emancipation of the serfs, and it was the burgeoning and increasingly literate lower classes in Russian cities who were the regular readers of the lightweight comic journals which flourished at this time. The St Petersburg weekly *Fragments* immediately became the most popular publication when it was founded in 1881. Like other such journals, it was full of cartoons, corny jokes, amusing little stories, and vignettes of contemporary life. There were no pretensions to literary merit. This was the arena in which Chekhov learnt his craft as a writer.

Chekhov began contributing to magazines like the *Dragonfly* and the *Alarm Clock* because he needed to help support his impoverished family. The fee he was paid for each piece printed was so small that like other impecunious contributors, he had to write a lot in order to earn anything, and this necessitated the adoption of a number of pseudonyms. The writing was a sideline, of course—Chekhov was a full-time medical student at Moscow University from 1879 to 1884—but he proved astonishingly adept at dashing off stories in his spare time. His prodigious comic gifts also ensured his success in the medium. In 1882 Chekhov started writing for *Fragments*, and he soon became its most popular contributor. Three years later he was headhunted by a St Petersburg newspaper, and shortly after that he was taken up by Alexey Suvorin, the proprietor of Russia's biggest daily newspaper, *New Times*. Most Russian newspapers had a small fiction section, often in their Saturday supplements, and this is where Chekhov's stories started appearing. Suvorin insisted that Chekhov now write under his own name, rather than as Antosha Chekhonte, his most common pseudonym. Chekhov had hoped one day to use his real name for writing medical articles, wary that disclosure of the identity of his comic alter ego might harm his reputation as a doctor and scientist, but he acquiesced. By the time Chekhov's first story appeared in *New Times* in early 1886, he had written almost 400 stories and features. The esteem in which he later held his juvenilia is apparent from the fact that he discarded two-thirds of these early writings when he came to compile his own collected works at the end of his life. None of the stories he had written in the first two years made the cut.

As Chekhov's literary talents developed in the early 1880s, he had begun to chafe at having to write to strict deadlines, adhere to fixed word limits, and be unfailingly witty. From being a means to an end (feeding his family), the fiction-writing started to become an end in itself. Chekhov was the first to recognize that the restrictions imposed by his editors had provided him with an excellent training, and an appreciation for the values of concision, if nothing else, but he wanted to explore new ground. The brief story 'The Huntsman', published in the summer of 1885, represents one of his first attempts at writing serious fiction. It also strikes one of the first notes of elegy in Chekhov's writing. As the publications in which Chekhov published became more high-profile, he took increasing care in crafting his stories, particularly when he started signing them with his own name. As a result, he started to attract critical attention from the literary establishment. And after he received a letter from a venerable Petersburg writer Dmitry Grigorovich exhorting him to take his literary endeavours seriously, Chekhov realized his future really did lie in writing rather than in medicine.

Finally, in 1887, when he was 27, Chekhov was invited to submit a story to one of Russia's prestigious literary journals. After the publication of 'The Steppe' early the following year in the *Northern Messenger*, Chekhov's career was meteoric. When he won the Pushkin Prize in 1888, soon after making his debut in a 'thick journal', as the serious literary monthlies were called (and which still remain the most important outlets for the publication of *belles lettres* in Russia), Chekhov joked to his friend Suvorin that second- and third-rate magazine writers ought to put up a statue to him or at the very least present him with a silver cigarette case. 'I have paved the way for them to the thick journals, and into the hearts and approbation of respectable people,' he wrote proudly (and with his usual dose of irony).[1] It was quite unprecedented for a Russian writer to begin a literary career in such an unpretentious way. Publication in the 'thick journals' denoted Chekhov's endorsement as a major writer. He now changed his work patterns accordingly. Once he was given carte blanche with word limits and no longer had the threat of a deadline hanging over him, he significantly expanded the length of his stories and significantly decreased his output. Where he had previously

[1] Letter to Suvorin, 10 Oct. 1888, in *Anton Chekhov: A Life in Letters*, ed. R. Bartlett (London, 2004).

been publishing an average of at least two stories a week, that figure was now reduced to a handful of stories a year. The number of stories Chekhov wrote declined still further when he concentrated on writing plays in the last years of his life. His last great prose work is, by common consent, considered to be 'The Bishop', which was published two years before his death in 1902.

In the 588 pieces of fiction Chekhov wrote between 1880 and 1902, he ranged more widely than any Russian writer before him had in terms of subject matter. His upbringing in Taganrog gave him an unparalleled insight into life in Russian provincial towns, which were to provide the setting for so many of his fictional masterpieces. His pious family background provided him with an intimate knowledge of the Russian Orthodox Church and its clergy. His medical practice brought him into contact with a huge cross-section of the Russian population, whose poorer members he could identify with because of his own humble origins. His life as a small-time landowner acquainted him intimately with rural life. His education bought him an entrée into the upper sections of Russian society. Chekhov rarely mingled with the high aristocracy, but he found a natural milieu amongst the educated members of the declining gentry class who are the most common protagonists of his stories and plays—the so-called intelligentsia. His literary and dramatic talent, meanwhile, brought him into Russia's artistic world. This rich diversity is reflected in the pages of Chekhov's stories, whose characters range from priests and schoolboys to peasant wives and princesses.

What is immediately striking about Chekhov's stories is his even-handed approach to his characters. What interests him as a writer are individual human qualities (or the lack thereof); social hierarchies recede into the background. Much of Tolstoy's fiction is taken up with persuading the Russian educated public of the virtues of simple peasant living, but it remains aristocratically centred. By contrast, it is entirely typical that Chekhov's story 'In the Cart' focuses on the downtrodden village schoolteacher rather than the roué landowner. As Diaghilev's cousin, the critic Dmitry Filosofov, noted in 1910, Chekhov not only noticed inconspicuous people, but he had a deep affection for them, and it was this quality which endeared him to the Russian public when his stories first appeared. A writer like Tolstoy may have noticed inconspicuous people, but it is equally character-istic of the very different nature of his fiction that they are invariably transformed into giants in his hands, the peasant Karataev in *War and Peace*, for example, emerging as a philosopher spouting Confucius-like wisdom.[2] It is Chekhov's compassion which led Petr Bitsilli in 1930 to speak of his writing being suffused with the 'unclear, warm, even light of Russian Orthodoxy': it is a religion in which a high value is placed on humility and forgiveness. Chekhov stopped going to church when he was an adult, but he exhibited far more Christian qualities than many self-consciously religious writers. His compassion was all-encompassing, but never sentimental. As Bitsilli comments: 'He has pity on his heroes, tiresome, awkward, incapable of loving and of being heroic; he has pity on the steppe, pity on its sunburnt grass, pity on a lone poplar standing on a hill.'[3]

## The Biographical Context

The stories in this collection have been chronologically arranged so that is possible to follow Chekhov's evolution as a writer. The earliest story, 'The Huntsman', was written on a hot summer's day in 1885, while the Chekhov family was staying at a dacha in the Moscow countryside. Chekhov wrote it while he was sitting on a riverbank, and had either just been swimming, or was about to do so. It was this story, about the futile attempt of an unhappy peasant woman to persuade the huntsman who had married her when he was drunk to live with her, that prompted the writer Dmitry Grigorovich to write his famous fan letter to Chekhov on 25 March 1886: 'About a year ago I happened to read a story by you in the *Petersburg Newspaper*; I don't remember what it was called now; I just remember that I was struck by qualities of particular originality, but mainly by the remarkable authenticity and truth in the depiction of the characters and the descriptions of nature. Since then I have read everything signed by *Chekhonte*.'[4] Chekhov had been writing professionally under his Chekhonte and other pseudonyms for five years when 'The Huntsman' was published. He claimed that he never

[2] Dmitri Filosofov, 'Lipovyi chai', in M. Scmenov and N. Tulupov, *Chekhovskii yubileinyi sbornik* (Moscow, 1910), 199; repr. in *A. P. Chekhov: Pro et Contra*, ed. I. Sukhikh (St Petersburg, 2002).

[3] Petr Bitsilli, 'Chekhov', *Chisla*, 1 (1930), 167; cited in Andrew Field, *The Complection of Russian Literature* (London, 1971), 173.

[4] Bartlett, *Anton Chekhov: A Life in Letters*.

spent more than a day on anything he wrote, but the qualities
remarked upon by Grigorovich suggest that this slight work was not
dashed off quite as casually as Chekhov claimed.

By contrast, the story 'On the Road' took Chekhov a full three
weeks, during which time he suffered the creative agony of four false
starts, and a great deal of anxiety. He readily admitted that he had
first started engaging in 'self-criticism' after being invited to contribute to *New Times* by its proprietor Alexey Suvorin in early 1886.
Now that he was publishing stories under his own name, in a prestigious daily newspaper, he was taking the writing process much
more seriously. 'On the Road' was submitted to *New Times* at the end
of that year, and was published on Christmas Day, echoing the sea-
sonal theme in the story. It was the longest short story Chekhov had
ever written for *New Times*, and by far the most ambitious. Set in the
southern Russia of Chekhov's childhood during a night-time blizzard, it portrays a larger-than-life, ruined landowner who has spent
his life in thrall to one passion or another, to the detriment of both
his livelihood and his personal life. Chekhov was nervous about how
the story would be received, but his fears proved to be groundless:
his brother wrote to him from St Petersburg to tell him 'On the Road'
had created a furore in the capital. It was one of Chekhov's
first stories, indeed, to win him wide recognition, and so inspired
Rachmaninov that in 1893 he wrote an orchestral fantasy (op. 7, *The
Rock*) based on it. Critics immediately made a connection between
the quixotic main character Likharyov and earlier incarnations of the
literary type of the Russian 'superfluous man'.

'The Letter', which was published in April 1887 (this time under
his own name), is one of Chekhov's many stories about the clergy.
Having grown up in a typically devout merchant family, Chekhov
knew the rites of the Russian Orthodox Church backwards. He was
made to sing in church choirs when a boy and also came into close
contact with priests through his pious father, whose idea of happiness
was attending every possible religious service. Chekhov largely lost
his faith as an adult, but his depictions of religious figures are almost
unfailingly sympathetic, as in this story. It was 'The Letter' which
first drew Tchaikovsky's attention to Chekhov—he had it read aloud
to him twice, because it made such an impression. The composer
wrote an admiring letter to the author soon afterwards, and later
came to visit Chekhov at home in Moscow, leaving his cigarette case

behind. Chekhov's admiration for Tchaikovsky was reflected in his dedication of his next short story collection to the composer.

'Fortune' was the first story Chekhov wrote after returning from his travels in the south of Russia in 1887. He had been invited to write a story for one of the Petersburg 'thick journals', and he immediately knew that he wanted to make his literary debut with a story about the steppe, the landscape that had entranced him from the time when he was a small boy growing up on its edges. Chekhov undertook the journey in the spring of 1887 in order not to 'dry out'; he wanted to resurrect in his memory things grown dim, so that his writing might become more vivid. Before he summoned up the courage to start writing 'The Steppe' for the prestigious literary journal the *Northern Messenger*, he experimented with 'Fortune'. As he explained to a friend, the story was about 'the steppe: the plain, night-time, a pale dawn in the east, a flock of sheep and three human figures talking about treasure'. Chekhov was not one for false modesty, and he proclaimed 'Fortune' to be the best story he had written at that time; it was to remain one of his favourite pieces of prose. The story certainly scored an immediate success with his readers: his brother in St Petersburg told him that issues of the newspaper it had been published in were still being passed from hand to hand in the city's cafés a week after publication, and were getting very worn.

'Gusev' was written on board the steamer carrying Chekhov home from the Siberian island of Sakhalin in 1890, and completed in Ceylon (Sri Lanka). No other story by Chekhov has such an exotic location or such a surreal ending: witnessed by a shoal of pilot fish, the corpse of the deceased peasant soldier Gusev is depicted sinking to the seabed, about to be consumed by a shark.

The euphoria which Chekhov felt at the purchase of his first property, a small country estate outside Moscow, led him to give in to the demands of his former editor Nikolay Leikin for some more comic stories. 'Fish Love', published in *Fragments* in the summer of 1892, was one of the results. Set in a pond outside a dacha, it was clearly inspired by Chekhov's own acquisition of a pond which, as a keen angler, he immediately filled with fish. The sophistication of his comic writing in the 1890s when compared to his work of the 1880s is immediately apparent. Particularly amusing—in the light of the criticism that his own work attracted—is the attitude to literary pessimism demonstrated in this story.

'The Black Monk' (1894) is another story which reflects Chekhov's life at his country estate in Melikhovo. But although he was a keen gardener, readers should be wary of identifying the author with the character of the horticulturalist Pesotsky in the story. This is one of his most ambiguous works, in which Chekhov seems to subvert the reader's expectations at every turn. None of the three main characters seems to fit the images projected onto them by the others.

Chekhov filled his writing with characters from all walks of Russian life. 'Rothschild's Violin' (1894) features a Jew, and is a sensitive exploration of Russian anti-Semitism. With its main character a coffin-maker who calculates that being dead will be more profitable than being alive, it is also one of Chekhov's most darkly humorous stories.

'The Student' (1894) is set in a provincial Russian landscape, but was written in the Crimea. This story, about a seminary student who suffers a temporary lapse of faith on Good Friday, the bleakest day in the Russian Orthodox year, was regarded by Chekhov as one of his most polished works, and also his favourite story. A parable about the power of art, it ends on a note of epiphany, its final, deliberately long sentence of exaltation definitively proving, in Chekhov's opinion, that he was not the cold-blooded pessimist his critics made him out to be.

Chekhov wrote 'The House with the Mezzanine' (1896) under the inspiration of visits to numerous dilapidated country estates, which were a source of continual poetic inspiration for him. It is an example of a story in which he pits opposing points of view: that of an indolent landscape artist and of a serious young woman who has dedicated her life to educating the peasantry. Chekhov was sympathetic to both. He valued time and leisure as vital to human happiness, aware that absorption in work can obscure one's ability to see, but he also highly respected the commitment of idealistic young people, and himself built three schools in the area where he lived.

'In the Cart' (1897) was written during Chekhov's nostalgic months in Nice, where he had gone in an attempt to preserve his deteriorating health. He knew only too well the miserable conditions provincial schoolteachers had to work under. Not only was he well acquainted with several local teachers in Melikhovo (one came to help in the decorating of Chekhov's house, in order to supplement his meagre income), but he worked variously as a school trustee, examiner, and inspector in the Melikhovo area.

'The Man in a Case' (1898), 'Gooseberries' (1898), and 'About Love' (1898) are a trilogy of stories linked by the figures of two men out on a summer hunting trip. All three have to do with limitations, imposed from within and without, and the theme of freedom. The trilogy becomes gradually more lyrical and elegiac in tone, with the satirical story that Burkin tells about the man in the case providing a sharp contrast with the lyrical night-time scene which frames it. Chekhov also includes a very subtle visual joke in 'The Man in a Case'. At the beginning of the story Ivan Ivanych, the vet, is described as tall and thin with a long moustache, while at the very end we learn that the teacher Burkin is short, fat, and bald, with a beard that reaches to his waist. Chekhov leaves it up to the readers who notice these small details to conjure up the humorous image of the two friends strolling through the countryside together with their hunting dogs.

Chekhov's most famous story, 'The Lady with the Little Dog' (1899), was completed just after he had moved into his new house in Yalta, where it is set. It is a classic example of a story in which there is an open ending, raising questions about love and marriage to which there are no easy answers. Like 'About Love' this story also provides an oblique commentary on the moral ideas preached by Tolstoy in *Anna Karenina*.

With the touching story 'At Christmas Time' (1900), Chekhov returned to the style of his earlier writing. It was written at the request of the editor of the *Petersburg Newspaper* (for which Chekhov had last written in 1887), and so the language, word-length, and topic were adjusted accordingly. The story is much shorter and straightforward than a typical story in a literary journal, and was written with a much less highbrow readership in mind. Its Christmas theme coincided with its publication on New Year's Day. It has been suggested that one of the Chekhov family's servant girls at his country estate in Melikhovo provided the inspiration for this story about the peasant Yefimya, who ends up unhappily married to someone who never posts her letters home to parents in the village.

Like many of the stories in this collection, 'The Bishop' (1902) is about death. Chekhov had mulled over the subject of a bishop dying at Easter-time for fifteen years before he finally sat down to write the story. When he did so, his own impending death was very much in his mind. Although this is a story about a member of the Russian Orthodox clergy, Chekhov's attention is focused (as in the early story 'The Letter') more on his character as a human being and less on him as a bishop. It is one of Chekhov's most autobiographical pieces of writing, reflecting aspects of his own relationship with his mother, his love of the Easter service and the sound of church bells, the long periods abroad when he was homesick for Russia, and the alienation he felt when people treated him as a famous writer rather than as a human being.

## The Literary Context

Giving an overview of Chekhov's career as a fiction writer is relatively straightforward. Defining his work in literary terms is an altogether trickier task, however, as the Futurist poet Vladimir Mayakovsky made clear in a typically provocative article (laced with the odd neologism), which he wrote in opposition to the many eulogies published to mark the tenth anniversary of Chekhov's death:

Of course, you will be offended if I say:
 'You don't know Chekhov!'
 'I don't know Chekhov?'
And you will immediately pull out a stock phrase from some dusty newspaper.
 'Chekhov is a deeply committed poet-haired lyric-reporter—he is a singer of the twilight.'
 'He's a devastating satirist.'
 'He's a comic writer.'
And a bard in a Russian shirt will rhyme:

> *He loved people with such a tender love*
> *Like a woman loves, like only a mother can love.*[5]

While Mayakovsky advanced the cause of Chekhov as a sober-minded artist-craftsman, there were critics who firmly anchored him as the successor of great Russian realists such as Tolstoy, and others who claimed him for the Symbolist camp. And after Chekhov was first introduced to the English-speaking world by Constance Garnett, he was seen as a pioneer of modernism. The ambiguity

[5] Vladimir Mayakovsky, 'Dva Chekhova', *Novaya zhizn'*, 7 (1914); repr. in *A. P. Chekhov: Pro et Contra*.

surrounding the question of how we interpret Chekhov has led to the word 'elusive' becoming a cliché in criticism of his writing.

From the very beginning, Chekhov's stories disconcerted readers. One of the very first English-language assessments of Chekhov's prose came from the pen of an erudite journalist and adventurer who later became Professor of Comparative Philology at Kharkov University. In 1891 Émile Dillon characterized Chekhov in a London literary journal as a 'miniaturist who courageously dives into the mysterious depths of the ocean of human life, and brings up—shreds and seaweed'.[6] Several decades later an even less flattering marine analogy occurred to the poet Anna Akhmatova, who condemned Chekhov's universe as 'uniformly drab'—a 'sea of mud with wretched human creatures caught in it helplessly'.[7] Dillon was writing when Chekhov was still at the start of his career as a major writer. Sensing that the young physician had most of his greatest works ahead of him, he was nevertheless already impressed by Chekhov's 'considerable insight', and by his 'unruffled calm and artistic objectivity'. As he rightly observed, it was a quality in which his colleagues were 'sadly deficient'. This was a shrewd appraisal. Akhmatova's views about Chekhov crystallized in the darkest years of Stalinist Russia; even with the full panoply of his works to choose from, Chekhov's tragicomic stories about unhappy lives were not always favoured reading in Russia in the bleak period of the purges. Akhmatova may have chosen the small-scale lyrical form as the preferred medium for her own writing in the past, but when it came to reading, she clearly felt a need for something more heroic in those troubled times.

Akhmatova was not alone in her impatience with the malaise which seems to pervade Chekhov's stories. During his lifetime Chekhov had grown used to people criticizing him for writing in a predominantly minor key, and for dwelling on pessimistic subjects. He was seen as a 'sick talent', a creator of 'autumnal moods', a destroyer of human hopes. Chekhov's younger contemporary Vladimir Nabokov perhaps presented the most eloquent articulation of this view when he came to prepare his undergraduate lectures on

[6] E. J. Dillon, 'Recent Russian Literature', *Review of Reviews* (July–Dec. 1891); cited in Victor Emeljanow, *Chekhov: The Critical Heritage* (London, 1981), 57.

[7] Isaiah Berlin, 'Meetings with Russian Writers', *Personal Impressions*, ed. Henry Hardy (London, 1980), 188.

Russian literature in the early 1940s. As an aristocrat from a distinguished family in St Petersburg, and a master of linguistic inventiveness, Nabokov was in many respects Chekhov's antipode. He was a strong admirer of Chekhov's writing, but nevertheless, what sprang first into his mind when he thought about it were the 'bleak landscapes, the withered sallows along dismally muddy roads, the grey crows flapping across grey skies, the sudden whiff of some amazing recollection at a most ordinary corner'. Magnanimously, he conceded that 'all this pathetic dimness, all this lovely weakness, all this Chekhovian dove-grey world' was 'worth treasuring'.[8]

There is, of course, an elegiac mood to most of Chekhov's writing: nearly all of the stories in this collection exhibit it. Chekhov himself confessed that he was prone to feeling elegiac when his house guests played the piano all day in the room next to his study while he was trying to write. The wistful Russian landscapes most people find depressing inspired him, and he was also unusual in seeing beauty in the monotonous expanses of the steppe. Above all, he spent most of his short adult life knowing he was going to die prematurely, having developed the symptoms of tuberculosis when he was 24. No matter how much he bravely suppressed the evidence, the impact this realization had on the general mood of his writing is incalculable; the serious note in his work begins at precisely this point. But after his death astute readers began noticing that there was more to Chekhov than elegy. As he is supposed to have once said to Maxim Gorky, 'to live in order to die is not all that funny, but to live knowing you are going to die prematurely is just totally stupid'. His constant awareness of the absurdities of the human condition ensured that there was at least one level of irony in his writing. To categorize it as 'pessimistic', therefore, is both reductive and redundant, as the English critic William Gerhardie observed in his 1923 critical study of Chekhov (one of the earliest in any language): life for Chekhov 'is neither horrible nor happy, but unique, strange, fleeting, beautiful and awful'.[9]

To surrender to the familiar clichés about Chekhov's short stories is, in effect, also to miss their point—which is that there perhaps is

---

[8] Vladimir Nabokov, *Lectures on Russian Literature* (London, 1983), 255.

[9] William Gerhardie, *Anton Chekov: A Critical Study* (London, 1923), 14; cited in Rene Wellek, introduction to *Chekhov: New Perspectives*, ed. R. and N. D. Wellek (Englewood Cliffs, NJ, 1984), 22.

no point, or at least not the point one might expect. Coming from a culture in which writers were seen also as teachers and moral guides, early Russian readers in particular were frustrated that Chekhov's stories asked questions, but gave no answers. But if there is any point to Chekhov's stories, it is that readers should themselves seek answers, as he repeatedly made clear in his letters. It was his duty as an artist to hold up a mirror to the world, but it was up to his readers to reflect on what they saw. 'Man will only become better when you make him see what he is like', Chekhov once jotted down in one of his notebooks. Reading a Chekhov story should not be akin to the sensation of drowning in mud, or even scouring the seabed and finding only seaweed and shreds; ideally, the experience should be like taking a bracing dip in the sea, or perhaps jumping into the snow after a Russian steam bath.

## Chekhov the Modernist

The stories of Chekhov's mature period seem straightforward at first glance, but as Virginia Woolf pointed out in her first review of his writing in 1918, there is invariably another view reflected in some mirror in the background.[10] It is for this reason untenable to see Chekhov wholly as a 'realist' writer in the great tradition of his predecessors Tolstoy and Turgenev, which has been the traditional view. While the distinguished critic Prince Dmitri Sviatopolk-Mirsky was arguing that the work of Chekhov marked 'the crest of a second wave in the history of Russian realism' in the 1920s,[11] writers such as Woolf were at the same time locating in it absurdity, random pathos, and irony—qualities we associate with modernism. Chekhov 'is not heroic', she writes; 'he is aware that modern life is full of nondescript melancholy, of discomfort, of queer relationships which beget emotions that are half-ludicrous and yet painful and that an inconclusive ending for all these impulses is much more usual than anything extreme'. Katherine Mansfield was another writer who championed Chekhov precisely because he had no answers to the existential questions he poses. In a letter she sent to Woolf about Chekhov in 1919, she writes: 'What the writer does is not so much

---

[10] Virginia Woolf, review of *The Wife and Other Stories*, *Times Literary Supplement*, 16 May 1918; cited in Wellek, *Chekhov*, 19.

[11] D. S. Mirsky, *Modern Russian Literature* (London, 1925), 91.

*solve* the question but . . . put the question. There must be the question put. That seems to me a very nice dividing line between the true and the false writer.'[12] From our twenty-first-century vantage point it is difficult to appreciate just how revolutionary Chekhov's stories were when they were first published, but John Middleton Murry was quite explicit about this in an article of 1922: 'Tchehov's breach with the classical tradition is the most significant event in modern literature . . . Tchehov wanted to prove nothing, because he profoundly believed there was nothing to be proved. Life was neither good nor bad; it was simply Life, given, unique, irreducible.'[13]

As the twentieth century proceeded, a different view of Chekhov began to emerge alongside the strangely persistent but hackneyed image of the writer whose works exuded the atmosphere of the *fin de siècle*, and who was even identified with his hopeless, struggling characters. This new view placed Chekhov firmly as the founder of the modern short story—the contemporary (in artistic terms) of Joyce, Conrad, and James. This subtle author became a 'writer's writer' furthermore, as can be attested by the steady stream of major names in English, Irish, and American fiction over the course of the last century who have come under his influence. As well as those already mentioned, Tennessee Williams, William Faulkner, Flannery O'Connor, Somerset Maugham, Frank O'Connor, and more recently Elizabeth Bowen, Eudora Welty, John Cheever, Raymond Carver, Andre Dubus, V. S. Pritchett, Sean O'Faolain, William Trevor, Richard Ford, and Tobias Wolff have all recognized him as a master. Raymond Carver, in fact, whose own late story 'Errand' (1987) is about Chekhov's last hours, unequivocally called him the 'greatest short story writer who has ever lived'.[14]

Chekhov's modernism lies not only in his sophisticated treatment of themes like human alienation, but also in his innovatory approach to structure, and it was characteristic of his fierce independence as a writer (he valued freedom above all else) that the story with which he made his literary debut in a 'thick journal', 'The Steppe', was as

---

[12] *Collected Letters of Katherine Mansfield*, ed. V. O'Sullivan with Margaret Scott, 4 vols. (Oxford, 1984–96), ii. 320; cited in Adrian Hunter, 'Constance Garnett's Chekhov and the Modernist Short Story', *Translation and Literature* (Spring 2003), 71.

[13] J. Middleton Murry, 'The Method of Tchehov', *Athenaeum*, 8 Apr. 1922; cited in Hunter, 'Constance Garnett's Chekhov and the Modernist Short Story', 70.

[14] Raymond Carver, 'The Unknown Chekhov', in *No Heroics Please: Uncollected Writings* (New York, 1992), 146.

experimental as anything he ever wrote. Closer to a prose poem than a story, its eight long chapters follow a 9-year-old boy's journey across the steppe, but there is no plot. As the earlier stories in this collection show, however, this was a revolution begun even before Chekhov joined the ranks of 'serious' writers. In 'Fortune', for example, which was the 'dress-rehearsal' for 'The Steppe', there is no 'event' other than a conversation three people have about buried treasure, and the story begins and ends in silence. Discarding the traditional plot-driven structure of the short story liberated Chekhov from having to observe other conventions. It meant that he could begin and end his stories inconclusively, for example, and challenge his readers' perceptions of what made up a short story. As Woolf observed in her essay 'Tchehov's Questions', the initial discomfort the reader feels at Chekhov's steadfast refusal to provide answers, as well as 'the choice of incidents and of endings', gives the impression 'that the solid ground upon which we expected to make a safe landing has been twitched from under us'. But somehow, she continues, things imperceptibly 'arrange themselves, and we come to feel that the horizon is much wider from this point of view; we have gained an astonishing sense of freedom'.[15] Chekhov would no doubt have nodded his head in approbation.

Plotlessness certainly does not amount to formlessness. Chekhov was a meticulous craftsman who exhorted his protégés to work continually on improving their style. Twentieth-century writers recognized this, and were to benefit hugely from Chekhov's innovations. As Eudora Welty has commented:

The revolution brought about by the gentle Chekhov to the short story was in every sense not destructive but constructive. By removing the formal plot he did not leave the story structureless, he endowed it with another kind of structure—one which embodied the principle of growth. And it was one that had no cause to repeat itself; in each and every story, short or long, it was a structure open to human meaning and answerable to that meaning. It took form from within.[16]

Another aspect of Chekhov's craftsmanship is evident in his use of language. When Tolstoy famously said that Chekhov was 'Pushkin

[15] Virginia Woolf, 'Tchehov's Questions', *The Essays of Virginia Woolf*, ed. Andrew McNeillie, 4 vols. (London, 1987), ii. 245.

[16] Eudora Welty, *The Eye of the Story: Selected Essays and Reviews* (New York, 1978), 74.

in prose', he had in mind the ability of both writers to achieve maximum expressiveness with the minimum of means, and their beguiling simplicity and clarity. What is also remarkable about both Pushkin and Chekhov is the apparent timelessness of their writing; when reading their works, one often has the impression that they are our contemporaries, so modern does their language seem. And this is what Mayakovsky had in mind when he wrote his astringent anniversary tribute:

Chekhov's language is as precise as 'Hello!' and as simple as 'Give me a glass of tea.' In his method of expressing the idea of a compact little story, the urgent cry of the future is felt: 'Economy!'

It is these new forms of expressing an idea, this true approach to art's real tasks, that give us the right to speak of Chekhov as a master of verbal art.

Behind the familiar Chekhovian image created by the philistines, that of a grumbler displeased with everything, the defender of 'ridiculous people' against society, behind Chekhov the twilight bard we discern the outlines of the other Chekhov: the joyous and powerful master of the art of literature.[17]

## Lyricism

Chekhov's prose is also Pushkinian in its lyricism. Irony came as second nature to both writers in their prose, but was sometimes suspended in favour of straightforward, heartfelt sentiment. In Chekhov's case, the two are also sometimes combined. It is no coincidence that the artist-narrator in 'The House with the Mezzanine' is a indolent landscape painter, for example. Tone is what is important in this story—one of lyricism, elegy, and nostalgia, but shot through with an ambivalence created by the irony directed at all the characters, but particularly at the narrator, so that the story never becomes too portentous. Lyricism for Pushkin and Chekhov did not mean the self-conscious application of 'poetic' effects, but pellucidity and lightness. Moments of epiphany in Chekhov are thus invariably understated, as in the last paragraph of 'The Student', which is in fact one long, carefully measured sentence whose impact is vital for the story's overall effect:

---

[17] Vladimir Mayakovsky, 'The Two Chekhovs' (1914); cited in Simon Karlinsky, 'Introduction: The Gentle Subversive', *Anton Chekhov's Life and Thought*, tr. Michael Henry Heim in collaboration with Simon Karlinsky (New York, 1973), 31.

And when he was crossing the river on the ferry, and then when he was walking up the hill, looking down at his own village and across to the west, where the cold crimson sunset was glowing in a narrow band, he realized that truth and beauty, which had guided human life in that garden and at the high priest's, had continued to do so without a break until the present day, and had clearly always constituted the most important elements in human life, and on earth in general; and a feeling of youth, health, and strength—he was only twenty-two years old—and an inexpressibly sweet expectation of happiness, of unfathomable, mysterious happiness, gradually overcame him, and life seemed entrancing and miraculous to him, and full of sublime meaning.

It is perhaps because D. S. Mirsky defined Chekhov first and foremost as a realist in the 1920s that he was immune to the beauties of his language. Chekhov's Russian, according to Mirsky, is 'colourless and lacks individuality. He had no feeling for words. No Russian writer of anything like his significance used a language so devoid of all raciness and nerve.'[18] Chekhov's words are certainly very plain; there are few metaphors or similes, and the linguistic register seems as homely as the characters in his stories. The beauty of his language lies not in the words themselves, however, but in the way they are put together. In keeping with the often modernist form of Chekhov's fiction, his prose is often musical rather than naturalistic. A key element of this musicality is the creation of a particular tone and prose rhythm in which no word or phrase is wasted, but on the contrary used in a very deliberate way. Rhythm is achieved through phrasing and carefully inserted pauses, as in the following passage from 'Gooseberries':

They returned to the house. And only when they had lit the lamp in the large drawing room upstairs, and Burkin and Ivan Ivanych were sitting in armchairs dressed in silk robes and warm shoes, and Alyokhin was walking about the room, freshly washed and with his hair brushed, in a new frock-coat, clearly enjoying the feeling of being warm and clean and wearing dry clothes and light shoes, and the beautiful Pelageya was offering tea with jam on a tray, treading noiselessly on the carpet and smiling gently, only then did Ivan Ivanych begin his story, and it seemed that it was not just Burkin and Alyokhin listening to it, but also the young and old ladies and officers who were looking at them sternly and calmly from their golden frames.

---

[18] D. S. Mirsky, *A History of Russian Literature from its Beginnings to 1900* (New York, 1958), 382.

Neither the long sentences often found in Chekhov's stories (which sometimes fill entire paragraphs), nor their clauses punctuated by strings of commas and semi-colons are thus to be viewed as evidence of stylistic negligence. Chekhov was characteristically reticent about his own methods, but a letter he wrote to an aspiring author in 1897 is revealing. He exhorted her 'to learn the correct and literate use of punctuation marks because in a work of art they often play the part of notes in a musical score, and you cannot learn them from a text book, but only from instinct and experience'.[19] The care that Chekhov took in constructing his cadences can be seen with particular clarity in his late story 'The Bishop':

The monks' singing that evening was harmonious and inspired; there was a young monk with a black beard leading the service; and as he heard about the bridegroom who cometh at midnight, and about the bridal chamber being adorned, the bishop did not feel repentance for his sins, or sorrow, but a spiritual calm, a quietness, and he was carried away by thoughts of the distant past, of his childhood and youth, when they had also sung about the bridegroom and the bridal chamber, and now that past seemed vivid, beautiful, and joyful, as it had probably never been.

Rhythmical phrasing is also created through particular combinations of long and short sentences and sentences which end in rows of dots. This is particularly marked in a haunting and poetic story like 'Gusev', where the open-ended, imprecise style of narration intentionally mirrors the semi-conscious state of the story's characters as they lie dying in the sick bay of a ship carrying them home to Russia. The rows of dots, after all, also have a role in contributing to the creation of mood:

And again there is stillness... The wind is running through the rigging, the screw propeller is throbbing, waves are crashing, bunks are creaking, but the ear has grown used to all this long ago, and it seems that everything all around is sleeping and staying silent. It is dull. The three sick people who played cards all day—two soldiers and a sailor—are already asleep and delirious.

It feels like the sea is becoming rough. Underneath him, Gusev's bunk goes slowly up and down as if it is sighing: once, twice, three times... Something hits the floor with a clang: a mug must have fallen.

---

[19] Bartlett, *Anton Chekhov: A Life in Letters.*

Another kind of musical structure is built up through the use of Wagnerian-style leitmotifs, as William Gerhardie noted in his 1923 study.[20] On one level there is the varied repetition of the colour grey in 'The Lady with the Little Dog': Anna has grey eyes, she wears a grey dress, the hotel room Gurov stays in is grey, and his hair is turning grey. On another level there is the complex pattern of associations that is created in 'The Student', in which the student Ivan's loss of faith is juxtaposed with Peter's betrayal of Christ, for example, and a link created between the widows' bonfire and the fire which burns on the night of Christ's betrayal. Musicality of a different variety can also be detected in Chekhov's stories through his (probably) unconscious use of a kind of sonata form. An exposition-development-recapitulation structure is particularly noticeable in stories such as 'Fortune', 'The Black Monk', and 'The House with the Mezzanine'.[21]

Although in the English-speaking world Chekhov's fame as a dramatist began to eclipse his standing as a prose writer early on (this has interestingly never been the case in Russia), it is important to recognize the extent to which the success of his plays rests on techniques he had refined through writing stories. This is particularly true of his ability to create mood and atmosphere by means of the lyrical devices outlined above. As critics like Donald Rayfield have commented, 'Chekhov remains a story writer when he composes drama'.[22] The four great plays of Chekhov's last years were written when a great number of his prose masterpieces were already behind him, but they are closely related to the stories both in terms of their subject matter and their themes. During a particularly long pause in the middle of *The Cherry Orchard*, his last work, for example, we hear the mysterious sound of a breaking string. The play's romantic dreamers typically refuse to believe the rational explanation that 'a bucket must have broken loose in the mines somewhere far away'. Chekhov had first heard this sound when he was a young man, while he was staying with friends who lived near the mining area in the hills north of Taganrog. He first introduced

---

[20] Gerhardie, *Anton Chekhov*, 14

[21] See R. Bartlett, 'Sonata Form in Chekhov's "The Black Monk" ', in Andrew Wachtel (ed.), *Intersections and Transpositions: Russian Music, Literature and Society* (Evanston, Ill., 1998), 58–72.

[22] Donald Rayfield, *Understanding Chekhov* (London, 1999), 240.

the sound of the breaking string into 'Fortune', the story written immediately following his travels in the steppe in 1887. Recalling that line in *The Cherry Orchard*, completed less than a year before he died, was Chekhov's veiled way of alluding to his own life, to the austere landscape which had inspired some of his most poetic writing, and to his earlier work—in particular, one of the stories he had written which he had been most pleased with from an artistic point of view. No wonder the stage directions indicate that the sound is distant, 'as if it had come from the sky', and 'dying away, sad'.

# NOTE ON THE TRANSLATION

Translation is at best an approximate art—an ongoing process that (thankfully) can never be permanently fixed. Foreign works of literature need the periodic transfusion of new translations in the way that musical compositions need to be continually re-interpreted by performers in order for them to live. This is particularly true when the works in question seem to invite radically different approaches in interpretation, as in the case of Chekhov's prose. While the position with translations of the classic nineteenth-century Russian realist novels remains relatively stable, Chekhov's ambiguity and contemporaneity have justified the need for new translations from each successive generation ever since the pioneering versions of Constance Garnett (*The Tales of Tchehov*, 1916–22). If Garnett's translations convey well the flavour of the era in which the stories were written, they nevertheless seem very archaic now, and contain occasional mistakes and lacunae. Later versions are more accurate, but are also ineluctably rooted in particular time periods. In seeking to create something timeless, by choosing locutions which might enable Chekhov's language to transcend both the era in which his stories were written, and that of the translation, in so far as it is possible (the rationale, after all, which lies behind the frequent new translations of Chekhov's plays), new translators of Chekhov must at the same time be aware of the finite life-span of their own versions.

Raymond Carver's well-justified belief that Chekhov's stories 'are as wonderful (and necessary) now as when they first appeared'[1] perhaps holds the key to presenting them in a new translation at the beginning of the twenty-first century, namely in a modernist light. Not only the delicate irony with which Chekhov probes the absurdity and tragedy of human existence, but the poetry and musicality of his prose risk being lost in translation if viewed exclusively through the prism of realism, which has often been the case in the past. The aim of these new translations is to render Chekhov's spare and unadorned language with as much precision as possible, bringing out its modernist, non-naturalistic qualities, while at the same time

[1] Raymond Carver, 'The Unknown Chekhov', in *No Heroics Please: Uncollected Writings* (New York, 1992), 146.

shaping the prose in an idiomatic way. It is for this reason that some of Chekhov's most lyrical and poignant prose has been selected for this anthology. The present collection brings together stories from across the range of Chekhov's literary career which have a particular focus on the themes of love and loss.

Chekhov's language is direct and straightforward, and the temptation to 'poeticize' it has been resisted, out of a conviction that it is lyrical enough as it stands. Translators can also succumb to 'improving' the original by smoothing phrasing and the repetition of certain words, as if this was carelessness on the author's part, rather than deliberate intention, and that temptation has also largely been resisted here. With a view to transposing Chekhov's prose rhythms, which contribute so subtly to the creation of atmosphere, his combinations of long and short sentences have in most cases also been preserved. The translator of Chekhov needs to be sensitive to his cadences and overall sense of form, paying as much attention to phrasing and sentence length as to the creation of a particular tone or mood. These translations also seek to remain faithful to Chekhov's idiosyncratic use of punctuation (which is interestingly echoed in his private correspondence), particularly the numerous commas and semi-colons that provide the breathing spaces in his long sentences, and the impressionistic rows of dots with which many of his sentences end.

The texts used for these translations are to be found in the Academy of Sciences edition of Chekhov's complete collected works (Moscow, 1974–83).

# SELECT BIBLIOGRAPHY

## Editions

A. P. Chekhov, *Polnoe sobranie sochinenii i pisem v tridsati tomakh*, ed. N. F. Belchikov *et al.* (Moscow, 1974–83).

Peter Constantine (tr.), *The Undiscovered Chekhov: Thirty-Eight New Stories* (New York, 1998).

Constance Garnett (tr.), *The Tales of Tchehov*, 13 vols. (London, 1916–22).

Ronald Hingley (tr.), *The Oxford Chekhov* (complete mature works), 9 vols. (Oxford, 1972).

Patrick Miles and Harvey Pitcher (trs.), *Early Stories* (Oxford, 1994).

## Letters

Rosamund Bartlett (ed.), R. Bartlett and A. Phillips (trs.), *Anton Chekhov: A Life in Letters* (London 2004).

Simon Karlinsky (ed. and intr.), *Anton Chekhov's Life and Thought: Selected Letters and Commentary*, tr. Michael Henry Heim in collaboration with Simon Karlinsky (New York, 1973).

Gordon McVay (ed. and tr.), *Chekhov: A Life in Letters* (London, 1994).

## Biographies

Rosamund Bartlett, *Chekhov: Scenes from a Life* (London, 2004).

Ronald Hingley, *A New Life of Anton Chekhov* (London, 1976).

V. S. Pritchett, *Chekhov: A Spirit Set Free* (New York, 1988).

Donald Rayfield, *Anton Chekhov: A Life* (London, 1997).

Ernest J. Simmons, *Chekhov: A Biography* (Boston, 1962).

## Background Reading

Edward Acton, *Russia: The Tsarist and Soviet Legacy*, 2nd edition (London, 1986).

D. S. Mirsky, *A History of Russian Literature from its Beginnings to 1900* (New York, 1958).

Charles Moser (ed.), *The Cambridge History of Russian Literature*, revised edition (Cambridge, 1992).

Hans Rogger, *Russia in the Age of Modernisation and Revolution: 1881–1917* (London, 1983).

David Saunders, *Russia in the Age of Reaction and Reform: 1801–1881* (London, 1992)

Victor Terras, *A History of Russian Literature* (New Haven, 1991).

### Criticism and Interpretation

Petr M. Bitsilli, *Chekhov's Art: A Stylistic Analysis*, tr. Toby W. Clyman and Edwina Jannie Cruise (Ann Arbor, 1983).

A. P. Chudakov, *Chekhov's Poetics*, tr. Edwina Jannie Cruise and Donald Dragt (Ann Arbor, 1983).

J. Douglas Clayton, *Chekhov Then and Now: The Reception of Chekhov in World Culture* (New York, 1997).

Toby W. Clyman, *A Chekhov Companion* (Westport, Conn., 1985).

Paul Debreczeny and Thomas Eekman (eds.), *Chekhov's Art of Writing* (Columbus, Ohio, 1977).

Julie W. de Sherbinin, *Chekhov and Religious Culture: The Poetics of the Marian Paradigm* (Evanston, Ill., 1997).

Thomas A. Eekman, *Critical Essays on Anton Chekhov* (Boston, 1989).

Victor Emeljanow, *Chekhov: The Critical Heritage* (London, 1981).

William Gerhardie, *Anton Chehov: A Critical Study* (London, 1923).

Vera Gottlieb and Paul Allain (eds.), *The Cambridge Companion to Chekhov* (Cambridge, 2000).

Adrian Hunter, 'Constance Garnett's Chekhov and the Modernist Short Story', *Translation and Literature* (Spring 2003), 69–87.

Robert Louis Jackson (ed.), *Chekhov: A Collection of Critical Essays* (Englewood Cliffs, NJ, 1967).

—— (ed.), *Reading Chekhov's Text* (Evanston, Ill., 1993).

R. L. Johnson, *Anton Chekhov: A Study of the Short Fiction* (New York, 1993).

Vladimir Kataev, *If Only We Could Know! An Interpretation of Chekhov*, tr. and ed. Harvey Pitcher (New York, 2002).

Virginia Llewellyn-Smith, *Anton Chekhov and 'The Lady with the Little Dog'* (Oxford, 1973)

Janet Malcolm, *Reading Chekhov: A Critical Journey* (New York, 2002).

Charles W. Meister, *Chekhov Criticism: 1880 through 1986* (Jefferson, NC, 1989).

L. M. O' Toole, 'Chekhov: *The Black Monk*', *Structure, Style and Interpretation in the Russian Short Story* (New Haven, Conn., 1982), 161–79.

—— 'Chekhov's "The Student" ', in Joe Andrew (ed.), *The Structural Analysis of Russian Narrative Fiction* (Keele, 1984), 1–25.

Cathy Popkin, *The Pragmatics of Insignificance: Chekhov, Zoshchenko, Gogol* (Stanford, 1993).

Donald Rayfield, *Chekhov: The Evolution of his Art* (London, 1975).

—— *Understanding Chekhov* (London, 1999).

Savely Senderovich and Munir Sendich (eds.), *Anton Chekhov Rediscovered: A Collection of New Studies with a Comprehensive Bibliography* (East Lansing, Mich., 1987).

Rene and Nonna D. Wellek (eds.), *Chekhov: New Perspectives* (Englewood Cliffs, NJ, 1984).

Thomas Winner, *Chekhov and His Prose* (New York, 1966).

### Further Reading in Oxford World's Classics

Anton Chekhov, *Early Stories*, trans. Patrick Miles and Harvey Pitcher
—— *Five Plays*, ed. and trans. Ronald Hingley.
—— *The Princess and Other Stories*, ed. and trans. Ronald Hingley.
—— *The Russian Master and Other Stories*, ed. and trans. Ronald Hingley.
—— *The Steppe and Other Stories*, ed. and trans. Ronald Hingley.
—— *Twelve Plays*, ed. and trans. Ronald Hingley.
—— *Ward Number Six and Other Stories*, ed. and trans. Ronald Hingley.

Nikolai Gogol, *Dead Souls*, ed. and trans. Christopher English, introd. Robert A. Maguire.

# A CHRONOLOGY OF ANTON CHEKHOV

1855 Alexander II becomes tsar of Russia.

1860 Chekhov is born on 17 January in Taganrog, a town on the Azov Sea in southern Russia, the third son of the merchant Pavel Yegorovich Chekhov (1825–98) and Evgeniya Yakovlevna Chekhova (1835–1919). Chekhov's parents married in 1854: of their seven children, five boys and two daughters, only the youngest, Evgeniya (1869–71), did not survive infancy.

1861 Emancipation of the serfs; Turgenev's *Fathers and Sons* published.

1864 Legal reforms; establishment of local government (*zemstvo*).

1865–9 Tolstoy's *War and Peace* published.

1866 Dostoevsky's *Crime and Punishment* published.

1868 Chekhov accepted as a pupil at the Taganrog Classical Gymnasium, following an unsuccessful first year at the Greek Parish school.

1873 Attends the theatre for the first time.

1873 Tolstoy's *Anna Karenina* published; Repin paints *The Volga Bargehaulers*.

1874 Mussorgsky's *Boris Godunov* first performed.

1876 Chekhov's father is declared bankrupt and flees with his family to Moscow, leaving Anton behind in Taganrog to finish school.

1879 Moves to Moscow and becomes a student in the Medical Faculty of Moscow University; Tchaikovsky's *Eugene Onegin* first performed.

1880 Chekhov's first story published in a St Petersburg comic journal; meets the artist Levitan, who becomes a close friend.

1880 Dostoevsky's *The Brothers Karamazov* published.

1880 Pobedonostsev becomes Procurator of the Holy Synod and is responsible for increase in censorship.

1881 Assassination of Alexander II; accession of Alexander III; deaths of Dostoevsky and Mussorgsky.

1882 Chekhov is invited to contribute to the leading St Petersburg comic journal *Fragments* by its editor, Nikolay Leikin.

1883 Death of Turgenev.

1884    Chekhov graduates from medical school; first signs of tuberculosis; writes almost 300 stories over the course of the year; publication of first book of stories, *Tales of Melpomene*; serialization of only novel, *Drama at a Shooting Party*, in a Moscow newspaper.

1885    Invited to write for the *Petersburg Newspaper*.

1886    Invited to write for *New Times* by its owner Alexey Suvorin, who becomes a close friend; first story published in Suvorin's newspaper is also under his own name; letter from Dmitry Grigorovich exhorting Chekhov to take his writing more seriously.

1887    Travels back to Taganrog and the steppe landscapes of his childhood.

1888    Publication of 'The Steppe' in the *Northern Messenger*—the first story to appear in a serious literary journal; awarded the Pushkin Prize by the Imperial Academy of Sciences; first performance of his play *Ivanov* in Moscow.

1889    Death of brother Nikolay from tuberculosis during a summer spent in the Ukrainian countryside.

1890    Travels across Siberia to the island of Sakhalin, where over a period of three months and three days he completes a census of its prison population; returns by sea.

1891    First trip to Western Europe with Suvorin: six-week tour to Vienna, Venice, Bologna, Florence, Rome, Naples, Nice, and Paris; assists with famine relief; Trans-Siberian Railway begun.

1892    Purchases small country estate at Melikhovo, 50 miles south of Moscow, and moves there with his parents. Works as a doctor to prevent cholera epidemic; publishes 'Ward No. 6'.

1893    Opening of Tretyakov Gallery in Moscow, the first public collection of Russian art. In 1897 Tretyakov commissions Yosif Braz to paint a portrait of Chekhov.

1893    Death of Tchaikovsky soon after the premiere of his Sixth Symphony.

1894    Death of Alexander III; accession of Nicholas II.

1895    Chekhov's first meeting with Tolstoy; *The Island of Sakhalin* published as a book.

1896    Builds the first of three schools in the Melikhovo area, and starts sending books to the Taganrog library. Disastrous first performance of *The Seagull* at the Imperial Alexandrinsky Theatre in St Petersburg.

1897    Falls seriously ill; publishes *The Peasants*, whose unvarnished depiction of rural life causes a furore; spends winter in Nice, and takes serious interest the Dreyfus Case.

1898    Meets Olga Knipper; death of father; successful first performance of *The Seagull* at the Moscow Art Theatre; Diaghilev founds a new journal, *The World of Art*, which Chekhov later declines to edit.

1899    Moves into house built for him in Yalta; first performance of *Uncle Vanya* at the Moscow Art Theatre; publishes 'The Lady with the Little Dog'.

1900    Elected an honorary member of the literary section of the Imperial Academy of Sciences; the first volumes of the Marx edition of his collected works are published.

1901    First performance of *Three Sisters* at the Moscow Art Theatre; marries Olga Knipper later in the year; excommunication of Tolstoy; assassination attempt on Pobedonostsev; student riots lead to closure of universities; Lenin's *What Is To Be Done?* published.

1904    First performance of *The Cherry Orchard* at the Moscow Art Theatre; worsening of medical condition leads to decision to seek treatment in Germany; dies in Badenweiler on 15 July (2 July according to Russian calendar).

# ABOUT LOVE
## AND OTHER STORIES

# THE HUNTSMAN

A sweltering, muggy midday. Not a cloud in the sky... The scorched grass looks dejected and hopeless: even if there were to be rain, it is too late for it to turn green now... The forest stands motionless and silent, as if the tops of the trees are looking somewhere or waiting for something.

A tall, narrow-shouldered man of about forty, wearing a red shirt, high boots, and patched trousers handed down from his boss, is sauntering with a lazy swagger along the edge of the clearing. Now he is sauntering down the road. On the right is a mass of greenery, and on the left a gold ocean of ripened rye stretches as far as the eye can see. He is red-faced and sweating. A white cap with a straight jockey's peak, obviously a charitable gift from some gentleman, sits rakishly on his handsome head of fair hair. There is a game-bag swung across his shoulder in which there is a squashed black grouse. The man is holding a cocked double-barrelled gun in his hands and looking through narrowed eyes at his scraggy old dog which has run on ahead and is sniffing around in the bushes. Everything alive has hidden from the heat...

'Yegor Vlasych!' The huntsman suddenly hears a quiet voice.

He gives a start and frowns when he turns round. A pale-faced woman of about thirty, with a scythe in her hand, is standing beside him, as if she had just grown up out of the ground. She tries to look into his face and smiles shyly.

'Oh, it's you Pelageya!' the huntsman says as he comes to a stop and uncocks his gun. 'Hmm!... What are you doing here?'

'There's women from our village working here, so I came along with them... as a labourer, Yegor Vlasych.'

'Uh-huh...' Yegor Vlasych mumbles as he walks slowly on.

Pelageya follows him. They walk on about twenty paces without saying anything.

'I haven't seen you for a long time, Yegor Vlasych...' says Pelageya, looking tenderly at the huntsman's moving shoulder-blades. 'You dropped in to our hut to get drunk on vodka in Holy Week, but we haven't seen you since... You just dropped in for a minute or two in Holy Week, and when I think of the state you were in... all drunk you were... Swore at me you did, and beat me, and then you left... And I'd been waiting and waiting... Keeping a look out, waiting for you... Ah, Yegor Vlasych, Yegor Vlasych! You might have stopped by just once!'

'And what's there for me to do at your place?'

'Well, there's nothing much to do, of course, but you know... there's the housekeeping... You could look over things... You're the master... Hey, I see you've shot a grouse. Yegor Vlasych! You should sit down and have a rest...'

Pelageya laughs like a fool as she says all this, then she looks up into Yegor's face... Happiness is just radiating from her face...

'Sit down? Could do...' Yegor says in an indifferent tone, as he chooses a spot between two fir trees growing together. 'Well, what are you standing there for? You sit down, too!'

Pelageya sits down a little way off in the full glare of the sun, and covers her smiling mouth with her hand, embarrassed by feeling so happy. A couple of minutes pass in silence.

'You might have stopped by just once!' Pelageya says softly.

'Why?' says Yegor with a sigh, taking off his cap and wiping his red brow with his sleeve. 'There's no point. Dropping in just for an hour or so would be a waste of time and you'd just get upset, and I certainly couldn't put up with living in the village the whole time... I've been spoilt, as you know... I need a bed to sleep in, good tea and nice conversations... everything's got to be proper, whereas where you are in the village it's just poverty and soot... I wouldn't last a day. Just supposing there was an order that I absolutely had to live with you—I'd either burn down the hut or take my own life. I've liked fine things ever since I was a boy, and there's nothing you can do about it.'

'So where you are living these days?'

'At Dmitry Ivanych, the master's place, as a huntsman. I bring game to his table... but mostly he just likes having me around.'

'That's not proper work, Yegor Vlasych... That would be just playing games for other people, but it's like that's your trade... your actual job...'

'You don't understand, you fool,' says Yegor, looking dreamily up at the sky. 'You've never understood what kind of a person I am, nor will you in a million years... You just think I'm a mad person who has thrown his life away, but for people who know, I'm the best marksman in the district. The gentlemen round here all know it; they've even written about me in a magazine. There's no one who can compete with me where hunting is concerned... And it's not pride or being spoilt that makes me loathe all your village work. I haven't known anything apart from guns and dogs since when I was young, you know. Take the gun from me, and I'll pick up a fishing rod; take that away and I'll use my hands. Well, maybe I've done a bit of horse-dealing too, and I used to roam the fairs when there was money, but you should know yourself that it's goodbye to the plough whenever a peasant starts hunting or getting into horses. Once the free spirit has taken hold of a man, there's no way of getting it out of him. It's just like if one of the gentlemen goes off to act in plays or does something else artistic; he can't be an office person or a landowner after that. You're a woman and you don't understand, but you should understand.'

'I do understand, Yegor Vlasych.'

'Well, I don't think you can, seeing as you are about to start crying...'

'I'm... I'm not crying...' says Pelageya, turning away. 'It's a sin, Yegor Vlasych! You could at least have the heart to spend one day with me. It's twelve years since I got married to you, and... there hasn't been love between us once! I'm... I'm not crying...'

'Love...' mumbles Yegor, scratching his arm. 'There can't be any love. We might officially be man and wife, but is that what we really are? To you I'm someone wild, and for me you're just a simple woman who doesn't understand anything. Do you really think we are a couple? I'm an idler, I'm spoilt and free to roam, but you're a labourer, a peasant; you live in filth and you're always bent over double. To see things your way, I might be the best huntsman around, but you just look at me in pity... How can we be a couple?'

'But we were wed, Yegor Vlasych!' says Pelageya, sobbing.

'Not of our own free will... You surely haven't forgotten? It's Count Sergei Pavlych you can thank... and yourself too. The count plied me with drink for a whole month out of envy that I was a better shot than he was, and you can be lured even into changing religion when you're drunk, not just into getting married. And so he went and married me to you when I was drunk to get his own back... A huntsman marrying a cowherd! You saw that I was drunk, so why did you marry me? You're not a serf, after all, you could have put up some resistance! I can see it's a dream come true for a cowherd to marry a huntsman, but you've got to use your head. Of course you're suffering and crying now. The count's laughing, and you're crying... well, you're banging your head against a wall...'

Silence ensues. Three wild ducks fly over the clearing. Yegor looks up at them and follows them with his eyes until they turn into three barely visible dots and come down to land way beyond the forest.

'What are you living on?' he asks, transferring his gaze from the ducks to Pelageya.

'I go out to work at the moment, but in the winter I take in a little baby from the orphanage to feed with a bottle. I get paid a rouble and a half a month.'

'I see...'

There is silence again. A quiet song carries across from the strip where peasants are working, but breaks off almost before it has begun. Too hot to sing...

'I've heard you've built Akulina a new hut,' says Pelageya.

Yegor Vlasych does not say anything.

'You must have a liking for her.'

'Well, that's fate for you!' says the huntsman as he stretches. 'You're just going to have to put up with your lot. Anyway, I've got to be going, I've been talking too long. I have to be in Boltovo by evening...'

Yegor stands up and stretches, then slings his rifle over his shoulder. Pelageya gets up.

'So when are you coming to the village then?' she asks quietly.

'Don't have any reason to come. I'll never come sober, and I'm not much use to you when I'm drunk. I get angry when I'm drunk. So goodbye!'

'Goodbye Yegor Vlasych...'

Yegor pulls his cap on to the back of his head, calls to his dog, and carries on his way. Pelageya stays behind and watches him walking off... She watches his shoulder-blades moving, the raffish way his cap sits on the back of his head, his casual, indolent stride, and her eyes fill with sadness and tender affection... Her gaze runs along her husband's tall, thin body, caressing it fondly... He is silent, but from his face and tensed shoulders Pelageya can see that he wants to say something to her. She goes up to him and looks at him entreatingly.

'Here you are!' he says, turning away.

He gives her a worn rouble note and walks off quickly.

'Goodbye, Yegor Vlasych!' she says, taking the rouble mechanically.

He walks down the road, which is as long and as straight as an outstretched belt... Pale and motionless as a statue, she stands there following every step he takes with her eyes. But now the red colour of his shirt is merging with the dark colour of his trousers, his strides cannot be seen, and you can no longer tell his dog from his boots. Only his cap is visible, but... Yegor suddenly takes a sharp right turn into the clearing and his cap disappears amongst the foliage.

'Goodbye, Yegor Vlasych!' whispers Pelageya, and she stands on tiptoe to see if she can catch one last glimpse of his white cap.

# ON THE ROAD

A little golden cloud spent the night
On the breast of a giant boulder...

(Lermontov)*

In the room which the Cossack innkeeper Semyon Chistoplyui himself called 'the travellers' room', since it was intended exclusively for
people passing through, there was a tall, broad-shouldered man of
about forty sitting at the large, unpainted table. With his elbows
resting on the table and his head propped up on his fist, he was
sleeping. A sallow candle stuck in a pomade jar lit up his light brown
beard, his thick, broad nose, his weather-beaten cheeks, and the
thick black brows which hung over his closed eyes... Taken separ-
ately, his nose, his cheeks, and his eyebrows were crude and cumbersome, like the furniture and the stove in the travellers' room, but
together they combined to look harmonious and even handsome.
That is the hallmark of the Russian face, so they say: the larger and
sharper its features, the softer and more kind-hearted it seems. The
man was wearing a gentleman's jacket which was shabby but edged
with new piping, a plush waistcoat, and baggy black trousers stuffed
into tall boots.

On one of the benches that stretched all the way along the wall,
sleeping on a fox-fur coat, was a girl of about eight, dressed in a
brown frock and long black stockings. She had a pale face, fair hair,
narrow shoulders, and a body that was thin and frail, but her nose
stuck out in a fat and unattractive lump, like the man's. She was fast
asleep and so did not notice the crescent-shaped comb which had
fallen out of her hair and was pressing into her cheek.

The travellers' room had a festive appearance. There was a smell
of freshly scrubbed floors in the air, for once there were no cloths
hanging off the rope that stretched diagonally right across the room,
and the icon lamp was flickering above the table, throwing a red
patch onto the icon of St George the Victor.* A row of cheap prints
stretched along the wall in both directions from the icon corner,
observing a strict and careful progression from the holy to the secu-
lar. The pictures seemed like one long strip covered with black

smudges in the dim light of the candle and the red icon lamp, but when the tiled stove decided to sing in unison with the weather, drawing air into itself with a wail, and when the logs sparked into bright flames, grumbling angrily as if they had just woken up, red patches started darting about the timbered walls, and then it became possible to see looming over the head of the sleeping man first the Elder Serafim, then the Persian Shah Nasreddin,* then a fat brown baby with goggle eyes, whispering something into the ear of a girl with an extraordinarily dim-witted and impassive face...

There was a storm raging outside. Something furious and ill-tempered, but deeply unhappy, was tearing round the inn with the frenzy of a wild animal, trying to break in. Banging the doors, knocking on the windows and the roof, and scratching at the walls, it by turns threatened, cajoled, and subsided briefly, only to throw itself down the chimney the next moment with a joyful, treacherous whoop; but the logs in the stove were blazing, and the fire confronted its enemy with the ferocity of a chained dog—a fight began, then after it came sobbing, screaming, and an angry growl. You could also hear in all this a resentful sorrow, an unsated hatred, and the wounded powerlessness of one formerly used to victory...

Bewitched by this wild, inhuman music, the travellers' room seemed to be cut off forever. But then the door screeched, and the boy who worked in the inn entered, wearing a new calico shirt. Limping on one leg, his sleepy eyes blinking, he trimmed the candle with his fingers, put some logs on the fire, and went out. Just at that moment the bell started ringing to mark midnight at the church in Rogachi, three hundred feet away from the inn. The wind played with the sounds of the bell as if they were snowflakes; chasing after the chimes, it spun them out in the huge space, so that some were broken up or stretched out into a long wave of sound, while others just disappeared in the general din. One chime sounded so clearly in the room, it was as if the bell was being rung right underneath the windows. The girl sleeping on the fox-fur gave a shudder and lifted her head. She looked at the dark window for a minute in a daze, and at Nasreddin, across whose face a crimson light from the stove was flitting just then, before turning her gaze to the sleeping man.

'Papa!' she said.

But the man did not move. The girl knitted her brows angrily, then lay down and drew her legs up close to her body. Someone let

out a long, loud yawn behind the door in the inn. Soon it was followed by the screeching of the door as it was opened, and muffled
voices. Someone came in and started stamping felt boots, trying to
get snow off them.

'What d'you want?' asked a lazy female voice.

'Madam Ilovaiskaya is here...'* replied a bass voice.

The door screeched again. The sound of the wailing wind could be
heard. Someone, probably the lame boy, went up to the door which led
into the travellers' room, coughed respectfully, and raised the latch.

'This way, milady,' said the singing female voice. 'We've got everything nice and clean in here, my lovely...'

The door swung open and a bearded peasant, covered in snow from
head to toe, appeared on the threshold in a coachman's long kaftan
and with a large suitcase on his shoulder. Following him in was
a small female figure, scarcely half the size of the coachman, all
wrapped up like a bundle, with no sign of a face or hands, and also
covered with snow. The girl noticed that the coachman and the bundle
gave off a damp smell like a cellar, which made the candle flicker.

'How idiotic!' said the bundle angrily. 'The road was fine! We only
had eight miles to go, mostly through the forest, and we would not
have got lost...'

'It wasn't a question of getting lost or not, milady, the horses just
won't go on!' answered the coachman. 'Wasn't as if I stopped
deliberately!'

'Heaven knows where you've brought us... But sshh... It seems
there are people sleeping here. Off you go...'

The coachman put the suitcase on the floor, sprinkling layers of
snow from his shoulders, made a plaintive sound through his nose,
and went out. The girl then saw two small hands emerging from the
middle of the bundle, stretching upwards and angrily undoing the
mass of shawls, scarves, and wraps. A large shawl fell onto the floor
first, then a hood, and after that a white knitted headscarf. Having
freed her head, the new arrival took off her mantle and immediately
shrank by a half. Now she wore only a long grey coat with large
buttons and sticking-out pockets. From one pocket she pulled out a
paper parcel with something in it, and from the other a cluster of
large, heavy keys, which she put down so carelessly that the sleeping
man shuddered and opened his eyes. For a while he looked around
from side to side as if not understanding where he was, then he

shook his head, went over to the corner, and sat down... The new arrival took off her coat, which again made her shrink by a half, removed her velvet boots, then also sat down.

Now she no longer looked like a bundle. She was a small, slim brunette, about twenty years old, as thin as a serpent, with a long, white face and curly hair. Her nose was long and pointed, her chin was long and pointed, her eyelashes were long, the corners of her mouth were pointed, and the expression on her face seemed spiky because everything else in it was so sharp. Buttoned up in a black dress, a mass of lace around her neck and sleeves, with pointed elbows and long, pink fingers, she was reminiscent of those portraits of medieval English ladies. Her serious, concentrated expression increased the similarity even more...

The brunette looked around the room, cast a sidelong glance at the man and the girl, and then went and sat by the window, shrugging her shoulders. The darkened windows were shaking from the raw west wind. Large, shining white snowflakes were landing on the glass but immediately vanishing, carried away by the wind. The wild music became stronger still...

After a long silence the girl suddenly changed position and said, angrily enunciating every word:

'Oh goodness, I am so unhappy! More unhappy than anyone in the world!'

The man got up and walked delicately over to the girl in a guilty manner, which did not go with his huge frame and large beard at all.

'Can't you sleep, sweetheart?' he asked in an apologetic voice; 'What do you want?'

'I don't want anything! My shoulder hurts! You're a bad man, Papa, and God will punish you! Just you wait, you'll be punished!'

'I know your shoulder hurts, sweetheart, but what can I do, my love?' said the man in the kind of tone adopted by drunk husbands apologizing to their strict wives. 'It's because of the journey that your shoulder hurts, Sasha. We'll reach where we are going to tomorrow and get some rest and then it'll be better...'

'Tomorrow, tomorrow... You always say tomorrow. We're going to be travelling for twenty more days!'

'But we will get there tomorrow, sweetheart, I give you a father's word. I never tell lies, and it's not my fault if we've been held up by the snowstorm.'

'I can't bear it any more! I can't bear it!'

Sasha swung her legs abruptly and filled the room with an unpleasantly shrill bout of crying. Her father waved his hand and looked in dismay at the brunette. She shrugged her shoulders and went timidly over to Sasha.

'Listen, dear,' she said; 'what's the point of crying? I know it's not nice if your shoulder is hurting, but what can be done?'

'The thing is, madam,' broke in the man quickly, as if to vindicate himself, 'we haven't slept for two nights, and we have been travelling in a really wretched carriage. So it's not surprising that she is not well and feeling miserable... And then we had this drunk coachman too, you know, and our suitcase got stolen... and there's been the blizzard all the time, but there is no point in crying is there, madam? Sleeping sitting up has really exhausted me, though, and I feel almost drunk now. Goodness me, Sasha, everything is bad enough already, but to have you crying too!'

The man shook his head, waved his hand, and sat down.

'Of course you shouldn't cry,' said the brunette. 'Only babies cry. If you're not feeling well, dear, you should get undressed and go to sleep... Come on, let's get you undressed!'

When the little girl was undressed and had calmed down, silence returned. The brunette sat by the window, looking in bewilderment at the room, the icon, and the stove... She obviously found everything very strange: the room, the girl in the short boy's shirt, with her large nose, and also her father. This strange person was sitting in the corner, looking around him in confusion, as if he was drunk, kneading his face with the palm of his hand. He sat there silently, blinking, and it was hard to imagine, looking at his guilty face, that he would start talking soon. But he was indeed the first one to start talking. He smoothed his trousers, gave a cough, grinned, then said:

'What a comedy this is, goodness me... I can't believe my eyes: what wood demon sent me to this wretched inn? What was the idea? Life throws up such slings and arrows that all you can do is toss your hands up in amazement. May I ask, are you travelling far, madam?'

'No, not far,' the brunette replied. 'I'm travelling from our estate, which is about twelve miles away, to our farmstead, where my brother and father live. My name is Ilovaiskaya, and that's the name of our farmstead, eight miles from here. What unpleasant weather!'

'Dreadful!'

The lame boy came in and put a new candle in the pomade jar.

'You could light the samovar for us, lad!'

'Who is drinking tea now?' said the lame boy contemptuously. 'It's a sin to drink before going to church.'

'Never mind, young lad, we're the ones who are going to burn in hell, not you...'

The new acquaintances got into conversation while they were drinking their tea. Ilovaiskaya discovered that the person she was talking to was called Grigory Petrovich Likharyov, that he was a brother of the famous Likharyov who served as marshal in one of the neighbouring districts, and that he had been a landowner himself at one time, but had managed to ruin himself in princely fashion. Likharyov, meanwhile, found out that Madam Ilovaiskaya's first name was Marya Mikhailovna, that her father's estate was huge, but that she had to manage it on her own since her father and brother were irresponsible, had their heads in the sand, and were too fond of borzois.

'My father and brother are all on their own at the farmstead,' said Ilovaiskaya, fluttering her fingers (she had a habit of fluttering her fingers in front of her spiky face while she spoke, and she licked her lips with her pointed little tongue after every phrase). 'Those men are a useless lot, and they won't lift a finger even to help themselves. I know who will have to provide the meal to break the fast* for them! My mother is no longer around, and our servants won't even lay the table without me there to chivvy them. You can imagine their situation now! They won't have a meal to break the fast with, and I have to sit here all night. It's all very strange!'

Ilovaiskaya shrugged her shoulders, gulped from the teacup, and said:

'There are some holidays which have a certain smell to them. At Easter, Trinity Sunday, and Christmas the air always smells special. Even people who don't believe love these holidays. My brother, for example, says there is no God, but he is the first to run off to church at Easter.'

Likharyov raised his eyes to Ilovaiskaya and laughed.

'People say that God does not exist,' Ilovaiskaya continued, also laughing, 'but then tell me, why do all the famous writers, scholars, and generally all the most clever people start believing at the end of their lives?'

'People who haven't been able to believe in their youth won't be able to believe in their old age either, madam, whatever their background.'

To judge from his cough, Likharyov was a bass, but he was speaking in a tenor voice, probably because he was afraid to speak loudly, or because he felt excessively shy. After pausing for a while, he sighed and said:

'I believe that faith is a capacity of the spirit. It is like talent: you have to be born with it. As far as I can judge from my own experience, the people I have encountered during my lifetime, and from everything that has gone on around me, this capacity for faith is something that Russian people possess in the highest degree. Russian life consists of an endless row of beliefs and passions, and it has not gone anywhere near lack of faith or rejection of it yet, if you want to know. If a Russian person does not believe in God, it means he believes in something else.'

Likharyov took a cup of tea from Ilovaiskaya, gulped down half of it straight away, and continued:

'I'll tell you about myself. Nature implanted an unusual capacity for faith in my soul. Although I should not confess such things so late at night, I've spent half my life belonging to the ranks of atheists and nihilists, but there has never been a single hour of my life when I did not have faith. Talents usually manifest themselves in early childhood, and my ability showed itself then too, when I was still small enough to walk underneath the table. My mother loved her children to eat a lot, and sometimes when she was feeding me, she would say "Eat up! Soup is the most important thing in life!" I believed her and ate soup ten times a day. I wolfed it down until I felt sick and faint. Our nanny told stories, and so I believed in house spirits, in wood demons, and all kinds of other creatures. I used to steal poison from my father, sprinkle it on gingerbread, and take it up to the attic, you know, so that the house spirits would eat it and die. And when I learned to read and started to understand what I was reading, then everything really went crazy! I tried running away to America, I went off to become a robber, I asked to be taken into a monastery, and paid some lads to persecute me in the name of Christ. And my faith was always active, never dead, note. Whenever I ran off to America it was never alone, I would drag someone else along, another fool like me, and I was glad when I froze beyond the town gates and was flogged; when I ran away to become a robber I would always come back with my face all cut up. It was a troubled childhood, I can tell you! And when I was sent to the gymnasium* and they started bandying about such truths as that the earth goes round the sun, or that white is not white at all but made up of the seven colours of the rainbow, my little head started spinning! Everything went all topsy-turvy in my life: Navin who stopped the sun in the Bible, my mother who rejected lightning conductors in the name of the prophet Elijah,* and my father, who was indifferent to the truths I was discovering. My insights inspired me. Like a madman, I would walk about the house and through the stables, preaching my truths; I was horrified by the ignorance around me, and I burned with hatred for those who only saw white as white... However, all that was just childish nonsense. My serious and, as it were, manly passions started in my university years. Have you had a higher education madam?'

'I was at the Mariinsky Institute* for young ladies, in Novo-cherkassk.'

'But you haven't had a university education? So you can't really know what science is. All the sciences across the world share the same *raison d'être*: the pursuit of truth! Every single one of them, even something bizarre like pharmocognosis,* is dedicated to the pursuit of truth, not to usefulness or comfort. It's wonderful! When you set out to study a branch of science, it is the beginning stage that astounds you most of all. Let me tell you, there is nothing more alluring or magnificent, there is nothing which can astonish or excite the human spirit like embarking on the study of science. You will be borne aloft by the brightest hopes after only the first five or six lectures, and you will feel as if you the possess the truth. I devoted myself to science as passionately and as wholeheartedly as if it was a woman I was in love with. I was a slave to science, and did not want to recognize any other source of knowledge. I studied day and night, never taking a break. I bankrupted myself buying books, and cried when I saw people exploiting scholarship for their own personal ends. But my passion did not last long. The thing is that every science has a beginning but no end, just like a recurring decimal. Zoology has discovered thirty-five thousand species of insects, and chemistry counts sixty elements. If in due course you add ten zeros to the end of these numbers, zoology and chemistry will be as far from their end as they are today, but all modern scientific work consists in the accumulation of numbers. I realized that when I discovered species number thirty-five thousand and one, and did not feel a sense of satisfaction. Well, actually I didn't really have time to experience any disappointment, as I was soon overpowered by a new faith. I got stuck into nihilism with all its proclamations, Black Re-Partition* organizations, and other sorts of things. I went to the people,* and I worked in factories oiling machinery, then as a barge-hauler. Then, when I was wandering about old Rus, I got a taste for Russian life, and I turned into a fervent devotee of this way of living. I loved the Russian people to distraction, I loved and believed in their God, in their language and their creativity... And so on and so forth... In my time I have been a Slavophile and have bombarded Aksakov* with letters, I've been a Ukraine fanatic, an archaeologist, a collector of folk crafts... I have been passionate about ideas, about people, about events and places... I have been endlessly passionate! Five years ago I was enthralled with the idea of rejecting personal property; my last faith was non-resistance to evil.'*

Sasha let out a shuddering sigh and changed position. Likharyov got up and went over to her.

'Would you like some tea, little one?' he asked tenderly.

'Drink it yourself!' the girl replied rudely.

Likharyov became embarrassed, and walked guiltily back to the table.

'So you've had a rich life,' said Ilovaiskaya. 'You've got some memories there.'

'Well, yes, it seems very rich when you are sitting and chatting to a kind lady over a cup of tea, but you might ask what all this richness cost me. What price did I have to pay for all this variety in my life? After all, madam, I didn't believe like a German doctor of philosophy or some pretentious person, I did not live out in the wilderness; each faith of mine has compelled me to submit, and torn me into pieces. Judge for yourself. I was rich like my brothers, but now I am a beggar. While I was in thrall to my passions I squandered my wife's fortune and my own—a great deal of other people's money. I am forty-two now, and old age is round the corner, but I have nowhere to shelter; I'm like a dog that has got separated from the wagon train at night. I have never known peace in my life. My soul has never ceased to languish and I've suffered even when I've been cherishing hopes... I've worn myself out from doing hard labour, I've put up with hardships, I've been to prison five times and roamed across Arkhangelsk and Tobolsk* provinces... it's painful to remember! I have lived, but in my state of intoxication I've never experienced the actual process of life. Believe me, I do not remember one single spring; I never noticed my wife's affection or my children being born. What else can I tell you? I have brought unhappiness to everyone who has loved me... My mother has been mourning for me for fifteen years now, and my proud brothers, who have had to suffer for me, blush and cringe with shame, and throw money at me, have finally come to find me as abhorrent as poison.'

Likharyov stood up and then sat down again.

'If I was just unhappy I would thank God,' he continued, not looking at Ilovaiskaya. 'My personal unhappiness fades into the background when I remember how clumsy I have often been in my passions; how far from the truth, how unfair and cruel and dangerous I have been! How often I have hated with all my soul and despised those I should have loved, and vice versa. I have betrayed people a thousand times. One day I believe and am ready to prostrate myself, then next day I am running like a coward from my current gods and friends, and silently going along with the scoundrel who follows me close behind. God alone has seen how often I have cried and gnawed the pillow from shame over my passions. I have never once in my life deliberately lied and done evil, but my conscience is not clean! I cannot even boast, madam, that I do not have someone's life on my conscience, as my wife, whom I wore out with my reckless ways, died in front of my eyes. Yes, my wife! Listen, we have two attitudes to women which predominate these days. Some people measure female skulls in order to prove that women are inferior to men; they seek out their faults so as to mock them, then they try to be clever in front of them and so justify their own beastliness. The others try with all their might to raise women to their level; what they do is make them study the thirty-five thousand species, and then get them to mouth and write the inanities they themselves mouth and write...'

Likharyov's face darkened.

'And I'll tell you, women have always been and will always be slaves to men,' he said in his bass voice, striking the table with his fist. 'A woman is a soft, delicate piece of wax from which man will make whatever he wants. Goodness me, for a man's worthless passion a woman will be ready to cut her hair off, abandon her family, and die abroad... And among the ideas for which she will sacrifice herself there will not be one that she can call her own! She will be a selfless, devoted slave! I have not measured skulls, but I'm telling you this on the basis of my own hard and bitter experience. If I have managed to inspire them, the proudest and most independent women have followed me without a moment's thought, asking no questions and doing everything I have wanted; there was a nun who I turned into a nihilist, who I later heard went and shot a policeman; my wife never left me in my wanderings for a minute, and changed her faith like a weather-vane whenever I changed mine.'

Likharyov leapt up and started walking round the room.

'Sublime, noble slavery!' he said, clasping his hands together. 'That is where the lofty meaning of female life lies! From the terrible muddle which has piled up in my head over the course of my relationships with women, it is not ideas, clever words, or philosophy that have remained intact in my memory, as if caught in a filter, but that extraordinary submissiveness to fate, that unbelievable charity and readiness to forgive...'

Likharyov clenched his fists, stared straight ahead of him, and then, with a kind of passionate intensity, as if he was chewing over every word, he said through clenched teeth:

'That... that magnanimous readiness to endure and remain true to the grave, all that poetry of the heart... The meaning of life lies precisely in that submissive martyrdom, in those tears which can soften stone, in that boundless, all-forgiving love which brings light and warmth into the chaos of life...'

Ilovaiskaya stood up slowly, took a step towards Likharyov, and fixed her eyes on his face. She could tell from the tears which shone on his eyelashes, from his tremulous, passionate voice and his flushed cheeks, that women were not an accidental or a casual topic of conversation. They were the subject of his new passion, or, as he himself put it, his new faith! For the first time in her life Ilovaiskaya saw before her a person of ardent, passionate faith. He seemed completely mad and deranged to her as he gesticulated, his eyes sparkling, but she felt so much beauty in the fire of his eyes, in his speech, and in the movements of his large body that she stood rooted to the spot before him without even realizing it, and was gazing into his face with rapture.

'Just consider my mother!' he said, stretching out his hands to her with an expression of entreaty on his face. 'I have poisoned her existence, and brought disgrace on the Likharyov family in her eyes; I have caused her the kind of harm that only the bitterest of enemies could cause, and what do you think? My brothers give her a few kopecks for prayers in church, and she violates her religious principles, saves up this money, and sends it secretly to her dissolute Grigory! That one detail alone nourishes and ennobles the soul more than theories, clever words, and thirty-five thousand species! I can give you a thousand examples. Well, let's take you! There is a blizzard outside, it's night, and you are travelling to see your brother and father in order to warm them up with some affection on the holiday, although they are perhaps not thinking about you, and may have even forgotten about you. And in a while, when you fall in love with someone, you will follow him to the North Pole. You will, won't you?'

'Yes, if... I fall in love.'

'There you are, you see!' Likharyov exclaimed joyfully, and he even stamped his foot. 'Goodness me, I'm so glad I have made your acquaintance! Fate is so kind to me; I keep meeting wonderful people. Never a day passes without me making the acquaintance of someone I would give my life for. There are many more good people in the world than bad ones. Isn't it amazing that we are being so open with each other, talking heart to heart as if we have known each other a hundred years? Let me tell you, sometimes you can hold out for about ten years, you can keep quiet and be secretive with your friends and your wife, but then you might meet some cadet in a train carriage and pour out your soul to him. I have the honour of seeing you for the first time in my life, and I have unburdened my soul to you the way I have never done in my life before. How can that be?'

Rubbing his hands together and smiling broadly, Likharyov walked up and down the room and started talking about women again. Just then the bell started ringing for the early morning service.

'Honestly!' exclaimed Sasha, bursting out crying, 'He won't let me sleep with his talking!'

'Ah, yes!' said Likharyov, recollecting himself. 'I'm sorry, my love. Go to sleep, go to sleep... Apart from her, I've got two boys,' he whispered. 'They live with their uncle, madam, but this one can't spend a day apart from her father. She suffers and grumbles and clings to me like flies stick to honey. But I've chuntered on, madam, and it would not be a bad thing for you to get some rest. May I make up a bed for you?'

Without waiting to be granted permission, he shook her wet mantle and stretched it out on the bench, fur side up, then gathered the scarves and shawls that had been discarded and put her rolled-up coat as a pillow at the head, doing all this silently, with an expression of beatitude on his face, as if he was dealing not with a woman's clothes but with fragments of holy relics. There was something guilty and sheepish about his whole person, as if he was ashamed of his height and strength in the presence of such a frail creature...

When Ilovaiskaya had lain down, he extinguished the candle and sat on a stool near the stove.

'So there you are, madam,' he whispered, as he lit a thick Russian cigarette and let its smoke be drawn into the stove. 'Nature has given Russian people an extraordinary capacity for faith, a questing mind, and a gift for abstraction, but when it comes up against carelessness, indolence, and impractical frivolity everything turns to dust... Ah yes...'

Ilovaiskaya looked into the darkness in surprise and could see only the red patch on the icon and the light from the stove flickering on Likharyov's face. The darkness, the sound of the bell ringing, the howl of the snowstorm, the lame boy, the petulant Sasha, and his long speech—all of these things became mixed up, fusing into one enormous impression, and God's world seemed fantastic to her, full of wonder and enchantment. What she had just heard was still ringing in her ears, and human life seemed to her to be a beautiful, poetic tale which had no end.

The enormous impression grew and grew, filling her consciousness, and then it turned into a sweet dream. But while Ilovaiskaya slept, she could still see the icon lamp and the fat nose with the red light dancing on it.

She heard crying.

'Dearest papa,' the child's voice was pleading tenderly. 'Let's go back to Uncle's! There's a Christmas tree there! And Styopa and Kolya are there!'

'What can I do, sweetheart?' replied the soft male bass voice, in an attempt to convince. 'You must understand my position! You must!'

And then the man's crying joined in with the child's. This voice of human sorrow amongst the howl of the storm graced the young woman's hearing with such sweet human music that the pleasure of listening to it was too exquisite, and she also started crying. She then saw a large black shadow coming quietly over to her, picking up a shawl which had fallen to the floor and wrapping it around her feet.

A strange howl awakened Ilovaiskaya. She jumped up and looked around in surprise. The blue light of dawn was appearing through the windows, which were half covered up with snow. The stove, the sleeping girl, and Shah Nasreddin were clearly visible in the grey twilight which hung in the room. The stove and the icon lamp had already gone out. Through the wide-open door you could see the main room of the inn, the counter and tables. A man with a vacant-looking gypsy face and a startled expression was standing in the middle of the room in a puddle of melted snow, holding a large red star on a pole.* He was surrounded by a crowd of little boys as motionless as statues, who were all encrusted with snow. The light of the star, shining through the red paper, was making their damp faces red. The crowd was roaring out a folk carol, though Ilovaiskaya could only distinguish one verse in the din:

> 'Hey you, little boy
> Take a little knife
> We'll kill the Jew
> The sorrowful son...'*

Likharyov was standing near the counter, looking with emotion at the singers and tapping his foot in time with the music. When he caught sight of Ilovaiskaya he grinned from ear to ear and went up to her. She also smiled.

'Happy Christmas!' he said. 'I could see you were fast asleep.'

Ilovaiskaya looked at him, did not say anything, and continued smiling.

After the night-time conversations he no longer seemed tall and broad-shouldered, but small, in the way that an enormous ship seems small after it has crossed the ocean.

'Well, I need to be going,' she said. 'I must get dressed. Tell me, where is it you are headed now?'

'Me? I'm going to Klinushka Station, from there to Sergievo, and from Sergievo twenty-five miles by carriage to some fool's coal-mines,* a general called Shashkovsky. My brothers have found a managerial job there for me... I'm going to go digging for coal.'

'Oh, I know those coal-mines. Shashkovsky is my uncle. But... why are you going there?' asked Ilovaiskaya, looking at Likharyov in surprise.

'To be a manager. I'm going to run the mines.'

'I don't understand!' said Ilovaiskaya, shrugging her shoulders. 'You are going to the mines? But it's just bare steppe there, it's deserted, and so boring you won't last a day! The coal is useless, no one buys it, and my uncle is a maniac, a despot, he's bankrupt... You won't be paid!'

'It doesn't matter,' said Likharyov indifferently. 'But thanks for letting me know about the mines.'

Ilovaiskaya shrugged her shoulders and walked anxiously around the room.

'I don't understand! I really don't understand!' she said, fluttering her fingers in front of her face. 'It's an impossible idea... complete folly! You've got to understand that it's... it's worse than exile, it's a living grave! Heavens above,' she said fervently, going up to Likharyov and fluttering her fingers before his smiling face; her upper lip was trembling and her spiky face had gone pale. 'Well, just imagine the bare steppe and all that loneliness. No one to talk to, and you... with your passion for women! Coal-mines and women!'

Ilovaiskaya was suddenly ashamed of the strength of her feelings and, turning her back to Likharyov, she went over to the window.

'No, you mustn't go there, you mustn't!' she said, tracing her finger quickly over the windowpane.

She felt, not only in her soul but also in the small of her back, that behind her stood an endlessly unhappy, hopeless, and wretched person, but he was looking at her and smiling warmly, as if he did not acknowledge his unhappiness, and as if it had not been him crying during the night. It would have been better if he had carried on crying! She walked anxiously up and down the room a few times, then went and stood in the corner and became lost in thought. Likharyov was saying something, but she did not hear him. With her back turned to him, she took out of her purse a twenty-five rouble note and crumpled it for a long time in her hands, but when she glanced at Likharyov she went red and put the note in her pocket.

The voice of the coachman could be heard behind the door. Ilovaiskaya started to get dressed, silently and with a severe, concentrated expression. Likharyov wrapped her up, chatting away merrily, but every word he said lay heavily on her soul. It is not funny to hear people who are unhappy or dying making jokes.

When the transformation of a living person into a formless bundle was complete, Ilovaiskaya looked round for a final time at 'the travellers' room', stood for a while in silence, then slowly walked out. Likharyov went to see her off...

Heaven knows why, but for some reason winter was still raging outside. Huge clouds of soft, large snowflakes were circling over the ground restlessly, unable to find a place to settle. The horses, the sleigh, the trees, and the bull tied to a post were all white, and seemed soft and fluffy.

'Well, God be with you,' murmured Likharyov as he helped seat Ilovaiskaya in her sleigh. 'Remember me kindly...'

Ilovaiskaya did not say anything. When the sleigh started moving and was going round a large snowdrift, she glanced back at Likharyov, looking as if she wanted to say something to him. He ran after her but she did not say a word, and just looked at him through long eyelashes, on which hung snowflakes...

Maybe his sensitive soul could read that glance, or perhaps his imagination deceived him, but it suddenly seemed to him that two or three more good, strong stories and that girl would have forgiven him his failures, his old age, and his poverty, and followed him like a shot, without even thinking about it. He stood there for a long time rooted to the spot, staring at the tracks left by the runners. Snowflakes landed eagerly on his hair, on his beard, and on his shoulders... Soon the tracks left by the runners disappeared, and he himself was covered in snow and beginning to look like a white boulder, but his eyes were still seeking something in the snowclouds.

# THE LETTER

Archdeacon Fyodor Orlov, a handsome portly man of about fifty, pompous and austere as always, with his habitual expression of self-worth now joined by one of extreme tiredness, was pacing up and down his small room thinking obsessively about one thing: when would his guest finally leave? It was wearing him down and he could not think about anything else. His visitor, Father Anastasy, a priest in one of the outlying villages, had come to see him about three hours earlier regarding some business concerning him which was very unpleasant and boring; he had stayed too long and was now sitting in the corner at the round table with his elbow resting on a fat accounts book and clearly not planning to leave, even though it was already after eight in the evening.

Not everyone has the gift of knowing when to be silent and when to leave. Even well-brought-up, tactful people sometimes do not notice that their presence is arousing in their tired or busy host a feeling akin to hatred, which is carefully concealed and covered up with lies. Father Anastasy could see and understand perfectly well that his presence was tedious and unwanted, that the archdeacon was worn out and needed to rest, having conducted a night-time service, and then a long mass at midday; he kept planning to get up and leave, but somehow it did not happen, so he just carried on sitting there, as if he was waiting for something. He was an old man of about sixty-five, prematurely decrepit, bony and stooping, with an old man's dark gaunt face, red eyelids, and a long narrow back like that of a fish; he was wearing a flamboyant pale lilac cassock which was too big for him (it had been given to him by the widow of a young priest who had recently died), a cotton kaftan with a wide leather belt, and a pair of clumsy boots, whose size and colour clearly showed that Father Anastasy made do without galoshes. Despite his office and advanced years, there was something pathetic, downtrodden, and oppressed in his tired red eyes, in the grey pigtail tinged with green which hung down from the back of his head and in the large shoulder-blades on his skinny back... He sat there silently without moving, and coughed with such circumspection that it was as if he was afraid the sound of his coughing would make his presence even more noticeable.

The old man had come to see the archdeacon on business. About two months earlier he had been forbidden to conduct services until further notice and was now being investigated. He had racked up a good number of sins. He did not lead a sober life, he did not get on with the clergy and the community, was careless about the church register and the bookkeeping—these were all things of which he had been formally accused, but in addition there had long been rumours that he had performed unlawful marriages for money and sold certificates showing proof of fasting* to civil servants and officers who came to him from the town. These rumours had persisted because he was poor and had nine children living off him who were failures just like he was. The sons were uneducated and spoilt and sat around doing nothing, while the unattractive daughters were not getting married.

Not possessing the strength to be frank, the archdeacon just walked up and down without saying anything, then tried to make a few hints.

'So you're not going home tonight?' he asked, pausing by the dark window and poking his little finger in at the sleeping canary whose feathers were all puffed up.

Father Anastasy gave a start, coughed circumspectly, and then said in a rush:

'Home? Never mind about that, Fyodor Ilyich. As you know, I can't hold services anywhere, so what will I do there? I don't want to have to look people in the eye; that's why I left. As you know, it's shameful not to be able to hold services. And I've got business here, Fyodor Ilyich. After breaking the fast tomorrow I want to have a good talk with the Father conducting the investigation.'

'I see...' said the archdeacon with a yawn. 'But where are you staying?'

'At Zyavkin's.'

Father Anastasy suddenly remembered that in about two hours the archdeacon would have to conduct the Easter service, and he became so ashamed of his unwelcome, disagreeable presence that he decided to get up at once and give the exhausted man some rest. The old man stood up in order to leave, but before beginning to say his farewells, he spent a minute coughing and looking searchingly at the archdeacon's back, his whole frame still expressing a sense of vague expectation; his face reflected a mixture of shame, timidity, and pathetic, forced merriment, of the kind exhibited by people who have no self-respect. Somehow managing to gesture decisively with his hand, he said with a hoarse, tinkling laugh:

'Father Fyodor, extend your charity right to the limit; to send me off, ask for me to be given... just a little glass of vodka!'

'This is not the time to be drinking vodka,' said the archdeacon severely. 'You should be ashamed.'

Father Anastasy became even more embarrassed, started laughing, and sank back down on to the chair, forgetting his decision to go home. The archdeacon looked at his bewildered, disconcerted face and at his hunched-up figure and felt sorry for the old man.

'The Lord will permit us to drink tomorrow,' he said, wishing to soften his harsh refusal. 'Everything in its own good time.'

The archdeacon believed in the possibility of people being reformed, but now that the feeling of pity had been aroused in him, it seemed to him that there was just no hope for this haggard old man under investigation, and entangled in sin and infirmities; there was now no power on earth which could straighten out his back, give his vision clarity, and restrain the disagreeable timid laugh which he deliberately employed in order to try to smooth over the abrasive impression he made on people.

The old man seemed to Father Fyodor to be not so much depraved and guilty as oppressed, abused, and unhappy; the archdeacon remembered his wife, his nine children, and Zyavkin's squalid rooms; he also remembered for some reason the people who revel in seeing drunk priests and convicted officials, and he thought that the best thing which could happen to Father Anastasy now would be for him to die as quickly as possible and leave this world forever.

Footsteps could be heard.

'Father Fyodor, are you resting?' came a bass voice from the hall.

'No, deacon, come in.'

Deacon Lyubimov, Orlov's colleague, came into the room. He was an old but hearty man with black hair, a large bald patch on the top of his head, and thick black brows like a Georgian. He bowed to Anastasy and sat down.

'What good tidings do you bring?' asked the archdeacon.

'There's no good news,' answered the deacon, continuing after a pause with a smile. 'Little children, little trouble, big children, big trouble. Father Fyodor, there is something that has happened and I just can't work out what to do. It would be funny if it weren't so sad.'

He was silent again, then smiled more broadly and said:

'Nikolay Matveyevich came back from Kharkov today. He was telling me about my Pyotr. He went to see him a couple of times.'

'And what he did tell you?'

'It's not his fault, but he's got me worried. He wanted to make me happy, but when I got to thinking about it, I realized there wasn't much to be happy about. I should be grieving rather than rejoicing... Your Petrushka, he said, is pretty sharp-witted; impossible to keep up with him. Well that's good, I said. I had lunch with him, he said, saw his way of life. It's a good life he has, he said, doesn't want for anything. I was curious, of course, so I asked: what he did he dish up for lunch? There was a fish course to begin with, he said, a sort of fish soup, then there was tongue with peas, and then, he said, roast turkey. Turkey during Lent? That's a piece of joy, that is, I said. Turkey during our great fast? Eh?'

'Nothing surprises me,' said the archdeacon, narrowing his eyes in a withering way.

Sliding the large fingers of both hands behind his belt, he pulled himself up to his full height, and in the tone he usually used for sermons or for teaching scripture to the children in the district school, he said:

'People who do not observe the fasts fall into two categories: there are those who are just irresponsible, and there are those who do not believe. Your Pyotr does not observe the fasts because of lack of faith. Ah, yes.'

The deacon looked timidly at Father Fyodor's stern face and said:

'There's more, it gets worse... They talked, got into discussion about this and that, and it also turns out that my heathen son is living with some madam, someone else's wife. She is living in his flat instead of a proper wife and mistress, pouring the tea, receiving guests, and all that kind of thing, as if they are wed. It's been three years he has been larking about with this viper. It would be funny if it weren't so sad. They have been living together for three years, and there are no children.'

'They must be living chastely then,' chuckled Father Anastasy, coughing huskily. 'There are children, Father Deacon, it's just that they aren't kept at home! They get sent off to foundling homes. Hee-hee-hee...' (Anastasy had a fit of coughing at this point.)

'Don't interfere, Father Anastasy,' said the archdeacon severely.

'Nikolay Matveyevich asked him: who is this madam sitting at table ladling the soup?' the deacon continued, peering gloomily at Father Anastasy's bent frame. 'And he says to him: that's my wife. And then he asked: Have you been married long? And Pyotr replies to him: we got married in Kulikov's cake shop.'

The eyes of the archdeacon blazed angrily, and colour appeared in his temples. Apart from his sinfulness, Pyotr was not someone he was fond of anyway. Father Fyodor had a bit of a grudge against him. He remembered him when he was a boy studying at the gymnasium; he remembered him clearly, because even then the boy had seemed abnormal to him. When he was a schoolboy, Petrusha had been ashamed of serving at the altar, he had taken offence if you were over-familiar with him, he had never crossed himself when entering the room, and most memorable of all, he had loved to talk volubly and passionately, and in Father Fyodor's opinion it was indecent and harmful for children to talk too much; apart from that, Petrusha was dismissive and critical of fishing, which the archdeacon and the deacon were both keen on. Pyotr did not go to church at all when he was a student; he slept until midday, looked down on people, and liked to raise sensitive, forbidden topics with a particular zeal.

'Well what exactly is it you want?' asked the archdeacon, as he walked up to the deacon and looked angrily at him. 'What do you want, eh? This is just what could have been predicted! I always knew and was quite sure that nothing good would come of your Pyotr! I told you then and I'm telling you now. What you sowed, you are now reaping! You must now reap!'

'But what did I sow, Father Fyodor?' asked the deacon quietly, looking up at the archdeacon.

'Well, who is guilty if not you? You're his parent; he's your progeny! You should have instructed him, inspired him with the fear of God. You have to teach! You have children, and you don't instruct them! It's a sin! It's bad! It's shameful!'

The archdeacon forgot his tiredness, and paced up and down as he continued to talk. Tiny beads of sweat appeared on the deacon's bald patch and on his forehead. He raised his guilty eyes to the archdeacon and said:

'But didn't I give him instruction, Father Fyodor? Heavens above, was I not a father to my child? You know yourself that I spared him nothing, and prayed all my life to God to do my best and give him a proper education. He had a classical education at the gymnasium, and I hired tutors, and he graduated from university. If I haven't been able to direct his mind, Father Fyodor, it's because I am simply not capable of it, judge for yourself! He used to come back here when he was a student, and I would try and instruct him as best I could and he wouldn't have any of it. I'd say to him: go to church, and he would answer: "Why? What's the point?" Or he would slap me on the back and say: everything in this world is relative, approximate, and contingent. I don't know anything, and neither do you, Papa.'

Father Anastasy started laughing huskily, then had a fit of coughing and waved his fingers in the air as if he was about to say something. The archdeacon looked at him and said severely:

'Don't interfere, Father Anastasy.'

The old man beamed as he laughed, obviously enjoying listening to the deacon; it was as if he was glad there were other sinners in the world apart from him. The deacon was talking sincerely, with a grieving heart, and there were even tears in his eyes. Father Fyodor started to feel sorry for him.

'You're the one who is to blame, deacon, you know,' he said, but less sternly and fiercely than before. 'If you were able to have a child, you should have been able to provide instruction. You should have instructed him when he was a child—it's hard to reform a student!'

Silence ensued. The deacon threw up his hands and said with a sigh:

'But I am the one who is going to have to take responsibility for him!'

'That's precisely the point!'

After a short pause, the archdeacon yawned and sighed at the same time, then asked:

'Who is reading the Acts of the Apostles?*

'Evstrat. Evstrat always reads them.'

The deacon stood up and asked, looking beseechingly at the archdeacon:

'Father Fyodor, what am I going to do now?'

'Do what you want. You're the father, not me. You know best.'

'But I don't know anything, Father Fyodor! Be merciful and teach me! Please believe me, my soul is weary! I can't sleep or even sit calmly at the moment; the holiday is not going to be a holiday at all for me. Please teach me, Father Fyodor!'

'Write him a letter.'

'What on earth am I going to write to him?'

'Write and tell him it won't do. Write a short letter, but make it strict and thorough, without easing or lessening his guilt. It's your duty as a parent. If you write to him you will be doing your duty, and then you will calm down.'

'It's true, but what on earth am I going to write to him? How do I phrase it? I'll write to him and he will just reply: Why? What for? Why is it a sin?'

Father Anastasy started his husky laugh again and wiggled his fingers.

'Why? What for? Why is it a sin?' he began saying in a shrill voice. 'I was hearing the confession of a gentleman one day and I told him that hoping too much for God's mercy was a sin, and he asked why. I was just about to answer him and then—Anastasy struck himself on the forehead—I had nothing in here to answer him with! Hee-hee-hee...'

Anastasy's remarks and his hoarse tinkling laugh about things which were not funny made an unpleasant impression on the arch-deacon and the deacon. The archdeacon was about to say to the old man 'Don't interfere', but then decided not to and just frowned.

'I can't write to him!' said the deacon with a sigh.

'Well if you can't, who can?'

'Father Fyodor!' said the deacon, inclining his head and putting his hand on his heart. 'I am an uneducated man and feeble-minded, but on you the Lord bestowed intellect and wisdom. You know everything, you understand everything, you can grasp everything with your mind; I can't say anything in words. Be generous and instruct me in the art of writing! Teach me how to do it, what to say...'

'What's there to teach? Nothing. You just sit down and write.'

'Father, please help me out! I beg you. I know a letter from you would scare him and make him obey, because you are educated too. Please! I'll sit down and you dictate to me. It would be a sin to write tomorrow, but now is just the right time, and then I can stop worrying.'

The archdeacon looked at the deacon's imploring face, remem-bered the unappealing Pyotr, and agreed to dictate. He sat the dea-con down at his desk and began:

'Well, start writing... Christ is Risen,* dear son... exclamation mark. Rumours have reached me, your father... then put in brackets... the source of which is of no concern of yours... close brackets... Have you got that?... that you are leading a life which is incompatible with God's laws and also with man's laws. Neither the material comforts, nor the social brilliance, nor the education with which you adorn yourself outwardly can conceal your pagan nature. You are a Christian by name, but you are a heathen in essence; just as pitiful and unhappy as all other heathens, even more pitiful, for heathens who do not know Christ perish from their ignorance, while you will perish because you possess riches but you do not cherish them. I will not list your flaws here, since you are already well aware of them; I will merely say that I see your lack of faith as the reason for your perdition. You imagine yourself to be worldly wise, and you brag of your scholarly knowledge, but you choose not to understand that scholarship without faith not only does not exalt a person, but even reduces him to the level of a lowly animal, for...'

The whole letter was in that vein. After he written it, the deacon read it aloud and jumped up, grinning from ear to ear.

'It's a gift, a true gift to be able to write like that!' he said, looking rapturously at the archdeacon and clasping his hands. 'What gifts the Lord sends, eh? Holy Mother of God! I don't think I could have written a letter like that in a hundred years! May the Lord preserve you!'

Father Anastasy was also in raptures.

'You need talent to write like that!' he said, getting up and twiddling his fingers. 'Oh yes! There is such beautiful rhetoric there that any philosopher could add a comma and offer it up as his own. The product of a clear mind! If you hadn't got married,* Father Fyodor, you would have been a bishop long ago—truly, you would!'

Having expressed his anger in the letter, the archdeacon felt some relief. His tiredness and exhaustion returned. The deacon was a close colleague, and so the archdeacon was not afraid to be frank:

'Well deacon, go with the Lord! I am going to have half-an-hour's nap on the couch, I need to rest.'

The deacon left and took Anastasy with him. As always on the eve of Easter Sunday, it was dark outside, but the whole sky was sparkling with bright, radiant stars.

The soft still air smelt of spring and holidays.

'How long did it take him to dictate that?' wondered the deacon in amazement. 'About ten minutes, not longer! Anyone else would need at least a month to write a letter like that. Don't you think? What a mind! I don't even know how to put words together to describe it! Amazing! Truly amazing!'

'Education!' said Anastasy with a sigh, lifting the hem of his cassock up to his belt as they crossed the muddy street. 'We can't hold a candle to him. Our fathers were sextons, but he has had learning. Oh yes. A real specimen of a human being, he is, no doubt about it.'

'And you just wait till you hear him read the Gospel in Latin* in mass tonight! He knows Latin, he knows Greek... Ah, Petrukha, Petrukha...' the deacon said, suddenly remembering his son. 'Now he'll have something to think about! He'll bite his tongue now! He's going to get his just deserts! He's not going to ask "why?" now. He's met his match! Ha ha!'

The deacon laughed loudly and happily. After the letter to Pyotr had been written, he had cheered up and calmed down. The awareness of having fulfilled his parental duty and his great faith in the letter's power had returned his sense of humour and bonhomie.

'If you translate Pyotr, it means stone,' he said as they approached his house. 'My Pyotr though is too spineless to be a stone. A viper has settled in his bosom and he is fussing over her and can't shake her off. Humph! God forgive me, but there are some dreadful women in the world! Don't you think? Where is her sense of shame? She's latched on to the lad and stuck fast; she's keeping him on a close rein... I wish we could see the back of her!'

'But maybe he is the one keeping her, rather than the other way around.'

'But she still doesn't have any shame! I'm not defending Pyotr, mind you... He's going to get it... He'll start scratching his head when he reads that letter! He'll be burning with shame!'

'The letter is wonderful, but it's just that... Maybe you shouldn't send it, Father! Let it be!'

'What?' exclaimed the deacon in alarm.

'Really, Father, don't send it! What good will it do? Well, if you send it, he will read it, and then... well, what then? You'll just worry him. Forgive him and forget about it!'

The deacon looked in amazement at Anastasy's dark face, at his billowing cassock which was flapping about in the shadows like a pair of wings, and shrugged his shoulders.

'How can I forgive him?' he asked. 'I'm the one who has to answer for him to God!'

'That may be, but you should still forgive him. Honestly! And God will forgive you for your kindness.'

'But he's my son. Aren't I supposed to teach him?'

'Teach him? No reason why you shouldn't. It's a good thing, but why call him a heathen? He'll be offended by that, Father...'

The deacon was a widower and lived in a tiny house with three windows. His elder sister was in charge of the household. She was an old spinster who had lost her legs three years before and was bedridden; he was afraid of her, obeyed her wishes, and did not do anything without consulting her. Father Anastasy came inside too. When he saw the table already covered with Easter cakes and red painted eggs, he for some reason started crying, probably because he was remembering his own home, but then he immediately started laughing huskily to make light of his tears.

'Yes, it will soon be time to break the fast,' he said. 'Yes... But I don't think it would be untoward to have a little glass of vodka, would it? I'll drink it so that the old lady doesn't hear,' he whispered, looking towards the door. The deacon silently pushed the bottle and a glass towards him, unfolded the letter, and started reading it out loud. He liked the letter just as much now as when the archdeacon was dictating it to him. He was beaming with pleasure and shaking his head as if he had just tasted something very sweet.

'That's a letter to end all letters!' he said. 'Petrukha couldn't even begin to imagine anything like it. Anyway, that's what he needs—to face the music.'

'You know what, Father? Don't send it!' said Anastasy while he poured himself a second glass, as if oblivious of his actions. 'Forgive him and just forget about it! It's a question of conscience, Father. If his own father won't forgive him, who will? Is he going to live without forgiveness? Think about it, Father: there are plenty of people who are going to punish him without you weighing in as well; you should be looking for people to be nice to him! I'll... I'll just have a little drink, my friend... Last one... Now you just take that letter and write: I forgive you Pyotr! He will understand! And he will get the message! I know he will, my friend... Father, I mean; I know from my own experience. I used to live like other people and didn't have too many worries, but now that I have fallen from the one true path, all I want is for kind people to forgive me. And think about it: it's not the people who live righteously who need forgiving but the sinners. Why should you forgive your old lady here if she is not a sinner? No, you should be forgiving the people who you feel pity for... really!'

Anastasy propped his head up on his fist and became lost in thought.

'It's awful!' he said with a sigh, clearly struggling with his desire for another drink. 'Awful! I was born in sin,* lived in sin, and will die in sin... Lord, forgive me! I have lost my way, Father! There is no salvation for me! And it's not as if I lost my way earlier in my life, but in old age, when I'm about to die... I...'

The old man waved his hand and downed another glass, then got up and settled himself in another part of the room. The deacon was walking up and down, still gripping the letter. He was thinking about his son. Dissatisfaction, sorrow, and fear no longer worried him: all that had gone into the letter. Now all he was doing was imagining Pyotr, picturing his face and remembering the olden times, when his son used to come to stay for the holidays. His head was filled with nice, warm, sad thoughts—the sorts of things you can spend your whole life thinking about without getting tired of them. Missing his son, he read the letter one more time and looked questioningly at Anastasy.

'Don't send it!' said the latter, with a wave of his wrist.

'No, all the same... I must. It really will do him some good to receive some instruction. It won't go amiss...'

The deacon took an envelope from his desk, but before putting the letter into it he sat down, smiled, and added at the bottom of the letter: 'They have sent us a new supervisor. He's a bit more lively than the last one. He's a dancer and a chatterbox, and is so good at everything that all the Govorov daughters are mad about him. Kostyrev, the army chief, is also apparently going to have to retire soon. About time!' Very pleased with himself, and not understanding that he had ended up undoing all the severity of the letter with his postscript, the deacon wrote out the address and put the letter in the most prominent place on the table.

# FORTUNE

*dedicated to Y. P. Polonsky*

A flock of sheep was spending the night by the wide steppe road known as the great highway. Two shepherds were watching over it. One of them, a toothless old man of about eighty with a shaking face, was lying on his stomach by the edge of the road with his elbows resting on dusty plantain leaves; the other, a clean-shaven young lad with thick black brows, his clothes made of the sort of hessian they use to make cheap bags with, was lying on his back with his hands beneath his head looking up at the sky, where right above his face stretched the Milky Way and dozing stars.

The shepherds were not alone. About a yard away from them in the shadows, blocking the road, was the dark shape of a saddled horse, and by it stood a man in high boots and a short kaftan leaning against the saddle; he looked as if he was a ranger from a nearby estate. To judge from his upright, motionless posture, his manner, and the way he behaved towards the shepherds and his horse, he was a serious, level-headed man who knew his own worth; even in the darkness you could make out traces of military bearing and the sort of graciously condescending expression that comes from frequent dealings with gentleman landowners and their stewards.

Most of the sheep were asleep. Against the grey background of the dawn's early light, which was already beginning to fill the eastern part of the sky, you could see silhouettes of the sheep who were not sleeping; they were standing with their heads bowed, thinking about something. Their unhurried, drawn-out thoughts, stimulated only by impressions of the broad steppe and the sky, and of days and nights, probably stunned and depressed them to the point of numbness. Standing there as if rooted to the spot, they were oblivious both to the presence of a stranger and the restlessness of the sheepdogs.

In the thick sleepy air hung a monotonous noise always present on summer nights in the steppe; grasshoppers were chirring continuously, quails were craking, and about a mile away from the flock, in a gully with willows and a running stream, young nightingales were singing indolently.

The ranger had stopped to ask the shepherds for a light for his pipe. He had lit up silently and smoked his pipe to the end, and then, without uttering a word, had lent his elbow on the saddle and become lost in thought. The young shepherd paid him no attention whatsoever; he continued to lie there staring up at the sky, but the old man examined the ranger for a long time then asked:

'You wouldn't be Panteley from the Makarovsk estate?'

'That's me,' replied the ranger.

'Of course it is. Didn't recognize you—means you'll be rich. Where have you come from?'

'From the Kovyly estate.'

'That's a long way off. Is the land leased?'

'Some of it. Some of it is leased, some of it rented out, and some of it used for growing fruit and vegetables. I'm going over to the mill now.'

A large, dirty-white, shaggy old sheepdog, with clumps of fur dangling round its eyes and nose, padded calmly round the horse three times, trying to appear indifferent to the presence of strangers, then suddenly threw itself at the ranger from behind with a bad-tempered and senile growl; the other dogs could not contain themselves and leapt up from their places.

'Be quiet, you cursed dog!' shouted the old man, raising himself on his elbow. 'Just shut up, you wretched creature!'

When the dogs had quietened down, the old man took up his previous position and said in a quiet voice:

'You know that Yefim Zhmenya died in Kovyly, right on Ascension Day? Shouldn't speak ill of the dead, but he was a foul old man. Suppose you heard about it?'

'No, I didn't.'

'Yefim Zhmenya was Stepka the blacksmith's uncle. Everyone round here knew him. Yes, he was a nasty piece of work! I knew him for about sixty years, from the time when they took Tsar Alexander*—the one who drove out the French—from Taganrog to Moscow on a wagon. We'd both set off to see the dead Tsar, but the great highway didn't go to Bakhmut then, but from Esaulovka to Gorodishche, and there were bustard nests where Kovyly is now— nests all over the place. Even back then I noticed that Zhmenya had ruined his soul and had an unclean spirit in him. I always think it's a bad sign when a peasant is quiet most of the time, gets involved with women's business, and seeks to live on his own, and Yefimka, you know, was dead quiet even when he was young; he'd scowl at you, and pout and strut about, like a cock in front of a hen. He wasn't one for going to church, hanging out with the lads, or sitting in the tavern; he would always be sitting on his own or whispering with the old women. He was young, but it was beekeeping and melon-growing that he earned his living by. Folk would come up to him to his plot, you know, and his melons and watermelons would start whistling. And then once he caught a pike in front of some folk, and it started laughing—ho ho ho! Just like that!'

'It can happen,' said Pantelcy.

The young shepherd turned on to his side and fixed his gaze intently on the old man, his black brows raised.

'So have you heard watermelons whistling?' he asked.

'God mercifully spared me from it,' said the old man with a sigh. 'But that's what people were saying. It's nothing to marvel at really... If an unclean spirit wants to, it can make a stone whistle. We had a big rock humming for three days and three nights in front of us before they gave us liberty.* I heard it myself. And the pike laughed because Zhmenya caught a demon, not a pike.'

The old man remembered something. He raised himself swiftly up onto his knees; shivering as if he were cold, and thrusting his hands into his sleeves nervously, he started babbling like an old woman:

'Lord have mercy on us! I was walking along the riverbank once to Novopavlovka. There was a storm brewing and Holy Mother of God, what a gale there was blowing... I was hurrying along as fast as I could, and between the blackthorn bushes—they were in blossom then—I saw a white ox walking down the path. And so I think: who does that ox belong to? Why has an evil spirit brought it here? It was walking along switching its tail and mooing. But the thing is, though, that when I caught up with it and went up close, I saw that it wasn't an ox, but Zhmenya. God have mercy! I made the sign of the cross, but he just looked at me with bulging eyes and muttered. I got scared, I tell you! We walked on together and I was too afraid to say a word to him—the thunder was rumbling away and lightning was slashing the sky, the willows were bent right down to the water, and then suddenly, God strike me down if I tell a lie, a hare runs across the path... It ran up, stopped, and said in a human voice to us: "Hello lads!" Oh get away, you cursed beast,' the old man shouted at the shaggy dog, which was circling the horse again; 'just clear off!'

'It can happen,' said the ranger, still leaning up against his saddle without moving; he spoke in the quiet, muffled voice of a person lost in thought.

'It can happen,' he said firmly and thoughtfully.

'Ugh, he was a wretched old man!' continued the old man with less emotion now. 'About five years after getting our liberty, we all had him flogged at the village office, so he got his own back by setting loose a throat infection all over Kovyly. People started dying like flies, thousands of them, like when we had cholera...'

'How could he let loose an illness?' asked the young man after a moment of silence.

'Well it's obvious, isn't it? You don't need to be all that clever, you just need the will. Zhmenya killed people with adder's oil. And that's not at all like ordinary oil, people can die just from smelling it.'

'That's true,' agreed Panteley.

'The lads wanted to kill him then, but the old folk wouldn't let them. You couldn't kill him, though, because he knew places where there was treasure. And no one apart from him knew about them. The treasure round here has a spell on it, so you might find the places where it's hidden, but you wouldn't be able to see it; he saw it though. He would be walking along the riverbank or through the wood, and underneath the bushes and the rocks there would be little lights everywhere... The lights were like they were made of sulphur. I saw them myself. Everyone was waiting for Zhmenya to show us the places, or dig them up himself, but it was like he was cutting off his nose to spite his face—he went and died: he didn't dig them up himself and he didn't show anybody where they were.'

The ranger lit his pipe, illuminating for a moment his large moustache and prominent nose, which was angular and pointed. Small rings of light jumped from his hands to his cap, ran across the saddle to the horse's back and disappeared in its mane up around its ears.

'There is a lot of treasure buried in these parts,' he said.

Drawing slowly on his pipe, he looked around, fixed his gaze on the white sky in the east, and added:

'There must be treasure.'

'Of course there is,' said the old man with a sigh. 'It's obvious to everyone, but there is no one to dig it up. No one knows the actual places, and you have to bear in mind that they all have a spell on them still. In order to find hidden treasure and be able to see it, you have to have a charm; you can't do anything without a charm. Zhmenya had charms, but do you think you could ask that devil for anything? He kept them to himself, so no one else could get hold of them.'

The young shepherd shifted a couple of feet over towards the old man, and propping his head on his clenched hands, fixed on him an unbroken stare. A childish expression of fear and curiosity lit up his dark eyes and the shadows seemed to stretch and flatten the features of his rough young face. He was listening intently.

'It says in books that there is a lot of treasure in these parts,' continued the old man. 'And it's all true. They showed one old Novopavlovka soldier in Ivanovka a scroll, and on that scroll was written the place were the treasure was buried, and how many pounds of gold there were, and what kind of pot it was in; they would have found the treasure long ago from that scroll, but the treasure has a spell on it and you can't get at it.'

'So why don't you go after it?' asked the young man.

'There must be some reason, but the soldier didn't say. It's got a spell on it... You need a charm.'

The old man talked with great emotion, as if he was pouring out his soul to complete strangers. He was speaking in a nasal drawl because he was unused to talking so much and so quickly; he was stuttering too, and trying to make up for the inadequacy of his speech by gesticulating with his head, his arms, and his scrawny shoulders; his linen shirt crumpled into wrinkles every time he moved, slipping down to his shoulders and revealing his back, which was black from sunburn and old age. He kept hitching it up, but it immediately slid down again. Finally, as if his patience was exhausted by his disobedient shirt, the old man jumped up and said with bitterness:

'There is treasure out there, but what is the use if it's buried in the ground? It will just be lost, without any use, like chaff or sheep droppings. But there is a lot of treasure, my boy, so much that there would be enough for the whole district, except that not a soul can see it! People will carry on waiting until the landowners dig it up or the government takes it. The landowners have already begun to dig up the kurgans...* They have sniffed them out! They are envious of the fortune which belongs to us peasants! The government has the same plan up its sleeve. It says in the law that if a peasant finds treasure, he has to report it to the authorities. Well, they are going to have to hang on a bit; they'll be waiting for ever! It's our treasure!'

The old man laughed contemptuously and sat down on the ground. The ranger listened attentively and agreed with him, but from the expression on his face and from his silence, you could tell that what the old man was telling him was not new to him, and that he had thought everything over long ago and knew much more about it all than the old man did.

'I've looked for a fortune about ten times in my lifetime, I have to confess,' said the old man, scratching his head bashfully. 'I was looking in the right places, but I just kept finding treasure that had a spell on it, you know. My father searched, and my brother searched, and they didn't find a thing, and so they died without finding their fortune. A monk revealed to my brother Ilya, God rest his soul, that there was treasure hidden underneath three particular stones in the Taganrog fortress, and that the treasure had a spell on it. And in those days—it was in thirty-eight, I remember—there was an Armenian living in Matveyev Kurgan who sold charms. So Ilya bought a charm, took two lads with him, and went off to Taganrog. But when my brother got to the fortress, there was a soldier standing there with a gun...'

A noise pierced the quiet air and echoed across the steppe. Something far off banged threateningly, hit against rock, and carried across the steppe with an echoing 'Takh! Takh! Takh! Takh!' When the sound died away, the old man looked questioningly at the impassive Panteley, who was standing not moving a muscle.

'That was a bucket breaking loose in the mines,'* said the young man.

It was already becoming light. The Milky Way had grown pale and was slowly melting like snow, losing its outline. The sky was becoming overcast and dull, so that it was difficult to tell whether it was clear or completely covered with clouds, and only the bright, glossy strip in the east and the few remaining stars here and there indicated what was happening.

The first morning breeze ran along the road without a murmur, cautiously rustling the euphorbia and the brown stubble of last year's wild steppe grass.

The ranger woke from his thoughts and shook his head. He rocked his saddle with both hands, adjusted the girth, and again became lost in thought, as if he could not make up his mind whether to get on his horse or not.

'Yes,' he said; 'so near and yet so far... There is fortune there to be had, but no way of working out how to find it.'

And he turned to face the shepherds. His stern face was sad and contemptuous, like that of someone who has encountered disappointment.

'Yes, we will die without finding a fortune, whatever it may be...,' he said slowly, as he lifted his left foot into the stirrup. 'Maybe someone younger will be lucky, but us lot will just have to give up.'

Stroking his long whiskers, which were covered with dew, he climbed heavily onto his horse and narrowed his eyes as he gazed into the distance, looking as if he had forgotten to say something or had somehow not finished what he had to say. Nothing stirred in the bluish distance, where the last visible hill merged with the mist; the kurgans, which towered here and there above the horizon and the endless steppe, looked severe and lifeless; in their mute immobility one could sense past centuries and complete indifference to human beings; another thousand years would go by, millions of people would die, and they would still be standing there, as they did now, neither sorry for those who had died, nor interested in the living, and not one soul would know why they stood there and what secrets of the steppe they contained.

Solitary rooks who had woken up were flying silently over the earth. There was no obvious point to the lazy flight of these long-lived birds, nor to the morning which repeated itself punctually every day, nor to the infinity of the steppe. The ranger smiled, and said:

'Heavens, what an expanse! You just try and go looking for a fortune. But it was likely round about here,' he continued, lowering his voice and putting on a serious expression, 'that two lots of treasure were found. The landowners don't know about them, but the old peasants certainly do, particularly the ones who were soldiers. Some robbers fell upon a convoy carrying gold here somewhere on this ridge (the ranger pointed with his whip); they were taking the gold from Petersburg to Emperor Peter, who was building his navy in Voronezh* at that time. The robbers beat up the waggoners and buried the gold, but then they couldn't find it. It was our Don

Cossacks who buried the other lot of treasure. They stole heaps of goods and silver and gold from the French back in 1812. When they were on their way home they heard that the government wanted to take the silver and gold from them. Rather than give up all their loot to the authorities for nothing, they were clever enough to go and bury it, so their children could have it, but no one knows where they buried it.'

'I've heard about those treasure troves,' the old man muttered gloomily.

'Yes,' said Panteley, lost in thought again. 'Indeed...'

Silence ensued. The ranger looked into the distance pensively, smiled, and then touched the reins with the same expression as before, as if he had forgotten something or not finished what he wanted to say. The horse reluctantly started walking. After about a hundred paces, Panteley shook his head vigorously, came out of his reverie, and set off at a trot, whipping his horse.

The shepherds were left alone.

'That's Panteley from the Makarov estate,' said the old man. 'He gets a hundred-and-fifty a year, and eats with the squire. Educated man...'

Not having anything better to do, the awakened sheep, all three-thousand of them, started eating the short, half-trampled grass. The sun had not yet risen, but distant Saur's Grave, with its pointed top which looked like a cloud, and all the other kurgans were already visible. If you climbed to the top of Saur's Grave, you could look out and see a plain that was as flat and boundless as the sky, manor houses and estates, German and Molokan farms,* villages; a far-sighted Kalmyk* would even be able to see the town and railway trains. Only from up here was it possible to see that there was another life in the world beyond the silent steppe and ancient kurgans, a life which was not concerned with buried treasure and the thoughts of sheep.

The old man felt around him for his crook, a long stick with a hook at the top, and got to his feet. He was silent and thinking. The childlike expression of fear and curiosity had not yet disappeared from the young man's face. He was still awestruck by what he had heard and was looking forward to new stories.

'What did your brother Ilya do with the soldier?' he asked, getting up and taking his crook.

The old man did not hear the question. He looked absent-mindedly at the young man and replied, mumbling through his lips:

'You know, Sanka, I've been thinking about the scroll they showed to the soldier in Ivanovka. I didn't tell Panteley, I wish him all the best, but there was a place indicated on the scroll which even a woman could find. You know where it is? In Bogataya Gully, you know, where there is a gully which splits into three like a goose's foot; it's in the middle one.'

'So are you going to go and dig it up?'

'I'll have a go at finding my fortune, sure...'

'And what will you do with the gold when you find it?'

'What am I going to do with it?' said the the old man, grinning. 'Hmm! I've got to find it first, and then... well, I'll show everyone... Hmm! I know what I'd do...'

The old man was not able to give an answer as to what he would do with the treasure if he found it. He had probably been asked this question for the very first time in his life that morning, and to judge from his nonchalant and indifferent expression, it did not seem to him to be important or worth reflecting on. Another confusing thought was stirring in Sanka's head: why was it that only old men looked for treasure, and what was the point of them finding a fortune on earth when they were just about to die from old age? But Sanka could not form his confusion into a question, and the old man would probably not have known what to answer him anyway.

The huge crimson sun appeared, enveloped in a light haze. As if pretending that they were not yet bored, broad bands of still, cold light started descending merrily to the earth and stretching out, basking in the dewy grass. Silvery artemisia, the blue flowers of wild allium, yellow rape, and cornflowers all burst into radiant colour, taking the sunlight as their own smile.

The old man and Sanka separated and went to stand at opposite ends of the flock. They both stood like columns without moving, staring at the ground and thinking. The former was still thinking about finding a fortune, while the latter was thinking about what had been discussed during the night; he was not so much interested in finding a fortune, which he did not want and could not really understand, as in marvelling at how human fortune was fantastic and wondrous.

A hundred or so sheep suddenly became jittery and then charged off from the flock in some inexplicable terror, as if responding to a signal. And Sanka started to charge off too, feeling the same incomprehensible animal terror, as if the sheep's long and leisurely thoughts had for a moment communicated themselves to him, but he immediately came to his senses and shouted out:

'Hey, you mad sheep! You've gone beserk; you should be properly punished!'

And when the sun started to burn the earth, promising a long, unconquerable sultriness, everything alive, everything which had moved and made noises at night, sank into somnolence. The old man and Sanka stood at opposite ends of the flock with their crooks; they stood there without moving, like fakirs at prayer, deep in thought. Wrapped up in their own lives, they were already oblivious of each other. The sheep were also lost in thought...

# GUSEV

## I

It has already grown dark, and soon it will be night.

Gusev, a private on indefinite leave, raises himself in his berth and says in a low voice:

'Pavel Ivanych, are you listening? A soldier in Suchan* told me that their ship hit a big fish out at sea which made a hole in its bottom.'

The person of unknown social status whom he is addressing, and whom everyone in the ship's sick bay calls Pavel Ivanych, remains silent, as if he cannot hear.

And again there is stillness... The wind is running through the rigging, the screw propeller is throbbing, waves are crashing, bunks are creaking, but the ear has grown used to all this long ago, and it seems that everything all around is sleeping and staying silent. It is dull. The three sick people who played cards all day—two soldiers and a sailor—are already asleep and delirious.

It feels like the sea is becoming rough. Underneath him, Gusev's bunk goes slowly up and down as if it is sighing: once, twice, three times... Something hits the floor with a clang: a mug must have fallen.

'The wind has broken its chain...' says Gusev, listening closely.

This time Pavel Ivanych coughs before answering irritably:

'One minute you've got a boat that has hit a fish, and next it's the wind that has broken its chain... So the wind is an animal is it, if it's breaking its chain?

'That's what people say.'

'Then people are as ignorant as you... You've got to keep your head on your shoulders and use your brain. You stupid man.'

Pavel Ivanych is prone to seasickness. When the ship rolls, he usually gets angry and is irritated by the slightest thing. But there is absolutely nothing to get angry about in Gusev's opinion. What is strange or weird about a fish or the wind breaking its chain, for instance? Suppose the fish is as big as a mountain, with a back as hard as a sturgeon's; or suppose that there are thick stone walls where the end of the world is, and ferocious winds chained to the walls... If they haven't broken their chains, why do they charge all over the sea like madmen, tugging as if they were dogs? And if they aren't chained up, where do they go when it is calm?

Gusev spends a long time thinking about fish as big as mountains and about thick, rusty chains, then he gets bored and starts thinking about his village, which he is now returning to after five years of service in the Far East. A picture of a huge pond covered with snow appears in his mind... On one side of the pond is the brick-coloured pottery, with a tall chimney and clouds of black smoke; on the other side is the village... Out of the yard—the fifth one along from the end—his brother Alexey is driving a sleigh; sitting behind him are his little son Vanka in big felt boots, and his little girl Akulka, also in felt boots. Alexey has been drinking, and Vanka is laughing, but you can't see Akulka's face because she is all wrapped up.

'He should watch out, or those children will catch their death,' thinks Gusev. 'May the Lord give them the good sense to honour their parents,' he whispers, 'and not be cleverer than their mother and father...'

'These need new soles,' says the sick sailor deliriously in his bass voice. 'Oh yes!'

Gusev's thoughts are cut short, and instead of the pond, a large bull's head without eyes suddenly appears in his vision for no apparent reason, and the horse and sleigh are no longer moving forward, but whirling round and round in black smoke. But he is still glad that he has seen his family. The pleasure of it quite takes his breath away, making his body tingle and his fingers tremble.

'The Lord ordained we should meet!' he mutters deliriously, but then he immediately opens his eyes and looks for water in the darkness.

He takes a drink then lies down, and once again he sees the sleigh being pulled along, then again the bull's head without eyes, the smoke and the clouds... And so it continues until dawn.

## II

A dark blue circle becomes visible in the darkness first—that is the round porthole; then little by little Gusev begins to his make out his cabin-mate, Pavel Ivanych. The man has to sleep sitting up, because he can hardly breathe when he lies down. His face is grey, his nose long and pointed, and his eyes are huge because he is so emaciated; his temples are sunken, his beard is sparse, and the hairs on his head are long... Looking at his face, it is impossible to work out his class: is he a gentleman, a merchant, or a peasant? To judge from his expression and his long hair, he looks as if he is on a fast, like a novice monk, but if you listen to what he says, he does not seem like a monk. He is exhausted from the pitching of the ship, from the lack of air, and from his illness; he is breathing with difficulty, moving his parched lips. Having noticed Gusev looking at him, he turns to face him and says:

'I'm beginning to work things out... Yes... I understand everything very well now.'

'What do you understand, Pavel Ivanych?'

'I'll tell you... It's always seemed strange to me that instead of being somewhere restful, all you people who are seriously ill have ended up on a steamship, where it's stuffy and hot and there is endless pitching, where everything is life-endangering basically, but now it's all clear to me... Yes... Your doctors have put you on to the steamer in order to get rid of you. They have got fed up with having to bother with you, all you cattle... You don't pay them any money, you just cause trouble, and then you go and mess up their figures by dying, so you must be cattle! But it's not difficult to get rid of you... To go about it, first of all a person needs to lack both a conscience and any philanthropic impulse, and then it is simply a question of deceiving the ship's management. There are no worries about the first requirement, as we have got that down to a fine art, and the second is a skill that can be acquired. In a crowd of four hundred healthy soldiers and sailors you won't notice five who are sick; so they herd you on to the boat, where you get mixed up with the people who are healthy; they do a quick count and don't notice anything fishy during all the commotion, and it's only when the ship leaves port that they notice paralytics and terminal consumptives lying about on deck...'

Gusev does not understand Pavel Ivanych; thinking that he is being reprimanded, he says in his defence:

'I was lying down on deck because I had no energy; when they transferred us from the barge to the ship I caught a chill.'

'It's outrageous!' Pavel Ivanych continues. 'The main thing, after all, is that they know perfectly well that you won't be able to withstand the long journey, and yet they still put you on board! Well, let's say you make it to the Indian Ocean, but then what? It's too awful to think about... And that's their gratitude for loyal, irreproachable service!'

Pavel Ivanych stares angrily, frowning with disgust, and says, gasping for breath:

'They are the ones who should be pummelled in the press until their feathers start flying!'

The two sick soldiers and the sailor have woken up and are already playing cards. The sailor is half lying down in his berth, with the soldiers sitting on the floor next to him, in the most uncomfortable positions. One of the soldiers has his right arm in a sling and his hand bandaged up in a thick lump, so he holds his cards under his right armpit or in the crook of his elbow, and uses his left hand. The ship is rolling heavily. It's impossible to stand up, drink tea, or to take medicine.

'Were you a batman?' Pavel Ivanych asks Gusev.

'Yes, a batman, that's right.'

'Lord, oh Lord!' says Pavel Ivanych, shaking his head sadly. 'To uproot a man from his home and drag him ten thousand miles, then make him work so hard he gets consumption and... well, what is the point of it all, I wonder? To make him a batman to some Captain Kopeikin or a Midshipman Dyrka?* That's very logical, that is!'

'It's not a difficult job, Pavel Ivanych. You get up in the morning, polish the boots, get the samovar going, and clean the rooms, but then there is nothing to do. The lieutenant spends all day drafting plans, and you can go off and say your prayers, or read a book, or go outside. Not everyone gets to have such a good life.'

'Yes, it's wonderful, isn't it? The lieutenant drafts plans, and you spend the whole day sitting in the kitchen feeling homesick... Plans... Human life is what is important, not plans! You only get one life, and you've got to respect it.'

'That's true, Pavel Ivanych, a bad person gets no respect at home or at work, but if you live honestly and do what you are told, why would anyone do you any harm? These are educated folk, they understand... I didn't get put in jail once in all five years, and I was only beaten once, if memory serves me right.'

'What for?'

'For fighting. I've got a heavy hand, Pavel Ivanych. There were these four Chinks who came into our yard; they were carrying firewood or something, I can't quite remember what. Well, I got bored and gave them a bit of a thrashing, and then blood starting coming out of one of the bastards' noses. The lieutenant was watching through the window and got angry and boxed my ears.'

'You are a sad, stupid man,' whispers Pavel Ivanych. 'You don't understand anything.'

He has become completely exhausted from the pitching of the ship and has closed his eyes; his head lolls backward then falls on to his chest. He tries lying down a few times, but it is no good: he starts suffocating.

'So what did you beat up those four Chinks for?' he asks, a little while later.

'Don't know. They came into the yard, so I beat them up.'

Silence descends... The card-players play for about two hours, with absorption and the odd bit of swearing, but the pitching even gets to them; they leave their cards and go and lie down. Gusev once more imagines the big pond, the factory, the village... The sledge is setting off again, Vanka is smiling and that foolish little Akulka has undone her fur coat and stuck her feet out: look, people, she is saying, my felt boots aren't like Vanka's, they're new.

'You'll be six soon, but you still haven't got any sense!' mutters Gusev deliriously. 'Instead of sticking your feet out, why don't you go and bring your uncle in the army a drink. I'll give you a present.'

Then comes Andron carrying a rabbit he has shot, with his flint-lock gun over his shoulder, and that decrepit little Jew Isaichik following behind, offering him a piece of soap in exchange for the rabbit; there is the little black calf just inside the front door, and there is Domna sewing a shirt and crying about something, and then that bull's head without eyes again, the black smoke...

Up above, someone gives a loud shout and several sailors run by; they seem to be dragging something cumbersome along the deck, or else something has fallen with a crash. They run past again... Has something bad happened? Gusev lifts up his head in order to listen, and he sees that the two soldiers and the sailor are playing cards again; Pavel Ivanych is sitting there, moving his lips. It is stifling, you do not have the energy to breathe and you are thirsty, but the water is warm and revolting... The ship does not stop rolling.

Suddenly something strange happens to the soldier playing cards...
He calls hearts diamonds, muddles up the score, and drops the cards;
then he looks round at them all with a frightened, inane smile.

'Just a minute, fellows...' he says, then lies down on the floor.

No one knows what to do. They call out to him, but he does not
respond.

'Maybe you're not feeling well, Stepan? Eh?' asks the other soldier
with the bandaged hand. 'Should we get the priest to come? What do
you think?'

'Stepan, you should drink some water...' says the sailor. 'Here you
are, mate, have a drink.'

'Well, what's the point of banging a mug against his teeth?' says
Gusev angrily. 'Can't you see, you dimwit?'

'What?'

'What!' mimics Gusev. 'He's not breathing, he's dead! What,
indeed! Good God, what a foolish lot you all are...'

## III

The ship has stopped rolling and Pavel Ivanych has cheered up. He is
not angry any more. There is a boastful, provocative, and sarcastic
expression on his face. It is as if he would like to say: 'Oh yes, I'm
about to tell you a joke that will make you split your sides with
laughter.' The round porthole is open, and a gentle breeze is blowing
on Pavel Ivanych. There is the sound of voices and oars flopping
against the water... Right underneath the porthole someone is whin-
ing in a horrible thin voice: it must be someone Chinese singing.

'We must be standing outside the harbour,' says Pavel Ivanych
with a sarcastic smile. 'Only about one more month and we'll be in
Russia. Oh yes, my esteemed privates. When I get to Odessa, I'm
going straight to Kharkov. I've got a friend who is a writer in
Kharkov. I'm going to turn up and say to him: right then, my friend,
it's time for you to put aside your vile plots about women's romances
and the beauties of nature for a while and expose the evils of two-
legged scum... Have I got some subjects for you...'

He spends a minute thinking about something, then says:

'Gusev, do you know how I duped them?'

'Who, Pavel Ivanych?'

'You know—them... There is only first and third class on this boat, you see, and what's more, they only let peasants travel third class—louts in other words. But if you are wearing a jacket and look remotely middle or upper class, then you have to sail first class, if you please. You've got to fork out those five hundred roubles if it kills you. So I asked them why they had to have this regulation. It surely wasn't about raising the prestige of the Russian intelligentsia. "Oh no," they said. "It's just that we can't let anyone respectable travel third class: it's far too squalid down there." Is that so? I'm so glad to see that you are taking such good care of respectable people, I said. Anyway, whether it's appalling down there or all right, I just don't have five hundred roubles. I haven't robbed a bank, I haven't exploited the natives, I haven't been doing any smuggling, I haven't flogged anyone to death, so what do you think: do I have the right to go first class, and therefore count myself as a member of the Russian intelligentsia? You can't fathom their logic... So I had to resort to trickery. I put on a rough coat and some tall boots, made myself look like a drunken lout, and went up to the agent. "Need a ticket, your excellency..." I told him.'

'And what class are you from in fact?' the sailor asks.

'The clergy. My father was an honest priest. He always told the plain truth to the grandees of this world and suffered a lot for it.'

Pavel Ivanych has become exhausted from talking and is short of breath, but he still carries on:

'Yes, I always tell people the truth too... I'm not afraid of anyone or anything. In that respect, there is a big difference between you and me. You people are ignorant, blind, and downtrodden, you don't see anything, and what you do see you don't understand... You get told that the wind has broken its chain, that you are beasts, savages, and you believe it all; they beat you about, and you go and kiss their hands; some brute in a raccoon coat swindles you and then tosses you fifteen kopecks as a tip, and all you can say is: "Let me kiss your hand, sir." You are outcasts, pitiful people... But I'm different. I live consciously; I see everything, like an eagle or a hawk flying above the earth, and I understand everything. I am protest personified. If I see despotism, I protest; if I see some swine getting away with something, I protest. And I'm invincible; no Spanish Inquisition is ever going to make me shut up. Oh yes... Cut out my tongue and I will protest in mime, lock me up in a cellar and I will shout so loudly you'll hear me a mile away, or I'll starve to death in order to weigh on their guilty consciences just that bit more; kill me and I'll come back to haunt them. Everyone I know tells me: "Pavel Ivanych, you're just unbearable!" I'm proud to have such a reputation. I served in the Far East for three years and will stay in people's memories for a hundred years: I fell out with everybody. My friends write from Russia: "Don't come back." But here I am, I'm coming just to spite them... Yes... That's a life I understand. That's a proper life.'

Gusev is not listening and is looking out through the porthole. A small boat is rocking on clear, soft, turquoise water, drenched in dazzling hot sunshine. Naked Chinese, holding up cages with canaries, are standing in it and shouting:

'Sings! Sings!'

Another boat runs into it, then a steam-launch goes past. And then another boat appears: there is a fat Chinaman sitting in it, eating rice with chopsticks. The water heaves lazily; white seagulls fly overhead lazily.

'I wouldn't mind having a go at that tub of lard...' Gusev thinks, looking at the fat Chinaman and yawning.

He starts dozing, and it feels like everything all around him is dozing too. Time passes quickly. The day passes imperceptibly, darkness descends imperceptibly... The steamship is no longer standing still but has resumed its journey.

## IV

Two days go by. Pavel Ivanych is no longer sitting up but lying down; his eyes are closed and his nose seems to have become more pointed.

Gusev calls out to him: 'Pavel Ivanych! Hey, Pavel Ivanych!'

Pavel Ivanych opens his eyes and moves his lips.

'Are you not feeling well?'

'I'm all right...' replies Pavel Ivanych, gasping for breath. 'I'm all right, quite the opposite almost... I'm feeling better... Look, I can already lie down... I'm getting better...'

'Well, thank goodness, Pavel Ivanych.'

'When I compare myself to you, I feel sorry for you... you poor wretches. My lungs are healthy, and it's just a gastric cough... I can put up with hell, so what is the Red Sea? Anyway, I've got a critical attitude to my illness and to medicines. But you... you're ignorant... It's hard for you; it's very, very hard!'

There is no pitching, the sea is calm, but it is suffocatingly hot, like in a steam bath, and not only talking but even listening is difficult. Gusev hugs his knees, rests his head on them, and thinks about home. Goodness, what a pleasure it is to think about snow and cold in such sweltering heat! He is back travelling on the sleigh. Suddenly the horses are frightened by something and they bolt... They gallop straight through the village with no thought to roads, ditches, or gullies: over the pond, past the factory, then across the field. 'Hold on!' the factory people and passers-by shout out at the tops of their voices; 'Hold on!' But why slow down? Let the piercing, cold wind strike your face and sting your hands, let the clumps of snow kicked up by the horses' hooves fall onto your hat, behind your collar, down your neck, down your front; let the runners screech and the tracers and crossbars snap—to hell with them! And what bliss when the sleigh overturns and you go hurtling into a snowdrift and land face-down in the snow; and then you get up all white, with icicles on your moustache; no hat, no mittens, your belt undone... There are people laughing and dogs barking...

Pavel Ivanych half-opens one eye, looks at Gusev with it, and asks quietly:

'Gusev, did your commanding officer steal?'

'Who knows, Pavel Ivanych! We don't get to hear about that sort of thing.'

And then a long time passes in silence. Gusev thinks about things, becomes delirious, and now and again drinks some water; it is hard for him to talk and hard to listen, and he's afraid someone will start speaking to him. An hour goes by, then another, and another; evening descends, then night, but he does not notice, and carries on sitting there, thinking about the frost.

It sounds as if someone has come into the sick bay; voices are heard, but after about five minutes everything goes quiet.

'May the kingdom of Heaven be his, God rest his soul,' says the soldier with his arm in a sling. 'That man was troubled!'

'What?' asks Gusev. 'Who?'

'He died. They've just taken him up.'

'Oh, right,' mumbles Gusev with a yawn. 'God rest his soul.'

'What do you think, Gusev?' asks the soldier with the sling after a pause. 'Will he go to heaven or not?'

'Who do you mean?'

'Pavel Ivanych.'

'Of course... he suffered for such a long time. And besides, he was from the clergy, and priests have lots of relatives. They'll all start praying.'

The soldier with the sling sits on Gusev's bunk and says softly:

'You're not long for this world either, Gusev. You won't get to Russia.'

'Why, did the doctor or the orderly say something?' asks Gusev.

'No one said anything, one just has to look at you... It is easy to tell when a person is going to die soon. You aren't eating, you aren't drinking, and you're wasting away—it's dreadful to look at you. Consumption, in a word. I'm not saying this to upset you, but because you might want to receive the sacrament and last rites. And if you have any money, you could give it to the senior officer.'

'I haven't written home...' says Gusev with a sigh. 'I'll die and they won't find out.'

'They'll find out,' says the sick sailor in his deep voice. 'When you die, they will make a note in the ship's log, then they will pass a record on to the military commander in Odessa, and he will write to your district or something...'

Gusev is terrified by this conversation and starts hankering for something. He drinks some water but that's not it; he stretches over to the round porthole and breathes in some hot, humid air, but that's not it either; he tries thinking about home, about snow, and that's not it... if he spends just one more minute in the sickbay, he will definitely suffocate.

'Can't breathe, fellows...' he says. 'I'm going up on deck. Help take me up, in the name of Christ!'

'All right,' says the soldier with the sling. 'You won't make it on your own, so I'll carry you. Hang on to my neck.'

Gusev puts his hands round the soldier's neck, and the soldier gets hold of him with his good arm and carries him up. Discharged soldiers and sailors are sleeping side by side on deck; there are so many of them it is difficult to make their way through.

'Get down now,' says the soldier with the sling quietly. 'Hold on to my shirt and just follow me slowly.'

It is dark. There are no lights on deck or on the masts, or anywhere around them on the ocean. The watch stands right on the bow, as motionless as a statue, but it looks as if he is sleeping too. It feels as if the steamship has been left to its own devices and is going wherever it wants.

'They're going to throw Pavel Ivanych into the sea now...' says the soldier with the sling. 'Into a bag first and then overboard.'

'Yes. That's what they do.'

'But it's better to lie in the earth at home. At least your mother can come to the grave and cry.'

'Of course.'

There is a smell of manure and hay. There are bullocks standing on the deck, hanging their heads. One, two, three... eight in all! And a little pony. Gusev stretches out his hand to pat it, but it shakes its head, bares its teeth, and tries to bite his sleeve.

'Damn you...' says Gusev angrily.

Both he and the soldier quietly make their way up to the bow of the ship, then stand by the rail, looking silently up above and then down below. Up above is deep sky, clear stars, and silence, exactly like at home in the village, but down below there is darkness and disorder. For no fathomable reason the huge waves are making a lot of noise. Whichever wave you look at, each one tries to go higher than all the others, chasing after and pounding the one before it; a third, just as ferocious and wild, will fall upon it noisily, with its white mane shimmering.

The sea has neither reason nor pity. If the steamship was smaller and not made of solid iron, the waves would have crushed it without the slightest feeling of remorse, devouring all the people without even bothering to sort saints from sinners. The steamship also has a senseless and cruel expression. The large-nosed monster is surging forward, cutting through millions of waves on its path; unperturbed by space and loneliness, it fears neither the darkness nor the wind; it simply does not care. If oceans had people, this monster would crush them and also not bother to sort saints from sinners.

'Where are we now?' asks Gusev.

'I don't know. In the ocean, I suppose.'

'You can't see land...'

'Of course not! They say we will only see land in seven days time.'

Both soldiers look at the white foam and its phosphorescent gleam, saying nothing and thinking. Gusev is the first to break the silence.

'There is nothing to be frightened of,' he says. 'It's just scary, like being stuck in a dark forest, but suppose they let down a boat on to the water right now and an officer ordered me to go fishing sixty miles away, I would go. Or say a Christian fell overboard right now— I'd go after him. I wouldn't rescue a foreigner or a Chinese, but I'd save a Christian.'

'Are you afraid of dying?'

'I am. It's my family I feel sorry for. My brother back home isn't very responsible, you know; he drinks, he doesn't honour our parents and he beats his wife up for no good reason. Everything will collapse without me, and my father and his old lady will end up begging, I know it. Actually, my legs are a bit wobbly and it's a bit stuffy here... Let's get some sleep...'

## V

Gusev returns to the sick bay and lies down on his bunk. He is tormented like before with a vague desire for something, but he cannot work out what it is that he wants. His chest feels tight, his head is throbbing, and his mouth is so dry he can barely move his tongue. As he dozes he becomes delirious, and after being tormented by nightmares, coughing, and the lack of air, he finally falls into a deep sleep as morning approaches. He dreams that they have just taken the bread out of the oven at the barracks, and he has climbed into the oven as if it is a steam bath and is beating himself with birch twigs. He sleeps for two days, and on the third, at noon, two sailors come down to the sick bay and carry him out.

They sew him up in sailcloth and put in a couple of iron weights to make him heavier. He starts to look like a carrot or a radish once he has been sewn up in the sailcloth: wide at the top where his head is and narrow at the bottom... They carry him up on deck before sunrise and put him on a plank; one end of the plank sits on the ship's rail, and the other on a box which has been put on a stool. Discharged soldiers and the ship's crew stand with their caps in their hands.

'Blessed is the Lord,' begins the priest; 'now, always, and for ever more!'

'Amen!' sing three sailors.

The discharged soldiers and the crew cross themselves and look out towards the waves. It is strange to think that a person has been sewn up in sailcloth and is about to go headlong into the waves. Could that really happen to anyone?

After sprinkling Gusev with earth, the priest bows. They sing 'Eternal Rest'.

The sailor on duty lifts the end of the board, Gusev slides off it, plunges head-first, somersaults in the air, and—plop! The foam covers him, and for a moment he seems to be shrouded in lace, but the moment passes and he disappears beneath the waves.

He descends quickly to the bottom. Will he go all the way? They say it is three miles to the bottom. After he has travelled about eight to ten fathoms, he starts going slower and slower, rocking gently from side to side as if deliberating; drawn by the current, he starts moving more sideways than straight down.

And now on his journey he meets a shoal of little pilot fish. When they see the dark body, they stop dead in their tracks, then they suddenly all turn round and disappear. But within less than a minute they are homing in on Gusev again as swiftly as arrows, zigzagging around him...

Then another dark body appears. It is a shark. It glides underneath Gusev grandly and nonchalantly, as if not noticing him, and Gusev lands on its back; it then turns belly up, basks in the warm, clear water and lazily opens its jaws, showing two rows of teeth. The pilot fish are thrilled; they stop and look to see what is going to happen next. The shark teases the body a little, then nonchalantly places its mouth underneath it, carefully grazes it with its teeth and the sailcloth is ripped along the whole length of the body from head to toe; one of the weights falls out and frightens the pilots by striking the shark on its side before descending quickly to the seabed.

But meanwhile up above, clouds are clustering together over where the sun is rising; one cloud is like a triumphal arch, another like a lion, and a third like scissors... A broad green strip of light emerges from behind the clouds and stretches out to the middle of the sky; a little later a violet one joins it, then a gold one, then a pink one... The sky turns a delicate lilac colour. The ocean frowns at first as it looks at this magnificent, mesmerizing sky, but it too then takes on those tender, radiant, passionate colours which are difficult to describe in human terms.

# FISH LOVE

Strange as it may seem, the solitary carp living in the pond near General Pantalykin's dacha fell head over heels in love with Sonya Mamochkina, who had come to stay. But actually, what is so strange about that? Lermontov's Demon fell in love with Tamara,* after all, and the swan fell in love with Leda, and do not bureaucrats sometimes fall in love with the daughters of their bosses? Sonya Mamochkina came to bathe every morning with her aunt. The love-struck carp swam along the water's edge and watched. The water in the pond had long ago turned brown because of being next door to the Krandel and Sons foundry, but the carp could still see everything. He could see white clouds and birds in the blue sky, lady holidaymakers undressing and young men peeping at them from behind the bushes on the edge of the pond. He could also see the plump aunt, who would spend about five minutes sitting on a stone before going into the water, patting herself contentedly and saying: 'Who do I take after to look like such an elephant? It's awful just to look at me.' After taking off the light clothes she was wearing, Sonya would rush into the water with a squeal and swim about, shivering with cold, and there would be the carp; he would swim up to her and begin greedily kissing her feet, her shoulders, her neck...

After bathing, the holidaymakers would go home to have tea and buns, while the lonely carp would swim around the pond, thinking:

'Of course there is absolutely no chance of reciprocation. Could such a beautiful woman fall in love with me, a carp? No, a thousand times no! Don't tempt yourself with dreams, you contemptible fish! Only one destiny awaits you—death! But how to die? There aren't any revolvers or phosphorous matches in the pond. There is only one death open to carp and that is via the jaws of a pike. But where can I get hold of a pike? There actually was a pike in the pond at one point, but it died of boredom. Oh, how unfortunate I am!'

Reflecting on death, the young pessimist buried himself in slime and wrote his diary...

One day in the late afternoon Sonya and her aunt were sitting on the edge of the pond fishing. The carp swam amongst the floats and could not tear his eyes away from the girl he loved. Suddenly an idea struck his brain like lightning.

'I will die by her hand!' he thought, his fins sparkling happily. 'What a wonderful sweet death it will be!'

So he swam up to Sonya's hook and took it in his mouth.

'Sonya, you've got a bite!' her aunt squealed. 'You've got a bite, darling!'

'Oh! Oh!'

Sonya jumped up and pulled with all her might. Something gold glittered in the air and plopped into the water, creating circles.

'It got away!' both exclaimed at once.

They looked at the hook and saw a fish's lip on it.

'Oh darling,' the aunt said. 'You shouldn't have tugged so hard. Now the poor little fish has been left without a lip...'

My hero was stunned when he broke away from the hook, and for a long time could not work out what had happened; then when he realized, he groaned:

'I've got to live again! Again! How you mock me, fate!'

When he noticed that he was missing his lower jaw, the carp went pale and gave a wild laugh... He went mad.

I fear my wanting to occupy the attention of serious readers with the fate of such an insignificant and uninteresting creature as a carp might seem strange. But actually, what is strange about it? Ladies in literary journals describe gudgeons and snails, which no one wants to read about. I'm just copying them. And maybe I am a lady myself and am just hiding behind a male pseudonym.

So the carp went mad. The unfortunate creature is still alive to this day. Carp generally like to be fried with sour cream, but my hero is now keen on any kind of death. Sonya Mamochkina married the owner of a chemist's shop, and her aunt went to live with her married sister in Lipetsk.* There is nothing strange about that, because the married sister has six children and they all love their aunt.

But there is more. At the Krandel and Sons foundry the director is an engineer called Krysin. He has a nephew called Ivan who, as everyone knows, writes poems and publishes them in all the journals and newspapers. At noon, one sultry day, the young poet was walking past the pond and decided to go for a dip. So he got undressed and slipped into the water. The mad carp took him for Sonya

Mamochkina, swam up to him, and kissed him tenderly on his back. That kiss had fatal consequences: the carp infected the poet with pessimism. The poet got out of the water not suspecting anything untoward, and set off home, laughing wildly. In a few days he went to Petersburg; after visiting various editorial offices, he infected all the poets there with pessimism too, and from that time onwards all our poets have been writing dark and gloomy poems.

# THE BLACK MONK

## I

Andrey Vasiliyevich Kovrin, master of arts, was exhausted and on the edge of a nervous breakdown. He did not go for treatment, but over a bottle of wine managed to have an informal chat with a doctor friend, who advised him to spend the spring and the summer in the country. As it happened he had just received a long letter from Tanya Pesotskaya, who wanted him to go and stay at Borisovka. So he decided that he ought indeed to go.

At first—this was in April—he went to Kovrinka, his own estate, and spent three weeks in solitude there. Then, when the roads became passable, he set off by carriage to stay with his former guardian and tutor Pesotsky, a horticulturist renowned throughout Russia. It was only about forty miles from Kovrinka to Borisovka, where the Pesotskys lived, and it was a real pleasure to travel on soft spring roads in a quiet sprung carriage.

Pesotsky's house was enormous, with columns and lions with stucco mouldings, and liveried servants at the front door. The old park, sombre and austere, was laid out in the English manner* and stretched over half a mile from the house to the river, where it ended abruptly in a steep clay bank, on which grew pine trees with bare roots that looked like furry paws. The water below glinted unsociably, there were sandpipers flying about, squeaking mournfully, and somehow the atmosphere down there always made you feel like sitting down and writing a sad ballad. Near to the house, however, in the courtyard and in the orchards, which along with the nurseries occupied about eighty acres, it was always bright and cheerful, even in bad weather. Kovrin had never seen such amazing roses, lilies, and camellias as the ones Pesotsky had, or such tulips in every imaginable colour, from snow white to jet black; in fact he had never seen such an incredible profusion of flowers anywhere else. Spring had only just begun and the most opulent blooms were still hiding away in hothouses, but what was blossoming along the paths and in the flower-beds was enough to make you feel that you were in a kingdom of delicate colours as you wandered about the garden, especially in the early morning when dewdrops sparkled on every petal.

The decorative part of the garden, which Pesotsky himself dismissed contemptuously as unimportant, used to have a magical effect on Kovrin when he was a child. There was no end to the whimsy, refined disfigurement, and mockery of nature to be found here! There were espaliered fruit trees, such as a pear tree in the form of a pyramidal poplar, there were spherical oaks and lime trees, an apple tree shaped like an umbrella, as well as trees in the form of arches, monograms, candelabra, and even a plum tree shaped into the number 1862, which was the year that Pesotsky took up horticulture. Then there were beautiful slim saplings with trunks as strong and as straight as palm trees, and it was only when you examined them closely that you could see they were actually goose-berries or blackcurrants. But the most cheerful aspect of the garden, and what made it seem so lively, was the constant activity. From early morning until dusk there were people with wheelbarrows, hoes, and watering-cans bustling about like ants around the trees and bushes, and in the paths and flower-beds...

Kovrin arrived at the Pesotskys' house in the evening, after nine. He found Tanya and her father Yegor Semyonich in a state of great agitation. The clear starry sky and the thermometer forecast frost the following morning, but Ivan Karlovich the gardener had gone into town and there was no one else they could rely on. At supper all they could talk about was the morning frost, and it was decided that Tanya would stay up; at one o'clock she would go into the garden to check that everything was all right, and Yegor Semyonich would get up at three or even earlier. Kovrin sat with Tanya all evening and then set off with her after midnight into the garden. It was cold. In the courtyard there was already a strong smell of burning. In the main orchard, the commercial orchard as it was called, which brought Yegor Semyonich several thousands each year in pure profit, a thick, black, acrid smoke had spread out along the ground and enveloped the trees, thus saving all those thousands from the frost. These trees were arranged like a draughts board, in regular straight rows like soldiers on parade, and this strict, pedantic regularity and the fact that all the trees were the same height and had identical foliage and trunks, made them monotonous and even boring to look at. Kovrin and Tanya walked along the rows, where there were bon-fires of manure, straw, and bits of rubbish smouldering, and occasionally they met gardeners wandering about in the smoke like shadows. Only the cherry trees, plum trees, and a few sorts of apple tree were in blossom, but the whole orchard was drowning in smoke and Kovrin could only breathe properly near the nursery beds.

'The smoke here used to make me sneeze when I was a child,' said Kovrin, shrugging his shoulders. 'And I still do not understand how the smoke stops the frost.'

'When there aren't any clouds, the smoke takes their place...,' Tanya answered.

'And why do you need clouds?'

'There isn't any frost when the weather is overcast and cloudy.'

'I see!'

He laughed and took her by the hand. He was moved by her wide, very serious, cold face, by her thin black eyebrows, by the raised collar of her coat which prevented her from moving her head freely, and by her lean and slender frame, clad in a dress which she had hitched up to stop it getting wet with dew.

'Goodness, she is so grown up already!' he said. 'When I left here the last time, five years ago, you were still a child. You were so scraggy, with your long legs, your plain hairstyle, and your short dresses, and I used to tease you about looking like a heron... Just look what time does!'

'Yes, it's been five years,' said Tanya with a sigh. 'A lot of water has flowed under the bridge since then.' She started talking animatedly, looking straight at him. 'Tell me Andryusha, honestly, do you feel a bit estranged from us now? I'm sorry, that is a stupid question. You are a man, you have an interesting life to lead, you are very eminent... You are bound to feel estranged. But despite all that, I would like to feel that you saw us as family, Andryusha. I think we have a right to that.'

'I do see you as family, Tanya.'

'Honestly?'

'Yes, honestly.'

'You were surprised today to see that we had so many photographs of you. But you must know how much my father adores you. Sometimes I think that he loves you more than me. He is so proud of you. You are a scholar, you are an exceptional person, you have had a brilliant career, and he is convinced that you have become what you are because he brought you up. I don't argue with him. Let him think that.'

Dawn was already breaking, and this was especially noticeable in the way the clouds of smoke and the tops of the trees were becoming more clearly outlined in the air. There were nightingales singing, and you could hear the croaks of quails coming from across the fields.

'Anyway, it's time for some sleep,' Tanya said. 'And it's cold too.' She took his arm. 'Thank you for coming, Andryusha. Our friends are dull, and there aren't very many of them anyway. All we have is gardening, gardening, and gardening—and nothing else. Standard, half-standard,' she laughed; 'pippins, rennets, winter apples, grafting, germination... Our whole lives have gone into gardening, and all I dream about are apple and pear trees. It's all wonderful and useful, I know, but you can't help wanting something else, some variety. I remember when you used to come here for the holidays, or just to visit, and the house always became brighter and more airy, as if the dust covers had been taken off the chandeliers and the furniture. I was a girl then, but I still could notice the difference.'

She talked for a long time and with great feeling. For some reason it suddenly occurred to him that over the course of the summer he might become rather attached to this small, frail, talkative creature; he might become attracted to her and fall in love; it would be so possible and so natural for them both in their position! This idea moved him and made him laugh. He leant close to her sweet, worried face and sang softly:

> 'Onegin, I don't want to hide it,
> You see, I love Tatyana madly...'*

When they arrived home, Yegor Semyonich had already got up. Kovrin did not want to sleep, so he started talking to the old man, and went back into the gardens with him. Yegor Semyonich was tall and broad-shouldered, with a large belly and a problem with breathlessness, but he always walked so fast it was difficult to keep up with him. He seemed to be in a hurry to get somewhere and he looked extremely preoccupied; his expression gave the impression that everything would be ruined if he was late by even one minute!

'So this is the problem, my friend,' he began, as he stopped to catch his breath. 'There is frost at ground level, as you can see, but if you lift the thermometer on the stick a few feet higher, it's warm... Why is that?'

'I really don't know,' said Kovrin with a laugh.

'Hmm... I suppose you can't know everything... However spacious our brains are, they can't fit everything in. You are still doing more with philosophy these days, aren't you?'

'Yes. I teach psychology, but my work generally is in philosophy.'

'You don't get bored of it?'

'On the contrary. It's what I live for.'

'Well, let's hope it stays that way...', said Yegor Semyonich, stroking his grey sideburns thoughtfully. 'Let's hope it stays that way. I'm very glad for you... very glad, my friend...'

Suddenly he started listening out for something, and with a terrible expression on his face he ran off and soon vanished in the clouds of smoke behind the trees.

'Who tied the horse to the apple tree?' came his desperate, heart-rending shriek. 'Which wretched scoundrel dared to tie a horse to the apple tree? Oh God, oh God! They've spoiled it all, they've let the frost in, they have mucked it up, they've fouled everything! The gardens are ruined! They are lost! Oh God!'

When he came back to Kovrin, he looked exhausted and deeply wounded.

'So what is one to do with these godforsaken people?' he said in a plaintive voice, throwing up his hands. 'Stepka was carting the manure last night, and he tied the horse to the apple tree! The miserable wretch tied up the reins so tightly that the bark has been rubbed off in three places. What do you think of that? I had a word with him, but all he does is stand there like an idiot and look blank. Hanging is too good for them!'

When he had calmed down he embraced Kovrin and kissed him on the cheek.

'Well, let's keep our fingers crossed... let's hope things will work out,' he muttered. 'I am very glad that you have come. I can't tell you how glad I am... Thank you.'

Then, at the same hurried pace and with the same anxious expression, he went round all the gardens, showing his former ward all the conservatories, the hothouses, the sheds for storing compost, and his two apiaries, which he called the miracle of the century.

While they were walking round the sun came out and flooded the gardens with light. It became warm. Sensing that it would be a long, clear, happy day, Kovrin remembered that it was only the beginning of May after all, and he had ahead of him the whole summer, which would be just as long and clear and happy, and he suddenly felt stirring in his chest the feelings of youth and joy he used to have when he ran about the gardens as a child. He embraced the old man and kissed him affectionately. Feeling rather overcome with emotion, they both went into the house and drank tea from old porcelain cups, with cream and thick pastries, and these small things again reminded Kovrin of his childhood and youth. The glorious present was fusing with the impressions of the past awakening in him; it was all rather overwhelming, but he felt good.

He waited for Tanya to wake up, drank a cup of coffee with her, and went for a stroll, then he went to his room and sat down to work. He read carefully, making notes; occasionally he lifted his eyes to look out through the open windows, or at the freshly cut flowers, still wet with dew, which were standing in vases on his desk, then he would turn his gaze back to his book again, and he felt as if every vein in his body was trembling and dancing with pleasure.

## II

He continued to lead the same nervous and restless life in the country as in the city. He read and wrote a great deal, taught himself Italian, and looked forward to resuming work when he was out walking. He slept so little that everyone was astonished; if he happened to fall asleep for half an hour during the day, he would then not sleep all night, but he would feel cheerful and happy after a sleepless night, as if it were nothing untoward.

He talked a lot, drank wine, and smoked expensive cigars. The young ladies who lived nearby came to visit the Pesotskys often, almost every day, and they would play the piano and sing with Tanya; sometimes the young man who lived nearby and who played the violin well also came to visit. Kovrin listened to the music and the singing with rapt attention and it exhausted him; this was physically expressed by his eyelids half-closing and his head lolling on one side.

There was one time after evening tea when he was sitting on the balcony reading. In the drawing room they were learning the famous Braga serenade*—Tanya was singing soprano, one of the young ladies had taken the alto part, and the young man was playing the violin. Kovrin listened attentively to the words—they were in Russian—but he just could not work out what they meant. Finally, after he had put down his book and listened very carefully he understoood: a girl with a febrile imagination hears some mysterious sounds one night in the garden, which are so beautiful and strange that she feels compelled to identify them as a sacred harmony incomprehensible to us mortals, which must therefore fly away back to the heavens. Kovrin's eyes were starting to close. He got up and walked through the drawing room and the ballroom in a state of intense fatigue. When the singing stopped he took Tanya by the arm and went out on to the balcony with her.

'There is a legend that has been in my mind ever since I got up this morning,' he said. 'I can't remember whether I read it somewhere or if I heard about it, but it's a strange sort of legend, unlike any other. To begin with, it's not at all straightforward. A thousand years ago a monk dressed in black was apparently walking in the desert, somewhere in Syria or Arabia... A few miles from where he was walking some fishermen saw another black monk moving slowly across the surface of the lake. This second monk was a mirage. Now forget all the laws of optics, which the legend does not seem to recognize, and listen further. The mirage produced another mirage, then another, so the image of the black monk started being transferred from one level of the atmosphere to another. He was seen in Africa, then in Spain and in India and in the Far North... Eventually he went beyond the perimeters of the earth's atmosphere and now he roams the entire universe, never able to find the right conditions which would allow him to evaporate. Maybe he can be sighted now somewhere on Mars or on one of the stars of the Southern Cross. But the whole point of the legend, my dear, is that exactly a thousand years after the monk first went walking through the desert, the mirage is supposed to enter the earth's atmosphere again and appear to people. And apparently those thousand years are almost up... According to the legend we ought to see the black monk any day now.'

'That's a strange kind of mirage,' said Tanya, who did not like the legend.

'But the most amazing thing,' said Kovrin with a laugh, 'is that I can't for the life of me remember how the legend came into my head. Did I read about it somewhere? Was it something I heard? Or perhaps I dreamt about the black monk? I swear to God, I can't remember. But the legend has been in my mind. I've been thinking about it all day.'

After he had let Tanya go back to her guests, he went out of the house and walked near the flower-beds, lost in thought. The sun was already setting. Because the flowers had just been watered, they were releasing a moist fragrance that made one's nose wrinkle. The singing started up again in the house, and from far away the violin sounded like a human voice. Focusing his thoughts in order to try and remember where he had heard or read about the legend, Kovrin set off for the park at a leisurely pace, and before he knew it he had reached the river.

Following the path which ran down its steep bank past the bare roots, he came to the water's edge, where he disturbed some sandpipers and frightened a couple of ducks. The last rays of the setting sun were still throwing light on the gloomy pines here and there, but it was definitely already evening on the river's surface. Kovrin crossed to the other bank on the footbridge. In front of him now lay a broad field covered with young rye, not yet fully grown. There was neither a house nor any living soul visible for far around, and it seemed that if you went along the path, it would lead you straight to that unknown, mysterious place where the sun had just set, and where the far-reaching evening twilight was glowing so majestically.

'There is so much space and freedom and quiet here!' thought Kovrin as he walked along the path. 'It feels like the whole world is looking at me, holding its breath and waiting for me to comprehend it...'

Just then ripples ran along the rye and a light evening breeze gently grazed his uncovered head. A minute later there was another gust of wind, but stronger this time—the rye started rustling and a muffled whisper came from the pines behind him. Kovrin stopped in astonishment. A tall black column had appeared on the horizon, stretching from the ground to the sky like a whirlwind or a sandstorm. Its contours were not clear, but from the very first moment you could see that it was not standing still but moving at a terrifying speed, and moving in his direction, straight towards him; as it came closer it became smaller and more distinct. Kovrin jumped out of the way, into the rye, in order to give it room to pass, and just in the nick of time...

A monk dressed in black, with grey hair and black eyebrows, his arms crossed over his chest, sped past... His bare feet did not touch the ground. After he had gone on about six yards, he looked back at Kovrin, nodded his head, and gave him a smile that was both warm and rather arch. But what a pale face, what a terribly pale, thin face! Growing larger again, the figure flew over the river, noiselessly hit the clay bank and the pines, and after going straight through them vanished into thin air like smoke.

'So there you are, you see...', murmured Kovrin. 'The legend was true.'

Without trying to explain this strange event to himself, and content simply to have seen not only the monk's black habit but also his eyes and his face so close up and so distinctly, he returned home in a pleasant state of excitement.

There were people calmly walking about in the park and in the gardens, and music was being played in the house, which meant that only he had seen the monk. He was dying to tell everything to Tanya and Yegor Semyonich, but he realized they would probably think he was hallucinating, and that would frighten them; it was better to remain silent. He laughed uproariously, sang, danced the mazurka, and enjoyed himself, and everyone, both Tanya and her guests, thought that there was something special, radiant, and inspired about the way he looked that night, and they found him very interesting.

III

After supper, when the guests had left, Kovrin went up to his room and lay down on the couch; he wanted to think about the monk. But Tanya came in a minute later.

'Here you are, Andryusha; some articles by my father for you to read,' she said, as she handed him a sheaf of pamphlets and offprints. 'They are wonderful articles. He writes beautifully.'

'Well, I don't know about that!' said Yegor Semyonich, forcing a laugh as he came in behind her; he felt embarrassed. 'Don't listen to her, and please don't feel you have to read them! Although actually if you want to fall asleep, then maybe you should read them: they have excellent sleep-inducing properties.'

'I think they are superb articles,' said Tanya with deep conviction. 'Read them, Andryusha, and persuade Papa to write more often. He could write an entire horticultural textbook.'

Yegor Semonyich chuckled awkwardly and blushed, and then began coming out with the sorts of statements that diffident authors are prone to make. Eventually he started to give in.

'In that case read Gaucher's article first,* and these Russian pieces here,' he mumbled as he sorted through the pamphlets with shaking hands; 'otherwise nothing will make sense. Before you read my objections, you ought to know what it is I am objecting to. Anyway, it's all nonsense... deeply boring. And it's bedtime, I think.'

Tanya went out. Yegor Semyonich sat down by Kovrin on the couch and gave a deep sigh.

'So my friend...' he began after a brief silence. 'My dear, learned friend. Here I am writing articles, taking part in shows, receiving medals... Pesotsky's apples are as big as your head, they say, Pesotsky's made a fortune for himself out of his orchard, they say. Basically, I've done very well for myself. But you can't help wondering what the point of it all is. The gardens really are wonderful, absolutely first class... They are not gardens but an institution of great state importance, because they are a step on the road to a new era of Russian agriculture and Russian industry. But what is it all for? What is the point?'

'Surely it speaks for itself.'

'That's not what I mean. What I want to know is: what will happen to the gardens when I die? They won't even last a month in the state in which you are seeing them now without me. The whole secret of success lies not in the fact that the gardens are huge and that there are many people working in them, but in the fact that I love my work—you understand?—I love it maybe even more than myself. Look at me: I do everything myself. I work from morning to night. I do the grafting myself, I do the pruning myself, and I do the planting myself; I do everything myself. When people help me I become possessive and then so irritated that I start being rude. The secret to it all is love—I mean keeping a watchful, proprietorial eye, and being your own manager, and the feeling you get when you are invited out for an hour or two, and you sit there but your heart's not in it, you're not at ease because you're worried something might happen in the gardens. And who is going to look after it all when I die? Who is going to do the work? The gardener? The workmen? You think so? Well, let me tell you something, my dear friend: our worst enemy in this business is not the hare, and it's not the cock-chafer or the frost, it's outsiders.'

'What about Tanya?' asked Kovrin with a laugh. 'I can't believe she is worse than a hare. She cares for the business and understands it.'

'Yes, it's true; she does. If she inherits the gardens after my death and takes over, I couldn't wish for anything better. But what if, heaven forbid, she goes and gets married?' whispered Yegor Semyon-ich, looking at Kovrin in alarm. 'That's the worry! She'll get married and have children, and then there will be no time to think about the gardens. What I most fear is her marrying some young fellow who will become greedy, and rent the gardens out to any old market-women, and then everything will be ruined in the first year! Women are a nightmare in this business!'

Yegor Semyonich sighed and was silent for a moment.

'It may be selfish of me, but I will be open about it: I don't want Tanya to get married. I'm scared! There is one upstart who pays visits and scratches away on his violin; I know Tanya won't marry him, I am sure of that, but I can't bear seeing him! I'm generally pretty eccentric, my friend. I have to admit it.'

Yegor Semyonich got up and walked about the room agitatedly, and it was obvious that there was something very important he wanted to say and that he did not quite know how to start.

'I love you dearly and am going to be frank with you,' he began finally, sticking his hands in his pockets. 'I like to deal with certain tricky questions in a straightforward way and say exactly what I think, and I can't abide it when people tiptoe around them. I'll be blunt: you are the only person who I wouldn't mind giving my daughter away to. You're intelligent and you've got a good heart and you wouldn't let my beloved work be destroyed. But the main reason is that I love you like a son... and I'm proud of you. If romantic feelings were ever to develop between you and Tanya, then—why not? I would be very glad and even happy. I am saying this openly, like an honest person, it's not pretend.'

Kovrin laughed. Yegor Semyonich opened the door in order to leaave, and stopped on the threshold.

'If you and Tanya were to have a son, I'd make him a gardener,' he said after a moment's thought. 'But anyway, that's just an idle dream... Goodnight.'

Now that he was left alone, Kovrin lay down more comfortably and started reading the articles. One was called 'On Intermediate Culture', another was called 'A Few Words in Response to Mr. Z on Digging Double Trenches in a New Garden', and another 'Further Thoughts on Grafting with Dormant Buds'—they were all in that vein. But what a restless, uneven tone, and what agitated, almost neurotic fervour! Here was an article which seemed to have the most innocuous title and inoffensive content: it was about Russian Antonovka apples. But Yegor Semyonich had begun it with 'audiatur altera pars' and finished it with 'sapienti sat',* and in between these two sayings there was a whole stream of poisonous invective aimed at the 'scholarly ignorance of our supposed gentlemen horticulturalists who observe nature from the heights of their university chairs', or at Mr Gaucher, 'who owes his success to ignoramuses and dilettantes'; and then there was also a protracted and insincere expression of regret that peasants could no longer be birched for stealing fruit and damaging trees while they did so.

'It's a nice, fine, healthy business to be in,' thought Kovrin, 'but there are passions and wars raging here too. I suppose people with ideas are always neurotic, whatever sphere they are in, and it is oversensitivity which makes them stand out. It needs to be that way probably.'

He thought about Tanya, who had liked Yegor Semyonich's articles so much. Small, pale, and so scrawny you could see her shoulder-blades; wide-open, dark, intelligent eyes, always darting about, looking for something; a hurried, quick walking pace like her father's. She talked a lot and loved arguing, and she accompanied even the most insignificant phrase with expressive movements and gestures. She had to be extremely neurotic.

Kovrin read some more, but he did not understand anything so he put the articles down. The pleasant feeling of excitement he had experienced dancing the mazurka and listening to the music had now begun to tire him, and was stimulating many thoughts in his head. He got up and started walking about the room, thinking about the black monk. It occurred to him that if he was the only one to have seen the strange, supernatural monk, he must be ill, and was already having hallucinations. This realization frightened him, but not for long.

'But I feel well, and I'm not harming anybody, so there cannot be anything bad about my hallucinations,' he thought, starting to feel better again.

He sat on the couch and clasped his head in his hands, trying to contain the unfathomable joy filling his entire being, then paced about again before sitting down to work. But the ideas in the book he was reading did not satisfy him. He wanted something massive, uncontainable, earth-shattering. Towards morning he undressed and reluctantly got into bed: he really did need to get some sleep!

When he heard Yegor Semyonich walking down to the gardens, Kovrin rang and ordered the servant to bring him some wine. He drank a few glasses of Lafite with relish, then tucked himself up; his thoughts became foggy and he fell asleep.

## IV

Yegor Semyonich and Tanya frequently fought and said unpleasant things to each other.

One morning they started quarrelling about something. Tanya started crying and went up to her room. She did not come down for lunch or for tea. To begin with, Yegor Semyonich walked about feeling self-righteous and peeved, as if to show that justice and order were the most important things in the world, but he could not keep it up and became miserable. He wandered dolefully about the park, constantly sighing and saying 'Oh heavens, heavens!', and did not have even a scrap to eat at lunch. Finally, feeling guilty and tormented by his conscience, he knocked at the locked door and called out timidly:

'Tanya! Tanya!'

And from behind the door, a faint but also firm voice worn out from crying answered:

'Just leave me alone!'

The Pcsotskys' misery was felt by the whole household, even by the people working in the gardens. Kovrin was immersed in his interesting work, but eventually he too started to feel uncomfortable and off-colour. In order to try and defuse the general bad mood, he decided to intervene and went to knock on Tanya's door before evening fell. He was let in.

'Now, now, this won't do!' he started saying jovially as he looked in surprise at Tanya's sorrowful, tear-stained face, covered with red blotches. 'Surely it's not that serious? Dear, dear!'

'But if you knew how he torments me!' she said, and tears, hot, copious tears, splashed from her large eyes. 'He's driven me insane!' she continued, wringing her hands. 'I didn't say anything to him... anything... I just said that there was no need to keep on... extra people, if... when you need to, you can hire casual labour. I mean those workmen have not done anything for a whole week now... That... that was all I said, and he flew off the handle and said a lot of hurtful and... deeply insulting things to me. What did I do?'

'Come on, stop now,' said Kovrin, as he straightened her hair. 'You've quarrelled, you've cried, and that's enough. You shouldn't stay angry for a long time, it's not good... particularly since he loves you.'

'He... he has ruined my whole life,' Tanya continued, between sobs. 'All I hear from him are insults and... and complaints. He doesn't have any need for me here. And you know what? He is right. I'm going to leave tomorrow and go and work in the telegraph office... So be it...'

'Hey, come on now... There is no need to cry, Tanya. There really isn't, my dearest... You are both hot-tempered and irritable and you are both in the wrong. Come on, let's go; I'm going to get you to make up.'

Kovrin spoke gently and convincingly, but she continued to cry, wringing her hands as if some terrible misfortune really had befallen her, her shoulders shaking convulsively. He felt all the more sorry for her, since the cause of her pain was not serious, but she was suffering deeply. What trivial incidents were enough to make this creature unhappy for a whole day, and perhaps her whole life! As he comforted Tanya, Kovrin thought that apart from this girl and her father, he would have to hunt high and low to find people who would love him as if he were family; he had lost his mother and father in early childhood, and if it were not for these two people, he might have lived his entire life without knowing true affection and that naive, unconditional love which you only feel for people very close to you, to whom you are related. And he felt that his highly strung and half-diseased nerves were responding to the nerves of this tearful, trembling girl like iron filings are drawn towards a magnet. He could never learn to love a strong, healthy, rosy-cheeked woman now, but he was attracted to frail, ashen-faced, unhappy Tanya.

And so he took pleasure in stroking her hair and her shoulders, holding her hands and wiping away her tears... Eventually she stopped crying. She continued to complain for a long time about her father and about her hard, unbearable life in the house, beseeching Kovrin to see things from her point of view; then little by little she started to smile and to sigh, saying that God had given her a bad personality, and then finally she burst out laughing loudly and called herself a fool, and went running out of the room.

When Kovrin went out into the garden a little later, he found Yegor Semyonich and Tanya walking side by side down the path as if nothing had happened; they were eating rye bread and salt, since they were both hungry.

## V

Happy to have been so successful in the role of peacemaker, Kovrin set off for the park. As he was sitting on the bench thinking, he heard the noise of carriages and women's laughter—guests had arrived. When the evening shadows started settling in the gardens, the sounds of a violin and voices singing could be heard faintly, and he was reminded of the black monk. In what country or planet was that optical illusion travelling now?

He had only just remembered the legend and was sketching in his mind the dark spectre he had seen in the rye field, when from behind a pine tree, right opposite him, emerged silently, without the slightest rustle, a man of medium height, with his grey hair uncovered; he was dressed all in black and was barefoot like a beggar, and his black eyebrows were sharply etched on his pallid, almost deathly face. Nodding his head in greeting, this beggar or wanderer came silently up to the bench and sat down, and Kovrin recognized him as the black monk. They looked at each other for a minute—Kovrin in astonishment, and the monk with a mixture of affection and archness, as before, and a guarded expression.

'But you are a mirage,' said Kovrin. 'How can you be here, sitting in one place? That doesn't fit with the legend.'

'That doesn't matter,' the monk replied slowly in a quiet voice as he turned to face him. 'The legend, the mirage, and I are all products of your heightened imagination. I am a ghost.'

'So you don't exist?' asked Kovrin.

'Think what you like,' said the monk, smiling wanly. 'I exist in your imagination, and your imagination is a part of nature, so that must mean I also exist in nature.'

'You have a very old, intelligent, highly expressive face, just as if you really have lived for more than a thousand years,' said Kovrin. 'I was not aware that my imagination was capable of creating such phenomena. But why are you looking at me with such delight? Do you like me?'

'I do. You are one of the few people who can genuinely be called one of God's chosen people. You serve eternal truth. Your thoughts and intentions, your astounding scholarship and your whole life have a heavenly, celestial bearing, since they are dedicated to all that is rational and beautiful, that is, everything which is eternal.'

'You said "eternal truth"... But is eternal truth accessible to people or necessary to them if there is no such thing as eternal life?'

'There is eternal life,' said the monk.

'Do you believe people are immortal?'

'Yes, of course. A great and dazzling future awaits all of you people. And the more people there are like you on earth, the sooner that future will materialize. Mankind would be nothing without those of you who serve the highest ideals, living consciously and freely; if mankind followed its natural course it would have to wait a long time for the culmination of its existence on earth. You are bringing mankind into the kingdom of eternal truth several thousand years ahead of time, and that is your greatest contribution. You are the incarnation of God's blessing, which is immanent in humanity.'

'But what is the goal of eternal life?' asked Kovrin.

'The experience of delight, like in any other life. True experience of delight comes from consciousness, and eternal life presents innumerable, endless sources for consciousness; that is what is meant by "In my Father's house there are many dwelling places".'*

'If you knew how enjoyable it is to hear you speak!' said Kovrin, rubbing his hands together with pleasure.

'I am very glad.'

'But I know that when you leave, I'm going to be bothered by the problem of your existence. You are a ghost, a hallucination. Does that mean I am mentally unwell and abnormal?'

'Something like that. But there is nothing to be embarrassed about. You are unwell because you have worked too hard and have worn yourself out, which means you have sacrificed your health to pursuing your ideal, and the time is approaching when you will give up your whole life to it. What could be better? It is generally what all divinely gifted people strive towards.'

'But can I believe in myself if I know that I am mentally ill?'

'And how do you know that the brilliant people respected by all of society have also not seen ghosts? Scholars are now saying that genius is closely related to mental derangement. Only ordinary, herd-like people are healthy and normal, my friend. Ideas about neuroticism, over-exhaustion, degeneration, and so forth can only seriously worry people who live for the present—herd-like people, in other words.'

'The Romans said "mens sana in corpore sano".'*

'Not everything the Romans and the Greeks said is true. An exalted mood, excitement, ecstasy—everything which distinguishes prophets, poets, and those who martyr themselves for an ideal, from ordinary people—is inimical to a person's animal nature, that is, his physical health. As I said before, if you want to be healthy and normal, join the herd.'

'It's strange; you are repeating ideas that often occur to me,' said Kovrin. 'It's as if you looked inside me and heard my most sacred thoughts. But let's not talk about me. What do you mean by eternal truth?'

The monk did not reply. Kovrin looked at him and could not see his face: his features had become hazy and were evaporating. Then the monk's head and arms started to disappear; his body merged with the bench and the evening shadows and then disappeared completely.

'The hallucination is over!' said Kovrin with a laugh. 'What a pity.'

He went back to the house, feeling happy and in good spirits. What little the black monk had said to him did not flatter his vanity, but rather his whole soul, and his whole being. What a noble, wonderful destiny to be one of the elect, to serve eternal truth, and to be one of those who will make mankind worthy of the kingdom of

God a couple of thousand years ahead of schedule, in other words to deliver people from several thousand unnecessary years of struggle, sin, and suffering, to sacrifice everything—youth, strength, and health—for the ideal and be prepared to die for the common good! His past life—uncorrupted, sensible, and full of hard work—flashed through his memory; he remembered what he had learnt and what he himself had taught others, and decided that there had not been any exaggeration in what the monk had said.

Tanya was walking towards him in the park. She was wearing a different dress.

'So this is where you are!' she said. 'We've been looking for you all over the place... But what's going on?' she asked in surprise, seeing his glowing, thrilled expression and his eyes full of tears. 'You're very strange, Andryusha.'

'I'm very contented, Tanya,' said Kovrin, placing his hands on her shoulders. 'I'm more than contented, I'm happy! Tanya, dearest Tanya, you are an extraordinarily lovely creature. Dearest Tanya, I'm so happy, so happy!'

He kissed both her hands warmly and then continued: 'I have just had a radiant, miraculous, unearthly experience. But I cannot tell you everything, because you will think I am mad, or you just won't believe me. Let's talk about you. Dearest, wonderful Tanya! I do love you, and I've already grown used to loving you. Being near you and meeting you ten times a day has become necessary to my soul. I don't know how I will manage without you when I go home.'

'Well! I think you will have forgotten about us in about two days!' said Tanya laughing. 'We are humble folk, but you are a great man.'

'No, come on, let's be serious!' he said. 'I'll take you with me, Tanya. Will you say yes? Will you come with me? Will you be mine?'

'Well!' said Tanya; she wanted to laugh again, but the laughter did not come and red blotches appeared on her face instead.

She started breathing rapidly and then walked off very quickly, not towards the house, but further away into the park.

'I haven't thought about that... I just haven't thought about it!' she said, wringing her hands as if in despair.

Kovrin walked behind her and said with the same radiant, thrilled expression:

'I want a love which will envelop me completely, and only you can give me a love like that, Tanya. I am happy! I am so happy!'

She was stunned; she seemed to stoop and shrivel up as if she had suddenly aged about ten years, but he found her beautiful and expressed his joy loudly: 'How lovely she is!'

## VI

When he found out from Kovrin that not only had a romance begun, but that there would be a wedding, Yegor Semyonich spent a long time walking up and down trying to conceal how agitated he was. His hands started to shake, his neck swelled and turned crimson, and eventually he ordered the racing trap to be harnessed and drove off somewhere. Watching him whip the horses and pull his cap almost right down over his ears, Tanya immediately understood what he was going through, and she went and locked herself up in her room and cried the whole day.

The peaches and plums had already ripened in the conservatories, and the packing and sending off to Moscow of this soft and fragile load required a great deal of attention, hard work, and trouble. Because the summer had been very hot and dry, every tree had needed watering; much time and energy had been devoted to it, and then hundreds of caterpillars appeared, which the gardeners and even Yegor Semyonich and Tanya squashed between their fingers, to Kovrin's great distaste. And while all this was going on it was necessary to take orders for fruit and trees to be delivered in the autumn and deal with a voluminous correspondence. And at the most pressured time, when it seemed that no one had a minute free, the work in the fields began, and took away more than half the workforce from the gardens; deeply sunburned, worn out, and irritable, Yegor Semyonich kept racing from the gardens to the fields, yelling that he was being torn into pieces and was going to end up shooting himself.

And then there was the business with the dowry, which the Pesotskys attached a good deal of significance to; the snipping of scissors, the whirring of sewing machines, the fumes from hot irons, and the whims of the dressmaker, a touchy, nervous lady, all made everyone's head spin. And then, just to make life even merrier, there were visits every day from guests who had to be entertained, fed, and even put up for the night. But all these dreadful labours went by unnoticed, as if in a fog. Tanya felt as though love and happiness had caught her unawares, although she had for some reason been sure from the age of fourteen that she would be the one that Kovrin would marry. She was astounded, confused, and unsure of herself... One minute she would experience such a surge of joy that she wanted to fly up to heaven and pray to God, while the next she would suddenly remember that in August she would have to leave her family home and be parted from her father; and then, from heaven knows where, would come the idea that she was insignificant, shallow, and unworthy of a great man like Kovrin, and she would go to her room, lock the door, and cry bitterly for hours on end. When they had guests she would suddenly start thinking that Kovrin was extraordinarily handsome, that every woman was in love with him and was envious of her, and she would be filled with pride and pleasure, as if she had conquered the whole of society, but he just had to smile politely to a lady for her to tremble with jealousy, go off to her room, and start crying again. These new feelings took complete control of her, so she helped her father mechanically and did not notice the peaches or the caterpillars, or the gardeners, or how quickly time was passing.

There was something very similar going on with Yegor Semyonich. He worked from morning till night, was always hurrying off somewhere, losing his temper and getting annoyed, but it all happened in a kind of enchanted dreamlike state. It was as if there were two people inside him: one was the real Yegor Semyonich, who would get angry when Ivan Karlych the gardener told him about things that had gone wrong and would clutch his head in despair, and then there was the other one who was not real, who would break off a conversation at work in mid-sentence, put his hand on the gardener's shoulder, and start mumbling as if he was half-drunk:

'Bloodlines account for a lot, you know, whatever you might think. His mother was extraordinary, a most noble, clever woman. It was a pleasure to look at her kind, bright, blameless face; it was just like an angel's. She drew beautifully, she wrote poetry, she spoke five foreign languages, she sang... And the poor creature died of consumption, may she rest in peace.'

The unreal Yegor Semyonich would sigh and fall silent for a while, before continuing;

'When he was a boy growing up with me, he also had the same angelic face, all bright and full of goodness. His look, the way he moved and talked, was gentle and refined, just like his mother. And his brain? His brain always astonished us. Well he's not got his degree for nothing, you know! Absolutely not! And you just see what he is like in ten years' time, Ivan Karlych! You won't be able to touch him!'

But then the real Yegor Semyonich would come to his senses; he would pull a terrifying face, clutch his head and shout:

'The devils! They have ruined everything! They have made a mess of it all, they have fouled everything up! The gardens are ruined! They are lost!'

Meanwhile, Kovrin worked with his usual zeal and did not notice the commotion. Love just fanned the flames. After each meeting with Tanya he would go to his room, excited and happy, and would take up his book or his manuscript with the same passion with which he had just kissed Tanya and declared his love for her. What the black monk had said about people chosen by God, eternal truth, brilliant future of mankind, and so on, just endowed his work with an unusual, special significance, filling his soul with pride, and a consciousness of his own high calling. Once or twice a week he would meet the monk in the park or in the house and have long conversations with him, but this did not frighten him; on the contrary, it excited him, as he was already firmly convinced that only a few exceptional people who had dedicated themselves to serving an ideal were selected to experience such visions.

Once the monk appeared during dinner, and he went and sat down by the window in the dining room. Kovrin was delighted, and he skilfully steered a conversation with Yegor Semyonich and Tanya on to a topic that the monk might find interesting; the black-robed guest listened, nodding his head cordially, and Yegor Semyonich and Tanya also listened, with happy smiles, not suspecting that Kovrin was conversing with his hallucination, not with them.

The period of fasting for the Assumption* arrived, and then soon after that came the day of the wedding which, according to Yegor Semyonich's fervent wish, went off 'with a bang', that is to say, it was celebrated with pointless revelries which went on for two days. The guests consumed about three thousand roubles' worth of food and drink, but because of the terrible musicians who had been hired, the raucous toasts, the bustle of servants running about the place, the noise and the crush, no one appreciated the fine wines or elegant canapés ordered from Moscow.

## VII

One long winter night Kovrin was lying in bed reading a French novel. Poor old Tanya, who suffered from headaches in the evening because she was unused to living in the city, had long been asleep and was from time to time uttering meaningless phrases while she dreamt.

The clock struck three. Kovrin put out the candle and lay down; he lay for a long time with his eyes closed, but he could not fall asleep because Tanya was still talking in her dreams and it felt very hot in their bedroom. At half-past four he lit the candle again, and it was then that he saw the black monk sitting in the armchair by the bed.

'Hello,' said the monk. After remaining silent for a short while, he asked: 'What are you thinking about at the moment?'

'About fame,' answered Kovrin. 'In the French novel which I have just been reading, there is a man, a young scholar, who does some stupid things, and wears himself out with his longing for fame. I don't understand that kind of longing.'

'That's because you are clever. You aren't bothered by fame; it's like a toy which does not interest you.'

'Yes, that's true.'

'Fame does not attract you. What is desirable or funny or useful in having your name on a gravestone which time will erode, along with the gilt lettering? There are fortunately too many of you for your names to be preserved by the weakness of human memory.'

'That makes sense,' said Kovrin in agreement. 'And what is the point of remembering them anyway? But let's talk about something else. Happiness, for example. What is happiness?'

When the clock struck five, he was sitting on the bed with his legs dangling over the carpet and saying to the monk:

'There was one happy person in ancient times who ended up becoming so frightened of his happiness, because it was so intense, that in order to please the gods he brought them his favourite ring as a sacrifice. And do you know something? I'm beginning to worry slightly about my happiness like Polycrates* did. It seems odd that I only ever experience joy from morning to night. It overwhelms me and drowns out any other feelings. I don't know what sadness, sorrow, or boredom is. Look, I am not sleeping, I've got insomnia, but I am not upset. I'm serious you know, I'm beginning to wonder about all this.'

'But why?' asked the monk in amazement. 'Is joy a supernatural feeling? Shouldn't it be man's normal state? The greater a person's intellectual and moral development, the greater his freedom, and the greater the pleasure he will derive from life. It was joy that Socrates, Diogenes, and Marcus Aurelius experienced, not sadness. As the Apostle said, "Rejoice evermore. Rejoice and be happy."'*

'But what if the gods suddenly become angry?' joked Kovrin, laughing. 'If they take away my prosperity and force me to starve and freeze to death, I am not sure that would be quite to my taste.'

Tanya had meanwhile woken up, and was staring with amazement and horror at her husband. He was talking, making gestures, and laughing as he sat looking towards the armchair; his eyes were shining and there was something strange in his laughter.

'Andryusha, who are you talking to?' she asked, clutching the arm he had stretched out towards the monk. 'Who? Andryusha!'

'What? Who am I talking to?' said Kovrin in confusion. 'With him... sitting over there,' he said pointing to the black monk.

Tanya put her arms around Kovrin, drew him near to her as if to protect him from his visions, and covered his eyes with her hand.

'You're ill,' she sobbed, her whole body shaking. 'Forgive me, my dearest, my love, but I noticed a long time ago that something had unsettled you... You're mentally ill, Andryusha...'

Now he started shaking too. He looked again at the armchair, which was now empty, felt a sudden weakness in his arms and legs which scared him, and started getting dressed.

'There's nothing seriously wrong, Tanya, I promise...,' he muttered, trembling. 'I am actually a little unwell though... it's time I admitted it.'

'I've been aware of it for a long time now... and Papa has noticed it too,' she said, trying to stifle her sobs. 'You talk to yourself, you smile in a weird way... you don't sleep. Dear God, please save us!' she said in horror. 'Don't be frightened, Andryusha, just please don't be frightened...'

She also started getting dressed. It was only now as he looked at her that Kovrin grasped how dangerous his condition was, and understood what the black monk and the conversations with him meant. It was clear to him now that he was mad.

Without understanding why, both had got dressed and had gone into the drawing room, Tanya first and Kovrin following. They found Yegor Semyonich, who was staying with them, already standing there in his dressing-gown, candle in hand, having been woken up by all the crying.

'Don't worry, Andryusha,' said Tanya, shaking as if she had a fever. 'Don't worry... Everything will be fine, Papa, everything will be all right.'

Kovrin was so agitated that he could not speak. He tried to address his father-in-law in a joking way, and wanted to say 'You can congratulate me, as I seem to have gone mad,' but all he could do was move his lips and smile bitterly.

At nine o'clock in the morning they dressed him in his jacket and then his fur coat, wrapped him in a shawl, and took him to the doctor in a carriage. He started receiving treatment.

## VIII

Summer came round again and the doctor ordered a stay in the country. Kovrin had already recovered and had stopped seeing the black monk, and now it was just a matter of building up his strength again. While he was living with his father-in-law in the countryside he drank a lot of milk, worked only two hours a day, and did not drink or smoke.

They held Vespers in the house on the evening before St Elijah's Day* at the end of the summer. When the sexton handed the censer over to the priest, the huge old ballroom started smelling just like a cemetery, and Kovrin started to feel depressed. He went out into the garden. He walked round without noticing the gorgeous flowers, sat for a while on a bench, then set off to walk through the park; when he got to the river he walked down the bank and stood there lost in thought, staring at the water. The fir trees with furry roots, which had seemed so young, joyous, and cheerful the previous year, now did not whisper but stood motionless and dumb, as if they did not recognize him. And indeed his head was shaved now; he no longer had his beautiful long hair, his posture was sluggish, and compared to last summer his face had filled out and become much paler.

He crossed to the other bank on the footbridge. Where there had been rye last year, scythed oats now lay in rows. The sun had already set, and there was a broad red glow blazing on the horizon, presaging windy weather the next day. It was quiet. Kovrin stood for about twenty minutes looking in the direction of the spot where the black monk had first appeared last year, and then the evening light began to fade...

The service had already finished when he returned home, dissatisfied and listless. Yegor Semyonich and Tanya were sitting on the steps of the terrace drinking tea. They were talking about something, but when they saw Kovrin they immediately fell silent and he concluded from their expressions that their conversation had been about him.

'I think it's about time you drank some milk,' said Tanya to her husband.

'No, it's not about time...', he answered, sitting down on the bottom step. 'You drink it. I don't want any.'

Tanya exchanged a nervous glance with her father and said in a guilty voice:

'But you've said yourself that milk is good for you.'

'Yes, very good for me!' sneered Kovrin. 'Well done: I've put on another pound since Friday.' He clasped his head in his hands and said sadly: 'Why, oh why did you cure me? Bromide preparations, rest, warm baths, observation, a timid fear over every mouthful I swallow, every step I take—it's eventually going to make me into a complete idiot. Maybe I was going insane, maybe I had delusions of grandeur, but I was good company, I was cheerful, even happy; I was interesting and original. Now I've become more down to earth and sensible, but I'm just like everybody else: I am a mediocrity, life is depressing... You've been so cruel to me! So what if I had hallucinations—who cared? I am asking you: who cared?'

'God knows what you are on about!' said Yegor Semyonich with a sigh. 'It's depressing just listening to you.'

'Don't listen then.'

Other people, especially Yegor Semyonich, now really irritated Kovrin; he answered him abruptly, coldly, and even rudely, and could only look at him with withering hatred; Yegor Semyonich felt awkward and coughed guiltily, although he did not in fact feel guilty in the least. Unable to understand why their affectionate, easygoing relationship had changed so dramatically, Tanya clung to her father and looked with anxiety into Kovrin's eyes: she wanted to understand, but could not, and all that was clear was that their relationship was deteriorating further every day, that her father had recently aged a great deal, and that her husband had become ill-tempered, capricious, prickly, and uninteresting. She could not sing or laugh any more, she ate nothing for lunch, she did not sleep for whole nights on end, expecting something awful to happen, and she worked herself up into such a state that one day she fainted after lunch and lay unconscious until evening. During Vespers she thought her father was crying, and now she was trying hard not to think about that while the three of them were sitting there on the steps.

'The Buddha, Mohammed, and Shakespeare were fortunate not to have their relatives and doctors cure them of their ecstasy and inspiration!' said Kovrin. 'If Mohammed had taken potassium bromide for his nerves, worked only two hours a day, and drunk milk, then he would have left as much to posterity as his dog. Doctors and devoted relatives will eventually make mankind duller, mediocrity will be seen as genius, and civilization will perish. If you only knew how grateful I am to you!' said Kovrin sarcastically.

He was feeling extremely irritated, and so he stood up and walked into the house so as not to say anything further. It was quiet, and the sweet scent of tobacco plants and beauty-of-the-night came wafting in through the open windows from the garden. Moonlight lay in green patches on the floor and on the grand piano in the darkened ballroom. Kovrin remembered the delights of the previous summer, when there had also been the scent of beauty-of-the-night and the moonlight had also shone in through the windows. In an attempt to try and resurrect his mood of the previous year, he marched up to his study, lit a strong cigar, and ordered the servant to bring him some wine. But the cigar tasted horrible and bitter in his mouth, and the wine did not have the taste it had the previous year. Talk about growing unaccustomed to things! His head was spinning from the cigar, and two mouthfuls of wine started giving him palpitations, so he had to take some potassium bromide.

Before bedtime, Tanya told him:

'Father adores you. You are angry with him about something and it's killing him. Just look at him: he is ageing not so much by the day but by the hour. I beg you Andryusha, for the love of God, for your late father's sake, for my peace of mind, please be kind to him!'

'I can't and I won't.'

'But why?' Tanya asked, as her whole body began to shake. 'Just tell me why?'

'Because I don't like him, and that's all there is to it,' said Kovrin casually, shrugging his shoulders. 'But let's not talk about him: he's your father.'

'I just can't understand it!' said Tanya, pressing her fingers to her temples and staring blankly ahead. 'Something incomprehensible and awful is going on in our home. You have changed and become quite unlike yourself... You are an intelligent and unusual person, but you now fly off the handle at the slightest provocation and you interfere in quarrels... You get worked up by such petty things that sometimes I am amazed and can't believe that it's really you. Look, don't be angry, please don't be angry,' she continued, kissing his hands, frightened by what she had said. 'You are good and clever and generous, I know you are. And you will be decent to him, I know. He is such a kind person!'

'He is not kind, he's just good-natured. Comic old men like your father, with their smug, good-natured physiognomies, effusive hospitality, and little eccentricities used to make me laugh—whether it was in stories, on the stage, or in real life. I found them quite touching too, but now I can't bear them. They are egotistical in the extreme. What I find most disgusting is their smugness and their sort of gastric optimism, as if they were bulls or pigs.'

Tanya sat down on the bed and then put her head on the pillow.

'This is torture,' she said, and you could tell from her voice that she was utterly drained and found it difficult to speak. 'There hasn't been one peaceful minute since the winter. My God, this is just awful! It's so painful...'

'Yes, yes, of course, I am like Herod,* and you and your Papa are the Egyptian infants. Of course!'

Tanya found his face unattractive and unpleasant. Hatred and sarcasm did not suit him. She had actually already noticed that there was something wrong with his face; it was as if it had changed when he had had his head shaved. She was about to say something insulting to him, but immediately became aware of her hostile feelings, was frightened, and left the bedroom.

## IX

Kovrin was given his own chair. His inaugural lecture was set for the second of December and notice of it was posted in the university corridor. But on the appointed day he informed the student administrator by telegram that he would be unable to read the lecture due to illness.

There was blood coming from his throat. He had been spitting blood before, but it was now flowing copiously once or twice a month, and when it did so he became incredibly weak and fell into a drowsy state. The illness did not particularly worry him, because he knew that his late mother had lived with exactly the same illness for ten years, even longer; the doctors had assured him it was not dangerous, and had advised him simply not to get overexcited, to lead a healthy life, and talk less.

The lecture also did not take place in January for the same reason, and in February it was already too late to begin the course. It had to be postponed until the following year.

He was now no longer living with Tanya but with another woman, who was two years older than him and looked after him as if he was a child. His frame of mind was calm and submissive: he readily acquiesced to her authority, and when Varvara Nikolayevna—as his friend was called—suggested that she take him to the Crimea, he agreed, although he sensed that nothing good would come of the trip.

They arrived in Sevastopol in the evening, and stayed in a hotel overnight in order to get some rest before travelling on to Yalta* the next day. They were both tired from the journey. Varvara Nikolayevna had a cup of tea, went to bed, and soon fell asleep. But Kovrin stayed up. An hour before setting off for the station, while they were still at home, he had received a letter from Tanya, but he had been unable to bring himself to unseal it, and now it sat in his jacket pocket and the thought of it was making him anxious. If he was honest with himself, he now felt deep down that his marriage to Tanya was a mistake, and was glad he had finally separated from her; his memory of the woman who had eventually turned into a walking skeleton, and in whom everything seemed to have died except those large, intelligent, intensely staring eyes, aroused only his pity and disappointment with himself. The handwriting on the envelope reminded him of how he had been unfair and cruel two years ago, and how he had unburdened all his emotional emptiness, boredom, loneliness, and all his dissatisfaction with life, onto people who were completely innocent. And then he was reminded of how he had torn his dissertation and all the articles he had written during his illness into shreds and thrown them out of the window, and how the scraps of paper had been carried off by the wind and had attached themselves to trees and flowers; in every line he had seen strange, groundless pretension, frivolous passion, impertinence, and delusions of grandeur, and it had had the effect of making him feel he was reading a description of his flaws; but when the last notebook had been torn up and tossed out of the window he had suddenly felt a sense of bitter disappointment, so he had gone to his wife and said all kinds of horrible things to her. Goodness, how he had tormented her! Once, when he wanted to cause her pain, he told her that her father had played an unattractive role in their courtship, as he had asked him to marry her; Yegor Semyonich happened to overhear this and had stormed into the room, but he felt so wretched he could not say a single word, and he had just stood there stamping his foot and mumbling strangely, as if his tongue had been removed. Tanya gave a piercing cry when she saw her father, and promptly fainted. It was disgraceful.

All this came back to him when he saw the familiar handwriting. Kovrin went out onto the balcony; the weather was calm and mild and you could smell the sea. The glorious bay reflected the moon and the lights and had a colour that was difficult to pin down. It was a soft, gentle mixture of blue and green; in some parts the colour of the water was like copper sulphate, while in others it seemed that the moonlight had condensed and filled the bay instead of water; but what a harmony of colours in general; what a peaceful, calm, and sublime mood!

The windows were probably open on the floor beneath the balcony, because women's voices and laughter could be heard clearly. There was obviously a party going on.

Kovrin summoned his courage to open the letter, and started reading as he walked back into the room:

'My father has just died. I have you to thank for this, as it was you who killed him. Our gardens are going to ruin, there are already other people running them, so basically everything my poor father feared is coming to pass. I have you to thank for this too. I hate you with all my heart and hope you die soon. How I suffer! My heart is consumed with an unbearable pain... May you be cursed. I took you for someone who was extraordinary and brilliant and grew to love you, but you turned out to be insane...'

Kovrin could not read further; he tore up the letter and threw it away. He was overcome by an uneasiness bordering on fear. Varvara Nikolayevna was sleeping behind the screen and he could hear her breathing; the sound of women's voices and laughter was coming up from the floor below, but he had the sensation that he was the only living soul in the entire hotel. He felt dreadful that the unhappy, grief-stricken Tanya had cursed him in her letter and hoped he would die; he looked briefly over towards the door, as if afraid that the mysterious force which had brought about so much destruction in his life and in the life of those close to him over the previous two years was about to enter the room and take control of him again.

He knew from experience that work was the best way of dealing with strained nerves. What he had to do was to sit down at the desk and, no matter what was going on, force himself to concentrate on some idea or other. He got out a notebook from his red briefcase, in which he had sketched an outline for a small anthology, conceived in case he found himself bored without something to do. He sat down at the desk, started thinking about the outline, and began to feel that his peaceful, submissive, and detached mood was returning to him. The outline in his notebook even prompted him to ponder the question of earthly vanity. He thought about the high price life exacts for the insignificant or very ordinary benefits it can give a person. In order to be appointed to a chair by the age of forty, for example, to be an ordinary professor and articulate ordinary ideas, other people's ideas moreover, in a language which was stilted, boring, and lifeless—in other words, to reach the position of an average scholar, Kovrin had to study for fifteen years, work day and night, suffer a serious psychiatric illness, experience an unsuccessful marriage, and do a lot of stupid and unfair things which it would be better not to remember. Kovrin now clearly recognized that he was a mediocrity, and he willingly reconciled himself to this, since it was his opinion that people ought to be happy with the way they were.

Working on the anthology would have succeeded in calming him down, but the white scraps of the torn-up letter were lying there on the floor, preventing him from concentrating. He got up from the desk, picked up the scraps of the letter, and threw them out of the window, but a light breeze was blowing in from the sea and just scattered them along the window-sill. Once again a state of unease, bordering on fear, overcame him, and he started to feel as if he was the only living soul in the whole hotel... He went out onto the balcony. The bay looked at him, with a multitude of sapphire, turquoise, and fire-coloured eyes, as if it was alive, luring him. It was hot and stuffy actually, and going for a dip would not have been a bad thing.

Suddenly a violin started playing on the floor below and two soft female voices began singing. It was something familiar. The song they were singing below was about a girl with a febrile imagination, who hears mysterious sounds in the garden at night and decides that this is a celestial harmony which we mortals cannot understand... Kovrin held his breath as his heart was gripped by sadness, and then his chest started vibrating with a wonderful sweet joy, such as he had long forgotten.

A tall black column like a whirlwind or tornado appeared on the other side of the bay. It was coming across the bay with terrifying speed and making for the hotel, becoming smaller and darker, and Kovrin barely had time to duck out of its way... A monk with black eyebrows and a bare head of grey hair, barefoot, arms crossed on his chest, rushed past him and then stopped in the middle of the room.

'Why did you not believe me?' he asked reproachfully, looking with affection at Kovrin. 'If you had believed me back then when I said that you were a genius, then these two years would not have been so miserable and unfulfilling for you.'

Kovrin already believed again that he had been chosen by God, that he was a genius, and he vividly remembered all his previous conversations with the black monk and wanted to speak, but blood was pouring from his throat straight onto his chest; at a loss to know what to do, he was moving his hands up and down his chest and his shirt-cuffs were becoming soaked with blood. He wanted to call out to Varvara Nikolayevna who was sleeping behind the screen, and he made an effort but said:

'Tanya!'

He fell onto the floor, and raising himself onto his arms, he called out again:

'Tanya!'

He was calling out to Tanya, calling out to the large gardens with their luxurious flowers, sprinkled with dew, he was calling out to the park, to the fir trees with the furry roots, to the rye field, to his wonderful scholarship, to his youth, to his daring, to his joy, and he was calling out to his life which was so beautiful. He could see a large pool of blood on the floor near his face, and he was so weak that he could not even say a single word, but an inexpressible, boundless happiness was filling his whole being. Underneath the balcony on the floor below they were playing the serenade, while the black monk was whispering to him that he was a genius, and that he was dying only because his weak human body had lost its equilibrium and could no longer serve as the vessel for genius.

When Varvara Nikolayevna woke up and came out from behind the screen, Kovrin was already dead, and a beatific smile had frozen on his lips.

# ROTHSCHILD'S VIOLIN

The town was very small—worse than a village really—and the people who lived in it were mostly old folk who died so rarely it was quite annoying. There was a very low demand for coffins from the hospital and from the jail. So things were pretty bad, basically. If Yakov Ivanov had been a coffinmaker in a proper town, then he would probably have had his own house and people would have called him Yakov Matveyich, but here in this little town they just called him Yakov, and for some strange reason he also got called Bronza by everybody. He lived in poverty like an ordinary peasant, in a little old hut with just one room, which had to accommodate him, Marfa, the stove, a double bed, the coffins, a workbench, and all their household goods.

Yakov did make good solid coffins. For peasants and lower-class people he measured them according to his own height and was never wrong, because there was no one taller or stronger than him any-where, not even in the jail, even though he was already seventy years old. For those who were more well-to-do and for women he took measurements, using an iron ruler. He did not like taking orders for children's coffins at all, and would go straight ahead and make them without measurements, with a sneer, and when he was paid for his work, he would say: 'I have to confess, I don't like having to bother with such trivial things.'

As well as his trade, his violin playing also brought him a small income. A Jewish band usually played at weddings in the town, run by Moisey Ilyich Shakhkes the tinsmith, who used to keep more than half the takings for himself. Since Yakov played the violin very well, especially Russian songs, Shakhkes sometimes invited him to play with the band at a rate of fifty kopecks a day, not including tips from the guests. When Bronza sat in the band his face would first become all sweaty and red. It would be hot, there would be an overpowering smell of garlic, the violin would squeal, a double bass would wheeze away by his right ear, and by his left would wail a flute, played by a red-haired, skinny yid who had a whole network of red and blue veins on his face and bore the name of the famous millionaire Rothschild. This wretched Jew managed to play even the most lighthearted tune mournfully. For no good reason, Yakov had gradually been filled with a hatred and contempt for Jews, and especially for Rothschild. He began picking on him and swearing at him using unpleasant words, and once he was on the point of beating him up, but then Rothschild got very upset and said, glaring at him ferociously: 'If I didn't have respect for your talent, I would have hurled you through the window a long time ago.'

Then he started crying. So Bronza did not get invited to play with the band very often, in fact only at times of extreme necessity, when one of the Jews could not make it.

Yakov was never in a good mood, because he had to put up with terrible losses the whole time. On Sundays and public holidays, for example, it was a sin to work, then Mondays were always hard, and so that meant there were about two hundred days in the year when you had to put your feet up whether you liked it or not. That was a dreadful loss! And if someone in the town had a wedding without music, or Shakhkes did not invite Yakov, that was also a loss. The police chief had been ill for two years and was on his last legs, so Yakov had been impatiently waiting for him to die, but he had decided to travel into the city for treatment and then he had gone and died there. That was a loss all right, at least ten roubles or so, because it would have been an expensive coffin, with brocade. Thoughts about losses particularly got to Yakov at night; so he used to put his violin next to him on the bed, and whenever his head began to fill with any kind of nonsense he could touch the strings, the violin would make a noise in the darkness and he would feel better.

On the sixth of May the previous year, Marfa had suddenly fallen ill. The old woman was breathing with difficulty and drinking a lot of water and she was unsteady on her feet, but she still got the stove going in the morning, and even went to fetch water. By evening she had taken to bed. Yakov played the violin all day; when it was completely dark, he picked up the book in which he recorded his losses every day and started totting up the annual total out of sheer boredom. It came out at more than one thousand roubles. He was so devastated by this that he flung all his accounts on the floor and stamped on them. Then he picked them up and again spent ages making calculations, sighing deeply with the strain of it all. His face was crimson and wet with perspiration. He realized that if he had put those wasted thousand roubles into the bank, he would have got the minutest amount of interest—forty roubles. So those forty roubles were a loss then too. Basically, whichever way you looked at it, it was just losses everywhere, nothing but losses.

'Yakov!' called out Marfa suddenly. 'I'm dying!'

He looked round at his wife. Her face was pink with fever, and extraordinarily clear and radiant. Bronza now felt embarrassed, as he was used to seeing her look pale, timid, and unhappy. It looked as if she really was dying and was glad to be finally leaving forever the hut, the coffins, and Yakov... She was looking at the ceiling and moving her lips and her expression was happy, as if she had seen death, her deliverer, and was whispering to it.

It was dawn already and the morning sun was shining through the window. As he looked at the old woman, Yakov for some reason recalled that over the course of their lives together he had never once caressed her or felt compassion for her; not once had he thought of buying her a scarf or bringing her home a piece of cake from a wedding. All he had done was shout at her, blame her for the losses, and shake his clenched fists at her. It is true that he had never actually hit her, but he had certainly scared her, and she froze with fear every time. He had also forbidden her to drink tea, because their outgoing expenses were already heavy, so she had to just drink hot water. And he understood why she now had such a strange and joyful expression, and he started to feel terrible.

When morning came, he borrowed his neighbour's horse and took Marfa to the hospital. There were not very many patients there, and so he did not have to wait long, only about three hours. He was very pleased to learn that it was not the doctor seeing patients that day, as he was sick himself, but the medical attendant Maxim Nikolayevich. He was an old man and everyone in the town said about him that although he drank and got into fights, he knew more than the doctor.

'Your good health sir,' said Yakov, as he brought the old woman into the surgery. 'Sorry to be troubling you with our trifling concerns, Maxim Nikolayevich, sir. It's my companion here who has been taken ill, you see. My better half, as they say, pardon the expression...'

Wrinkling his grey eyebrows and stroking his sideburns, the attendant started to examine the old woman, who was sitting hunched over on the stool. Emaciated and sharp-nosed, with her mouth open, she looked in profile like a bird wanting to drink.

'Hmm... I see,' said the orderly slowly. He sighed. 'Influenza, but maybe it is a fever. There is a lot of typhoid going round the town at the moment. Anyway, the old lady has done pretty well for herself, praise the Lord. How old is she?'

'A year off seventy, sir.'

'Well, then. She has done all right for herself... Time for her to say her farewells.'

'It's totally right, what you are remarking upon, Maxim Nikolayevich, sir,' said Yakov, smiling out of politeness. 'And we thank you most deeply for your kindness, sir, but if you will permit me to say so, every little insect wants to live.'

'Don't I know it!' said the attendant, in such a way as if the old woman's life or death depended on him. 'Well, I tell you what, my friend, you just go and put a cold compress on her head and give her some of these here powders twice a day. Right, bye-bye for now, bonjour.'

Yakov could see from the expression on his face that the situation was bad, and that no amount of powders were going to help; it was clear to him now that Marfa would die very soon, in fact any day now. He tapped the attendant on the elbow, winked at him, and whispered:

'Hey, Maxim Nikolayevich, oughtn't she to have some cupping-glasses put on her?'

'No time for that, absolutely not, my friend. Now you just take your old woman off home and God bless you. Cheerio.'

'Wouldn't you be so kind, though?' Yakov asked beseechingly. 'You must know yourself—if it was her stomach hurting or something inside like, then you give powders and drops, but it's a chill she's got after all! The first thing you do with a chill is get the blood going, Maxim Nikolayevich.'

But the orderly had already called in the next patient, and a woman had come in with her little boy.

'Come on, it's time you were off,' he said to Yakov, frowning. 'No point in dragging it out.'

'In that case, you could at least put some leeches on her! Give us a reason to pray eternally to God!'

The attendant lost his temper and shouted:

'One more word and I'll... Wretched idiot!'

Yakov also lost his temper and turned completely crimson, but he did not say a word. Instead he took Marfa by the hand and led her out of the room. Only when they were already sitting in the cart did he look back at the hospital, and say:

'What a lot of frauds they've got in there! I'm sure they'd put glass cups on someone well-off, but they can't even spare a single leech for someone poor. The brutes!' When they arrived home, Marfa went into the hut, and then stood for about ten minutes, holding on to the stove. She thought that if she lay down Yakov would start talking to her about losses, and tell her off for lying down and not wanting to work. But Yakov was looking at her with complete boredom and remembering that tomorrow was the feast day of St John the Evangelist, then the day after that was St Nicholas the Miracle-Worker,* and then it was Monday, which was a bad day. He would not be able to work for four days, and Marfa was bound to die on one of them; which meant he had better make the coffin today. He picked up his iron ruler and went up to the old woman to take her measurements. Then she lay down, and he crossed himself and started working.

When he had finished the job, Bronza put on his glasses and wrote in his book:

'Marfa Ivanovna—one coffin—2 roubles, 40 kopecks.'

He sighed. The old woman had been lying there silently all the time with her eyes shut. But in the evening, when it had got dark, she suddenly called the old man over.

'Yakov, do you remember?' she asked, looking radiantly at him. 'Do you remember fifty years ago when God gave us a little baby with blonde curly hair? We used to sit on the riverbank all the time and sing songs... underneath the willow tree.' Then with a grimace she added: 'But our little girl died.'

Yakov searched his memory, but could not for the life of him remember any little baby, or willow.

'You've been dreaming,' he said.

The priest came and administered the sacrament and extreme unction. Then Marfa started mumbling something unintelligible, and towards morning she died.

The old women from next door washed and dressed her and laid her in the coffin. Yakov read the psalms himself so as not to pay the deacon anything extra, and he was not charged for the grave either, because the cemetery caretaker was a relative. Four men carried the coffin to the cemetery, but out of respect, not because they were paid to. Old women, beggars, and two holy fools* followed the coffin, and the people they passed on the way crossed themselves devoutly... And Yakov was very pleased that everything was so honourable, decent, and cheap, and not a nuisance to anyone. As he said goodbye to Marfa for the last time, he patted the coffin with his hand and thought: 'Good workmanship!'

But when he was coming back from the cemetery he was overcome by a deep sorrow. He did not feel quite well: his breathing was fevered and short, his legs felt weak, he needed to drink. All sorts of thoughts were going through his head. He remembered again that he had never once in his life felt compassion for Marfa. He had never caressed her. The fifty-two years that they had lived in the same hut had gone by incredibly slowly, but it had somehow turned out that he had not once thought about her in all that time; he had paid her no more attention than if she was a cat or a dog. But she had kept the stove going every day, she had cooked and baked, gone for water, chopped wood, slept in the same bed as him, and whenever he had come home drunk from a wedding, she had always hung up his violin on the wall with reverence and put him to bed, and she had done all this silently, with a timid, concerned expression.

Walking in Yakov's direction was Rothschild, all smiles and bows. 'I've been looking for you!' he said. 'Moisey Ilyich is sending his regards and wanting you to go and see him straight away.'

Yakov was not feeling up to it. He wanted to cry.

'Go away!' he said, and walked on.

'What do you mean?' asked Rothschild anxiously, running ahead of him. 'Moisey Ilyich will get upset! He wants you to come at once.'

Yakov was revolted by this out-of-breath, blinking yid with so many red freckles. And it was horrible looking at his green frock-coat with dark patches and at his fragile, delicate frame.

'Why are you bothering me, garlic breath?' Yakov shouted. 'Keep away from me!'

The Jew started to get cross. 'Just you be quiet please or I'll send you flying over the fence!' he shouted.

'Get out of my sight!' yelled Yakov and went at him with his fists. 'Can't get away from you wretched people!'

Frozen with fear, Rothschild crouched down low and started

waving his arms over his head as if to protect himself from the blows, then he jumped up and ran away as fast as he could. As he ran he jumped up and down, flinging up his arms, and you could see his long, thin back shuddering convulsively. The little boys enjoyed the spectacle and ran after him, shouting 'Yid! Yid!' at him. The dogs also chased after him, barking. Someone started laughing, then gave a whistle and the dogs started barking louder and in unison... Then a dog must have bitten Rothschild because a desperate shriek of pain filled the air.

Yakov wandered along the meadow, then walked aimlessly through the outskirts of the town, with the little boys shouting: 'Bronza's coming! Bronza's coming!' And then he arrived at the river. There were sandpipers squeaking as they flew over and ducks quacking. The sun was shining very brightly and the water was so dazzling it was hard to look at it. Yakov walked along the path by the riverbank and saw a plump, red-cheeked lady getting out of the bathing pool, and he thought: 'Goodness! Just like an otter!' Little boys were fishing for crayfish with bits of meat not far from the bathing pool, and when they saw him they started shouting maliciously 'Bronza, Bronza!' Then he came to a broad old willow tree with a huge trunk and crows' nests in it. And suddenly the blonde, curly-haired baby and the willow that Marfa had spoken about came vividly back into his memory. Yes, this was the same willow—all green, quiet, and sad... how old the poor thing had grown!

He sat underneath it and memories started flooding back. He remembered there had once been a large birch wood on the other bank, where there was now a water meadow, and an ancient blue pine forest on the bare hill just visible in the distance. There had been barges on the river too. And now everything was flat and smooth; on the other bank there was just one birch tree, young and slim like a fine lady, and on the river there were just ducks and geese, and it was difficult to imagine that there had ever been barges. It seemed that there were fewer geese than before too. Yakov closed his eyes and huge gaggles of white geese flew into his imagination, one after the other.

He wondered how it had come about that he had never once gone down to the river during the past forty or fifty years of his life, or if he had by chance, how he could have failed to notice it? It was a decent-sized river after all, not just any old river; he could have done some fishing and sold the fish he caught to merchants, town officials, and the café owner at the station, and then put the money in the bank. He could have rowed a boat from one country estate to the next and played his violin, and all kinds of people would have paid him money; he could have tried barge-hauling again—it would have been better than making coffins. He could even have bred geese for slaughter and sent them to Moscow in the winter. You could probably get about ten roubles a year just for the down. But he had failed to take the initiative and had done none of these things. What losses! What terrible losses! If he had managed to do all those things together—fish, play the violin, haul barges, and slaughter geese, just think how much capital he would have built up! But there was none of that, not even in his dreams; life had gone by without purpose, without pleasure of any kind; it had been wasted in vain; it was not even worth a sniff of tobacco. There was nothing left to look forward to now, and if you looked back there was nothing to see but losses, and such awful ones that it gave you the shivers. Why couldn't people live without these losses and all this waste? Why did they have to chop down the birch wood and the pine forest? Why was the meadow so bare? Why do people always do the opposite of what they ought to do? Why had Yakov spent his whole life cursing, snarling, and going at people with his fists? Why had he been mean to his wife and what was the point of frightening and insulting that Jew just now? Why do people stop each other from getting on with their lives? It brings such losses! Such awful losses! If there was no hatred or anger, people would be an enormous help to one another.

All evening and all night he thought about the little baby, the willow, the fish, the slaughtered geese, and Marfa, who in profile had looked like a bird wanting to drink. And he thought about the pale, pitiful face of Rothschild, and then other ugly faces started coming at him from all directions, murmuring about losses. He tossed from side to side and got out of bed about five times to play the violin.

In the morning he forced himself to get up and go to the hospital. The same Maxim Nikolayevich told him to put a cold compress on his head and gave him some powders, but Yakov could tell from the expression on his face and from the tone of his voice that things were very bad and that no amount of powders were going to help. As he walked home, he realized that being dead would bring only profit: he would not need to eat or drink, pay tax, or offend people, and since people get to lie in their graves for not just one, but for hundreds and thousands of years, then you would make a huge profit if you added it all up. From life you just made a loss, but from death you made a profit. This was, of course, a reasonable way of looking at things, but it was annoying and painful to come to terms with it: why was the world set up in such a strange way so that life, which a human being only gets once, brings no profit?

He was not sad about dying, but as soon as he saw his violin at home, he was overcome with emotion and then he did become sad. He could not take his violin into the grave with him, and now it would be an orphan and would suffer the same fate as the birch wood and the pine forest. Everything in the world had disappeared and would continue to disappear! Yakov went out of the hut and sat by the threshold hugging his violin to his chest. As he thought about his lost, wasted life, he began to play; he did not know what he was playing, but it was mournful and touching, and tears started running down his cheeks. And the deeper his thoughts, the sadder his violin sang.

The latch squeaked a couple of times, and Rothschild appeared at the gate. He walked boldly across the first half of the yard, but when he saw Yakov he stopped dead and cowered. He started making signs with his hands as if he wanted to show on his fingers what time it was, no doubt from fear.

'Come over, it's all right,' said Yakov gently, beckoning him to come nearer. 'Come over here!'

Looking around distrustfully and in fear, Rothschild began to approach him, stopping about a yard away.

'Look, please, just don't hit me!' he said as he squatted down. 'Moisey Ilyich has sent me over again. Don't be scared, he said, go and see Yakov again, he said, and tell him that we can't do without him. There is a wedding on Wednesday... Yes, there is! Mr Shapovalov is giving away his daugher to a fine man... And the wedding will be very smart,' added the Jew, screwing up one eye.

'I can't...,' Yakov said, breathing heavily. 'I've been taken poorly, my friend.'

He started playing again, and the tears splashed from his eyes onto the violin. Rothschild listened intently, standing to one side, his arms folded on his chest. The frightened, confused expression on his face gradually changed to one of grief and suffering. He rolled his eyes, as if experiencing exquisite pain, and said: 'Aaagh!' And tears started slowly running down his cheeks and falling onto his green frock-coat.

And then Yakov lay down all day and felt sorrowful. When the priest came in the evening to administer the last rites, he asked him whether he could remember any particular sin in his life. Straining his fading memory, he again remembered Marfa's unhappy face and the Jew's desperate cry when he was bitten by the dog, and, barely audibly, he said:

'Give my violin to Rothschild.'

'Very well,' replied the priest.

And now everyone in the town wonders where Rothschild got such a good violin. Did he buy it or steal it, or did someone perhaps pawn it? He stopped playing the flute a long time ago, and now he only plays the violin. The same mournful sounds that used to come out of his flute now pour from his bow, but when he tries to repeat what Yakov played when he was sitting on the porch, what comes out is so mournful and sad that it makes people cry, and by the end even he is rolling his eyes and saying: 'Aaagh...!' People in the town like this new song so much that merchants and officials are always inviting him over to their houses and making him play it ten times over.

# THE STUDENT

The weather was fine and still at first. There were thrushes singing, and in the marshes nearby something alive was whistling mournfully, as if blowing into an empty bottle. A lone woodcock flew over, and the shot fired at it rang out with a resounding brightness in the spring air. But when it grew dark in the wood, an unseasonable cold and biting wind started blowing from the east and everything fell silent. Ice needles stretched across the puddles and the wood became bleak, desolate, and empty. It began to smell of winter.

Ivan Velikopolsky, a seminary student, son of a sexton, had been following the path along the water meadow as he returned from shooting. His fingers had turned numb and the wind was making his face burn. It seemed to him that this sudden cold spell had broken the order and harmony of everything, that nature itself was scared, and that was why the evening shadows had gathered more quickly than they needed to. Everything seemed desolate and somehow particularly gloomy. The only fire burning was in the widows' vegetable gardens near the river; everything else had completely dissolved into the cold evening mist, including the village about three miles away. The student remembered that when he had left the house, his mother had been sitting barefoot in the doorway cleaning the samovar, while his father lay coughing on the stove; because it was Good Friday there was no cooking at home, and he was ravenous. And now, shivering from the cold, the student thought about how exactly the same sort of wind must have blown in the times of Ryurik, Ivan the Terrible, and Peter the Great,* and how in their day there would have been exactly the same desperate poverty and hunger, the same thatched roofs with holes in them, the same ignorance and misery, the same wilderness all around, the same gloom and feeling of oppression—all these awful things existed back then, existed now, and would continue to exist, and life would be no better after another thousand years had passed. And he did not want to go home.

The vegetable gardens were called the widows' gardens because they were tended by two widows, a mother and daughter. A bonfire was burning brightly with a crackle, lighting up the ploughed earth far around it. The widow Vasilisa, a tall, stout old woman in a man's sheepskin jacket, was standing by it and staring into the flames, while her daughter Lukerya, small, with a pitted and stupid-looking face, was sitting on the ground washing a pot and spoons. They had obviously just eaten supper. Men's voices could be heard—local labourers were watering their horses down by the river.

'Well, it looks like winter's come back,' said the student as he walked over to the bonfire. 'Hello there!'

Vasilisa gave a start, but immediately recognized him and smiled warmly.

'Goodness, I didn't recognize you,' she said. 'That means you're going to be rich.'

They talked. Vasilisa, a worldly woman, who had once served with the gentry as a wet-nurse and then as a nanny, expressed herself gracefully, and a gentle, serene smile never left her face; her daughter Lukerya, a peasant woman who had been battered by her husband, simply looked at the student through narrowed eyes and remained silent, and her expression was strange, like that of someone deaf and dumb.

'Peter the Apostle warmed himself by a fire on a cold night just like this,' said the student, holding out his hands in front of the fire. 'So it must have been cold then too. That was a terrible night, wasn't it? An utterly miserable, long night.'

He looked around him at the shadows, shook his head vigorously, then asked: 'You were at the twelve gospel readings* yesterday, I expect?'

'Yes, I was,' said Vasilisa.

'If you remember, at the Last Supper, Peter said to Jesus: "I am ready to go with you, both to prison and to death."* And the Lord replied to him: "I tell you Peter, that before the cock has finished crowing today, thou shalt—I mean, you will—deny knowing me three times." After the supper, Jesus went through the agony of death in the garden and prayed, while poor Peter was weary in spirit; he grew weak, his eyelids were heavy, and he just could not fight off sleep. He slept. Then you heard how that same night Judas kissed Jesus and betrayed him to his tormentors. They took him bound to the high priest and beat him, while Peter, who was exhausted and tormented with fear and worry, you see, not having got enough sleep, followed them with a premonition that something awful was about to happen in the world... He loved Jesus passionately and with complete devotion, and now from afar he could see them beating him...'

Lukerya left the spoons and fastened her gaze on the student.

'They came to the high priest,' he continued, 'and started to question Jesus, and meanwhile some attendants had started a fire in the courtyard because it was cold, and were warming themselves. Peter stood with them near the fire, warming himself as well, like I am doing now. One woman said when she saw him, "He was with Jesus too"; in other words, she was saying that he should also be taken for questioning. And all the attendants who were standing near the fire must have looked at him suspiciously and harshly, because he was confused, and said, "I do not know him". A little later someone again recognized him as one of Jesus' disciples and said, "You are one of them too". But again he denied it. And for the third time someone said to him, "Didn't I see you with him in the garden today?" He denied it a third time. And then the cock began to crow at once, and Peter, having looked at Jesus from afar, now remembered what he had said to him at the supper... He remembered, realized what he had done, left the courtyard, and began to cry bitterly. In the gospel it says: "And he went out and shed bitter tears." I can imagine the garden being totally still and dark, with just a faint sound of muffled sobbing in the silence...'

The student gave a sigh and became pensive. Continuing to smile, Vasilisa suddenly started sobbing, and copious large tears started flowing down her cheeks; she hid her face from the fire with her sleeve, as if ashamed of her tears, while Lukerya, whose eyes had been fixed on the student, blushed, and her expression became tense and strained, like that of someone stifling severe pain.

The labourers were returning from the river, and one of them, on horseback, was already close; the light from the fire was quivering on him. The student said goodnight to the widows and walked on further. And once again the shadows drew in, and his hands began to grow cold. A fierce wind was blowing, winter really had returned and it did not seem like Easter was the day after tomorrow.

The student began to think about Vasilisa: if she had started crying, it meant that everything that had happened to Peter on that terrible night related to her in some way...

He looked back. The solitary fire was flickering peacefully in the darkness, and the people by it were no longer visible. The student started thinking again that if Vasilisa had started crying, and her daughter had felt embarrassed, then obviously the events he had just recounted, which had happened nineteen centuries ago, must also relate to the present—to the two women, probably to this deserted village, and to himself and to all people. If the old woman had started crying, it was not because he was able to speak movingly, but because she felt close to Peter, and because she was completely absorbed with what was going on in Peter's soul.

And then suddenly there was a frenzy of joy in his soul, and he had to stop for a minute to catch his breath. The past, he realized, was linked to the present by an unbroken chain of events, which flowed from one into another. And it seemed to him that he had just seen both ends of this chain: he had touched one end and the other had moved.

And when he was crossing the river on the ferry, and then when he was walking up the hill, looking down at his own village and across to the west, where the cold crimson sunset was glowing in a narrow band, he realized that truth and beauty, which had guided human life in that garden and at the high priest's, had continued to do so without a break until the present day, and had clearly always constituted the most important elements in human life, and on earth in general; and a feeling of youth, health, and strength—he was only twenty-two years old—and an inexpressibly sweet expectation of happiness, of unfathomable, mysterious happiness, gradually overcame him, and life seemed entrancing and miraculous to him, and full of sublime meaning.

# THE HOUSE WITH THE MEZZANINE
## (AN ARTIST'S STORY)

### I

It all happened about six or seven years ago when I was living in one of the districts of T. province,* on the estate of a landowner called Belokurov—a young man who used to get up very early, go around in traditional Russian dress,* drink beer in the evenings, and complain to me the whole time that no one appreciated anything he did. He lived in the grounds, in one of the annexes, while I was in the old mansion, in a vast ballroom with columns, which had no furniture except the large divan I used to sleep on, and a table at which I played patience. The old pneumatic stoves* always used to moan, even when the weather was calm, but during thunderstorms the entire house would start shaking, as though it was about to break into pieces. It was quite frightening, especially at night, when all ten of the large windows would suddenly be lit up by lightning.

I was doomed by fate to lead a life of complete idleness, and so I did absolutely nothing with myself. I spent hours on end looking out through my windows at the sky and the birds and at the avenues in the park; I read everything that arrived by post, and I slept. And every now and then I would leave the house and go wandering off somewhere until late in the evening.

Once when I was returning home, I happened to stray into an estate I had never come across before. The sun was already beginning to disappear, and evening shadows stretched along the flowering rye. Two rows of old and very tall fir trees planted closely together stood like solid walls, forming a dark, beautiful avenue. I climbed over the fence without any difficulty and set off down this avenue, slipping on the needles which lay on the ground several inches thick. It was quiet and dark, except high up at the tops of some of the trees, where there was a glimmer of bright golden light which made rainbows in the spiders' webs. The scent from the needles was so strong it was almost overpowering. Then I turned down the long linden avenue. Here too there were signs of neglect and old age; last year's fallen leaves rustled sadly under my feet, and shadows hid in the twilight between the trees. To my right, in an old orchard there was an oriole singing, reluctantly and feebly; it was probably old too. But at this point the lindens came to an end; I walked past a white house with a veranda and a mezzanine, and before me suddenly unfolded a vista of the house's front courtyard, a large pond with a bathing area and a cluster of green willows, a village on the other side, and a tall, narrow bell-tower, at the top of which was a cross, which looked as if it was on fire as it reflected the rays of the setting sun. For a second I was bewitched by the sensation that all of this was something familiar and cherished—as if I had seen this exact vista at some point in my childhood.

By the white stone gateposts which led from the courtyard into the fields two girls were standing in front of a pair of sturdy old gates with lions on them. One of them—older, thin, pale, very pretty, with a great mop of chestnut hair on her head and a small, stubborn mouth—had a stern expression and barely cast a glance at me. The other one, who looked quite young still—about seventeen or eighteen, no more than that—was also thin and pale, and had a large mouth and large eyes. She looked at me in surprise as I walked past, said something in English, and then immediately became embarrassed. It seemed that I had known these two lovely faces for a long time too. I returned home feeling I had woken up from a pleasant dream.

Soon afterwards, at around noon one day, as Belokurov and I were out for a stroll near the house, a sprung carriage suddenly swept into the courtyard, making the grass rustle. In it sat one of those girls I had seen; the elder one. She had come with a subscription list in aid of the victims of a fire. Without looking at us, she told us earnestly and in profuse detail about how many houses had burned down in the village of Siyanovo, how many men, women, and children had been left without a roof over their heads, and what were the immediate steps to be taken by the fire committee, of which she was now a member. After giving us the list to sign, she tucked it away and immediately started saying goodbye.

'You have been neglecting us, Pyotr Petrovich,' she said to Belokurov, as she held out her hand to him. 'You should come over. And if Monsieur N. (she pronounced my surname) is interested in seeing how admirers of his work live round here, and would like to pay a visit, then Mama and I would be very glad.' I bowed.

When she had gone, Pyotr Petrovich started telling me about her. She was a girl from a good family, according to him, and was called

Lidiya Volchaninova. And the estate where she lived with her mother and sister was called Shelkovka, which was also the name of the village on the other side of the pond. Her father had once held a prominent post in Moscow and had attained the rank of privy councillor when he died. Despite their affluence, the Volchaninovs lived in the village all year round, both summer and winter, and Lidiya was a teacher in the local district school in Shelkovka and earned twenty-five roubles a month. This was the only money she spent on herself, and she was proud of being able to live on her wages. 'They are an interesting family,' said Belokurov. 'Maybe we should go and call on them one day. They would be very pleased to see you.'

After lunch one feast day, we remembered about the Volchaninovs and set off to visit them in Shelkovka. The mother and both her daughters were at home. Yckaterina Pavlovna, the mother, had obviously once been pretty, but now looked older than her years, was short of breath, sad, and absent-minded. She tried to start a conversation about painting with me. Having heard from her daughter that I might visit Shelkovka, she had hurriedly recalled a couple of my landscape paintings that she had seen at exhibitions in Moscow and was now asking me what I had wanted to express in them. Lidiya, or Lida, as they called her at home, spoke more to Belokurov than to me. With an unsmiling and earnest expression she was asking him why he did not serve on the zemstvo,* and why he still had not attended a single meeting.

'It's not good, Pyotr Petrovich,' she said. 'Not good. Shame on you.'

'You're right Lida,' her mother said. 'It's not good.'

'Our whole district is at the mercy of Balagin,' Lida continued, turning to me. 'He runs the office and he has given all the jobs in the district to his nephews and nieces. He does whatever he wants. We've got to put up a fight. The young people round here ought to join forces, but you can see what kind of young people we have round here! Shame on you, Pyotr Petrovich!'

The younger sister Zhenya was silent while we were talking about the local zemstvo. She did not take part in serious discussions, since she was not considered grown-up. They called her Missius, as if she were a little girl, because that was what she had called her governess, instead of 'Miss'. She looked at me with curiosity the whole time, and as I looked through a photograph album, she placed her finger on each of the portraits, explaining: 'That's my uncle... that's my godfather...' Like a child, she leaned her shoulder against me, and I could see up close her delicate young breasts, her narrow shoulders, her plaited hair, and her thin little body, tightly held in by a belt.

We played croquet and lawn-tennis, walked around the garden, drank tea, then took a long time over dinner. After the huge expanse of the ballroom with its columns, I enjoyed being in this small, comfortable house, where there were no imitation oil paintings on the walls, and where they were polite to the servants. Everything in it seemed young and pure, thanks to the presence of Lida and Missius, and there was an atmosphere of integrity. Lida talked about the zemstvo again to Belokurov at dinner, about Balagin, and about the school libraries. She was a lively, sincere girl with strong convictions, and it was interesting to listen to her, although she talked a great deal and in a loud voice, probably because that was what she was used to doing at her school. Good old Pyotr Petrovich, on the other hand, who had retained from his student years the habit of turning every conversation into an argument, was boring, monotonous, and long-winded when he spoke, but he was obviously intent on appearing clever and forward-thinking. He knocked over the sauce-boat with his sleeve as he was making a gesture, and a large puddle formed on the tablecloth, but no one apart from me appeared to notice.

It was dark and quiet when we returned home.

'Good breeding is not about whether you spill sauce on the table-cloth or not, but about not noticing someone else doing it,' said Belokurov with a sigh. 'Yes, what a fine, cultured family they are! I've lost touch with good people, I really have! It's just work, work, work, all the time!'

He talked about how hard one had to work in order to become a model farmer. Meanwhile I was thinking what a lazy and tiresome fellow he was! Whenever he talked about anything serious he would drag out his sentences unbearably, and the way he worked was just like the way he talked—slowly, always behind schedule and with scant regard for deadlines. I already had little faith in his ability to get things done, because he would carry around the letters I had asked him to mail for me in his pocket for weeks on end.

'And the hardest thing of all,' he muttered, as he walked along beside me; 'the hardest thing is that you do all this work, and no one ever appreciates it! Never any appreciation!'

## II

I started spending time at the Volchaninovs. I would usually just sit on the bottom step of the veranda, tormented by dissatisfaction with myself, and sad that my life was passing by so fast and so uneventfully. I kept wishing I could just pluck out my heart, because it had become so heavy. And all the while I would hear people talking on the veranda, dresses rustling, and the pages of a book being turned. In the afternoons I soon got used to seeing Lida treat sick people, give out books, and often walk bareheaded into the village with a parasol. Then in the evenings she would usually talk loudly about the zemstvo and the schools. This slim, pretty, and unrelentingly puritanical girl with the small, perfectly formed mouth would always tell me drily, whenever the conversation turned to her work:

'This won't be interesting to you.'

I did not appeal to her. She did not like me because I painted landscapes instead of depicting social problems, and because I was indifferent to all the things she so strongly believed in, or so it seemed to her. I remember once when I was travelling along the shores of Lake Baikal, I met a Buryat girl,* dressed in a shirt and blue trousers made of Chinese calico, sitting astride a horse. I asked her if she would sell me her pipe, and while we were talking she looked at my European face and at my hat with complete derision. She was bored with talking to me after less than a minute, and she just gave a whoop and galloped off. Lida despised me as someone alien in just the same way. She never expressed her dislike of me out in the open, but I could sense it, and would become irritated while sitting on the bottom step of the veranda. I said that to treat peasants without being a doctor was to deceive them, and that it was easy to do good works when you owned thousands of acres.

But her sister Missius had no cares at all and spent her days in complete idleness, just like me. As soon as she got up she would pick up a book and read, sitting on the veranda in a deep armchair, with her feet barely touching the ground, or she would hide away with her book in the linden avenue, or walk through the gates into the field. She read the whole day, with her eyes glued to the page, and it was only because she sometimes looked tired and rather dazed, and her face became extremely pale, that you could tell that all that reading mentally exhausted her. Whenever I appeared, she would blush and put down her book. With her large eyes fixed on me, she would tell me what had been going on, that the chimney had caught fire in the servants' quarters, for example, or that one of the labourers had caught a big fish in the pond. During the week she would usually wear a light-coloured blouse and a navy skirt. We went for walks together, picked cherries to make jam, and went boating, and when she jumped up to reach a cherry or was pulling on the oars, her thin, frail arms showed underneath her wide sleeves. At other times I would do some sketching, and she would stand nearby and watch with delight.

One Sunday, at the end of July, I arrived at the Volchaninovs in the morning, at around nine o'clock. Keeping some way off from the house, I walked through the park looking for white mushrooms, which were in abundance that summer, and put markers by them so I could pick them later with Zhenya. There was a warm wind blowing. I saw Zhenya and her mother coming home from church, both wearing smart summer dresses, and Zhenya holding on to her hat because of the wind. Then I heard them having tea on the veranda.

For me, a person without cares, forever seeking justification for my life of permanent idleness, these summer weekend mornings at our country estates are always extraordinarily pleasant. With the green garden still damp with dew and basking happily in the sunlight, the scent of mignonette and oleander surrounding the house, and the young people drinking tea in the garden, just back from church, everyone in their Sunday best, and in good spirits, and with the knowledge that all these healthy, well-fed, attractive people will do nothing all day long, one cannot help wishing that life would always be like this. And that is precisely what I was thinking as I walked round the garden that day, ready to carry on walking without aim or purpose for the whole day, or the entire summer.

Zhenya arrived with a basket; she looked as if she knew or had sensed that she would find me in the garden. We picked the mushrooms and talked, and when she asked me about something, she would walk in front of me so she could see my face.

'A miracle took place in our village yesterday,' she said. 'Pelageya, the cripple, has been ill the whole year; no doctors or medicines were any help, and yesterday an old woman just whispered something and she got better.'

'That's nothing,' I said. 'You shouldn't just look for miracles that happen with sick people and old women. Isn't good health a miracle? And what about life itself? Anything you can't understand is a miracle.'

'But aren't you scared of things you don't understand?'

'No. I have a healthy attitude to things I don't understand and don't give in to them. I'm above them. Human beings should acknowledge themselves as being above lions, tigers, stars—above everything in nature, in fact even above things which are incomprehensible and seem miraculous, otherwise we are not human beings but mice, frightened of everything.'

Zhenya thought that I must know a lot since I was an artist, and that I could just guess the answer to things I didn't know. She wanted me to transport her into the realm of the eternal and beautiful, to the higher world where she thought I resided, and she would talk to me about god, about eternal life, and about heaven. Meanwhile, refusing to entertain the thought that I and my imagination would perish forever after my death, I would reply: 'Yes, people are immortal', 'Yes, eternal life does await us.' And she listened, believed what I said, and needed no proof.

When we were walking back towards the house, she suddenly stopped and said: 'Lida is a remarkable person, don't you think? I love her so much, and would gladly sacrifice my life for her. But tell me,' Zhenya then asked, touching my sleeve with her finger; 'why do you argue with her all the time? Why do you get so annoyed?'

'Because she is wrong!'

Zhenya shook her head and tears appeared in her eyes. 'I just don't understand!' she said.

Lida had just then returned from somewhere. Standing by the porch with a riding crop in her hands, looking slim and pretty and all bathed in sunlight, she was giving instructions to a workman. After briskly attending to a few people requiring medical attention, to whom she talked in a loud voice, she walked through the house with a businesslike, preoccupied look, opening one cupboard after another, and then disappeared into the mezzanine. It took a long while to find her and call her down to lunch, and by the time she appeared we had already finished our soup. For some reason I have fond memories of all these tiny details, and can recall the day vividly, even though nothing special happened. After lunch, Zhenya read, recumbent in her deep armchair, and I sat on the bottom step of the veranda. We did not talk. The whole sky was now full of clouds, and it began to rain with a fine, light drizzle. It was hot, the wind had long since dropped, and it seemed that the day would never end. Still drowsy, Yekaterina Pavlovna came out onto the veranda with a fan.

'Oh Mama, you know it isn't good for you to sleep in the daytime,' said Zhenya, kissing her hand.

They adored one another. When one of them went out into the garden, the other would immediately go and stand on the veranda and call out in the direction of the trees, 'Zhenya, dear!' or 'Mama, where are you?' They always prayed together and shared a strong faith, and they understood each other, even when they were silent. And they interacted with people in the same way. Yekaterina Pavlovna just as quickly got used to me and became fond of me, and if I did not appear for two or three days, she would send someone to find out whether I was ill. She also delighted in looking at my sketches and would inform me, just as ingenuously and talkatively as Missius, what had being going on, often entrusting me with her domestic secrets.

She was in awe of her elder daughter. Lida was never affectionate and always talked about serious matters. She lived her own particular life, and for her mother and her sister she was as sacred and slightly mysterious a creature as an admiral who always sits in his cabin must seem to his sailors. 'Lida really is a remarkable person,' her mother would often say; 'don't you think?'

We began to talk about Lida while it was spitting rain.

'She really is a remarkable person,' said her mother, and then, looking round warily, added in a whisper, in a furtive tone: 'You won't find another like her, but I do begin to worry a bit, you know. The school, the medicines, the books—it's all very well, but why does it have to be so extreme? She is twenty-four already, after all; it's time she thought about herself. If you get caught up in books and handing out medicines you might not notice life going by... She ought to get married.'

Pale-faced from all her reading, and her hair in a mess, Zhenya looked up and said, as if to herself, but looking at her mother:

'Everything depends on God's will, Mama darling!'

Then she buried herself in her book again.

Belokurov arrived, decked out in his embroidered peasant shirt and coat. We played croquet and lawn-tennis, then spent a long time over supper when it grew dark, and Lida again talked about the schools and about Balagin, who had taken control of the whole district. As I left the Volchaninovs that evening, I carried away with me an impression of an incredibly long day spent in complete idleness, as well as a sad recognition that everything in this world must come to an end, no matter how long it lasts. Zhenya accompanied us as far as the gates, and perhaps because she had spent the whole day with me, from morning until night, I then felt rather lonely without her, and I realized that all her lovely family were dear to me. For the first time that summer I had an urge to paint.

'So why do you lead such a dull, monochrome life?' I asked Belokurov as we walked home. 'My life is difficult, dull, and monotonous because I am an artist. I know I am peculiar; ever since I was young I have been tormented by envy, dissatisfaction with myself, and a lack of faith in what I do. I am always hard-up, and will never be settled, but you, on the other hand, are a normal, healthy person, a landowner, a gentleman—why do you live so uninterestingly, why don't you get more out of life? I mean, why haven't you fallen in love with Lida or Zhenya yet?'

'You're forgetting that I love another woman,' answered Belokurov.

He was referring to his friend Lyubov Ivanovna, who lived with him in the annex. I used to see this lady walking every day with a parasol in the garden, in traditional Russian costume complete with beads, while the servant would periodically invite her to come and eat or drink tea. She was plump and chubby-faced, like a fattened-up goose, and vain too. About three years before, she had rented one of the annexes for the summer, and had just stayed on, living with Belokurov on a permanent basis, or so it appeared. She was about ten years older than him and kept him on a tight leash, so that he had to ask permission if he wanted to go anywhere. She would often start sobbing in a deep masculine-sounding voice, and then I would have someone inform her that I would move out unless she stopped; and then she did.

When we got home, Belokurov sat down on the sofa, his brows furrowed in thought, while I paced up and down the room, feeling quietly excited, as if I was in love. I wanted to talk about the Volchaninovs.

'Lida could only love someone on the zemstvo, who is as mad as she is about hospitals and schools,' I said. 'But for a girl like that, most men would not think twice about becoming a member of the zemstvo; they would be ready to wear out a pair of iron boots,* like in the fairy tale. Then there's Missius, of course. She's so lovely!'

Belokurov began a long diatribe about pessimism, the sickness of the age, complete with heavy sighs. He talked forcefully, as if I was arguing with him. Even endless miles of bleak, empty, scorched steppe are less depressing than a person who just sits and talks for ever and ever. 'But the problem isn't pessimism or optimism,' I said finally, with irritation; 'but that ninety-nine per cent of people don't have brains.' Belokurov thought I was talking about him, took offence, and left.

### III

'The prince is staying at Malozyomovo and sends his regards,' said Lida to her mother, as she took off her gloves after returning from somewhere. 'He had some very interesting things to say... He promised to raise the question of the medical centre again at the county meeting, but he said there was little hope of success.' And turning me to me, she said: 'I'm sorry, I always forget that this can't be of any interest to you.'

I was annoyed.

'What do you mean?' I asked, shrugging my shoulders. 'You're not keen to know my opinion, but I can assure you that I take a lively interest in this subject.'

'Really?'

'Really. In my opinion, a medical centre in Malozyomovo is quite unnecessary.'

My irritation was transferred to her; she looked at me through narrowed eyes and asked:

'What is necessary then? Landscape paintings?'

'Landscapes aren't necessary either. Nothing is needed there.'

She finished pulling off her gloves and opened the newspaper which had just been brought from the post office. A minute later she said quietly, with obvious self-restraint:

'Last week Anna died in childbirth, but if there had been a

medical centre nearby she would have survived. I think gentlemen landscape painters ought to have some views on this subject.'

'I have some very definite views on this subject, I can assure you,' I replied. She closed the newspaper as if she did not want to listen. 'In my opinion, medical centres, schools, libraries, and first-aid kits can only prolong enslavement under current conditions. The poor are bound by a huge chain, and you aren't breaking that chain, just adding new links. There you are—that's my view.'

She raised her eyes to me, and smiled sarcastically while I continued, trying to elucidate my main idea.

'The issue is not whether Anna died in childbirth, but that all these Annas, Mavras, and Pelageyas are bent double from dawn till dusk, getting ill from overwork. They constantly worry about their hungry, sick children, they are constantly scared of death and disease, they constantly have to take medication, they fade early, they grow old early, and then they die amidst dirt and stench. Their children repeat the whole cycle when they grow up, and so it goes on for hundreds of years, with millions of people living worse than animals in a permanent state of fear—and all for the sake of earning a living. Surely the most awful thing about their position is that they never have time to think about their souls, or even remember that they are human beings. Hunger, coldness, visceral fear, and endless work all block them like snowdrifts from pursuing a spiritual life, which is the one thing that distinguishes human beings from animals and makes life worth living. You turn up to help them with hospitals and schools, but that isn't going to clear their path, it's just going to enslave them more, because when you bring into their lives new standards, you increase the number of their needs, and that's quite apart from the fact that they have to pay the zemstvo for the ointments and books, forcing them to work even harder.'

'I'm not going to get into an argument with you,' said Lida, putting the newspaper down. 'I've heard all this before. I'll say only one thing to you, which is that you can't just sit there and do nothing. It's true that we are not going to save mankind, and are mistaken in many respects, but we are doing what we can, and we are right to do so. Our greatest and noblest duty as educated people is to serve our fellow human beings, and we are trying to do that as best we can. You don't like it, but then one can't please everybody, can one?'

'You're right, Lida, absolutely,' her mother said.

She always became shy in Lida's presence, and would look at her anxiously while she was speaking, afraid of saying something superfluous or out of place; she never contradicted her, but was always in agreement: you're right, Lida, absolutely.

'Peasant literacy, books with pathetic homilies and sayings, and first-aid kits can't reduce ignorance or mortality, just as the light from your windows cannot light up this huge garden,' I said. 'You aren't contributing anything by interfering in these people's lives; you are just creating new needs, and new reasons why they have to work.'

'Oh, for heaven's sake, one has got to do something though,' said Lida in annoyance. I could tell from the tone of her voice that she despised my argument and found it worthless.

'People should be freed from heavy physical labour,' I said. 'We need to lighten their load and give them some breathing-space, so that they don't spend their entire lives by the stove, at the trough, or in the field, but have time to think about their souls, about God, and can develop spiritually. The greatest duty of any person with a spiritual life must be to keep searching for truth and for the meaning of life. Make all this crude physical labour unnecessary, give them a taste of freedom, and then you will see how ridiculous all these books and first-aid kits are. As soon as people acknowledge their true vocation, it will be satisfied only by religion, science, or art, and certainly not by these petty things.'

'Free them from work!' snorted Lida. 'You think that's really possible?'

'Yes. Take a share of their work. If all of us town-dwellers and people from the countryside agreed without exception to share out the work expended by humanity on the satisfaction of our physical needs, then no one would have to work more than two or three hours a day. Just imagine all of us, rich and poor, working only three hours a day—we would have the rest of the time free. And imagine if we invented machines to replace physical labour, so we wouldn't have to depend on our bodies so much and could work less, and could also try to reduce our needs to a minimum. We would harden ourselves, and our children, so they wouldn't be afraid of going hungry or being cold and we wouldn't constantly fret about their health, as Anna, Mavra, and Pelageya do. Just imagine us not having to take medicines, not having to run pharmacies, tobacco factories, or distilleries—think how much free time we would have! We could collaborate in devoting this leisure time to science and the arts. Like the peasants who sometimes join forces to mend the roads together, we would join forces to seek the truth and the meaning of life together, and—I am quite convinced of this—the truth would be revealed to us very rapidly; people would rid themselves of this constantly agonizing and oppressive fear of death, and even from death itself.'

'But you are contradicting yourself,' said Lida. 'You keep talking about science, but you reject literacy.'

'The kind of literacy when a person can only read signs on taverns and the occasional book he can't understand has been around since the vikings.* Gogol's Petrushka* learned to read a long time ago, but the villages are just the same as they were under Ryurik. We don't need more literacy, but the freedom to develop our spiritual potential to the full. We don't need schools, we need universities.'

'But you reject medicine too.'

'Yes. It should be necessary only for the study of diseases as natural phenomena, not for finding their cure. If you are going to cure something, then it shouldn't be the disease, but its cause. If you remove the main cause—manual labour—then there won't be any disease. I don't recognize science which just provides treatment,' I continued breathlessly. 'True science and true art are never about the ephemeral and the individual, but about the eternal and universal. We are talking about truth and the meaning of life, God, and the soul, but if art and science have to get embroiled with contemporary needs and problems, with medical supplies and libraries and the like, then we just end up making life more complicated and burdensome. We have plenty of doctors, pharmacists, and lawyers, and there are lots of literate people out there now, but there aren't enough biologists, mathematicians, philosophers, and poets. All that intellect and emotional energy goes towards satisfying temporary, transient needs... Scientists, writers, and artists work round the clock, and thanks to them our home comforts are increasing by the day. The body's needs increase, but truth is still a long way off, and human beings are still the most predatory and slovenly animals on earth. Everything is leading to the degeneration of most of mankind and the permanent loss of any vitality. The life of an artist does not have any point under these conditions, and the more talented the artist, the stranger and more incomprehensible his role becomes, since it turns out that he is working for the amusement of a predatory, slovenly animal, while just maintaining the status quo. So I don't want to work, and I am not going to... We don't need anything; let the country go back to the Tatars!'*

'Missius, dear, would you leave us?' said Lida to her sister, obviously worried about the effect of what I was saying on such a young girl.

Zhenya looked sadly at her sister and at her mother and went out.

'People usually voice such charming sentiments when they want to justify their own indifference,' said Lida. 'It's easier to denigrate hospitals and schools than to treat people and teach them.'

'That's right, Lida,' said her mother; 'absolutely.'

'You threaten not to work,' Lida continued. 'So it's obvious that you value your painting highly. Let's stop arguing. We will never see eye to eye, since I value even the most imperfect libraries and first-aid kits, to which you refer so dismissively, more highly than all the landscape paintings in the world.' And turning to her mother, she immediately added, in quite a different tone, 'The prince has got very thin and has changed a great deal since the last time he was with us. He's being sent to Vichy.'*

She was talking to her mother about the prince to avoid having to talk to me. Her face was burning, and in order not to let me see how upset she was, she leant closely over the table, as if she was short-sighted, and pretended to read the newspaper. My presence was not welcome. I said goodbye and set off home.

## IV

It was quiet in the courtyard. The village on the other side of the pond had already gone to sleep, and there was not a single light to be seen, just a few pale reflections from the stars glimmering dimly on the surface of the pond. Zhenya was standing motionless by the gates with lions, waiting to say goodbye to me.

'Everyone is asleep in the village,' I said to her, trying to make out her face in the darkness, and seeing a pair of dark, sad eyes focused on me. 'The innkeeper and the horse-thief are sound asleep, while respectable people like us get irritated with each other and argue.'

It was a wistful August night—wistful because there was already a hint of autumn in the air. The moon had risen, but was obscured by a purple cloud, and barely illuminated the road and the dark fields of winter crops growing on either side. There were many shooting stars. Zhenya walked along the road beside me, trying not to look up at the sky so she would not see the shooting stars, which for some reason frightened her.

'I think you are right,' she said, shivering from the night's dampness. 'If people could just work together and devote themselves to spiritual concerns then we would soon know about everything.'

'Of course. We are superior beings, and if we could actually realize the extent of human genius and live for higher goals, then we would eventually become like gods. But this won't ever happen—humanity is degenerating and there won't be any trace of genius left soon.'

When the gates were no longer visible, Zhenya stopped and shook hands with me hurriedly.

'Goodnight,' she said, shivering. Her shoulders were covered with only a thin blouse and she was hunched up from the cold. 'Come tomorrow.'

The prospect of being left alone, irritated, fed up with myself and others, was too ghastly, and even I tried not to look at the shooting stars now.

'Spend one more minute with me,' I said. 'Please.'

I loved Zhenya. I think I loved her because whenever I went to visit, she would always come out to meet me, and accompany me part of the way home, and because she looked at me with such obvious affection and appreciation. Her pale face, her slender neck, her slender hands, her frailty, her indolence, and her books all had a poignant beauty. And her mind? I suspected she had an exceptional mind; certainly the breadth of her views amazed me, perhaps because she had a different outlook from the severe, beautiful Lida, who had no liking for me. Zhenya liked me because I was an artist; I had won her heart with my talent, and I passionately wanted to paint just for her. I dreamed she was my own little queen, and that one day we would own the trees and fields, the mists and the dawns, and all this wonderful, enchanting countryside, where I still felt so desperately useless and lonely. 'Just stay one more minute,' I entreated her. 'Please.'

I took off my coat and covered her frozen shoulders with it, but she giggled and then threw it off, because she was afraid of looking stupid and unattractive in a man's coat. It was then that I put my arms round her, and began to cover her face, her shoulders, and her hands with kisses.

'I'll see you tomorrow!' she whispered, putting her arms around me carefully, as if she was afraid of disturbing the night's silence. 'We don't keep secrets from each other, so I'll have to tell Mama and my sister everything now... I'm scared! Mama will be all right, because she is very fond of you, but think about Lida!'

She ran off back towards the gates.

I could hear her running for a few minutes. I did not feel like going home, and there was not much reason to go back anyway. I stood for a while thinking, then quietly sauntered back once more to look at the house she lived in. That charming, naive old house seemed to be peering at me through the windows of its mezzanine, which were like eyes, comprehending all. I walked past the veranda, sat on the bench near the tennis-court in the darkness, beneath the old elm, and gazed at the house from there. A bright light was shining in the windows of the mezzanine, where Zhenya slept, which then turned to a subdued green as the lamp was covered with a shade. The shadows moved... I was brimming with tender feelings, and felt serene and content with myself for once because I had succeeded in becoming attracted to someone and had fallen in love. At the same time I felt uneasy, since Lida, who did not love me, and maybe even hated me, was also in one of the rooms of the house, just a few feet away. I sat waiting to see if Zhenya would come outside, and when I listened I thought I could hear the sound of people talking in the mezzanine.

About an hour went by. The green light went out and the shadows disappeared. The moon was already high above the house and lit up the sleeping garden and the paths. The dahlias and roses in the flower-bed in front of the house were very distinct, and they seemed to be all the same colour. It had become very cold, so I left the garden, picked up my coat from the road, and trudged off home.

When I turned up at the Volchaninovs after lunch the next day, the glass door into the garden was wide open. I sat down on the veranda, expecting Zhenya to appear any minute on the patio behind the flower-bed, or on one of the paths, or for her voice to be heard in one of the rooms of the house. I went into the sitting room and the dining room. There was no one about. From the dining room I walked down the long passageway to the hall, and then back again.

Several doors opened off the passageway, and Lida's voice could be heard emanating from behind one of them.

'God sent the crow...', she said loudly in a lilting voice, probably dictating a Krylov fable.* 'Sent-the-crow... A piece of cheese... God... sent... Who is there?' she then suddenly called out, hearing my footsteps.

'It's me.'

'Oh! I'm afraid I can't come out just now as I am in the middle of teaching Dasha.'

'Is Yekaterina Pavlovna in the garden?'

'No, she and my sister left this morning to visit my aunt near Penza.* And they will probably go abroad in the winter...', she added after a pause. 'God sent the crow... a piece... of cheese. Have you written that?'

I went to the front door and stood there, my mind empty of thoughts. As I looked across to the pond and the village, I could hear behind me:

'God sent the crow... a piece... of cheese...'

I left the estate by the same path I had followed the first time, but in the opposite direction. From the courtyard to the garden first, past the house, then along the linden avenue... A little boy caught up with me just then and handed me a note: 'I told my sister everything and she insists that I have to part from you,' I read. 'I don't feel I can let her down by being disobedient. May God grant you happiness. Forgive me. If you only knew how much Mama and I have been crying!'

Then the dark avenue of fir trees, the rickety fence... In the field where the rye had bloomed, and quails had cried, there were now cows, and horses wearing halters. Bright, green winter crops were sprouting here and there on the hills. A sober, weekday kind of mood descended on me and I became ashamed of everything I had said at the Volchaninovs. My life became boring again, like it had been before. When I got home, I packed and left that evening for Petersburg.

I never saw the Volchaninovs again. I met Belokurov recently in a train when I was travelling down to the Crimea. He was dressed in his traditional Russian coat and embroidered shirt as usual, and when I asked him how he was, he replied that he was in fine fettle.

We fell into conversation. He had sold his estate and had bought a smaller one somewhere else in Lyubov Ivanovna's name. He had little to report on the Volchaninovs. According to him, Lida was still living in Shelkovka and teaching children at the school. She had gradually managed to establish a circle of like-minded people around her. They had joined forces, and at the last zemstvo elections they had managed to do something about Balagin, the man who had the whole district under his thumb—he had finally been 'sent packing'. All that Belokurov could say about Zhenya was that she was not living at home, but he did not know where she was.

I am already beginning to forget about the house with the mezzanine, but just once in a while while I am painting or reading, for no particular reason I will suddenly remember the green light in the window, or the sound of my steps in the field when I returned home that night in love, rubbing my hands together from the cold. Even more occasionally, when I am feeling lonely and sad, dim memories will resurrect themselves, and for some reason I will begin to imagine that there is someone out there also remembering me— waiting for me, believing that we will meet again...

Missius, where are you?

# IN THE CART

They left town at half past eight in the morning.

The road was dry and the beautiful April sun was very warm, but there was still snow lying in the ditches and in the forest. The long, dark, mean winter was not long past, and spring had arrived suddenly, but neither the sunshine, nor the thin listless forests warmed by the breath of spring, nor the black flocks flying over enormous puddles which were like lakes in the fields, nor the glorious sky into whose boundless expanses one could have joyously disappeared seemed new or interesting to Marya Vasilievna sitting there in the cart. She had been a teacher for thirteen years and had lost count of the number of times she had travelled to town for her wages; whether it was spring, like now, or a rainy autumn evening, or winter—it was all the same to her, and each time she only ever wanted one thing: to get the trip over as quickly as possible.

She felt as if she had been living in these parts for ages and ages, a hundred years at least, and it seemed as if she knew every single stone and every single tree on the road from the town to her school. Here was her past and her present and she could imagine no other future than school, the journey to town and back, more school, the journey again...

She had already got out of the habit of recalling her life before she became a schoolteacher, and had forgotten almost everything about it. At one point she had a father and mother; they lived in Moscow near the Red Gates, in a large apartment, but all that was left of that life was a dim, blurred memory like a dream. Her father had died when she was ten years old, and her mother had died soon after... Her brother was an officer and they had corresponded at first, but then he got out of the habit of writing and stopped answering her letters. All she had left from her former possessions was a photograph of her mother, but it had faded because the school was so damp, and now all you could see was her hair and her eyebrows.

When they had travelled a few miles, old Semyon, who was holding the reins, turned round and said:

'They've arrested an official in town. Sent him off to jail. People are saying apparently he and some Germans killed Mayor Alekseyev in Moscow.'

'Who told you that?'

'People were reading about it in the newspaper at Ivan Ionov's inn.'

They were silent again for a long time. Marya Vasilievna was thinking about her school and about the exam coming up at which she would be presenting four boys and one girl. And just as she was thinking about exams, Khanov the landowner overtook her in his four-horse carriage—the same man who had examined at her school the year before. As he drew level he recognized her and nodded his head in greeting.

'Hello there!' he said. 'You homeward bound?'

This man Khanov, who was about forty and had a haggard face and a sluggish expression, had already begun to age noticeably, but he was still handsome and attractive to women. He lived by himself on his large estate and did not have a job; people said that he did nothing at home except play chess with his old servant and walk around whistling. People also said that he drank a lot. In fact, at the exams last year even the papers he brought with him stank of wine and cologne. Everything he had worn then was brand new and Marya Vasilievna had been very attracted to him; she had felt completely tongue-tied while she was sitting next to him. She had grown used to cold and formal examiners at her school, but this one could not remember a single prayer and did not know what questions to ask; he was exceptionally polite and considerate and gave everyone top marks.

'I'm on my way to see Bakvist,' he continued, turning to Marya Vasilievna, 'but I've heard he is not at home!'

They turned off the highway onto the road leading to the village, Khanov in front and Semyon following behind. Khanov's four horses plodded along the road, straining to drag the heavy carriage through the mud. Semyon, meanwhile, was weaving about, going over hillocks and through the meadows in order to avoid the road, and he kept having to get off the cart to help the horses. Marya Vasilievna was still thinking about school and whether the exam would be difficult or easy. And she was feeling annoyed with the local zemstvo* because there had been no one in the office when she stopped by the day before. What disorder! She had been asking them for two years now to dismiss the caretaker, who did not do his job, was rude to her, and beat the schoolchildren, but no one ever listened to her. It was difficult to get hold of the head of the zemstvo when he was at work, and even when you did, he would just tell you with tears in his eyes that he was too busy; the school inspector only came once every three years, and did not understand anything because he had worked in excise before and had got the job through the back door; the board of governors met very infrequently and no one knew where they met; the school's trustee was an uneducated peasant who ran a tanning business and was rude, slow-witted, and in cahoots with the caretaker, so goodness knows to whom she was supposed to address complaints and enquiries...

'He really is good-looking,' she thought, glancing at Khanov.

The road was getting worse and worse... They had entered a forest. There was nowhere to turn off here; the ruts were very deep, and there was gurgling water streaming along them. Prickly branches were hitting her face.

'How do you like the road?' asked Khanov with a laugh.

The teacher looked at him and could not understand why this odd person lived here. What possible use was there for his money, his interesting appearance, and his fine manners in this boring, muddy place in the middle of nowhere? He was not getting anything out of life, and here he was just like Semyon, having to plod along this frightful road and put up with the same discomforts. Why did he live here when he could live in Petersburg or abroad? And you would have thought a rich man like him might have considered it worth improving this dreadful road so as not to have to put up with this nightmare, and not have to see the despair etched on the faces of his coachman and Semyon; but he just laughed; he clearly could not care less and had no interest in living better. He was a gentle, naive, and kind man who did not understand this crude life, and his knowledge of it was as poor as his knowledge of the prayers they said at exams. All he gave the school were globes of the world, and he genuinely thought he was being useful and doing a lot to improve national education. But what use were his globes here!

'Hold tight, Vasilievna!' said Semyon.

The cart tilted heavily and almost keeled over; something heavy fell onto Marya Vasilievna's feet—it was her shopping. Now there was a steep climb up the hill through mud as thick as clay; noisy streams were running down the winding ditches, and it was as if the water had been eating away at the road—travelling here was dreadful! The horses were snorting. Khanov climbed out of his carriage and started walking along the edge of the road. He was hot.

'How do you like the road?' Khanov asked again with a laugh. 'My carriage is going to be wrecked at this rate.'

'No one is making you travel in weather like this, are they?' said Semyon severely. 'You should have stayed at home.'

'It's boring at home, old man. I don't like staying at home.'

He seemed slim and sprightly next to old Semyon, but there was something in his bearing, barely noticeable, which gave him away as a person who was already done for, weak and close to ruin. And just then the forest suddenly started smelling of wine. Marya Vasilievna started to feel afraid and sorry for this person who was going into decline for no apparent reason, and it occurred to her that if she was his wife or his sister, she would probably devote her whole life to saving him from ruin. If she was his wife? Life had ordained that he should live on his own on his large estate and she should live on her own in a remote village, but even just the thought that she and he could be equals and intimate with each other seemed impossible and ridiculous for some reason. Life was generally arranged in such an incomprehensible way and relationships with people were so compli-cated that you ended up feeling terrified, with your heart sinking, however you looked at it.

'And it's impossible to understand,' she thought, 'why God gives beauty and charm and such sweet, sad eyes to such useless, weak, and unhappy people, and why they are so attractive.'

'We're turning to the right here,' said Khanov as he got into his carriage. 'Goodbye then! All the best!'

And again she started thinking about her pupils, about the exam, about the caretaker and the board of governors; and when the wind brought the sound of the receding carriage over from the right, these thoughts started mingling with the previous ones. She wanted to think about beautiful eyes, about love, about the happiness she would never have...

Be a wife? It was cold in the morning, there was no one to light the stove, the caretaker was never there; the schoolchildren would start arriving at first light, bringing snow and mud and noise; everything was so uninviting and cheerless. Her home was just one room with a kitchen in it. Her head ached every day after classes, and after dinner she felt a burning sensation in her chest. She had to collect money from her pupils to pay for firewood and for the caretaker, take it to the school trustee, and then beg that self-satisfied, brazen peasant to be so kind as to deliver the firewood. Then at night she would dream of exams, peasants, and snowdrifts. And this life had aged her and made her coarse and unattractive; she had become awkward and clumsy, as if she were filled with lead; she was afraid of everything, and in the presence of a councillor or the school trustee she would stand up, not daring to sit down again, and when she referred to them in conversation she would be needlessly deferential. No one liked her, and her life was passing by miserably, without affection, without the sympathy of friends, and without any interesting acquaintances. What a terrible thing it would be if she fell in love in her position!

'Hold on tight, Vasilievna!'

Another steep climb up a hill...

She had trained as a teacher out of necessity rather than any sense of vocation; she had never actually thought about a vocation, or the benefits of learning; it always seemed to her that the most important thing in her job was not pupils or education but exams. And anyway, when did she have the time to think about a vocation or the benefits of learning? With all the work they have to do, teachers, hard-up doctors, and medical assistants never even have the consolation of thinking that they are devoting themselves to an ideal or helping the people, because their heads are always full of thoughts about firewood, getting enough to eat, bad roads, and illnesses. Life is difficult and uninteresting, and only docile carthorses like Marya Vasilievna put up with it for long; lively, sensitive, impressionable people who talk about their vocation and dedication to ideals soon become worn out and give up.

Semyon was doing his best to drive on ground that was dryer, taking short cuts through the fields and back ways; but either the peasants did not always let them through, or there was the priest's land and that was no thoroughfare, or there was the land that Ivan Ionov had bought from the landowner and dug a trench around. Sometimes they had to turn back.

They arrived at the little town of Lower Gorodishche.* Near the inn, on ground strewn with manure underneath which there was still snow, stood carts which had been transporting large drums of oil of vitriol. There were a lot of people in the inn, all drivers, and it smelt of vodka, tobacco, and sheepskin. The conversation was loud and the weighted door kept slamming. Behind the partition in the shop someone was playing an accordion continually. Marya Vasilievna sat drinking tea, while at the next table some peasants were drinking vodka and beer, red-faced from all the tea they had drunk and the stuffiness in the inn.

'Hey, Kuzma!' some unruly voices shouted out. 'What's going on? God save us! Ivan Dementich, I can sort things! You watch!'

A small peasant with a short black beard and a pitted face, long drunk, was suddenly taken off guard by something; he let out a string of curses.

'What's all that swearing for? Hey, you!' Semyon called out angrily from the far corner where he was sitting. 'Surely you can see there's a lady here!'

'A lady...' mimicked someone in the opposite corner.

'You swine!'

'Look, we didn't mean any harm,' said the small peasant in embarrassment. 'Sorry. We'll keep to our patch, and let the lady do the same... Good morning to you!'

'Hello,' said the teacher.

'Thank you most kindly.'

Marya Vasilievna enjoyed her tea and went red in the face like the peasants, and she started thinking again about the firewood and the caretaker...

'Hang on!' came a voice from the next table. 'She's the teacher from Vyazovye... we know her! She's a good lady.'

'Honourable!'

The weighted door kept banging as people came in and out. Marya Vasilievna sat and thought about the same old things while the accordion played on behind the partition. There were patches of sunshine on the floor; then they transferred to the counter and onto the wall, and then they completely disappeared, which meant the sun had crept past midday. The peasants at the next table started getting ready to move. Tottering slightly, the small peasant went up to Marya Vasilievna and shook her hand; seeing this, the others also shook her hand to say goodbye as they left one by one, and the door squeaked and banged ten times.

'Come on, Vasilievna, time to get going,' called Semyon.

They set off. And again they had to walk.

'They built a school here not long ago, in Lower Gorodishche,' said Semyon, turning round. 'That was a bad business!'

'Why?'

'Apparently the zemstvo chief pocketed a thousand, and the trustee took a thousand too, and the teacher got five hundred.'

'But building a whole school only costs a thousand. It's not good to speak ill of people. That's all nonsense.'

'I don't know... That's what people said.'

But it was clear that Semyon did not believe the teacher. The peasants never believed her; they thought she was paid far too much—twenty-one roubles a month (when five would have been enough)—and they thought that she kept most of the money she collected to pay for firewood and the caretaker. The trustee thought the same as all the peasants; he earned a bit on the side himself from the firewood, and he received a salary from the peasants for being trustee, which was something the authorities did not know about.

The forest had come to an end, thank goodness, and now it was flat all the way to Vyazovye. And there was not much further to go; they had to cross the river, then the railway line, and Vyazovye was immediately after that.

'Where are you going?' Marya Vasilievna asked Semyon. 'You ought to take the road to the right, over the bridge.'

'What? We'll be all right this way. It's not too deep.'

'Watch out, we don't want to drown the horse.'

'What?'

'There's Khanov going across the bridge,' said Marya Vasilievna, seeing a coach-and-four a long way over to the right. 'That is him, isn't it?'

'Yes, that's him. Bakvist can't have been at home. What a fool he is, heaven help us, going that way for no good reason, when it's two miles shorter this way.'

They arrived at the river. In summer it was not much more than a stream, which was easy enough to ford and had usually dried up by August, but now after the floods it was a river about forty feet across, fast-flowing, turbulent, and cold, and there were fresh tracks on the bank by the water's edge—people had obviously been crossing here.

'Giddy up!' shouted Semyon angrily and with anxiety, pulling hard on the reins and waving his elbows up and down like a bird flapping its wings. 'Giddy up!'

The horse walked into the water up to its belly and stopped, then started again at once, straining every muscle, and Marya Vasilievna felt a sharp coldness in her feet.

'Giddy up!' she also shouted out, as she stood up. 'Come on, giddy up!'

They reached the other bank.

'And anyway, what's the point of all this, for heaven's sake?' mumbled Semyon, adjusting the harness. 'It's downright murder having to deal with that zemstvo.'

Her shoes and galoshes were full of water, the bottom of her dress and her coat and one of her sleeves were dripping wet, and the sugar and flour were sodden—that was more upsetting than everything else and Marya Vasilievna just threw up her hands in despair and said:

'Ah, Semyon, Semyon!... Really!'

The barrier was lowered at the railway crossing: the express train was coming from the station. Marya Vasilievna stood by the crossing and waited for the train to pass, her whole body trembling with cold. You could already see Vyazovye—the school with its green roof, and the church with its crosses blazing as they reflected the evening sun; the windows in the station were also blazing, and there was pink smoke coming from the railway engine... And it seemed to her that everything was shivering with cold.

Here was the train. Its windows were flooded with bright light like the crosses on the church, and it hurt to look at them. On the platform at the end of one of the first-class carriages stood a lady, and Marya Vasilievna glanced at her fleetingly: it was her mother! What a resemblance! Her mother had the same luxuriant hair, the same forehead, and her head was inclined in the same way. And with amazing clarity, for the first time in all these thirteen years, she was able vividly to remember her mother and father, her brother, the apartment in Moscow, the aquarium with the little fish, and everything else down to the smallest detail; suddenly she heard the sound of the piano being played and her father's voice; she felt as if she was young, pretty, and well-dressed, in a bright, warm room, surrounded by her family as she had been then; a feeling of joy and happiness suddenly enveloped her and she pressed her palms to her temples in rapture and called out softly in supplication:

'Mama!'

And for no apparent reason she burst into tears. Just at that moment Khanov drove up in his coach-and-four, and when she saw him she imagined the happiness she had never had and smiled at him, nodding her head as if she was a close acquaintance and his equal, and it felt to her as if her happiness, her exultation, was reflected in the sky, in all the windows, and in the trees. No, her father and mother had never died, and she had never been a teacher; it had just been a horrible, long, bizarre dream, and she had just woken up...

'Vasilievna, get in!'

And suddenly it all vanished. The barrier was slowly rising. Shivering and numb with cold, Marya Vasilievna got into the cart. The coach-and-four crossed the tracks, and Semyon followed. The guard at the crossing took off his hat.

'Here's Vyazovye. We're home.'

# THE MAN IN A CASE

Some huntsmen had belatedly set up camp for the night in Elder Prokofy's barn, right at the edge of the village of Mironositskoe. There were only two of them: the veterinary surgeon Ivan Ivanych and the schoolteacher Burkin. Ivan Ivanych had a rather strange two-part surname—Chimsha-Gimalaisky—which did not suit him at all, and people throughout the province just called him by his first name and patronymic; he lived on a stud farm near the town and had come on this hunting trip to breathe some fresh air. Burkin the schoolteacher, meanwhile, stayed every summer with Count P.'s family, and was very much at home in these parts.

They were still awake. Ivan Ivanych, a tall, thin old man with a long moustache, was sitting outside by the barn door and smoking a pipe; he was lit up by the moon. Burkin was inside, lying on the hay, and you could not see him in the darkness.

They were telling various stories. Amongst other things, they talked about the Elder's wife Mavra, a healthy and not unintelligent woman who had never once in her life been out of the village she was born in; she had never seen the town or the railway, and for the last ten years had just sat by the stove, only going out at night.

'But it's not all that unusual!' said Burkin. 'There are quite a few people of a solitary disposition in the world who spend their entire lives trying to retreat into their shells like hermit crabs or snails. Maybe it's something atavistic, and we are witnessing a return to the times when our forebears lived alone in their lairs and were not yet social animals, or maybe it's just one of the varieties of the human character—who knows? I am not a scientist and it's not for me to delve into such questions; all I mean is that there are quite a few people like Mavra around. In fact, you don't have to look very far: someone called Belikov, a Greek teacher who was one of my colleagues, died about two months ago in our town. You're bound to have heard of him. He was famous for always carrying an umbrella and wearing galoshes even in fine weather, and he also never failed to wear a warm coat with a lining. He had a case for his umbrella, and a case for his watch made of grey suede, and when he took out his penknife to sharpen his pencil even that had a little case; his face also seemed to be in a case, because he kept it hidden in his raised collar. He wore dark glasses and a sweater, he stuffed his ears with cotton wool, and whenever he took a cab, he ordered the hood to be raised. Basically, he was someone who had a constant and overwhelming need to envelop himself in a protective cover, to create a kind of case for himself which would isolate and protect him from external influences. Reality irritated him; it scared him and kept him in a permanent state of alarm, and maybe he always praised the past and things which had never existed because he wanted to justify his timidity and his aversion to the present; the classical languages he taught were also just like his galoshes and umbrella really, hiding him from real life.

' "How melodious and beautiful the Greek language is!" he would say, smiling sweetly; and as if to prove the truth of his words, he would half-close his eyes, raise his finger, and say "Anthropos"!

'Belikov even tried concealing his ideas in a case. All he could understand clearly were regulations and newspaper articles in which something was forbidden. A regulation forbidding pupils from being out after nine o'clock in the evening, or some article or other prohibiting carnal love was clear and well-defined in his eyes; the thing was forbidden and there was no more to be said. But there was always a dubious element lurking in permissions and authorizations for him—something disturbing and incomplete. Whenever they permitted a drama circle in the town, or authorized the opening of a reading room or a tea shop, he would shake his head and say quietly:

' "It's all very well, this kind of thing, but just think where it might lead."

'Every kind of infringement, deviation, or departure from the rules depressed him, although you might wonder what business it was of his? If one of his colleagues was late for prayers, or if rumours of a schoolboy prank reached him, or if a lady from the school was seen out late one evening with an officer, he would become very agitated and repeatedly ask where it all might lead. And at teachers' meetings he would drive us to despair with his circumspection and suspiciousness, and his absurd man-in-a-case sort of ideas about, for example, how badly the young people behaved in the boys' and girls' schools and how they made too much noise—oh and what if the school authorities found out, oh and where might it all lead?—and how it would be a good thing if Petrov could be expelled from the second year, and Egorov from the fourth. And what do you think happened? He oppressed us all so much with his sighs and his moans, and those tinted spectacles on his pale little face—his face was really small, you know, like a polecat's—that we ended up giving in; we gave Petrov and Egorov the lowest marks for behaviour, we put them in detention, and eventually we managed to expel both Petrov and Egorov. He used to have a strange habit of visiting us at home. He would arrive at a teacher's apartment, sit down, not say anything, but just look around. And he would sit like that without saying anything for an hour or so and then leave. He called this "maintaining good relations with his colleagues", but he clearly found coming to see us and just sitting there a trial, and only did it because he considered it his collegial duty. We teachers were all afraid of him. Even the head of the school was scared of him. Our teachers are a pretty decent lot, you know, thoughtful people brought up on Turgenev and Shchedrin,* and can you imagine, this little homunculus with his galoshes and his umbrella had the whole school under his thumb for fifteen whole years! And not just the school. The whole town! Our ladies could not put on amateur shows on Saturdays for fear of him finding out, and the clergy were afraid to eat meat or play cards in front of him. Under the influence of people like Belikov, over the last ten to fifteen years people in our town have started to be afraid of everything. They are afraid to talk loudly, send letters, make new acquaintances, read books; they are afraid of helping the poor, teaching people to read and write...'

Ivan Ivanych cleared his throat in preparation for saying something, but first he drew on his pipe and looked up at the moon; then he said between pauses:

'Yes. Decent, thoughtful people who read Shchedrin, Turgenev, Buckle,* and whoever else, and they just capitulate and put up with it... That just about sums it up.'

'Belikov lived in the same building as me,' Burkin continued. 'On the same floor in fact; his door was opposite mine, so we saw each other often, and I knew what his life at home was like. And it was exactly the same story in his apartment: dressing-gowns, nightcaps, shutters, bolts, a whole load of prohibitions and restrictions—well, you never know where things might lead! He thought that Lenten food was harmful, but non-Lenten food was forbidden, and so in order to prevent people saying that he did not observe the fasts,

Belikov ate perch cooked in butter, which is not Lenten food, but it wasn't exactly non-Lenten either. He didn't have any female servants because he was afraid of what people might think, but he did have a cook called Afanasy, a permanently drunk, cretinous old man of about sixty, who had once been a batman in the army and could just about drum up a meal. Old Afanasy would usually stand by the door with his arms crossed, always mumbling the same thing and sighing deeply:

' "There's a lot of types like *them* about these days!"

'Belikov's bedroom was small, just like a box, and his bed had a curtain. When he went to bed, he wrapped himself up completely; it would be hot and stuffy, the wind would knock on the closed doors, and the stove would hum; meanwhile, sighs would come from the kitchen, ominous sighs...

'And he was afraid underneath his blankets. He was scared of what might happen, scared that Afanasy might stab him, or that thieves might break in, and all night he would have troubled dreams. Then in the morning, when we walked to school together, he was pale and withdrawn; it was clear that he found the crowded school he was walking to terrifying and inimical to his whole being, and walking next to me was also difficult for him because he was such a solitary person by nature.

' "They make such a lot of noise in the classrooms," he would say, as if trying to find an explanation for his negative feelings. "It's a disgrace."

'And can you imagine, this teacher of Greek, this man in a case, almost got married.'

Ivan Ivanych looked round quickly into the barn and said:

'You're joking!'

'Yes, he almost got married, as strange as it may seem. A new history and geography teacher was appointed at our school, a certain Mikhail Savvich Kovalenko, a Ukrainian. He did not come alone, but with his sister Varenka. He was a tall, dark young man with huge hands; you could see from his face that he had a bass voice, and his voice really did sound as if it came from a barrel: boom, boom, boom... She was not all that young, about thirty, but she was also tall and slim, with black eyebrows and red cheeks—a very handsome woman, basically—and so lively and noisy; she was always singing Ukrainian songs and laughing away. The slightest encouragement

and she would let forth a throaty laugh: ha-ha-ha! We first got to
know the Kovalenkos properly, I remember, at our principal's
birthday party. Amongst the dreary, terminally dull teachers who go
to birthday parties out of a sense of obligation, we suddenly saw a
new Aphrodite arising from the foam: hands on hips, laughing, singing, dancing... She sang "The Winds are Blowing" with real gusto,
then another song, and another, and she charmed us all—all of us,
even Belikov. He sat down next to her and said with a sweet smile:
"Ukrainian is like Ancient Greek in its softness and pleasant
sonority."

'This flattered her and so she started enthusiastically telling him
about the farmstead she had back home in the Gadyach* district,
where her dear mama lived; what pears they grew there, what
melons, what pumpkins! She explained that Ukrainians used the
Russian word for tavern to mean pumpkin, and that they had
another name altogether for taverns. And the bortsch they cooked
with tomatoes and aubergines was "just so incredibly, amazingly
delicious!"

'We listened and we listened and then suddenly an identical
thought occurred to all of us.

' "It would be good to marry those two off to each other," said the
principal's wife quietly to me.

'For some reason we had remembered that Belikov was not married, and now it seemed strange to us that we had completely neg-
lected to consider such an important detail in his life. What was his
attitude to women in general; how had he decided this central question? It had not interested us before; perhaps it had not even entered
our heads that a person who went about in galoshes whatever the
weather and slept behind curtains was capable of love.

' "He's well past forty and she's thirty..." the principal's wife went
on. "I think she would accept him."

'The things we get up to in the provinces from sheer boredom—
so many unnecessary and stupid things! And it is because we do not
do what actually needs to be done. Why did we suddenly feel we had
to marry off this man Belikov, whom it was impossible even to
imagine ever being married? But the principal's wife and the other
ladies in the school all perked up and even started looking more
attractive, as if they had suddenly discovered a purpose in life. The
principal's wife took a box in the theatre and we saw Varenka sitting

there with a fan, beaming away happily, and Belikov next to her, all hunched up and small, as if he had been extracted from his apartment with pincers. If I had a party the ladies would insist that I make sure to invite Belikov and Varenka. To cut a long story short, the machine was put into motion. It turned out that Varenka was not against getting married. She did not much enjoy living with her brother, as they were always arguing and being rude to each other. Here's a typical scene: Kovalenko would be walking down the street, a tall, lanky fellow in an embroidered shirt, with a lock of hair on his forehead escaping from his cap; in one hand he would be carrying a bundle of books and in the other a thick, knotted stick. His sister would be following him, also carrying books.

' "But you haven't read it, Mikhailik!" she would argue loudly. "I'm telling you, I swear you haven't read any of it!"

' "And I'm telling you that I have!" Kovalenko would shout, banging his stick on the pavement.

' "Really, Mikhailik! I don't see why you have to be so angry. This is a question of principle, after all."

' "But I am telling you that I have read it!" Kovalenko would shout even louder.

'And they would also start squabbling as soon as anyone came to see them at home. She probably found it all a bit wearing, and was wishing she had her own space, and then you have to take her age into consideration; she did not have the luxury of being able to choose, and she was ready to get married to anyone, even the Greek teacher. It's the same with most of our young ladies; they just want to get married; they are not fussed who to. Anyway, Varenka started to show obvious favour towards old Belikov.

'And what about old Belikov? He visited Kovalenko like he used to visit us. He would turn up, sit there, and say nothing. And while he sat there saying nothing, Varenka would sing "The Winds are Blowing" or look at him dreamily with her dark eyes, or suddenly burst out laughing: "Ha-ha-ha!"

'Suggestion plays an important role in affairs of the heart. My colleagues and all the ladies started to assure him that he ought to get married, and that getting married was the one thing which he had left to do in life; we all congratulated him, put on serious expressions, and mouthed a lot of platitudes, such as marriage being a serious step to take. Varenka was not bad-looking, moreover, and she was interesting; she was the daughter of a state councillor, and had a property in the country; but the main thing was that she was the first woman who had shown him any kindness or affection. His head was turned and he decided that he really should get married.'

'That's when you should have taken away his galoshes and his umbrella,' chipped in Ivan Ivanych.

'Would you believe it, it turned out to be impossible. He put Varenka's portrait on his desk, and kept coming to talk to me about Varenka, and about family life, and about how marriage was an important step, and he often went over to the Kovalenkos, but he did not change his way of life at all. It was almost the opposite—the decision to get married seemed to make him ill: he lost weight, he went all pale, and seemed to retreat even further into his shell.

' "I like Varvara Savvishna," he would tell me with his crooked little smile; "and I know everyone should get married, but... all this has come about rather suddenly, you know... I need to think about it."

' "What is there to think about?" I would ask him. "You just get married, that's all there is to it."

' "Oh no, marriage is a serious step and first you need to weigh up all the duties and responsibilities you will have... to avoid mishaps. It worries me so much I don't sleep at night. And I have to confess that I am rather afraid: she and her brother have a strange way of thinking; the way they discuss things is also strange, you know, and she's got such a lively personality. Who knows what trouble I might get into if I get married."

'And so he did not propose, but kept putting it off, to the great disappointment of the principal's wife and all the other ladies; he kept weighing up all the duties and responsibilities which lay ahead, but meanwhile he carried on taking walks with Varenka almost every day, perhaps thinking that was the correct thing to do in his position, and he kept coming to see me to talk about family life. And he probably would have eventually proposed and entered into one of those unnecessary, stupid marriages such as thousands of people enter into out of boredom and want of anything better to do, had there not suddenly been a *kolossalische Skandal*.\* I need to point out here that Kovalenko, Varenka's brother, loathed Belikov from the very first day they met and just could not stand him.

' "I just do not understand," he said to us, shrugging his shoulders, "I do not understand how you can put up with that horrible old sneak. The way you live, gentlemen! The atmosphere here is suffocating, it's totally vile. You think you are teachers, engaged in pedagogical work? You're time-servers, that's what. This is no sacred place of learning, it's more like a police station, and it smells as sour as a sentry box. I'll stay just a while longer with you, my friends, and then I'm going off to my house in the country to catch crayfish and teach young Ukrainians. I'm going, and I'll leave you here to your Judas, curse him."

'Or he would laugh, laugh till he cried, sometimes in a deep bass, sometimes in a squeaky high voice, and he would ask me, throwing up his hands:

' "Why does he have to sit at my place? What does he want? He just sits there staring."

'He even called Belikov "the vampire spider". Obviously, we avoided talking to him about his sister Varenka's plans to marry this "vampire spider". And when the principal's wife hinted one day to him that it would be a good idea to fix Varenka up with a reliable, well-respected man like Belikov, he frowned, and snarled:

' "It's nothing to do with me. She can marry a viper as far as I am concerned, I don't like involving myself in other people's business."

'Anyway, listen to what happened next. Some joker drew a cartoon: it showed Belikov in galoshes, wearing trousers with the ends turned up, walking under an umbrella with Varenka on his arm; underneath there was a caption: "Anthropos in love". And you know, his expression had been caught brilliantly. The artist must have spent more than just one night on it, because every teacher in the boys' and girls' schools, as well as the seminary teachers and all our officials received a copy. Belikov received one too. The cartoon had a terrible effect on him.

'There was one day when we had an outing—it was the first of May, as it happened, a Sunday, and all of us teachers and pupils had agreed to meet at school and then walk out of town to the woods. Just as we were leaving Belikov appeared, looking quite green, with an expression that was blacker than a storm-cloud.

' "What nasty, malicious people there are!" he said, his lips quivering.

'I even began to feel sorry for him. Well, we were walking along when suddenly, can you imagine, Kovalenko came rolling by on a bicycle, followed by Varenka, also on a bicycle, red-faced and tired out, but clearly looking as if she was enjoying herself.

' "We're going on ahead!" she shouted. "It's such lovely weather, it's glorious!"

'And they both disappeared. Belikov turned from green to white, and it was if he had been struck dumb. He stopped and looked at me...

' "May I ask, just what is the meaning of this? Or do my eyes deceive me? It cannot be proper for schoolteachers and women to ride bicycles."

' "What's improper about it?" I said. "I think they should cycle away to their heart's content."

' "I don't believe it!" he shouted, appalled at how unperturbed I was. "Do you realize what you are saying?"

'And he was so shocked that he did not want to walk any further; he just turned round and went home.

'He spent the next day rubbing his hands together nervously, and you could see from his face that he was not well. He left school early, which he had never done before in his life. And he did not have lunch. And then towards evening he wrapped up warmly, even though the weather was completely summery, and trudged off to the Kovalenkos. Varenka was out, so he found only her brother at home.

' "Do please take a seat," said Kovalenko coldly, with a frown; he looked very bleary-eyed, as he had just woken up from his afternoon nap and he really was not in a good mood.

'Belikov sat there without saying anything for ten minutes, then he began:

' "I have come to see you to take a weight off my mind. I'm very, very troubled. Some lampoonist drew a picture poking fun at me and another individual who is close to us both. I consider it my duty to assure you that it had nothing to do with me... I gave absolutely no grounds for such ridicule—the opposite in fact; I have always behaved like a respectable person."

'Kovalenko sat there fuming, but did not say anything.

' "And there is something else I have to say to you. I have been teaching for a long time, but you have just started your career, so I consider it my duty as your senior colleague to warn you. You have been riding a bicycle, and it is a pastime which is totally improper for an educator of young people."

' "Why is that?" asked Kovalenko in his bass voice.

' "Do I really have to spell out why it is unacceptable, Mikhail Savvich? If a teacher rides a bicycle, what can we expect of the pupils? They will be walking on their heads next! Since permission has not been granted in a regulation, it is forbidden. I was horrified yesterday! When I saw your sister I felt faint. To see a woman or a young girl on a bicycle is monstrous!"

' "What exactly is it you want?"

' "I want just one thing—to warn you, Mikhail Savvich. You are a young man with your future ahead of you, and you need to comport yourself very, very carefully, as you have been extremely negligent; oh, how negligent you have been! You walk around in an embroidered shirt, you are always out on the street with some book or other, and now there is the bicycle too. The principal will find out that you and your sister have been riding bicycles, and then it will get to the school's trustee..."

' "It's nobody's business that my sister and I ride on bicycles!" said Kovalenko, going crimson. "People who interfere in my private and family business can go to hell."

'Belikov went pale and stood up.

' "I cannot carry on if you are going to speak to me in that tone," he said. "And I must ask you never to speak in such a manner about our superiors while in my presence. You must have respect for authority."

' "And what have I said that is critical of the authorities?" said Kovalenko, looking at him angrily. "Please leave me in peace. I am an honest man and do not wish to talk to a gentleman like you. I do not like sneaks."

'Belikov started fidgeting nervously and then quickly put on his coat, with an expression of horror on his face. It was the first time in his life that he had heard someone being so rude, after all.

' "You may say whatever you want," he said, as he stepped from the hall onto the landing in the stairway. "But I do have to warn you that someone may have heard us, and lest our conversation is interpreted the wrong way, or there are repercussions, I will have to report the contents of our discussion to the principal... in general terms. I am obliged to."

' "You're going to write a report? Well, go ahead, write it!"

'Kovalenko grabbed him by the collar from behind and gave him a shove, and Belikov flew down the stairs, his galoshes thudding as he went. It was a long, steep staircase but he landed safely at the bottom. He stood up and touched his nose: were his spectacles broken? But just as he had been tumbling down the stairs Varenka had come in, accompanied by two ladies; they had stood at the bottom and watched, and for Belikov that was worse than anything else. He would have preferred to have broken his neck and both his legs to being made a laughing-stock; the whole town would know now, it would get to the principal and the school trustee—oh and where might it all lead!—someone would draw a new cartoon, and it would end in him being asked to submit his resignation...

'When he got up, Varenka recognized him, and as she looked at his funny face, and his crumpled coat, and his galoshes, not understanding what had happened but thinking he must have slipped, she could not restrain herself from bursting out laughing very loudly:

' "Ha-ha-ha!"

'And that booming, resonant "ha-ha-ha!" brought everything to an end: both the matchmaking and Belikov's earthly existence. He no longer heard what Varenka was saying, and could see nothing. When he returned home, he first of all removed her picture from his desk and then he went to bed and never got up again.

'Afanasy came to see me three days later to ask whether a doctor should not be called out, as there was something wrong with his master. I went over to see Belikov. He was lying behind his bed curtains, covered up with a blanket and not speaking; if you asked him anything, all he would answer was yes or no, but he made no other sound. He went on lying there while Afanasy wandered about gloomily with a scowl on his face, sighing deeply; he reeked of vodka like a tavern.

'Belikov died a month later. We all took part in burying him, that is to say, both the schools and the seminary. He had such a meek, pleasant, and even happy expression on his face lying in the grave that it was as if he was glad that he had finally been put in a case which he would never climb out of. Yes, he had reached his goal! And the weather on the day of his funeral was overcast and rainy, as if in his honour, and we all wore galoshes and carried umbrellas. Varenka also came to the funeral, and she shed a few tears when they lowered the coffin into the grave. I have noticed that Ukrainian women can only ever laugh or cry; there is no middle ground for them.

'I have to confess that burying people like Belikov is very pleasurable. When we came home from the cemetery we all had suitably pious faces of course—no one wanted to admit to feeling pleased, and I was reminded of those times long, long ago in childhood, when all the grown-ups would go out and we would be able to run round the garden for an hour or two, enjoying the feeling of being completely free! Ah yes, freedom! Even a hint of it, just the faintest hope of it, is enough to make one's spirit soar, don't you think?

'We came home from the cemetery in a good mood. But barely a week had gone by before everything went back to normal: the same grim, exhausting, pointless life in which things were not expressly forbidden, but not really permitted either; nothing had improved. We might have buried Belikov, but there were so many other people in cases still, and just think how many more there are going to be!'

'Yes, that just about sums it up,' said Ivan Ivanych as he lit his pipe.

'Just think how many more there are going to be!' Burkin said again.

The schoolteacher went out of the barn. He was a short, fat man who was completely bald, with a black beard that went almost down to his waist; he was followed by two dogs.

'Look at that moon!' he said, looking up.

It was already midnight. To the right one could see the whole village, and a long road stretching for about three miles into the distance. Everything had been plunged into a quiet, deep sleep; there was no movement and no sound, and it was hard to believe that such silence could exist in the countryside. Seeing that wide village street with its little houses, haystacks, and somnolent willows on a moonlit night, brought a sense of peace to one's heart; during its time of rest, sheltered by night's shadows from troubles, toil, and sorrow, it looked meek, sad, and lovely; it seemed that even the stars were gazing down tenderly and affectionately, that there was no more evil in the world and that all would be well. Open countryside began to the left of the village; one could see it stretching as far as the horizon, and there was no sound or movement coming from its great moonlit expanse either.

'Yes, that just about sums it up,' said Ivan Ivanych again. 'But what about the cramped, stuffy lives we lead in town, writing useless papers and playing cards—is that not living in a case too? And what about the way we spend our whole lives amongst idlers, pedants, and vain, stupid women, talking and listening to all sorts of rubbish—is not that a kind of case as well? There is a very instructive story I can tell you, if you would like.'

'No, it's time to go to sleep,' said Burkin. 'Let's leave it till morning!'

They both went into the barn and lay down on the hay. And they had both tucked themselves up and were starting to doze off when they suddenly heard light footsteps going tap, tap... Someone was walking near the barn, taking a few steps then stopping, and then starting again a minute later: tap, tap... The dogs started growling.

'That must be Mavra,' said Burkin.

The footsteps died away.

'To see and hear people lying,' said Ivan Ivanych, turning on to his other side, 'and then to be called a fool for putting up with it; to endure insults and humiliations but to be too scared to come out in the open and declare that you are on the side of honest, free people, and then to lie and smile ingratiatingly yourself, when it's all for the sake of a crust of bread, a roof over your head, and a pathetic little job in the service which is not worth anything—no, it's impossible to go on living like that!'

'Well that's a whole other story, Ivan Ivanych,' the teacher said. 'Let's get some sleep.'

And about ten minutes later Burkin was already asleep. But Ivan Ivanych kept tossing from side to side and sighing; then he got up and went outside again, sat down by the door, and lit his pipe.

# GOOSEBERRIES

Rain-clouds had filled the whole sky since early morning; it was quiet, not particularly warm, and dull, as so often on those grey, overcast days when dark clouds hang over the landscape for ages and you keep expecting it to rain but it never does. Ivan Ivanych the veterinary surgeon and Burkin the schoolmaster had already grown tired of walking, and the open countryside seemed endless. A long way ahead you could just about see the windmills in the village of Mironositskoe; to the right there was a series of hills which stretched away and then disappeared far beyond the village, and they both knew that this was the riverbank, where there were meadows, green willows, and estates; if you stood on the top of one of the hills you could see another equally enormous stretch of open countryside, as well as telegraph poles and a train creeping along in the distance like a caterpillar, while on clear days you could even see the town. Ivan Ivanych and Burkin were filled with love for this landscape in this subdued weather, with the whole countryside looking so meek and pensive, and both were thinking how magnificent and beautiful their country was.

'The last time we were at Elder Prokofy's barn,' said Burkin, 'there was a story you were going to tell.'

'Yes, I wanted to tell you about my brother.'

Ivan Ivanych let out a long sigh then lit his pipe in order to start his story, but just at that moment it started to rain. Within five minutes the rain was coming down steadily in a heavy downpour, and it was difficult to forecast when it was going to stop. Ivan Ivanych and Burkin paused to think for a moment; the dogs, who were already wet, stood wagging their tails, looking at them affectionately.

'We need to take shelter somewhere,' said Burkin. 'Let's go to Alyokhin's. It's nearby.'

'Let's go.'

They turned off their path and walked through the scythed field, sometimes in a straight line and sometimes making turns to the right until they got to the road. Soon there appeared poplars, an orchard, then the red roofs of barns; a river gleamed, and a view opened up of a wide stretch of open water with a windmill and a white bathing hut. This was Sofyino, where Alyokhin lived.

The windmill was working, muffling the sound of the rain, and the weir was shuddering. Near to the carts stood wet horses with bowed heads, and there were people who had covered themselves with sacks walking about. It was damp, muddy, and uninviting and the open water looked cold and malevolent. Ivan Ivanych and Burkin had started to feel wet, dirty, and uncomfortable all through their bodies and their feet had become heavy with mud; when they were walking past the dam and up to the barns belonging to the estate they were silent, as if they were angry with each other.

A winnowing-machine was whirring in one of the barns; the door was open and there was dust billowing out of it. Alyokhin himself was standing in the doorway; he was a man of about forty—tall and on the plump side, with long hair, and he looked more like a professor or an artist than a landowner. He was wearing a white shirt which had not been washed for a long time, shorts instead of trousers with a bit of rope for a belt, and there was mud and straw sticking to his boots. He recognized Ivan Ivanych and Burkin and was evidently very glad to see them.

'Please go on up to the house, gentlemen,' he said with a smile. 'I'll just be a minute.'

The house was large and on two storeys. Alyokhin lived downstairs, in two rooms with vaulted ceilings and small windows which the bailiffs had once lived in; they were furnished simply and smelt of rye bread, cheap vodka, and harnesses. He spent little time in the main rooms upstairs, and only used them when he had guests. Ivan Ivanych and Burkin were met at the house by a maid, a young woman who was so beautiful that they both stopped dead in their tracks and looked at each other.

'You can't imagine how glad I am to see you, gentlemen,' said Alyokhin, coming into the hall after them. 'What a surprise!' He turned to the maid. 'Pelageya, could you please give the guests something to change into. Actually, I will change too. But I have to go and wash first, as I feel as if I haven't had a wash since spring. How about nipping down to our bathing area on the river, gentlemen, while they get things ready?'

The beautiful Pelageya, so delicate and gentle-looking, brought towels and soap, and Alyokhin and his guests went down to the bathing hut.

'Yes, I haven't had a wash in ages,' he said as he undressed. 'I've got a wonderful place for bathing, as you can see—my father set it up, but I never seem to have the time to wash.'

He sat down on the step, putting soap on his long hair and on his neck, and the water around him turned brown.

'Yes, I have to admit...' said Ivan Ivanych meaningfully as he eyed his head. 'Haven't washed in ages,' repeated Alyokhin sheepishly, as he soaped himself again, the water around him this time turning indigo, like ink. Ivan Ivanych came out of the hut, plunged noisily into the water, and started swimming about in the rain, taking large strokes with his arms, and producing waves on which tossed white water-lilies; he swam right into the middle of the river then dived down and came up in another place a minute later; then he swam further out and kept diving underwater, trying to reach the bottom. 'Oh my goodness...' he kept repeating in deep enjoyment. 'Goodness me...' He swam up to the windmill, had a chat with the peasants there, and then turned round and lay floating on his back in the middle of the river with his face upturned beneath the rain. Burkin and Alyokhin had already got dressed and were ready to go, but he was still swimming about and diving underwater.

'Oh my goodness...' he was saying; 'Goodness gracious me.'

'Come on, that's enough!' Burkin shouted out to him.

They returned to the house. And only when they had lit the lamp in the large drawing room upstairs, and Burkin and Ivan Ivanych were sitting in armchairs dressed in silk robes and warm shoes, and Alyokhin was walking about the room, freshly washed and with his hair brushed, in a new frock-coat, clearly enjoying the feeling of being warm and clean and wearing dry clothes and light shoes, and the beautiful Pelageya was offering tea with jam on a tray, treading noiselessly on the carpet and smiling gently, only then did Ivan Ivanych begin his story, and it seemed that it was not just Burkin and Alyokhin listening to it, but also the young and old ladies and officers who were looking at them sternly and calmly from their golden frames.

'There are two of us brothers,' he began. 'There's me, Ivan Ivanych, and there's Nikolay Ivanych, who is two years younger. I was the more academic one, and I became a vet, while Nikolay started work in a government office when he was nineteen. Our father, Ivan Chimsha-Gimalaisky was a rank-and-file soldier who was eventually promoted to officer class, and so bequeathed to us hereditary nobility and a minuscule estate. The estate was taken to pay off debts after his death, but despite that we spent our childhood in the countryside in complete freedom. We were just like peasant children, outside in the woods and fields day and night; we kept horses, stripped bark for bast,* went fishing, that kind of thing... And you know, someone who has caught a ruff or seen the thrushes migrating south in flocks above the village in autumn on clear, cool days can never be happy in a town; he is going to long for the freedom of the countryside till the end of his days. My brother was miserable in his government office. The years were going by and he was still in the same place, filling out the same documents and thinking about one thing: how much he would like to be in the country. This longing gradually shaped itself into a particular desire—to carry out his dream of buying a property somewhere on the bank of a river or next to a lake.

'He was a kind and gentle man and I loved him dearly, but I could never understand his desire to closet himself away on his own estate for the rest of his life. People say that a person only needs six feet of earth.* But in fact it's a corpse that needs six feet of earth, not a person. And people also say these days that it's a good thing when members of our intelligentsia feel drawn to the land and want to live on country estates. But those country houses with their plots of land are nothing other than those six feet of earth. Leaving city life and all its struggles and stresses; leaving all that in order to lock oneself away in the country—that's no life, that's being selfish and lazy; it's a kind of monasticism, but monasticism without any sacrifice. People don't need six feet of earth, or even a house in the country, but the whole globe, the whole of nature in its entirety, so they can have the space to express all the capacities and particularities of their free spirit.

'While he was stuck in his office, my brother Nikolay would dream of being able to eat his own pickled cabbage, whose delicious smell he imagined wafting across the yard; he would dream of picnicking on green grass, taking an afternoon nap in the sunshine, and sitting for hours on end on a bench in front of his gateposts and looking at the fields and forests. Books about agriculture and the bits of advice you find in calendars were his greatest joy and his favourite spiritual food; he also loved reading newspapers, but only the notices advertising however many acres of arable land for sale with a meadow and a house and garden, plus a river, an orchard, a windmill, and well-drained ponds. And he would begin to draw up in his mind paths in the orchard, flowers and fruit, starling-boxes, carp in the ponds, and, well, you know, all that kind of stuff. These imaginary pictures changed according to the advertisements he came across, but for some reason they all featured gooseberry bushes. There was not one estate or poetic little spot that he imagined which did not include gooseberry bushes.

' "Country life has definitely got something to offer," he would say. "You can sit on the balcony drinking tea, with your ducks swimming in the pond, everything smelling so good and... and your gooseberry bushes growing."

'He would sketch out the plan of how his estate would look and each time it would turn out the same: (a) a house, (b) servants' quarters, (c) a vegetable garden, and (d) gooseberry bushes. He lived in a miserly manner, eating little, drinking little, dressing himself in goodness knows what, like a tramp, and all the time stashing away money in the bank. He was incredibly stingy. It was painful to look at him, and I used to give him things and send stuff over for the holidays, but he would squirrel them away too: once a person is fixed on a certain idea, there is nothing you can do about it.

'The years passed, he was transferred to another region, he had turned forty, and he was still reading advertisements in the newspapers and saving money. Then I heard that he had got married. Still set on buying an estate with gooseberry bushes, he had married an elderly and unattractive widow—not for love but simply because she had a lot of cash. He lived like a miser with her too, keeping her half-starved and putting her money in the bank in his name. She had been married to a postmaster before and had been used to cakes and liqueurs, but with her second husband she could not even eat as much black bread as she wanted; that kind of life made her start wasting away, and after about three years she gave up the ghost and died. And my brother of course never thought for one minute that he might have been responsible for her death. Money makes people behave weirdly, just like vodka. There was a merchant who lived in our town. Just before he died he ordered a dish of honey and went and ate up all his money and his lottery tickets with the honey so that no one else would get them. I was examining cattle at the station once, when a cattle-dealer fell under a train and got his leg chopped off. We took him to the casualty ward with blood pouring everywhere—it was terrible—and he kept asking people to search for his leg, and worrying that he would lose the twenty roubles in the boot he had been wearing.'

'Well, that's a whole other story,' said Burkin.

'After his wife died,' Ivan Ivanych continued, after pausing to think for thirty seconds, 'my brother started hunting out an estate for himself. Of course, you can spend five years looking but in the end you are bound to trip up and buy something which is not quite what you were dreaming about. Through an agent who organized a mortgage, my brother Nikolay bought three hundred acres with a house, servants' quarters, and gardens, but no orchard and no gooseberry bushes, and no pond with ducks in it; there was a river, but the water in it was the colour of coffee, because on one side of the estate there was a brick factory and a bone-ash works on the other. But my dear brother was not perturbed; he ordered up twenty gooseberry bushes, planted them, and started living the life of a landowner.

'I went to pay him a visit last year. I thought I would go and see how he was getting on. In his letters, my brother called his estate Chumbaroklov Wilderness, a.k.a. Gimalaiskoe. I arrived at "a.k.a. Gimalaiskoe" after midday. It was hot. There were ditches everywhere, and hedges, fences, and fir trees planted in rows, so it was difficult to work out where the entrance was and where to leave my horse. I walked up to the house and was met by a fat ginger-haired dog that looked like a pig. It wanted to bark but couldn't be bothered. The cook came out of the kitchen; she was barefoot and fat and she looked like a pig too; she said the master was having a rest after lunch. So I go in and find my brother sitting up in bed with a blanket over his knees; he had aged and filled out and looked bloated: his cheeks, nose, and lips were all protruding and he was grunting into the blanket.

'We kissed each other and shed a few tears of joy and also sadness at the thought that we had been young once, but were now both grey-haired and it was time for us to die. He got dressed and took me on a tour of his estate.

' "So how are you getting on here?" I asked.

' "Pretty well, really, can't complain; things are good." '

'He was no longer the timid, poverty-stricken official he used to be but a real landowner now, lord of the manor. He had already settled in, got used to his new life, and begun to enjoy it; he ate a lot, he went for saunas in the bath-house, he had put on weight, was already in litigation with the locals and with both the factories next door to him, and was very put out that the peasants did not call him "your excellency". And he took care of his soul in a respectable, lordly way, doing good works with ostentation rather than with discretion. And what were these good works? He treated the peasants for all their ailments with soda and castor oil, and on his name day held a service of blessing in the village, then put out large quantities of vodka, thinking that was what was required. All that vodka! One day a fat landowner is dragging peasants to the regional authorities for damaging crops, and the next day it's a celebration and he's giving them vodka, so they drink and shout hurrah, and bow down at his feet when they are drunk. Wealth, idleness, and a change in life for the better all produce in Russian people the worst kind of inflated self-opinion. Nikolay Ivanych, who in his government office had even been afraid of having his own views, now spoke only words of wisdom, and in a ministerial-like tone: "Education is vital, but it is premature for the populace", "Corporal punishment is generally harmful but in certain instances it is indispensable and useful." '

' "I understand the people and how to talk to them," he would say. "They like me. I just have to lift a finger and they will do anything I want." '

'And all this was said, mind you, with a knowing smile. He said about twenty times things like "we of the nobility" or "as a member of the nobility", and had obviously forgotten that our grandfather was a peasant and his father a soldier. Even our surname, Chimsha-Gimalaisky, which is basically absurd, now seemed sonorous, distinguished, and very pleasant to him.

'But the point of all this is not him but me. I want to tell you what change took place within me during those hours I spent on his estate. In the evening, while we were drinking tea, the cook brought a large plate of gooseberries to the table. They had not been bought, they were his own gooseberries, picked for the first time since the bushes had been planted. Nikolay Ivanych chuckled and looked at the gooseberries for a minute in silence, with tears running down his cheeks—

he was so excited he could not speak, then he put a gooseberry into his mouth, looked at me triumphantly, like a child who has finally been handed a favourite toy, and said: "How delicious!"

'He started eating greedily and saying over and over: "Ah, how delicious! You must try one!"

'They were hard and sour, but as Pushkin said, "the lie which exalts us is dearer to us than a host of truths."* I was watching a contented person, whose cherished dream had so clearly become a reality, who had achieved his aim in life, who had got what he wanted, and who was happy with his lot and with himself. There has always been some sadness mixed in with my thoughts about human happiness, and now, seeing this contented person, I was overcome by a dreadful feeling which was close to despair. It was particularly awful during the night. A bed was made up for me in the room next to my brother's bedroom, and I could hear that he was still awake and was getting up and going over to the plate of gooseberries and taking one after the other. I started thinking about how many contented, happy people there are in actual fact! What an oppressive force! Think about this life of ours: the insolence and idleness of the strong, the ignorance and bestiality of the weak, unbelievable poverty everywhere, overcrowding, degeneracy, drunkenness, hypocrisy, deceit... Meanwhile all is quiet and peaceful in people's homes and outside on the street; out of the fifty thousand people who live in the town, there is not one single person prepared to shout out about it or kick up a fuss. We see the people who go to the market for their groceries, travelling about in the daytime, sleeping at night, the kind of people who spout nonsense, get married, grow old, and dutifully cart their dead off to the cemetery; but we do not see or hear those who are suffering, and all the terrible things in life happen somewhere offstage. Everything is quiet and peaceful, and the only protest is voiced by dumb statistics: so many people have gone mad, so many bottles of vodka have been drunk, so many children have died from malnutrition... And this arrangement is clearly necessary: it's obvious that the contented person only feels good because those who are unhappy bear their burden in silence; without that silence happiness would be inconceivable. It's a collective hypnosis. There ought to be someone with a little hammer outside the door of every contented, happy person, constantly tapping away to remind him that there are unhappy people in the world, and that however happy he may be, sooner or later life will show its claws; misfortune will strike—illness, poverty, loss—and no one will be there to see or hear it, just as they now cannot see or hear others. But there is no person with a little hammer; happy people are wrapped up in their own lives, and the minor problems of life affect them only slightly, like aspen leaves in a breeze, and everything is just fine.

'That night I realized that I was contented and happy too,' Ivan Ivanych continued as he got to his feet. 'I also pontificated when I was at the dinner table and when I was out hunting, about how to live, how to practise the faith, and about how to deal with the people. I also used to say that learning was sacred, that education was vital but that learning to read and write was quite enough for simple people for the time being. Freedom is a good thing, I used to say; it is as necessary as the air we breathe, but we must bide our time. Yes, I used to talk like that, and now I am wondering what on earth it is that we are actually biding our time for?' Ivan Ivanych looked angrily at Burkin as he spoke. 'I'm asking you, what is it we are waiting for? What justification is there? People tell me you can't do everything at once, that every idea has to be put into practice gradually, in its own good time. But who are the people saying such things? Where is the proof that this is the right way to proceed? You refer to the natural order of things, and to natural phenomena, but where is the order, what is natural about me, a living, thinking person, standing in front of a trench, and waiting for it to grow over by itself or fill up with silt, when I could jump over it or throw a plank over it? Once again, you have to ask, what is the point of waiting—waiting when there is no energy for living? But we need to live, and there is such a strong desire to live!

'I left my brother early in the morning, and I've found it unbearable being in the town ever since. The peace and quiet depress me and I am afraid to look through people's windows, because the hardest thing for me is to see a happy family sitting round a table drinking tea. I am old, and not up to fighting now; I'm not even capable of hatred. I'm just in a state of mourning inside, I get angry and annoyed, and at night my head is filled with a mass of thoughts and I can't sleep... Oh, if only I was young!'

In his agitated state, Ivan Ivanych was pacing the room from one corner to the other, saying over and over again: 'If only I was young!'

Then suddenly he went up to Alyokhin and started clasping his hands, first one then the other.

'Pavel Konstantinovich,' he said in a beseeching voice. 'Never be satisfied, don't let yourself go! Don't tire of doing good while you are young and strong and active! Happiness does not exist and it should not exist, and if there is a meaning and purpose to life, then that meaning and purpose is certainly not for us to be happy, but something far greater and wiser. Do good!'

Ivan Ivanych said all this with a pitiful, pleading smile, as if he was asking him to do this for him personally.

All three then sat in their armchairs at different ends of the drawing room without saying anything. Neither Burkin nor Alyokhin found Ivan Ivanych's story satisfying. With the generals and the ladies gazing out of their golden frames and looking in the dusk as if they were alive, it was boring to listen to a story about a poor official who ate gooseberries. For some reason they would have liked to have heard and talked about elegant people, about ladies. Sitting in a drawing room where everything—from the chandelier in its dust-cover to the armchairs and the carpets under their feet—was a reminder of the fact that the very people who were now looking out of those frames once walked about here, sat down and drank tea, and where the beautiful Pelageya was now moving about silently, was far better than any story.

Alyokhin was desperate to go to bed; he had got up early to start work on the estate, before three in the morning, and he could barely keep his eyes open, but he was afraid that his guests might start talking about something interesting without him, so he did not leave. He could not work out whether the story Ivan Ivanych had just told was clever or fair; his guests were not talking about grain or hay or tar but about something which bore no direct relation to his life, and he was glad and wanted them to carry on...

'But it's time to sleep,' said Burkin, getting up. 'May I wish you goodnight.'

Alyokhin took his leave and went downstairs to his rooms while the guests remained upstairs. They had been given a large room for the night in which there were two old wooden beds with carved decorations and a crucifix made of ivory in the corner; the cool, wide beds which the beautiful Pelageya had made up smelt pleasantly of fresh linen.

Ivan Ivanych undressed silently and got into bed.

'Lord, forgive us sinners!' he said, covering his head.

There was a strong smell of tobacco smoke from his pipe which lay on the table; Burkin took a long time to go to sleep and he could not work out where that pungent smell was coming from.

The rain hammered against the windows all night.

# ABOUT LOVE

The next day for lunch delicious pies, crayfish, and lamb rissoles were served, and Nikanor the cook came upstairs during the meal to ask what the guests would like for dinner. He was an average-sized man, with a chubby face and small eyes; he was clean-shaven, and it looked as if his whiskers had been plucked out rather than shaved.

Alyokhin said that the beautiful Pelageya was in love with this cook. Since he drank a lot and could be violent at times, she did not want to marry him, but she had agreed to live with him. He was very devout, however, and his religious convictions did not allow him to live with her; he demanded that she marry him, and did not want it any other way; he would shout at her when he was drunk, and even hit her. She used to hide upstairs and cry when he was drunk, and Alyokhin and the servants would not go out of the house during those times, so that they could protect her if necessary.

The conversation turned to love.

'How love is born,' said Alyokhin; 'why, for example, Pelageya didn't go for someone more suited to her emotionally and physically, since personal happiness is so important in love, but instead developed an attachment to Nikanor, that great pig-snout—everyone calls him pig-snout around here—is completely unknowable, and you can analyse it any way you want. Only one indisputable truth has ever been uttered about love, which is that "this is a great mystery",* as it says in the Bible; nothing else that has been written and uttered about love has provided any kind of answer, but merely posed a set of problems which have remained without a solution. The explanation which seems to be right for one particular set of circumstances turns out to be wrong for a dozen others, and so the best one can do, as far as I can see, is to assess each situation on its own terms, without trying to generalize. As doctors say, you should treat each case individually.'

'Quite true,' agreed Burkin.

'We respectable Russians are drawn precisely to these problems which have remained without a solution. People of other nations poeticize love, or adorn it with roses and nightingales, but we

Russians have to adorn love with imponderable problems, and we always pick on the most uninteresting problems too. I once had a lady friend in Moscow when I was still a student, a charming woman, who was always thinking about how much money I was going to give her each month whenever I held her in my arms, or how much the current price of a pound of beef was. We're just the same where love is concerned; we can never stop asking ourselves questions as to whether we are being honest or not, whether we are acting wisely or stupidly, whether the relationship is going anywhere and so forth. I don't know whether all this is a good or a bad thing, but I do know that it holds us back; it's not rewarding, it's just a source of irritation.'

It seemed that he had a story he wanted to tell. People who live alone always have something or other that they want to get off their chests. Bachelors who live in towns make a point of going to the baths or to restaurants just to talk, and sometimes the stories they tell their bath attendants or waiters are very interesting. In the country they usually end up pouring their hearts out to their house guests. Through the window could be seen grey sky and trees wet with rain; since there was nowhere one could go in that kind of weather, there was nothing else to do but tell stories and listen.

'I've been living and working on the land in Sofyino a long time now,' began Alyokhin; 'since I left university in fact. My upbringing was not conducive to physical work, and my natural inclinations are towards books and papers. But when I came here, the estate was saddled with debts, and since my father had taken out loans partly because he had spent so much money on my education, I decided I would not leave; I'd stay and work until I had paid off the debt. I made my decision and started to work here, although not, I have to admit, without a certain amount of dread. The land around here does not yield very much, and in order for the farming not to make a loss, you need to use slave labour or take on casual workers, which amounts pretty much to the same thing, otherwise you have to put everything on to a peasant footing, which means you and your family working in the fields yourselves. There is nothing in between. But back then I did not go in for such fine distinctions. I didn't leave a single patch of earth untouched. I rounded up all the men and women labourers from the neighbouring villages and got them working like crazy. I also threw myself into the ploughing and the sowing and the reaping, but I found it very tedious and frowned with disdain, like the village cat, which finally gets so hungry it ends up eating the cucumbers in the vegetable patch. My body ached and I used to fall asleep on the job. At first I was under the impression that I could easily accommodate my cultural pursuits to this kind of working life, and I thought all I would need would be to maintain a certain amount of discipline. So I set up home in the smart rooms here upstairs, arranged to have coffee and liqueurs served after lunch and dinner, and then when I went to bed I used to read the *Messenger of Europe*\* into the early hours. But our priest Father Ivan came over one day and drank all my bottles of liqueur in one sitting, and then my *Messengers of Europe* started ending up with his daughters, because in the summer, especially when we were haymaking, I would not even manage to make it to my own bed, and used to fall asleep in the sleigh in the barn or in some forest hut—what reading was I going to do? I gradually ended up moving downstairs and eating in the servants' kitchen, and the only remnants of my former luxurious lifestyle are all the people here who used to work for my father, and I'd find it too painful to let them go.

'During my first few years here, I was elected to serve as an honorary justice of the peace. Every now and then I would have to go into town and take part in sessions at the assizes and at the regional court, and it kept me amused. After you have lived here for two or three months on end, especially during the winter-time, you end up beginning to miss seeing black frock-coats. And it wasn't just black frock-coats you could see at the circuit court, but uniforms and tail-coats—these were all lawyers, people who had been educated; there was always someone to talk to. After sleeping in the sleigh and sitting in the servants' kitchen, it was such a luxury to sit in an armchair, wearing a clean shirt and ankle-boots, with a chain around your neck!

'People in the town received me warmly, and I was keen to get to know them. Of all the acquaintances I made, the most lasting, and also the most pleasant, to be honest, was with my colleague Luganovich, the president of the circuit court. You both know him—he's an absolutely charming man. It was just after that famous arson case; the cross-examination went on for two days, and we were exhausted. Luganovich looked at me and said:

' "Look, why don't you come over for dinner?"

'It was unexpected, because I barely knew Luganovich; our

relationship had been purely formal up to that point, and I had never been to his home. I nipped back to my hotel room to change and set off for dinner. And that's when I had the opportunity to get to know Anna Alexeyevna, Luganovich's wife. She was still very young then, no more than twenty-two, and her first child had been born six months earlier. It's all in the past, and so I would find it hard now to define what exactly was so unusual about her, and what I liked so much about her, but back then at the dinner it was crystal clear. I saw a young woman—a beautiful, kind, intelligent, charming woman, who was unlike anyone I had ever met before. I immediately felt she was a kindred spirit, someone I already knew, as if I had seen her face and those warm, intelligent eyes back in my childhod, in the album which lay on my mother's dresser.

'In the arson case, four Jews had been accused of forming a conspiracy, but totally falsely in my opinion. I got very worked up at dinner because I felt so miserable about it, and I can't for the life of me remember what I said, but Anna Alexeyevna kept shaking her head and saying to her husband:

' "Dmitry, how on earth could this have happened?"

'Luganovich is a good-natured sort, and one of those straight-forward kind of people who strongly believe that if a person is brought to court he must therefore be guilty, and that expressing doubt in the correctness of the sentence can only be done in a legal manner, on paper, but certainly not over dinner, nor in private conversation.

' "Neither you nor I started the fire," he said gently, "and that's why they haven't taken us to court and sent us to prison."

'Both husband and wife pressed me to eat and drink more. From various small details, such as the way they made coffee together, for example, and the way they understood each other without finishing their sentences, I could see that they had a peaceful, happy relationship, and that they were glad to have a guest. After dinner we played duets on the piano, then it began to grow dark and I went home. This was at the beginning of spring. Then I spent the whole of the summer at Sofyino without once leaving, and I had no time even to think about the town, but the memory of the slender, fair-haired woman remained with me all those days; I didn't think about her, but it was as if her graceful shadow lay across my soul.

'In late autumn there was a charity performance in town. When I

went into the governor's box (I had been invited to stop by in the interval) who should I see but Anna Alexeyevna with the governor's wife,
and I was struck once again by the same impression of irresistible,
dazzling beauty and kind, gentle eyes, and again a feeling of intimacy.

'We sat next to each other and then went into the foyer.

' "You've lost weight," she said. "Have you been ill?"

' "Yes. I have a problem with my shoulder, and I sleep badly when
it rains."

' "You look run down. When you came to dinner in the spring you
seemed younger and in brighter spirits. You were inspired that evening and talked a great deal; what you said was very interesting, and I
have to confess that I even became a little bit carried away by you.
For some reason you came into my mind quite often during the
summer months, and today, when I was getting ready to come to the
theatre, I just had a feeling I would see you."

'And she started laughing.

' "But you look run down today," she said again. "It makes you
look older."

'I had lunch with the Luganoviches the next day, then after lunch
they went off to their dacha to get everything ready there for winter,
and I went with them. I returned to town with them too, and at
midnight sat drinking tea with them in their peaceful family home,
with the fire blazing and the young mother constantly going out to
check whether her little girl was asleep. After that I would go and
visit the Luganoviches whenever I went to town. They got used to me
and I got used to them. I would usually turn up without any advance
notice, as if I was one of the family.

' "Who is it?" From a far-off room would come that lilting voice I
found so lovely.

' "It's Pavel Konstantinovich," the maid or the nanny would
answer.

'Anna Alexeyevna would come to greet me with a concerned
expression, and would ask every time:

' "Why have you been away so long? Has something happened?"

'The look of her eyes, the refined, elegant hand she held out to me,
the dress she wore at home, her hairstyle, her voice, and the way she
walked always gave me the impression of something new, unusual,
and important in my life. We would talk for ages and be silent for
ages, each thinking our own thoughts, or else she would play the

piano for me. If no one was at home, I would stay and wait, talking to the nanny and playing with the baby, or I would go and lie down on the ottoman in the study and read the newspaper; when Anna Alexeyevna returned I would go and greet her in the hall, take her parcels from her, and for some reason I would always carry those parcels with as much love and solemnity as if I was a little boy.

'There is a saying: the woman had no cares, so she bought a pig. The Luganoviches had no worries, so they made friends with me. If I did not come to town for a long time, it meant I was ill or something bad had happened to me, and they both began to worry a great deal. They worried that instead of engaging in academic or literary work, here I was, an educated man who knew foreign languages, living in the countryside, running round and round like a hamster in a wheel, working fiendishly hard but never making any money. They thought I was unhappy, and that if I talked and laughed and ate, then it was only to cover up my unhappiness; I felt their anxious eyes on me even in more light-hearted moments, when I was in a good mood. Their concern was particularly touching when I really was going through a tough time, when some creditor was hounding me, or there was not enough money to pay an urgent bill; both of them, husband and wife, would whisper by the window, then he would come up to me and say with a serious expression:

' "If you need money at the moment, Pavel Konstantinovich, then my wife and I hope you won't feel shy about borrowing from us."

'And his ears would turn red with embarrassment. And sometimes after they had whispered by the window in just the same way, he would come up to me with his red ears and say:

' "My wife and I would sincerely like you to accept this gift."

'And he would give me cufflinks, a cigarette case, or a lamp, and in return I would send them from the country some slaughtered fowl, butter, and flowers. They were both very wealthy, by the way. In the early days I often took out loans, and was not particularly fussy about where I obtained them from, anywhere would do, but nothing in the world would have induced me to borrow from the Luganoviches. The very idea!

'I was unhappy. I thought about her at home, out in the fields, and in the barn; and I tried to unravel the mystery of how a young, beautiful, clever woman could marry an uninteresting man on the brink of old age (her husband was over forty) and have children with him. I also tried to unravel the mystery of this boring, good-natured, simple soul, who thought in such a boring sensible way, who only ever socialized with wealthy people at balls and parties, who was superfluous and inert, who wore a submissive and detached expression as if he had been put up for sale, but who believed, however, in his right to be happy and have children with her. I kept trying to understand why she had to meet him of all people, rather than me, and why such a dreadful mistake should have taken place in our lives.

'Each time I came into town, I could see from her eyes that she had been expecting me; and she herself would confess that she had felt something special all day, and had guessed that I was going to come. We would talk for a long time, and be silent for a long time, but we never confessed our love to each other, always hiding it shyly and jealously. We were frightened of everything that might betray our secret to each other. My love was tender and deep, but I tried to be rational, and wondered what might happen to our love if we didn't have the strength to contain it; it seemed impossible that my quiet, sad love could suddenly crudely destroy the happy flow of life of her husband, her children, and the whole household, where everyone was so fond of me, and trusted me. Would it be honest? She would have gone with me, but where would we go? Where could I take her? It would have been different if my life had been glamorous and interesting, if I had been fighting for the liberation of my country, for example, or was a famous scholar, an actor or an artist, but I would just be taking her from one tedious and ordinary way of life to another one exactly the same, or one that was even more tedious. And how long would our love last? What would happen if I got ill, or died, or if we simply stopped loving each other?

'She had clearly thought about everything in a similar way. She thought about her husband, about her children, and about her mother, who loved her husband like a son. If she gave in to her feelings, she would have to lie or tell the truth, and both options seemed equally terrible and awkward in her position. And she was tormented by the question of whether her love would bring me happiness, and whether it would only complicate my life, which was already difficult and full of misfortune. She felt that she was not young enough for me, and not hardworking or dynamic enough to begin a new life, and she often told her husband that I should get married to an intelligent, reliable girl, who would be a good housewife and helper to me, immediately adding that it would be practically impossible to find anyone like that in the town.

'Meanwhile, the years went by. Anna Alexeyevna now had two children. When I arrived at the Luganoviches, the maid would smile warmly, the children would shout that their Uncle Pavel Konstanti-novich had come and would throw themselves round my neck; everyone was glad to see me. They did not understand what was going on in my heart, and they thought I was glad too. Everyone saw me as a noble being. Both the adults and the children in the household felt that a noble being had entered their house when I arrived, and this added a particular charm to their relationships with me; it was as if their lives became somehow purer and more beautiful in my presence. Anna Alexeyevna and I would go to the theatre, always on foot; we would sit next to each other, with our shoulders touching, and I would silently take the opera glasses from her hands and feel during that time that she was close to me, that she was mine, and that we could not live without each other, but through some misunderstanding we would always say goodbye and part like strangers whenever we left the theatre. Goodness knows what people in town were saying about us, but there was never a grain of truth in anything they said.

'In the last years Anna Alexeyevna started to go to visit either her mother or her sister more often. She was in a bad state by this time; there were times when she felt dissatisfied, and thought that her life was ruined, when she did not want to see either her husband or her children. She had begun to be treated for her nerves.

'We continued, tight-lipped, to maintain our silence, and when others were present she started to experience a strange irritation with me; whatever I said she would disagree with, and if I got into an argument, she would always side with whoever I was arguing with. Whenever I dropped something, she would say coldly:

' "Well done."

'If I forgot the opera glasses when we were going to the theatre she would say:

' "I knew you would forget them."

'Luckily or unluckily, there is nothing in our lives which does not come to an end sooner or later. The time for separation came when Luganovich was appointed to be a judge in one of the western provinces. They had to sell their furniture, their horses, and their dacha. We were all sad on the day we went out to the dacha, and looked

around one last time at the garden and the green roof before returning home, and I realized that the time had come to part not just with
the dacha. It was decided that at the end of August we would send
Anna Alexeyevna off on her journey to the Crimea, where her doctors were sending her, and then a little while later the children would
accompany Luganovich to his western province.

'A great crowd of us went to see Anna Alexeyevna off. When she
had already said goodbye to her husband and her children, and there
was a minute left before they rang the third bell, I ran into her
carriage to put up on the rack a basket she had almost left behind,
and then we had to say goodbye. As soon as our eyes met while we
were standing there in the compartment, our emotional strength left
us and I embraced her; she pressed her face to my chest, and tears
ran down her face; as I kissed her face, her shoulders, and her hands,
which were wet with tears—oh, we were so unhappy!—I confessed
my love for her, and with a burning pain in my heart I realized how
unnecessary, petty, and deceptive everything which had got in the
way of our love had been. I realized that when you love someone,
your reasoning about that love should be based on what is supreme,
on what is more important than happiness or unhappiness, sin or
virtue, in the way that they are usually understood, otherwise it is
not worth reasoning at all.

'I kissed her for the last time, shook her hand, and we parted—
forever. The train was already moving. I went and sat in the next
compartment—it was empty—and sat there and cried until we got to
the next station. Then I went back home to Sofyino on foot.'

While Alyokhin had been talking the rain had stopped and the sun
had come out. Burkin and Ivan Ivanych went out on to the balcony,
from where there was a wonderful view onto the garden and the
river, which was now gleaming in the sun like a mirror. They enjoyed
the view, but they also felt sad that this man with the kind, intelligent
eyes, who had told them such a heartfelt story, really was just going
round and round here on this huge estate, like a hamster in a wheel,
instead of being engaged in scholarship or something else which
would have made his life more enjoyable; and they thought about
how sorrowful the young lady must have looked when he was saying
goodbye to her in the train and was kissing her face and shoulders.
They had both met her in town from time to time; Burkin was even
aquainted with her and thought she was beautiful.

# THE LADY WITH THE LITTLE DOG

## I

People were saying that someone new had appeared on the seafront: a lady with a little dog. Dmitry Dmitriyevich Gurov had been staying in Yalta for two weeks now, and had settled into its rhythm, so he too had begun to take an interest in new faces. As he was sitting in the pavilion at Vernet's* he watched the young lady walking along the seafront; she was not very tall, fair-haired, and she was wearing a beret; a white Pomeranian dog scampered after her.

Then he started bumping into her several times a day in the municipal garden and in the tree-lined square. She always walked by herself with the white Pomeranian, wearing the same beret. No one knew who she was and so she was simply called the lady with the little dog.

'If she is here without her husband and without friends,' reasoned Gurov, 'it would not be a bad thing to get to know her.'

He was not yet forty but he had a twelve-year-old daughter and two sons at the gymnasium. He had been married off early, when he was still in his second year at university, and now his wife seemed one-and-a-half times older than he was. She was a tall woman with dark eyebrows: very upright, pretentious, and worthy, and, as she put it herself, intellectual. She read a lot, dispensed with the old-fashioned hard sign* from words when she wrote letters, and called her husband Dimitry rather than Dmitry, while he secretly thought she was rather dull, small-minded, and graceless; he was afraid of her and did not like being at home. He had started being unfaithful to her a long time ago, had been unfaithful to her often, and it was probably for that reason that he almost always spoke negatively about women; when they were being talked about in his presence, he would always refer to them as 'the lesser species!'

He felt he had accrued enough bitter experience to call them whatever he wanted, but all the same he could not live without 'the lesser species' for more than a couple of days. In the company of men he was bored and did not feel comfortable; he was taciturn and cold, but when he was with women he felt relaxed and knew what to talk to them about and how to behave; even remaining silent with them was easy. There was something attractive and elusive in his appearance, in his character, and in his whole nature which predisposed women to him and drew them to him; he knew it, and some kind of power drew him to them as well.

Repeated experience, bitter experience, had long ago taught him that however much intimate relationships seem like a nice, light-hearted little adventure at first, adding a welcome bit of spice to one's life, they will eventually always turn into an excessively complex and intractable dilemma for respectable people—particularly Muscovites, who are phlegmatic and tend to vacillate; the situation always ends up becoming burdensome. But every time he met an interesting new woman, that experience somehow managed to vanish from his memory; he wanted to live, and everything just seemed straightforward and enjoyable.

One day in the late afternoon he was having dinner in the municipal garden, and who should walk up unhurriedly to sit down at the next table but the lady in the beret. Her expression, her bearing, her dress, and her hairstyle all told him that she was from a respectable background, was married, was in Yalta for the first time and alone, and was bored here... There was a great deal of untruth in the stories about local morals; he despised them and knew that they were mostly made up by people who would sin themselves given half the chance, but when the lady was sitting down at the neighbouring table three feet away from him, he recalled all those stories about easy conquests and trips into the mountains and was suddenly gripped by the seductive thought of a swift and brief relationship—a romance with an unknown woman whose name he did not even know.

He beckoned the Pomeranian over in a friendly fashion and then shook his finger at it when it came close. The Pomeranian started growling. Gurov again shook his finger.

The lady looked at him then immediately lowered her eyes.

'He doesn't bite,' she said, blushing.

'Can I give him a bone?' When she nodded her head, he asked:

'Have you been in Yalta long?'

'About five days.'

'And I'm already sitting out my second week.'

They were silent for a little while.

'Time passes quickly, but it's also so dull here!' she said, without looking at him.

'That's just because it's the done thing to say it's dull here. Your average inhabitant of some town like Belyov or Zhizdra* isn't usually bored, but as soon as he comes here, it's "Oh, it's so dull! Oh, the dust!" You would think he had come from Grenada.'

She laughed. Then they both continued to eat in silence, like strangers. But after dinner they walked off side by side and a playful, easygoing conversation started up—the sort of conversation between contented people who are at leisure, and who do not mind where they go or what they talk about. As they walked, they talked about how strangely the sea was lit: the water was a lilac colour, incredibly soft and warm, with a golden strip of moonlight running along it. They spoke about how humid it was after the day's heat. Gurov said that he was a Muscovite, who had studied literature but worked in a bank; he had at one time trained to sing at the private opera, but had given it up; he had two houses in Moscow... And from her he found out that she had grown up in St Petersburg, but had married in S., where she had been living for two years, that she would be in Yalta for a month, and that maybe her husband would come and join her here, as he also wanted a holiday. She could not explain where her husband worked—whether it was the regional government or the local government, and even she herself found that funny. Gurov also discovered that she was called Anna Sergeyevna.

He thought about her when he was back in his room, and about the probability of them meeting tomorrow. It was bound to happen. As he was going to bed he remembered that not so long ago she had been at the institute, studying just like his daughter; he remembered how timid and awkward her laughter still was in conversation with a stranger—it was no doubt the first time in her life that she was on her own in such surroundings, with people following her around, looking at her, and talking to her with a single hidden agenda, which she could not fail to divine. He remembered her slender, frail neck and her beautiful grey eyes.

'All the same, there is something pitiful about her,' he thought before falling asleep.


## II

A week had gone by since they had become acquainted. It was the weekend. Inside it was stuffy, but outside there was a gale throwing up clouds of dust and blowing people's hats off. They were thirsty all day and Gurov kept going to the pavilion to offer Anna Sergeyevna cordials and ice creams. They did not know what to do with themselves.

In the evening, when the wind had dropped a little, they went down to the jetty to watch the steamer come in. There were a lot of people strolling about the quayside; they had come to meet someone, and were holding bunches of flowers. There were two particularities of the well-dressed Yalta crowd which immediately stood out: the elderly ladies were dressed like young girls, and there were a lot of generals.

Because of the sea being rough, the boat came in late, when the sun had already set, and it took a long time turning round before mooring. Anna Sergeyevna looked through her lorgnette at the boat and at the passengers as if searching for people she knew, and her eyes shone when she turned to Gurov. She was talking a lot, her questions were disjointed, and she herself immediately kept forgetting what it was she had asked; then she lost her lorgnette in the crowd.

The throng of well-dressed people began to disperse until there was no longer anyone left; the wind had completely dropped, but Gurov and Anna Sergeyevna were still standing there as if they were waiting for someone to get off the boat. Anna Sergeyevna had fallen silent by now and was sniffing her flowers, not looking at Gurov.

'The evening has brought better weather,' he said. 'So where shall we go now? Shall we take a trip somewhere?'

She did not reply.

Then he looked at her intently, put his arms round her suddenly, and kissed her on the lips, and was enveloped by the scent and moisture of her flowers; he immediately looked around warily to see if anyone was watching.

'Let's go to your place...' he said quietly.

They started walking quickly.

Her room was stuffy and smelled of the perfume she had bought in a Japanese shop. As he looked at her now, Gurov was thinking: 'Life certainly does throw up some strange encounters!' He had memories from the past of good-natured, carefree women who enjoyed having love affairs, and were grateful to him for some happiness, even if it was very short-lived; he also had memories of women—such as his wife, for instance—who loved without sincerity and with needless conversations, who were affected and over-emotional, their expression implying that this was not love or passion, but something more significant; and he also had memories of a handful of very beautiful, cold women, on whose faces you would suddenly be able to detect a predatory expression and a wilful desire to take, to extract from life more than it is capable of giving; and these were women no longer in the first flush of youth, they were women who were capricious, irrational, overbearing, and unintelligent; and when Gurov cooled towards them, their beauty would arouse hatred in him and the lace on their underwear would seem like fish-scales.

But here was that timidity again, that youthful awkwardness, lack of experience, and a feeling of discomfort; his companion also seemed startled, as if someone had suddenly knocked at the door. Anna Sergeyevna, the 'lady with the little dog', seemed to regard what had happened in a particular and very serious way, as if it was her downfall—or so it seemed, and this was strange and inappropriate. Her face drooped and became expressionless, her long hair hung sadly down the sides of her face, and she sat there in a dejected pose, just like the sinner in an old-world painting, lost in thought.

'This is awful,' she said. 'You will be the first to lose respect for me.'

There was a watermelon on the table in the room. Gurov cut himself a slice and took his time eating it. At least half an hour passed in silence.

He found Anna Sergeyevna touching; she had the wholesome air of a respectable, naive woman with little experience of life; the solitary candle burning on the table barely illumined her face but it was clear that she felt terrible.

'Why on earth would I stop respecting you?'* asked Gurov. 'You yourself don't have any idea of what you are saying.'

'May God forgive me!' she said, as her eyes filled with tears. 'This is terrible.'

'You seem to want to justify yourself.'

'How can I justify myself? I am a bad and wretched woman, I despise myself; justification is the last thing on my mind. It's not my husband I've betrayed but myself. And not just now either: I've been betraying myself for a long time. Maybe my husband is a decent and good man, but he's a flunkey! I don't know what he does at the place where he works, or what the nature of his employment is, all I know is that he is a flunkey. I was twenty when I got married to him. I was bursting with curiosity, I wanted something better for myself—there has to be a better life, I kept telling myself. I wanted to live! I so wanted to live... I was consumed with curiosity... You won't be able to understand this, but I swear to God, I couldn't restrain myself any longer, something was happening to me; I couldn't stop myself, so I told my husband that I was ill and came here... And I've been walking around here all the time in complete ecstasy, like a madwoman... and now I have just become cheap and worthless, a woman whom anyone might despise.'

Gurov had already got fed up with listening; he was annoyed by the naive and penitential tone, which was so unexpected and so misplaced; without the tears in her eyes you might have thought she was joking or acting out a role.

'I don't understand,' he said quietly. 'What is it you want?'

She hid her face in his chest and clung closely to him.

'Please believe me, I beg you...' she said, 'I just want to live a decent, honest life; I can't bear sin and I don't know myself what I am doing. Country people talk about getting tangled up with an evil spirit. Now I can say about myself that I have got tangled up with an evil spirit.'

'Come on now, that's enough...' he murmured.

He looked at her scared, staring eyes, kissed her, spoke softly and tenderly, and she gradually calmed down; her good spirits returned and they both started to laugh.

Later on, when they went out, there was not a soul down on the seafront; the town with its cypresses looked totally dead, but the waves were still crashing noisily against the shore; there was just one fishing-boat tossing about on the sea, its light twinkling sleepily.

They found a cab and set off for Oreanda.*

'Just now in the lobby downstairs I found out what your surname is: there was a von Diederitz written up on the board,' said Gurov. 'Is your husband German?'

'No. I think his grandfather may have been German, but he was born Russian Orthodox.'

They sat on a bench not far from the church at Oreanda, looking down at the sea and not saying anything. Yalta was barely visible through the morning mist, and white clouds stood motionless on the tops of the mountains. The leaves on the trees did not stir, the cicadas were chattering, and the monotonous, muffled noise of the sea coming up from down below spoke of rest and of the eternal sleep which awaits us. It had made that noise down below when neither Yalta nor Oreanda existed, it was making that noise now, and would continue to make that noise in that same hushed and indifferent way when we are no longer here. And in that permanence, in that complete indifference to the life and death of each one of us, is perhaps concealed a guarantee of our eternal salvation, a guarantee of the constant movement of life on earth and of endless perfection. Sitting tranquilly next to a young woman who seemed so beautiful in the dawn light, entranced by this magical setting—the sea, the mountains, the clouds, the vast sky—Gurov was thinking that when you really reflect on it, everything is beautiful on this earth, everything that is, except what we think and do when we forget about the higher purpose of existence and about our human dignity.

Someone—most likely a nightwatchman—came up close, peered at them, and then went away. Even that detail seemed mysterious and beautiful too. They could see the steamer from Feodosia* arriving; it was lit up by the dawn and already without lights.

'There is dew on the grass,' said Anna Sergeyevna, breaking the silence.

'Yes. Time to go back.'

They returned to town.

Then they took to meeting up every day at twelve on the seafront, having lunch together, dining, going for walks, and admiring the sea. She complained that she was not sleeping well and that her heart was beating irregularly; she kept asking him the same questions, either out of jealousy or a fear that he did not respect her sufficiently. And often in the square or in the gardens, when there was no one about, he would suddenly draw her to him and kiss her passionately. He felt rejuvenated by the complete idleness and those kisses in the middle of the day, which were accompanied by furtive looks and the fear that they might be seen; he felt rejuvenated by the heat, by the smell of the sea, and by the constant flitting before his eyes of contented, elegantly dressed holidaymakers; he told Anna Sergeyevna how pretty and attractive she was, he was ardent and passionate and never left her side even for a minute, while she often became pensive and begged him to admit that he did not respect her or love her at all, and just saw her as a cheap woman. They went out of town almost every evening when it was getting late, either to Oreanda or to the water-fall;* and their excursions were always a success; the impressions they made were unfailingly beautiful and majestic.

They were expecting her husband to arrive. But a letter came from him in which he told her he had contracted an eye infection and begged her to come home as soon as possible. Anna Sergeyevna made haste.

'It's a good thing that I am leaving,' she said to Gurov. 'It's fate.'

She set off in a carriage to Sevastopol, and he accompanied her. It took all day. When she had settled into her compartment on the express train and the second bell had gone, she said:

'Let me look at you again... I want one last look. That's right.'

She was not crying, but she looked miserable, as if she was ill, and her face was trembling.

'I'll think about you... and remember you,' she said. 'God bless you, don't go yet. Think well of me. This is goodbye forever and it has to be that way, because we shouldn't have ever met. Well, God bless.'

The train departed quickly, its lights soon disappeared, and within a minute you could no longer hear any noise, as if a special arrangement had been made to bring this sweet oblivion, this insan-ity, to a swift end. As he stood alone on the platform looking into the far distance, Gurov listened to the crickets chirping and the hum-ming of the telegraph wires and felt as if he had just woken up. He thought about how this had been one more escapade or adventure in his life; it too had now come to an end and all that was left was a memory... He felt moved, sad, and slightly repentant; after all, the young woman whom he would never see again had not been happy with him; he had been friendly and sincere with her, but all the same, whenever he had been with her there had been a trace of mockery in his tone and in his endearments—the crude arrogance of a con-tented man who was, moreover, almost twice her age. She had kept saying he was kind, exceptional, noble; she had not divined his real personality, so he had unwittingly deceived her...

There was already a smell of autumn down at the station, and the evening was cool.

'It's time for me to go north too,' thought Gurov as he left the platform. 'Time to go north!'

## III

At home in Moscow everything was already on the winter timetable; the stoves were lit and it was dark in the mornings when the children were getting ready for school and drinking their tea; the nanny had to light the lamps for a while. There were frosts already. When the first snow falls, and when you travel by sleigh for the first time, how nice it is to see the ground and the rooftops all white; the air is soft and lovely, and it makes you start remembering the times when you were young. Clothed in white rime, the old lindens and birches have a good-natured appearance; they are more endearing than cypresses and palms, and being near them dispels any desire to think about sea and mountains.

Gurov was a Muscovite, and he arrived back in Moscow on a wonderful frosty day; when he put on his fur coat and warm gloves and walked down Petrovka,* and when he heard the church bells ringing on Saturday evening, his recent trip and the places he had visited completely lost their charm for him. Little by little he re-immersed himself in Moscow life; soon he was avidly reading three newspapers a day and saying he did not read Moscow newspapers on principle. Before long he was being lured to restaurants, clubs, dinners, and parties; he felt flattered that he was visited by famous lawyers and artists, and played cards at the doctors' club with a professor. And he was soon able to polish off a whole portion of cabbage stew served in the pan, Moscow style...

A month or so would go by, he had thought, and Anna Sergeyevna's image would become shrouded in mist; he would just dream of her touching smile from time to time, like he dreamed about all the others. But more than a month had gone by and winter had set in, and his memories were as clear as if he had parted from Anna Sergeyevna the day before. His memories grew more vivid, in fact. He might hear from his study the voices of his children doing their homework in the quiet of an evening, a song or an organ in a restaurant, or the howling of the snowstorm in the chimney, and all of a sudden everything would be resurrected in his mind: the time when they were at the jetty, that early misty morning in the mountains, the steamer from Feodosia, the kisses. He would spend hours walking about his room, remembering and smiling, and then his memories would turn into dreams and the past would fuse with the future in his imagination. Anna Sergeyevna did not appear in his dreams, but she followed him everywhere he went like a shadow, watching over him. As soon as he closed his eyes he would see her as if she were standing right there, and she would seem prettier, younger, and more affectionate than before; and he himself seemed better than he was back then in Yalta. In the evenings she would look across at him from the bookshelf, or from the fireplace or from the corner of the room; he could hear her breathing and the gentle rustle of her dress. Outside on the street he followed women with his eyes, looking to see if there was someone like her...

And he was overcome by a powerful desire to share his memories with someone. But he could not talk about his love at home, and there was no one anywhere else. He could not talk to the lodgers or to the people at the bank. And what would he say anyway? Had he really loved her back then? Was there really something beautiful, poetic, uplifting, or even simply interesting about his relationship with Anna Sergeyevna? All he could do was talk in vague terms about love and women, and no one guessed what was going on; his wife just knitted her dark eyebrows and said:

'You know, Dimitry, the role of the romantic really does not suit you.'

One night when he was coming out of the doctors' club with his partner at cards, an official, he could not restrain himself and said:

'You can't imagine what an enchanting woman I met in Yalta!'

The official got into his sleigh and drove off, but then suddenly he turned round and called out:

'Hey, Dmitry Dmitrich!'

'What?'

'You were right earlier: the sturgeon was off!'

Those very ordinary words for some reason suddenly made Gurov angry; they seemed degrading and dishonourable to him. What appalling manners, and what dreadful people there were! What meaningless nights and what uninteresting, unmemorable days! Frenzied games of cards, gluttony, drunkenness, and endless conversations always about one and the same thing. These pointless activities and conversations about one and the same thing took up the better part of your time and energy and eventually left you with an uninspired, restricted kind of life which was worth nothing, and which you could neither leave nor run away from; it was like sitting in a madhouse or behind bars!

Gurov could not sleep all night and he became angry, and then he had a headache all the next day. He slept badly the following nights too; he would sit up in bed and think, or he would pace about. He was fed up with his children, fed up with the bank, and he did not want to go anywhere or talk about anything.

In December, during the Christmas holidays, he packed a bag and told his wife that he was going to St Petersburg to try and intercede on behalf of a certain young man—but he actually went to S. Why? He himself did not really know the answer. He wanted to see Anna Sergeyevna and talk to her, arrange a meeting if possible.

He arrived in S. the next morning and took the best room in the hotel, whose floor was covered wall to wall with thick, grey military felt. On the desk there was an inkwell, grey with dust, which was shaped like a rider on a horse; the rider was raising his hat with his hand, but his head had been knocked off. The porter gave him the necessary information: von Diederitz lived on Old Goncharnaya Street, in his own house, not far from the hotel—he lived well, prosperously, had his own horses and was known by everybody in the town. The porter pronounced his name as Dridiritz.

Gurov set off unhurriedly along Old Goncharnaya Street, looking for the house. Just in front of it stretched a long, grey fence studded with nails.

'That's the kind of fence that makes you want to run away,' thought Gurov casting his eyes back and forth from the windows to the fence.

He figured that since this was not a working day, the husband would probably be at home. It would be tactless anyway to go into the house and cause embarrassment. If he were to send a message it might perhaps fall into the husband's hands and everything would be ruined. It would be better to count on the right opportunity presenting itself. So he walked up and down the street and along the fence, waiting for this opportunity. He saw a beggar walking through the gates and being attacked by dogs, then an hour later he heard a piano being played and faint, indistinct sounds floating out. It must have been Anna Sergeyevna playing. Then the front door suddenly opened and an old woman came out, with the familiar white Pomeranian running after her. Gurov wanted to call out to the dog, but his heart started beating wildly, and he was so nervous he could not remember what it was called.

As he walked up and down he started to hate the grey fence more and more; he was thinking with irritation that Anna Sergeyevna would have forgotten about him and maybe was seeing someone else, and it would be so natural for a young woman who was compelled to see that wretched fence from morning till night. He went back to his hotel room and sat for a long time on the couch, not knowing what to do; then he had lunch and went to sleep for a long time.

'This is all so stupid and pointless,' he thought, after he had woken up and was staring through the dark windows; it was already evening. 'Now I have gone and had a good sleep. But what am I going to do tonight?'

He sat on the bed, which was covered with a cheap grey blanket which looked as if it had come out of a hospital, and taunted himself with his feelings of disappointment:

'So much for your lady with the little dog... So much for your adventure... You can just sit here.'

At the station that morning he had noticed a poster advertising the first performance of *The Geisha** with very large letters. He remembered it, and set off for the theatre.

'It's quite possible that she goes to first nights,' he thought.

The theatre was full. As in most provincial theatres there was mist above the central chandelier and people in the gallery making a lot of noise. The local romeos stood in the front row before the performance started with their hands clasped behind their backs; in the governor's box the governor's daughter was sitting in the front row wearing a boa, with the governor himself modestly hiding behind the partition, so that only his hands were visible; the curtain was swaying and the orchestra was taking a long time tuning up. While the audience were coming in and finding their seats Gurov scoured the place with his eyes.

Anna Sergeyevna came in. She sat down in the third row, and when Gurov looked at her his heart leapt, and he understood clearly that there was now no person whom he cherished more, no one dearer or more important to him; lost in the provincial crowd, this small and in no way remarkable woman, with a vulgar lorgnette in her hands, now made up his whole life; she was his sorrow and his joy, the only happiness he now wanted for himself; and to the accompaniment of the sounds coming from the terrible orchestra and the wretched amateur violins, he thought about how lovely she was. He thought and dreamed.

A young man with short sideburns, very tall and stooping, had come in with Anna Sergeyevna and sat down next to her; at every step he had nodded his head and seemed to be constantly bowing. This was probably her husband, whom in Yalta in a rush of bitterness she had called a flunkey. There really was something deferential and flunkey-like in his long figure, his sideburns, and his small bald patch; he was smiling insipidly, and there was some kind of academic insignia glinting in his buttonhole just like a lackey's badge.

During the first interval the husband went out to smoke and she stayed in her seat. Gurov had also been sitting in the stalls and so he went up to her; in a shaking voice, forcing a smile, he said 'Hello'.

She looked up at him and went pale, then looked at him again with horror, not believing her eyes, clasping her fan and lorgnette tightly together and clearly doing her best not to faint. They said nothing. She sat and he stood, frightened by her embarrassment, and unsure as to whether he should sit down next to her. The violins and the flute had begun to tune up and it was suddenly horrifying; it felt as if the people in all the boxes were all looking at them. But then she got up and quickly headed towards the exit; he followed her and they both walked in confusion along corridors and then up and down staircases, while before their eyes flitted people in judicial, peda-gogical, and state uniforms, all with insignia, ladies, and fur coats on pegs; a draught was blowing which gave off a smell of cigarette ends. His heart beating wildly, Gurov was thinking, 'Heavens! Why do there have to be all these people here, and that orchestra...?' And at that moment he suddenly remembered that when he had seen Anna Sergeyevna off at the station that evening, he had told himself that it was all over and that they would never see each other again. But it was far from over in fact!

She stopped on a dark, narrow staircase where there was a sign saying: 'Entrance to the amphitheatre.'

'You gave me such a scare!' she said, breathing hard, still pale from the shock. 'Such a scare! I'm barely conscious. Why did you come here? Why?'

'You must understand, Anna, you must understand...' he said hurriedly in a hushed voice. 'You must understand, I beg you...'

She looked at him entreatingly with a mixture of fear and love, staring into his face so as to imprint his features more firmly in her memory.

'I've suffered so much!' she continued, without listening to him. 'I've thought about you all the time; all I've thought about is you. I wanted to forget about you, forget all about you. Why, oh why have you come?'

On the landing higher up, two schoolboys were smoking and looking down, but Gurov did not care; he drew Anna Sergeyevna to him and started kissing her face, her cheeks, and her hands.

'What are you doing? What are you doing?' she said in horror, pushing him away from her. 'We have both gone completely mad. You must leave today; you must leave now in fact... I swear to you by all that is holy, I beg you... There are people coming!'

There was someone walking up the stairs.

'You must leave....' Anna Sergeyevna continued in a whisper. 'Dmitry Dmitrich, are you listening to me? I'll come and see you in Moscow. I have never been happy, I'm not happy now and I will never ever be happy. Never! Don't make me suffer even more! I swear, I'll come and see you in Moscow. But we must part now! My dearest, beloved, dear friend, we must part!'

She pressed his hand and started briskly walking down the stairs, looking back at him all the time, and you could see from her eyes that she really was not happy. Gurov stood for a while, listening, and then when everything had gone quiet he looked for his coat-peg and left the theatre.

## IV

So Anna Sergeyevna started to come and visit him in Moscow. Every two or three months she would leave S., telling her husband she was going to see a consultant about a female complaint, and her husband both believed her and did not believe her. When she came to Moscow she stayed at the Slavyansky Bazaar Hotel* and would immediately send over someone in a red hat to let Gurov know. Gurov would come and see her and no one in Moscow knew about it.

He was going to see her on one of those occasions, one winter morning (the messenger had tried to find him the previous evening, but he had been out). With him was his daughter whom he wanted to take to school, as it was on the way. Snow was falling in thick, wet flakes.

'It's now three degrees above zero, but it's still snowing,' said Gurov to his daughter. 'But it's only the surface of the earth which is warm, you see; there is a quite different temperature in the upper layers of the atmosphere.'

'Papa, why aren't there thunderstorms in winter?'

He explained about that too. As he was talking, he was thinking about the fact that he was going to a rendezvous and that there was not one living soul who knew about it; probably no one ever would know about it. He had two lives: one was the public one, which was visible to everybody who needed to know about it, but was full of conditional truth and conditional deceit, just like the lives of his friends and acquaintances, while the other one was secret. And by some strange coincidence—perhaps it was just chance—everything that was important, interesting, and essential to him, in which he was sincere and did not deceive himself, and which made up the inner core of his life, was hidden from others, while everything that was false—the outer skin in which he hid in order to cover up the truth, like his work at the bank, for example, the arguments at the club, his 'lesser species', and going to receptions with his wife—was public. And he judged others to be like himself, not believing what he saw, and always supposing that each person's real and most interesting life took place beneath a shroud of secrecy, as if under the veil of night. Every individual existence is a mystery, and it is maybe partly for this reason that cultured people take such pains for their secrets to be respected.

Once he had taken his daughter to school, Gurov set off for the Slavyansky Bazaar. He took off his fur coat downstairs, and then went upstairs and knocked on the door. Anna Sergeyevna had been waiting to see him since the previous evening; she was wearing his favourite grey dress and was worn out from the journey and the anticipation of seeing him. She was pale and looked at him without smiling; barely had he walked in through the door when she threw herself on his chest. It was as if they had not seen each other for two years and their kiss was slow and protracted.

'So, how is life down there?' he asked. 'What's new?'

'Wait, I'll tell you in a minute... I can't now.'

She could not speak as she was crying. She turned away from him and pressed a handkerchief to her eyes.

'She must have a cry if she needs to; I'll just sit here for a minute,' thought Gurov and he went and sat down in an armchair.

Then he rang and asked for some tea to be brought up to him, and while he was drinking the tea she remained standing, in front of the window... She was crying because she was so upset, and because of the painful realization that their life had turned out so sadly; they saw each other only in secret, and had to hide from people like thieves! Their life really was a mess.

'Come on now, stop!' he said.

It was clear to him that the love they felt for each other would not come to an end any time soon; it was impossible to say when in fact it would end. Anna Sergeyevna was growing more attached to him, she adored him, and it would be unthinkable to tell her that it all would have to come to an end at some point; she would not have believed it anyway.

He went over to her and took her by the shoulders so he could caress her and make her laugh, and just at that moment he saw himself in the mirror.

His hair had already begun to go grey. He found it strange that he had aged so much in the last few years, and had lost his looks. The shoulders on which his hands were placed were warm, and they were shaking. He felt compassion for this life, still so warm and beautiful, but probably already on the point of fading and wilting, just like his own life. Why did she love him so much? He always seemed to women to be something other than what he was; it was not really him they loved, but a person created in their imagination whom they longed to have in their lives, and when they noticed their mistake they still carried on loving him anyway. And not one of them had been happy with him. Time had gone by, he had got to know women, he had become close to them and then parted from them, but he had never felt love; everything and anything but love in fact.

It was only now, when his hair was turning grey, that he had started to love someone truly and properly—it was the first time in his life.

He and Anna Sergeyevna loved each other like people who were related and very close, like husband and wife, or close friends; they felt that fate had intended them to be together, and found it impossible to understand why they were both married to other people; they were like two migratory birds, a male and a female, who had been caught and made to live in separate cages. They had forgiven each other for things they were ashamed of in their past, they forgave each other for everything in the present, and they felt that their love had changed them both.

In the past, when there had been moments of sadness, he had reassured her with the first rationalization which came into his head, but he had no time for rationalizations now; he felt deep compassion and wanted to be sincere and gentle...

'Stop it, my love,' he said. 'You've done enough crying now... Let's talk now, let's see what we can come up with.'

Then they spent a long time conferring and talking about how they could extricate themselves from the need to hide and deceive, from having to live in different towns and not see each other for long stretches. How could they free themselves from these unbearable bonds?

'How are we going to do it? How?' he asked, holding his head in his hands. 'How?'

And it seemed that in a little while a solution would be found and then a new, wonderful life would begin, but it was clear to both of them that the end was still a long way off and that the most complex and difficult part was only just beginning.

# AT CHRISTMAS TIME

## I

'What shall I write?' Yegor asked, dipping his pen.

Vasilisa had not seen her daughter for four years now. Her daughter Yefimya had gone to live in Petersburg with her husband after their wedding, and she had sent two letters, but then it was if she had disappeared without trace; there had been no news at all. And whether the old lady was milking the cow at sunrise, lighting the stove, or lying in bed awake at night, the only thing she ever thought about was how Yefimya was doing, whether she was alive or not. They needed to send her a letter, but her old man could not write, and there was no one to ask.

But then Christmas came, and Vasilisa could bear it no longer, so she went to the inn to see Yegor, the landlady's brother, who had been sitting at home in the inn doing nothing ever since he had finished his military service; people said he could write a good letter if you paid him enough. Vasilisa had a word in the inn with the cook, then with the landlady, and finally with Yegor. They settled on fifteen kopecks.

And now, the day after Christmas, here was Yegor sitting at the table in the kitchen in the inn, holding a pen in his hand. Vasilisa was standing in front of him, deep in thought, with an expression of sadness and worry on her face. With her had come her old man Pyotr, who was tall and very thin, with a bald patch in his brown hair; he stood there motionless, staring straight in front of him as if he was blind. There was some pork frying in a pan on the stove; it was spitting and hissing, and it sounded almost as if it was saying 'floo-floo-floo'. It was stuffy.

'What shall I write?' asked Yegor again.

'Hang on!' said Vasilisa, looking at him angrily and suspiciously. 'Don't rush me! It's not as if you are writing for nothing, we are paying you after all! Well all right, I'm ready now. Dear son-in-law Andrey Khrisanfych and our beloved only daughter Yefimya Petrovna, we bow deeply to you and send you our love and our parental blessing, which will be there always.'

'Right, got that. Fire away.'

'And we wish you a Happy Christmas, we are alive and well, and we hope you are too, with all the blessing of the Lord... the King of Heaven.'

Vasilisa stopped to think and exchanged glances with the old man.

'We hope you are too, with all the blessing of the Lord... the King of Heaven,' she said again and burst into tears.

She could say nothing more. Before when she had been lying there at night thinking, it had seemed to her that she would not be able to say everything there was to say even if she wrote ten letters. Much water had gone under the bridge since the time that her daughter and her husband had left. Her old folk had been living like orphans, and they sighed so deeply at night it was as if they had buried their daughter. And to think of all the events in the village during that time, all the weddings, and all the deaths! To think of all those long winters! And such long nights!

'It's hot!' said Yegor, unbuttoning his waistcoat. 'Must be getting on for seventy degrees. So what else?'

The old people were silent.

'What does your son-in-law do?' asked Yegor.

'He was in the army, if you remember,' replied the old man in a feeble voice. 'He finished his service the same time as you. He was a soldier, and now he's in Petersburg at a clinic where they have water treatments. The doctor treats sick people with water. He works for the doctor as the doorman.'

'It's all written here...' said the old woman, taking a letter from her handkerchief. 'We got it from Yefimya, goodness knows when. Maybe they aren't even alive anymore.'

Yegor thought for a while, then started writing quickly.

'At the present time,' he wrote; 'seeing that fate has sent you to the Milittary Spheere, we advise you to have a look at the Statutes of Dissiplinary Penelties and the Criminal Laws of the War Dipart-ment, and you will see in the Law there a sivilization of the Ranks of the War Dipartment.'

After he had written it all down, he read it out loud, and Vasilisa realized they ought to be writing about the hardships of the previous year, about the shortage of grain which had continued right up until Christmas, and how they had been forced to sell the cow. They ought to be asking for money, they ought to be writing about how her old husband was often sick, and would probably soon be giving up his soul to God... But how could you put that into words? What do you say before and afterwards?

'Pay attention to the fifth volume of the Milittary Regulations,' Yegor carried on writing. 'Soldier is a Common and Universel Term. The General at the Topp and the Private at the Bottom is called a soldier...'

The old man moved his lips and said softly:

'Wouldn't be a bad thing to see our grandchildren.'

'What grandchildren?' asked the old woman, looking at him crossly. 'Maybe there aren't any!'

'Grandchildren, you mean? But maybe there are. Who knows?'

'And so therefor you can tell,' hurried Yegor, 'who is our External enemy and who is our Innternal enemy. Our most Innternal Enemy is Bacchus.'

The pen scratched away, making great flourishes that looked like fish-hooks. Yegor was racing through it and reading out every line several times. He was sitting there on the stool, all well fed, chubby-cheeked, and healthy-looking, with a red neck, and his legs splayed out wide beneath the table. He was vulgarity itself—crude, arrogant, unassailable vulgarity, proud to have been born and brought up in an inn, and Vasilisa knew very well that that he was vulgar, but could not put it into words, and just kept looking at Yegor with anger and suspicion. Her head had started aching from his voice, the unintelligible words, the heat, and the stuffiness, her thoughts had become confused, she could not say anything, she could not think straight, and was just dying for him to finish all his scratching. But the old man was looking on with complete faith. He trusted his old woman, who had brought him here, and he trusted Yegor; and when he had mentioned the water treatment clinic just now, it was clear from the expression on his face that he trusted the clinic and the healing power of water.

When he had finished writing, Yegor stood up and read the whole letter out from the beginning. The old man did not understand anything, but he nodded his head trustingly.

'That's all right, that is; real smooth,' he said; 'Yes, it's all right. Your good health.'

They put three five-kopeck pieces on the table and left the inn;

the old man stared straight ahead of him, like a blind man, and there was complete trust written all over his face, but when they went outside Vasilisa raised her hand at the dog and said angrily:

'Ugh... what scum!'

Worried by her thoughts, the old woman could not sleep all night, then at dawn she got up and said her prayers and set off for the station to post the letter.

The station was eight miles away.

## II

Dr B. O. Moselweiser's Water Treatment Clinic was open for business at New Year just like on other days, and the only thing which was different was that the doorman, Andrey Khrisanfych, was wearing a uniform with new piping on his lapels, and his boots were particularly shiny; he wished everybody who arrived a Happy New Year and season's greetings.

It was morning. Andrey Khrisanfych was standing by the door and reading the newspaper. On the stroke of ten arrived the familiar figure of a general who was a regular visitor, followed by the postman. Andrey Khrisanfych helped the general off with his coat and said:

'Happy New Year and season's greetings to you, your excellency!'

'Thank you, my friend. And the same to you.'

As he was going up the stairs, the general nodded towards a door and asked (he asked every day and forgot every time):

'What's in this room?'

'That's the massage room, your excellency!'

When the general's footsteps had died away, Andrey Khrisanfych looked through the letters which had been delivered, and found one addressed to him. He unsealed it, read a few lines, and then, without hurrying, still looking at the newspaper, went along to his room, which was right there downstairs, at the end of the corridor. His wife Yefimya was sitting on the bed feeding a baby; another child, the eldest one, was standing by her, with his curly head resting on her lap, while a third child was sleeping on the bed.

As he came into the room, Andrey Khrisanfych held out the letter to his wife and said:

'Must be from the village.'

Then he went out, still not taking his eyes off the newspaper, and stood in the corridor, not far from the door. He could hear Yefimya reading the first lines in a shaking voice. She could read no further; just those lines were enough, her eyes had filled with tears; hugging her eldest child and kissing him, she started talking, and it was impossible to work out whether she was laughing or crying.

'It's from granny and grandpa...' she said; 'from the village... There will be snow all piled up beneath the roofs by now... the trees will be all white. The kiddies will be out on their little sledges... And bald old grandpa will be lying on the stove... with the little yellow dog... My dear family!'

As he was listening to this, Andrey Khrisanfych remembered that his wife had given him letters and asked him to send them to the village about three or four times, but something important had always got in the way and he had not sent them, so the letters were left lying about somewhere.

'And there will be little hares jumping in the fields,' lamented Yefimya, wiping away her tears and kissing her little boy. 'Grandpa is kind and gentle, Granny is kind too, and very understanding. They live a good life in the country, they fear God... And there is a little church in the village, and the men sing in the choir. Holy Mother of God, heavenly protector, if only you could take us away from here!'

Andrey Khrisanfych came back to his room for a smoke before anyone else arrived, and Yefimya immediately stopped talking and became quiet; she wiped her eyes, and only her lips continued to tremble. She was very scared of him, she was so scared of him!

Andrey Khrisanfych had lit his cigarette, but just at that moment the bell rang upstairs. He put out his cigarette, put on a serious expression, and sped off to the front door.

The general, looking all pink and fresh from his bath, was coming down the stairs.

'And what goes on in this room?' he asked, pointing to a door.

Andrey Khrisanfych stood up straight to attention and said loudly:

'The Charcot* shower-bath, your excellency!'

# THE BISHOP

## I

Vespers were being held on the eve of Palm Sunday in the Staro-Petrovsky Convent. When they started to hand out the branches of pussy-willow* it was already getting on for ten o'clock, the candles were growing dim, their wicks burned right down, and everything seemed to be in a fog. The crowd was heaving like the sea in the shadows of the church, and it seemed to Bishop Pyotr, who had been unwell for the last three days or so, that their faces—old, young, male, female—all looked identical, and that every person who came up for a branch of pussy-willow had the same expression in their eyes. The doors could not be seen through the fog, the crowd kept moving all the time, and it seemed that there would never be an end to it. There was a women's choir singing and a nun was reading the canon.

It was so stuffy, and so hot! Vespers had been going on for such a long time now! Bishop Pyotr was tired. His breathing was heavy and rapid, his mouth was dry, his shoulders ached with tiredness, and his legs were shaking. And the holy fool crying out occasionally from the gallery jarred his nerves. But then suddenly, as if in a dream or a delirium, it seemed to the bishop that his own mother Mariya Timofeyevna, whom he had not seen for nine years now, or an old woman who looked like his mother, had come up to him in the crowd, taken a branch of pussy-willow from him, and then walked away, still beaming at him with a warm, joyful smile until she merged back into the crowd again. For some reason, tears started pouring down his face. He was at peace in his heart, everything was fine, but his gaze was fixed on the left choir-stall where the reading was taking place, and where you could no longer make anyone out in the evening darkness, and he was crying. Tears glistened on his face and on his beard. Then someone near to him started crying, and another person further away as well, then more and more people started crying, until the whole church was full of quiet weeping. But after a little while, about five minutes later, the convent choir was singing, people had stopped crying, and everything was as it had been before.

Soon the service finished too. When the bishop got into his carriage in order to go home, the moonlit garden was flooded with the beautiful, festive pealing of precious, heavy bells. The white walls, the white crosses on the graves, the white birch trees, the black shadows, and the distant moon in the sky standing right above the convent all seemed to be living their own special life, which was incomprehensible but somehow strangely familiar. It was the beginning of April, and after a warm spring day it had become cool, with a touch of frost; but in the soft, cold air you could definitely feel the breath of spring. The road from the convent into the city went over sand, so they had to travel at a walking pace, and on either side of the carriage there were pilgrims trudging through the sand in the serene, bright moonlight. Everyone had become lost in thought and was silent, while everything all around—the trees, the sky, and even the moon—looked so young, friendly, and so close that it made you wish it would always be like this.

The carriage had finally entered the city and was going down the main street. The shops were already locked up, and only Erakin the merchant millionaire was experimenting with electric light, but it kept going on and off and a crowd of onlookers had gathered. Then came wide, dark streets, one after the other, all deserted, then the highway beyond the town, then fields and the smell of pine trees. A white indented wall loomed suddenly before his eyes, and behind it a tall belfry, all lit up; next to it were five large, shining gold cupolas—this was the Pankratiev Monastery where Bishop Pyotr lived. And the quiet, pensive moon was standing just as high above the monastery here too. The carriage drove in through the gates, making a crunching sound in the gravel; there were monks in black darting about in the moonlight, and footsteps could be heard on the flagstones...

'Your Mama turned up here while you were gone, your Reverence,' the lay brother reported when the bishop entered his rooms.

'My Mama? When did she arrive?'

'Before Vespers. First she asked where you were and then she went over to the convent.'

'So I really did see her in church just now! Oh Lord!'

And the bishop laughed with happiness.

'She asked me to let you know, your Reverence,' the lay brother continued, 'that she would come tomorrow. There is a girl with her, a grandchild, I suppose. They are staying at Ovsyannikov's Inn.'

'What time is it now?'

'Just after eleven.'

'Oh, what a shame!'

The bishop sat pondering for a while in his drawing room, not quite believing that it was already so late. His arms and legs ached and the back of his head hurt. He felt hot and uncomfortable. After a little rest, he went into his bedroom and sat down there for a while too, still thinking about his mother. He could hear the lay brother going out and Father Sisoy the monk coughing behind the wall. The monastery clock struck four.

The bishop changed and started reading his night-time prayers. He read the familiar old prayers carefully, thinking about his mother at the same time. She had nine children and about forty grandchildren. There was a time when she had lived with her husband, a deacon, in a poor village; she had lived there for a very long time, from when she was seventeen to when she was sixty. The bishop remembered her from when he was a small child, right from the age of about three, and how he had loved her! Dear, beloved, unforgettable childhood! Why did this irretrievable time, this time which had gone for ever, seem brighter, merrier, and more vibrant than it had ever really been? His mother had been so caring and attentive whenever he had been ill as a child! The prayers were now getting mixed up with his memories which were beginning to burn like flames, ever brighter, but the prayers did not stop him thinking about his mother.

When he had finished praying he got undressed and lay down, and as soon as it became dark all around him, his late father, his mother, and Lesopolye, the village he came from, immediately arose in his mind... The squeak of wheels, the bleating of sheep, church bells on clear summer mornings, gypsies under the window—oh, how sweet it was to think about it all! He remembered the Lesopolye priest, Father Simeon, who was gentle, meek, and good-natured; he was small and thin, but his son, a seminarist, was huge, and he spoke in a thundering bass voice. One day the priest's son got cross with the cook and yelled 'You ass of Jehudiel!' at her, and when Father Simeon heard this he did not utter a word, and was just ashamed that he could not remember where in the Holy Scriptures that particular ass was mentioned. After him the priest in Lesopolye had been Father Demyan, who drank a lot, sometimes to the point of seeing the green dragon, and he even had a nickname: Demyan the

Dragon-seer. The teacher in Lesopolye was Matvey Nikolayevich, who came from the seminary, and was a kind and intelligent man, but he too was a drunkard; he never hit his pupils, but for some reason there was always a bundle of birch rods hanging on the wall, and underneath them was a notice in Latin which was completely meaningless: *betula kinderbalsamica secuta*. He had a shaggy black dog which he called Syntax.

And the bishop started to laugh. Five miles from Lesopolye was the village of Obnino which had a wonder-working icon. In the summer they carried the icon in a procession from Obnino around the neighbouring villages and the bells were rung all day, first in one village and then in the next, and back then it had seemed to the bishop (he was called Pavlusha then) that the air was vibrating with joy, and he used to walk barefoot behind the icon without a hat, with naive faith and a naive smile, eternally happy. There were always a lot of people in Obnino, he remembered now, and the priest there, Father Alexey, used to make his deaf nephew Ilarion read the notes and pleas on the communion loaves 'for health' or 'for eternal rest' in order to save time during mass. Ilarion complied, occasionally receiving five or ten kopecks for a service, and only when he was grey and bald, when his life was over, did he suddenly come across 'You're a fool Ilarion!' written on a bit of paper. Up until the age of fifteen at least Pavlusha was a late developer and did badly at his studies, to the point that they had wanted to take him out of the ecclesiastical school and send him to work in a shop; once when he came to Obnino to collect the post, he had looked for a long time at the clerks and asked: 'Would you be so kind as to tell me whether you receive your wages monthly or daily?'

The bishop crossed himself and turned over onto his other side in order to stop thinking and go to sleep.

'My mother has come...' he remembered with a chuckle.

The moon looked in through the window, lighting up the floor and casting shadows on it. A cricket chirped. Behind the wall in the next door room Father Sisoy was snoring gently, and there was something lonely, forlorn, and even vagrant-like in his senile breathing. Sisoy had once been the steward for the diocesan bishop, and now he was called 'the former Reverend steward'; he was seventy years old, he lived in a monastery ten miles out of the city, but he also lived in the city when necessary. Three days earlier he had stopped by the

Pankratiev Monastery and the bishop had put him up in his rooms, so that he could have time to talk to him about things, and discuss monastery matters...

At half-past one the bells were rung for early matins. Father Sisoy could be heard coughing and grumbling in a discontented voice, then getting up and walking through the rooms barefoot.

'Father Sisoy!' the bishop called out.

Sisoy went back to his room and a little later appeared wearing boots and holding a candle; he was wearing a white cassock over his underclothes and a faded old skullcap on his head.

'I can't sleep,' said the bishop as he sat down. 'I think I must be ill. But I don't know what it is. I feel so hot!'

'You have probably caught a chill, your Reverence. We ought to rub you down with some tallow.'

Sisoy stood there for a moment and said with a yawn: 'Oh Lord, have mercy on me, sinner that I am!'

'They turned on the electricity at Erakin's today,' he added. 'Oh, I don't like it!'

Father Sisoy was old and scrawny and his back was hunched; he was always dissatisfied with something, and his eyes were angry and bulging, like a lobster's.

'I don't like it!' he repeated as he left. 'I just don't like it at all! Well, let him do as he likes, I don't care!'

## II

On Palm Sunday, the next day, the bishop celebrated the morning service in the city's cathedral, then he went to see the diocesan bishop, then to the very sick elderly wife of a general, and then finally he went home. He had some special guests to lunch at two o'clock: his old mother and his niece Katya, a girl of about eight. During lunch the spring sun poured in continuously through the windows from the courtyard outside, shining merrily on the white table-cloth and in Katya's red hair. Through the double window frames you could hear rooks cawing and starlings singing in the garden.

'It's nine years since we saw each other,' said the old lady, 'but yesterday in the convent, when I looked at you—good heavens! You haven't changed a bit; well, maybe you've lost a bit of weight and your beard is longer, but that's all. Holy Mother of God, Queen of the Heavens! And yesterday during Vespers everyone was crying, they couldn't help it. When I saw you I suddenly started crying too, but I couldn't tell you why. It was His holy will!'

Despite the tenderness with which she spoke these words, it was noticeable that she felt awkward, as if she did not know whether to address him formally or informally, and whether she should laugh or not, and it was if she felt more like a deacon's wife than a mother. Katya meanwhile stared at her uncle the bishop without blinking, as if trying to work out what kind of a person he was. Her hair had escaped from her comb and velvet ribbon and was standing up like a halo; she had a snub nose and crafty eyes. Before they had sat down to lunch she had broken a glass, and her grandmother was now moving tumblers and wine glasses away from her while she was talking. As the bishop listened to his mother he remembered that once, many, many years ago, she had taken him and his brothers and sisters to visit relatives whom she had regarded as wealthy; she had been busy with her children back then, and now it was grand-children she was looking after, and she had brought Katya along...

'Your sister Varenka has four children,' she said. 'Katya here is the eldest, and Lord only knows why, her father, my son-in-law Ivan, took ill, and passed away three days before the feast of the Assumption. And now my poor Varenka has been left penniless.'

'And how is Nikanor?' the bishop enquired after his eldest brother.

'Oh he's making ends meet, thanks be to God. The only thing is, his son Nikolasha, my grandson, didn't want to go into the church, and he's gone to the university to become a doctor. He thinks that's better, but who knows! It's God's heavenly will.'

'Nikolasha cuts up dead bodies,' said Katya and then went and spilt water onto her lap.

'Sit still, child,' said her grandmother calmly, taking the glass from her hand. 'Say a prayer when you eat.'

'It's been such a long time since we saw each other!' said the bishop as he tenderly stroked his mother's shoulder and arm. 'I missed you while I was abroad, Mama, I missed you a lot.'

'I'm grateful.'

'I'd be sitting by an open window in the evening, you know, all on my own, and music would start playing, and I'd suddenly get so homesick that I think I would have given anything just to go home, and see you...'

His mother smiled, beaming with pleasure, but then she immediately put on a serious expression and said:

'I'm grateful.'

At some point his mood suddenly changed. He looked at his mother and could not understand where all the respect and timidity in her voice and in her features came from, what the point of it was; he did not recognize her. He began to feel sad and irritated. And then his head was hurting just like yesterday too, his legs ached, the fish seemed tasteless and unappetizing, and he was thirsty all the time...

After lunch two wealthy lady landowners came and sat for about an hour-and-a-half with long faces, without saying anything; then came a business visit from the taciturn and somewhat deaf archimandrite. And then the bells rang for Vespers, the sun sank behind the forest, and the day was at an end. After returning from church the bishop hurriedly said his prayers, got into bed, and tucked himself up as warmly as he could.

It was unpleasant remembering the fish he had eaten at lunch. The moonlight bothered him, and then he heard a conversation. In another room, it must have been the sitting room, Father Sisoy was talking about politics:

'The Japanese have got a war on at the moment. They are fighting. The Japanese are just the same as the Montenegrins, you know, my dear, they're from the same tribe. They were all under the Turkish yoke.'

And then Mariya Timofeyevna's voice could be heard:

'So after we had said a prayer and had a cup of tea, we went off to Father Yegor's in Novokhatnoe, you know....'

Every now and then there was an 'after we had some tea' or 'we had just sat down for a cup', and it seemed that all she had done was drink tea. Dim memories of the seminary and the academy began slowly to return to the bishop. He had been a Greek teacher in the seminary for about three years, and already by that time he could not look at a book without glasses; then he had become a monk and had been made an inspector. Then he had written his dissertation. When he was thirty-two they had appointed him as head of the seminary and made him an archimandrite; life then was so easy and pleasant; it seemed incredibly long, and with no end in sight. But then he became ill, lost a lot of weight, and almost went blind; on the advice of doctors he was forced to give everything up and go abroad.

'And then what?' asked Sisoy in the next room.

'And then we had tea...' answered Mariya Timofeyevna.

'Father, you've got a green beard!' Katya suddenly said in amazement and started laughing.

The bishop remembered that the grey hairs in Father Sisoy's beard did have a green tinge and he laughed.

'Good gracious me, that girl should be properly disciplined!' said Sisoy loudly in an angry voice. 'How spoilt you are! Sit still!'

The bishop remembered the brand new white church he had led services in while he lived abroad, and he remembered the sound of the warm sea. His apartment had five bright rooms with high ceilings, and there was a new desk in the study and a library. He had read a great deal and also written a lot. And he remembered how he had been homesick for Russia, how a blind beggar girl had sung about love and played the guitar every day under his window, and how every time he listened to her he had for some reason always thought about the past. And then eight years had gone by, he had been summoned back to Russia, and now he was a bishop, and all his past had disappeared somewhere far away in a fog, as if it was all a dream...

Father Sisoy came into his room with a candle.

'Goodness me,' he said in surprise; 'you in bed already, your Reverence?'

'What's the matter?'

'It's just that it's early still, ten o'clock, not even that. I bought a candle today; I wanted to rub you down with some tallow.'

'I've got a fever...' said the bishop, sitting up. 'It would probably be good to do something though. My head does not feel right...'

Sisoy took off the bishop's shirt and started rubbing his chest and back with the tallow from the candle.

'There we are... there we are...' he said. 'Lord Jesus... There we are. I walked into town today, and went to see—what's his name?— Archpriest Sidonsky... I had a cup of tea with him... I don't like him! Oh Lord Jesus... There we are... Oh, I don't like him!'

## III

The diocesan bishop, who was old and very overweight, was suffering from rheumatism or gout, and had not got out of bed for a month now. Bishop Pyotr had been visiting him nearly every day and receiving his petitioners for him. And now that he was unwell, he was amazed by the emptiness and the shallowness of what people were petitioning for and crying over; their backwardness and their diffidence made him angry; the sheer weight of all this triviality and needlessness was oppressive, and he felt he could now understand the diocesan archbishop, who at some point when he was younger had written 'The Doctrine of Free Will', but now seemed to have submerged himself in pettiness, had forgotten everything, and did not think about God. Bishop Pyotr must have become unused to Russian life while he had been abroad, as it was not easy for him; the people seemed primitive, the women petitioners were dull and stupid, and the seminary students and their teachers were uneducated, even barbaric at times. And the documents that came in and were sent out ran into the tens of thousands—and what documents! Deans throughout the diocese evaluated the behaviour of priests, both young and old, and even their wives and children, as excellent or good, and sometimes only satisfactory, and then it was necessary to discuss it all, and to study and write serious reports. There was absolutely not one free minute, Bishop Pyotr's nerves were on edge all day, and he only calmed down when he was in church.

He just could not get used to the fear he involuntarily inspired in people, despite his quiet, humble manner. Everyone in the province seemed small, frightened, and guilty when he looked at them. They were all shy in his presence, even the old archdeacons; they all fell at his feet, and one petitioner recently, an old priest's wife from the country, had been so terrified she could not utter a single word, and left having achieved nothing. He could never bring himself to speak badly of a person or reproach anyone in his sermons because he felt sorry for them, but even he now lost his temper with petitioners, became angry, and threw their petitions on the floor. In all the time that he had been in the post, not one person had talked to him openly and simply in a down-to-earth way; even his old mother did not seem the same anymore, she was not remotely the same! Why was it that with Sisoy she could talk non-stop and laugh a lot, but be serious, tongue-tied, and embarrassed with her own son, which was not like her at all? The only person who was uninhibited in his presence and who said everything he wanted was old Sisoy, who had spent his whole life around bishops and had seen all their trials and torments at close hand. So for that reason it was easy being with him, although he was definitely a difficult and cantankerous character.

On Tuesday after the liturgy the bishop was in the episcopal palace, where he received petitioners and became upset and angry; then he went home. He still felt unwell and was longing to be able to go to bed, but barely had he walked through the door when he was informed that the young merchant and benefactor Erakin had come on very important business. He had to be received. Erakin sat for about an hour talking very loudly and almost shouting, and it was difficult to understand what he was saying.

'God grant it!' he said as he left. 'Absolutely unfailingly! According to circumstances, your most holy Reverence! I do so hope!'

After him came the abbess from a distant convent. And when she had gone, the bells were rung for Vespers and it was time to go to church.

The monks' singing that evening was harmonious and inspired; there was a young monk with a black beard leading the service; and as he heard about the bridegroom who cometh at midnight,* and about the bridal chamber being adorned, the bishop did not feel repentance for his sins, or sorrow, but a spiritual calm, a quietness, and he was carried away by thoughts of the distant past, of his childhood and youth, when they had also sung about the bridegroom and the bridal chamber, and now that past seemed vivid, beautiful, and joyful, as it had probably never been. And maybe in our next life we will remember the distant past and our life here on earth with the same feeling. Who knows! The bishop was sitting by the altar, where it was dark. Tears were running down his face. He was thinking that he had achieved everything possible for a man in his position, and he had faith, but still not everything was clear to him, something was missing, he did not want to die; it seemed to him that he was still missing something really important, something which he had dreamed about vaguely once long ago, and that same hope about the future stirred him now, as it had during his childhood, while he was at the academy and when he had been abroad.

'They are singing so beautifully today!' he thought as he listened to the choir; 'So beautifully!'

## IV

On Thursday he took the morning service in the cathedral and there was the washing of feet. When the service finished and people had gone home, it was radiantly warm and sunny, water was gurgling in ditches, and the unceasing tender song of larks wafted in from the fields outside the city, bringing a sense of peace. The trees had already come to life and were smiling amiably, while above them the vast, blue, fathomless sky disappeared heaven knows where into the unknown.

After he came home, Bishop Pyotr had some tea, then he got undressed, climbed into bed, and asked the lay brother to close the shutters. His bedroom darkened. Goodness, how tired he was, there was such pain in his legs and his back, a cold, heavy pain, and what a din there was in his ears! It seemed as if he had not slept for a long time, a very long time, and what was preventing him from falling asleep was some tiny thing which glimmered in his brain as soon as he shut his eyes. Voices and the sound of teaspoons clinking against glasses came through the walls of the next-door rooms as they had the day before... Mariya Timofeyevna was merrily recounting something to Father Sisoy with all kinds of funny sayings, and he was replying in a sullen, disgruntled voice: 'Never! I don't believe it! As if!' And the bishop once again started to feel annoyed and then offended that the old lady could behave in a normal and straightforward manner with strangers, while with him, with her own son, she was tongue-tied and shy, not able to say what she wanted to; she had even kept looking for an excuse to stand up in his presence these past few days, as she felt awkward sitting, or so it seemed to him. And his father? If he had been alive he probably would not have been able to say a single word in front of him...

Something fell and shattered in the room next door; Katya must have dropped a cup or a saucer, because Father Sisoy suddenly snorted and said angrily:

'Lord have mercy, but it's pure punishment having this girl around! Can't keep anything safe!'

Then it became quiet, and the only sounds that could be heard came from outside. When the bishop opened his eyes he saw Katya standing there motionless in his room, looking at him. Her red hair was sticking out from her comb as usual and standing up like a halo.

'Is that you Katya?' he asked. 'Who is it who keeps opening and shutting the door downstairs?'

'I can't hear anything,' she answered, listening out.

'Someone just walked past.'

'That's just in your tummy, uncle!'

He laughed and stroked her hair.

'So your cousin Nikolasha cuts up dead bodies, does he?' he asked after a pause.

'Yes. He's studying.'

'Is he a good cousin?'

'He's all right I suppose. But he drinks a lot of vodka.'

'And what illness did your father die of?'

'Papa was weak and he got ever so thin and then suddenly it was his throat. And then I was ill and my brother Fedya was ill—everyone's throat hurt. Papa died, but we got better, uncle.'

Her chin had started to wobble; tears appeared in her eyes and ran down her cheeks.

'Your holiness,' she said in a thin little voice, already crying bitterly, 'me and Mama have been left so unhappy, uncle... Please give us a little bit of money... Please be kind... dear uncle!...'

He also started crying, and for a long time he was so upset that he could not say a word, then he stroked her hair and patted her shoulder and said:

'Don't worry, child. Once Easter Sunday comes we will talk... I will help, of course I will...'

His mother came in quietly and timidly to pray to the icon. When she noticed he was not asleep she asked:

'Wouldn't you like a little soup?'

'No, thank you...' he answered. 'I don't feel like eating.'

'You don't seem very well... looking at you now. And how could you not fall ill! On your feet all day, from morning to night, goodness me, it's tiring just to watch you. Well, Easter Week is not far off and then you can have a rest, God willing, and we can talk, but I am not going to bother you with conversations now. Let's go Katya—let his Lordship get some sleep.'

And he remembered that she had talked to the dean in just the same half-playful, half-respectful tone when he was still a boy a very long time ago... Only from the unusually kind eyes and the shy, concerned look she threw him in passing as she left the room could one see that she was his mother. He shut his eyes and thought he had gone to sleep, but he heard the clock striking twice, and Father Sisoy coughing behind the wall. And his mother came in once more and spent a minute looking at him shyly. He could hear someone driving up to the porch in a coach or a carriage. Suddenly there was a knock and the door banged: the lay brother came into his room:

'Your Reverence!' he called out.

'What?'

'The horses have been sent round, it's time for the Lord's Passion.'

'What time is it?'

'Quarter-past seven.'

He got dressed and drove over to the cathedral. He had to stand motionless right in the middle throughout all the twelve passages from the gospel, and the first, the longest and most beautiful, was read by him. He suddenly felt cheerful and well. He knew this first gospel reading, 'Now is the son of man glorified',* by heart, and while he read it he occasionally lifted his eyes and saw on both sides an ocean of flames, and heard the sputtering of candles, but as in previous years he could not see any people, and it seemed that these were the same people who had been there back in his childhood and in his youth, and that they would be there every year until God only knows when.

His father had been a deacon, his grandfather had been a priest, his great-grandfather had been a deacon, and his family had maybe belonged to the clergy from the time that Rus adopted Christianity;* his love for church services, the clergy, and the sound of bells being rung was deep, innate, and ineradicable; he felt energetic, cheerful, and happy when he was in church, especially when he was taking part in the service himself. And so it was now. It was only when they finished the eighth gospel reading that he felt his voice had become weak, so that even his coughing was not audible; he had a terrible headache and he began to worry that he might keel over at any moment. His legs really had gone numb, so that he gradually lost all sensation in them, and he could not understand how he was managing to stand up, and why he was not falling over...

When the service finished it was a quarter to midnight. After arriving home, the bishop immediately got undressed and went to bed without even saying his prayers. He could not speak and would no longer be able to stand up, he thought. When he covered himself up with the blanket, he was suddenly gripped by a desire to go abroad—an incredibly intense desire! He felt he would give his life not to have to see these miserable cheap shutters and low ceilings, and endure this stifling monastery smell. If only there was one person whom he could talk to and unburden his soul!

He could hear someone walking about for a long time in the room next door, but he just could not remember who it might be. Finally the door opened and Sisoy came in with a candle and a teacup in his hands.

'You've already gone to bed, Your Reverence?' he asked. 'Well I've come to rub you down with vodka and vinegar. It can be a real help if you rub it in well. Oh Lord Jesus... There we are... There we are... I've just been over to our monastery... I don't like it, I really don't! I'm going to leave tomorrow, your Reverence, I don't want to stay any longer. Sweet Lord Jesus... There we are...'

Sisoy could never stay long in one place, and he felt as if he had already been living in the Pankratiev monastery for a whole year. But what was really hard to puzzle out listening to him was where his home was, whether there was anyone or anything he actually loved, and whether he believed in God... He himself did not understand why he was a monk, he certainly never thought about it, and the time when he took his vows had vanished from his memory so long ago that it was as if he had actually been born a monk.

'I'm leaving tomorrow. Stuff it! Stuff everything!'

'If I could just have a little talk with you... it's been difficult to find the time,' said the bishop softly, speaking with great effort. 'I don't know anyone here, you see, or anything...'

'All right, I will stay until Sunday, if I have to, but I'm not staying longer than that. Confound it all!'

'What sort of bishop am I?' the bishop continued softly. 'I ought to be a village priest, a sexton... or an ordinary monk... All this weighs me down... it weighs me down...'

'What? Lord Jesus... There we are... Well, time to get some sleep now, my Lord!... I don't know! Heavens above! Good night!'

The bishop did not sleep all night. And in the morning, at about eight, his intestine started bleeding. The lay brother was scared and ran first to the archimandrite and then to the monastery doctor, Ivan Andreyevich, who lived in the city. The doctor, a rotund old man with a long grey beard, examined the bishop for a long time, shaking his head as he did so and frowning, and then he said:

'You know what, your Reverence? You've got typhoid!'

In the hour following the haemorrhage the bishop became very thin and pale, his cheeks hollowed, his face wrinkled, his eyes grew larger, and it was as if he had grown old and had shrunk in size; it already seemed to him that he was thinner and weaker and more insignificant than everyone else, that everything that existed had gone somewhere very, very far away, and would never be repeated or continue.

'How wonderful!' he thought. 'How wonderful!'

His old mother arrived. When she saw his shrunken face and his large eyes, she took fright and fell to her knees by the bed, and started kissing his face, his shoulders, and his hands. And for some reason it seemed to her too that he was thinner, weaker, and more insignificant than anyone else; she had already forgotten that he was a bishop and was kissing him as if he was a child, her very own dear child.

'Pavlusha, sweetheart,' she said. 'Darling! My dear son! What's happened to you? Pavlusha, speak to me!'

Katya stood there looking pale and tight-lipped, not understanding what was wrong with uncle, why there was such suffering on her grandmother's face, and why she was saying such touching, sad words. And he could no longer say a single word nor understand what was happening, and was imagining himself as a simple, ordinary person, walking briskly and happily through the fields, tapping his stick, while up above him was the huge sky, drenched with sunshine; he was as free as a bird now and could go wherever he wanted!

'Pavlusha, dear son, please answer me!' said the old woman. 'What's the matter with you? My dearest!'

'Don't upset his Lordship,' said Sisoy angrily as he marched across the room. 'Let him get some sleep... Nothing you can do... there's no point!...'

Three doctors arrived and consulted with each other and then they went away. The day was long, unbelievably long, and then night fell and it went on and on, but towards morning on the Saturday the lay brother went over to the old lady, who was lying on the couch in the sitting room, and asked her to go into the bedroom; the bishop had passed away.

The next day it was Easter. There were forty-two churches and six monasteries and convents in the city, and the booming, joyous sound of bell-ringing hung over it from dawn to dusk without a break, stirring up the spring air; birds sang and the sun shone brightly. It was noisy in the main marketplace; there were swings going up and down, barrel organs playing, an accordion wheezing away, and drunken voices calling out. And then pony-rides began on the main street in the afternoon—it was all great fun, in a word; everything went well, just as it had the previous year, and as it probably would the following one.

A month later they appointed a new bishop, and no one remembered Bishop Pyotr any more. And then they completely forgot about him. The old lady, the dead man's mother, went to live with her son-in-law the deacon in a remote little district town, and it was only when she went out in the late afternoon to fetch her cow and meet up with the other women in the pasture that she talked about her children, her grandchildren, and about her son who had been a bishop; she spoke shyly, because she was afraid that people would not believe her...

And indeed, not everyone did believe her.

# EXPLANATORY NOTES

## THE HUNTSMAN [*Eger'*]

First published in the *Petersburg Newspaper* [*Peterburgskaya gazeta*], 18 July 1885.

## ON THE ROAD [*Na puti*]

First published in *New Times* [*Novoe vremya*], 25 December 1886.

8 *A little golden cloud . . . boulder*: the beginning of 'The Crag' ('Utes'), dating from 1841, by Mikhail Lermontov (1814–41).

*the icon of St George the Victor*: the third-century martyr credited with slaying the dragon.

9 *Serafim . . . Nasreddin*: the monk Serafim of Sarov (1759–1833), renowned for his asceticism, was canonized in 1903; Nasreddin (1831–96) became Shah of Persia in 1848. A Russian translation of a travelogue by him was published in St Petersburg in 1887.

10 *Madam Ilovaiskaya is here*: the Chekhov family's nanny, Agafya Kumskaya, was a serf of the Ilovaisky family, whose estates were situated in the Don steppe region, not far from Taganrog in southern Russia.

13 *break the fast*: a fast preceding Christmas morning.

15 *gymnasium*: the Russians adopted the German word for government-run secondary schools, and also their classical bias. Such schools were initially for the nobility only, but later admitted the children of merchants. Chekhov attended the gymnasium at Taganrog.

*Navin . . . prophet Elijah*: in Joshua 10: 12, Joshua (called Jesus, son of Navin in Slavonic) bids the sun to stand still. Russian peasants believed Elijah controlled storms and lightning. In 1 Kings 38 he brings down lightning to defeat the prophets of Baal.

*Mariinsky Institute*: the Mariinsky Don Institute was a private educational institution for young ladies of the nobility, founded in Novocherkassk in southern Russia in 1853.

*pharmocognosis*: the study of drugs and the plants from which they derive.

16 *Black Re-Partition*: an organization founded by revolutionary populists in 1879.

*went to the people*: a reference to the summer of 1874, when thousands of young radical populists left the cities to try to spread socialist ideas among the peasantry.

*Aksakov*: Konstantin Aksakov (1817–60) was a major figure in the

Slavophile movement, which rejected European influences on Russian society, and especially idealized the Russian peasant.

16 *rejecting personal property . . . non-resistance to evil*: respectively communist and Tolstoyan ideals.

17 *Arkhangelsk and Tobolsk*: remote areas of Russia, in the north and in Siberia respectively, to which opponents of the regime were traditionally exiled.

21 *'a large red star on a pole'*: a Christmas tradition in Russia.

*'Hey you, little boy . . . son'*: a folk carol published in A. Tereshchenko's *Life of the Russian People* (St Petersburg, 1848)

22 *coal-mines*: the reference to coal-mines further confirms that this story is set in southern Russia. The Don steppe region produced about half of the country's coal.


## THE LETTER [*Pis'mo*]

First published in *New Times*, 18 April 1887.

25 *proof of fasting*: of the many fasts in the Russian Orthodox calendar, the one most strictly observed is that during the seven weeks of Great Lent, when meat, eggs, and milk products are forbidden.

29 *reading the Acts of the Apostles*: readings from the fifth book of the New Testament are included as part of the Russian Orthodox Easter service.

31 *Christ is Risen*: this is the traditional Easter greeting in the Russian Orthodox Church, to which the reply is 'Truly He is risen'.

*If you hadn't got married*: only unmarried priests can be appointed as bishops in the Russian Orthodox Church.

32 *Gospel in Latin*: on Easter Saturday, before the Easter vigil, it is customary in the Russion Orthodox Church for the Gospel to be read in different languages.

34 *I was born in sin*: a paraphrase of Psalm 51: 5: 'I was born guilty, a sinner when my mother conceived me.'


## FORTUNE [*Shchast'e*]

First published in *New Times*, 6 June 1887.

36 *from the time when they took Tsar Alexander*: a reference to Alexander I's death in Taganrog in 1825.

37 *before they gave us liberty*: a reference to the Abolition of Serfdom (1861), the most important of Alexander II's reforms.

39 *the kurgans*: kurgan is the word for the Scythian burial mounds located across the steppe in southern Russia. The Scythians were buried together

with priceless gold ornaments, which gave rise to the confused myths of buried treasure that so entrance the old shepherd in the story.

40 *That was a bucket breaking loose in the mines*: the southern Russian steppe of the Donets Basin incorporated land extensively used for mining.

41 *Emperor Peter, who was building his navy in Voronezh*: Peter the Great originally planned to base his navy in Taganrog.

42 *German and Molokan farms*: the steppe was home to German Mennonite communities and members of the religious Molokan sect, which, like other sectarian groups, was officially banned by the tsarist government.

*a far-sighted Kalmyk*: Kalmyks were a Buddhist, nomadic people who lived on the steppe.

## GUSEV [*Gusev*]

First published in *New Times*, 25 December 1890, dated 'Colombo, 12 November'.

45 *Suchan*: town in Siberia, about 60 miles east of Vladivostok.

48 *Captain Kopeikin . . . Dyrka*: Kopeikin is a comic character in Gogol's novel *Dead Souls*, Part 1 (1842). Dyrka is a comic character in Gogol's play *The Marriage* (1842).

## FISH LOVE [*Ryb'ya lyubov'*]

First published in *Fragments* [*Oskolki*], 13 June 1892.

58 *Lermontov's Demon fell in love with Tamara*: in Lermontov's long poem *The Demon* (1839), the demon's kiss causes the death of Tamara, the girl he loves.

59 *Lipetsk*: town about 230 miles south of Moscow.

## THE BLACK MONK [*Chernyi monakh*]

First published in *The Artist* [*Artist*], January 1894

61 *in the English manner*: from the eighteenth century onwards, it became customary for Russian landowners to plant a part of their estates following the English fashion of 'natural' landscape gardening.

64 *'Onegin, I don't want to hide it. . . madly'*: from Tchaikovsky's opera *Eugene Onegin* (1879), based on Pushkin's novel in verse of the same name (1823–31). Pushkin's heroine is called Tatyana—often shortened to Tanya. The words Chekhov quotes come from an aria in which Prince Gremin proclaims his love for Tatyana, his wife, to the love-struck Onegin who once spurned her. Chekhov was particularly fond of this opera.

66 *the famous Braga serenade*: composition by Gaetano Braga (1829–1907) for soprano and piano.

70 *Gaucher's article first*: N. Gaucher, French-born horticulturalist, whose works were published in Russian translation in the late 1880s and 1890s.

72 *audiatur . . . sat*: *audiatur altera pars*: 'Let the other side be heard'; *sapienti sat*: 'A word to the wise.'

76 *'In my Father's house . . . places'*: John 14: 2.

77 *'mens sana in corpore sano'*: 'a healthy mind in a healthy body'.

81 *Assumption*: The feast of the Assumption falls on 15 August.

82 *Polycrates*: tyrant of Samos who was crucified *c.*522 BC. The story of the ring is in Herodotus, *Histories*, iii. 40–3.

83 *'Rejoice evermore . . . happy'*: 1 Thessalonians 5: 16.

84 *St Elijah's Day*: 20 July.

87 *I am like Herod*: a confused reference to Matthew 2: 16, which describes events after the birth of Jesus: 'When Herod saw that he had been tricked by the wise men, he was infuriated, and he sent and killed all the children in and around Bethlehem who were two years old or under.'

88 *Sevastopol . . . Yalta*: Sevastopol is a Crimean port and naval base; Yalta is a resort on the southern Crimean coast.

## ROTHSCHILD'S VIOLIN [*Skripka Rotschil'da*]

First published in *Russian Gazette* [*Russkie vedomosti*], 6 February 1894.

97 *St John . . . Miracle-Worker*: St John the Evangelist's Day is celebrated on 8 May, St Nicholas's on 9 May.

98 *two holy fools*: idiots or people feigning madness who are held to possess the gift of religious prophecy—a phenomenon which arose in the Russian Orthodox Church in the fourth century.

## THE STUDENT [*Student*]

First published in *Russian Gazette*, 15 April 1894, under the title 'In the Evening' [*Vecherom*].

103 *Ryurik . . . Peter the Great*: Ryurik was a viking prince of Novgorod in the late ninth century, and founder of the ruling Russian dynasty from 862 to 1598; Ivan the Terrible was Ivan IV, Tsar of Muscovy from 1533 to 1584; Peter the Great (Peter I), the first Russian emperor, ruled from 1682 to 1725.

104 *twelve gospel readings*: it is the custom in the Russian Orthodox Church for excerpts relating the story of Christ's passion from the four gospels to be read at the Maundy Thursday service.

104 *'I am ready to go with you . . . death'*: the student's telling of the story of
Peter's betrayal of Jesus draws on the gospels of Matthew (26: 75), Luke
(22: 33–4, 56–8), and John (18: 18, 26), sometimes quoting them almost
exactly.

## THE HOUSE WITH THE MEZZANINE [*Dom s mezoninom*]

First published in *Russian Thought* [*Russkaya mysl'*], April 1896, No. 4.

107 *T. province*: probably Tula province.

*traditional Russian dress*: Chekhov uses the word *poddyovka*—a sleeveless
coat, fastened at the side, worn by peasants and merchants.

*pneumatic stoves*: literally 'Amosov stoves', which were invented by
Major-General Amosov in 1835.

109 *zemstvo*: elective district councils, founded in 1864.

111 *a Buryat girl*: the Buryat were an indigenous Siberian tribe of Mongol
provenance. Chekhov crossed Lake Baikal, the largest lake in Siberia, on
his journey to Sakhalin island in 1890.

116 *a pair of iron boots*: in numerous Russian fairy tales, such as 'The Frog
Princess' and 'Fenist the Bright Falcon', the hero or heroine must wear
out at least one pair of iron boots on their journey to find their
beloved.

119 *since the vikings*: the vikings founded Russia's first ruling dynasty at the
end of the ninth century (see note on Ryurik, p. 103). They originally
came to Russia because it lay on the route to Byzantium, where they
wished to trade.

*Gogol's Petrushka*: Petrushka, Chichikov's servant in the novel *Dead Souls*
(1842) by Nikolai Gogol, was fond of reading things he did not
understand.

120 *let the country go back to the Tatars*: a reference to the 'dark years' of
Russia's occupation by the Tatar-Mongols, from 1238 to 1480, when
much of its early culture was destroyed.

*Vichy*: French spa town which became popular at the end of the
nineteenth century as a health resort.

123 *a Krylov fable*: the first line of one of the best-known fables by Ivan
Krylov (*c.*1769–1844), an adaptation of La Fontaine's *Le Corbeau et le
Renard*.

*Penza*: a provincial town about 500 miles south-east of Moscow.

## IN THE CART [*Na podvode*]

First published in *Russian Gazette*, 21 December 1897.

126 *the local zemstvo*: Russia's elective district councils founded and main-
tained jurisdiction over many of the village schools in each area.

130 *Lower Gorodishche*: there was a village called Old Gorodishche about 30 miles south-east of Melikhovo, where Chekhov lived.

## THE MAN IN A CASE [*Chelovek v futlyare*]

First published in *Russian Thought*, July 1898, No. 7.

136 *Turgenev and Shchedrin*: Ivan Turgenev, Russian novelist (1818–83), Saltykov-Shchedrin: satirical writer (1826–89).

*Buckle*: Henry Thomas Buckle: English social historian (1821–62).

138 *Gadyach*: a small town in the Ukraine, about 150 miles east of Kiev.

140 *kolossalische Skandal*: 'a colossal scandal' (German).

## GOOSEBERRIES [*Kryzhovnik*]

First published in *Russian Thought*, August 1898, No. 8.

150 *stripped bark for bast*: birch bark was traditionally used for making shoes, boxes, and ornaments in Russia.

*six feet of earth*: a reference to Tolstoy's short story *How Much Land Does a Man Need?* (1886).

154 *'the lie . . . hosts of truths'*: from the poem 'A Hero' (1830) by Pushkin.

## ABOUT LOVE [*O lyubvi*]

First published in *Russian Thought*, August 1898, No. 8.

158 *'this is a great mystery'*: Ephesians 5: 32.

160 *Messenger of Europe*: liberal monthly journal covering history, politics, and literature, founded in St Petersburg in 1866.

## THE LADY WITH THE LITTLE DOG [*Dama s sobachkoi*]

First published in *Russian Thought*, December 1899, No. 12.

167 *Vernet's*: a well-known café in the public garden at Yalta.

*hard sign*: letter of the Russian alphabet affecting pronunciation.

169 *Belyov or Zhizdra*: small towns, respectively 150 miles south and 200 miles south-west of Moscow.

171 *'Why on earth . . . you?'*: Gurov has switched from the formal *vy* (you) to the more intimate *ty*. Later on in the story he reverts to *vy* again.

172 *Oreanda*: the site of a former imperial palace about 5 miles along the coast south-west of Yalta, with a spectacular view of the bay.

173 *Feodosia*: town towards the eastern end of the Crimean coast.

174  *the waterfall*: the waterfall of Uchan-Su, about 6 miles north-west of Yalta, and a popular destination for excursions.

175  *Petrovka*: a street in central Moscow.

178  *The Geisha*: operetta by Sidney Jones, first produced in London in 1896.

180  *Slavyansky Bazaar Hotel*: large and popular hotel in central Moscow.


## AT CHRISTMAS TIME [*Na svyatkakh*]

First published in the *Petersburg Newspaper*, 1 January 1900.

188  *Charcot*: Jean Martin Charcot (1825–93), the French physician who pioneered psychotherapy.


## THE BISHOP [*Arkhierei*]

First published in *Journal for Everyone* [*Zhurnal dlya vsekh*], April 1902, No. 4.

189  *branches of pussy-willow*: these are used on Palm Sunday in the Russian Orthodox Church instead of palm branches.

198  *bridegroom who cometh at midnight*: Matthew 25: 1–6.

201  *'Now is the son of man glorified'*: John 13: 31.

    *the time that Rus adopted Christianity*: approximately AD 988, following the conversion of Vladimir, prince of Kiev.

| | |
|---|---|
| JANE AUSTEN | Emma |
| | Mansfield Park |
| | Persuasion |
| | Pride and Prejudice |
| | Sense and Sensibility |
| MRS BEETON | Book of Household Management |
| LADY ELIZABETH BRADDON | Lady Audley's Secret |
| ANNE BRONTË | The Tenant of Wildfell Hall |
| CHARLOTTE BRONTË | Jane Eyre |
| | Shirley |
| | Villette |
| EMILY BRONTË | Wuthering Heights |
| SAMUEL TAYLOR COLERIDGE | The Major Works |
| WILKIE COLLINS | The Moonstone |
| | No Name |
| | The Woman in White |
| CHARLES DARWIN | The Origin of Species |
| CHARLES DICKENS | The Adventures of Oliver Twist |
| | Bleak House |
| | David Copperfield |
| | Great Expectations |
| | Nicholas Nickleby |
| | The Old Curiosity Shop |
| | Our Mutual Friend |
| | The Pickwick Papers |
| | A Tale of Two Cities |
| GEORGE DU MAURIER | Trilby |
| MARIA EDGEWORTH | Castle Rackrent |

*The Oxford World's Classics Website*

**www.worldsclassics.co.uk**

- Information about new titles
- Explore the full range of Oxford World's Classics
- Links to other literary sites and the main OUP webpage
- Imaginative competitions, with bookish prizes
- Peruse the Oxford World's Classics Magazine
- Articles by editors
- Extracts from Introductions
- A forum for discussion and feedback on the series
- Special information for teachers and lecturers

**www.worldsclassics.co.uk**

American Literature

British and Irish Literature

Children's Literature

Classics and Ancient Literature

Colonial Literature

Eastern Literature

European Literature

History

Medieval Literature

Oxford English Drama

Poetry

Philosophy

Politics

Religion

The Oxford Shakespeare

A complete list of Oxford Paperbacks, including Oxford World's Classics, Oxford Shakespeare, Oxford Drama, and Oxford Paperback Reference, is available in the UK from the Academic Division Publicity Department, Oxford University Press, Great Clarendon Street, Oxford OX2 6DP.

In the USA, complete lists are available from the Paperbacks Marketing Manager, Oxford University Press, 198 Madison Avenue, New York, NY 10016.

Oxford Paperbacks are available from all good bookshops. In case of difficulty, customers in the UK can order direct from Oxford University Press Bookshop, Freepost, 116 High Street, Oxford OX1 4BR, enclosing full payment. Please add 10 per cent of published price for postage and packing.